D1263206

Praise for Thomas H. Block's Previous Thrillers

Mayday

"Fascinating, frightening, furiously paced . . . A story of almost unrelenting suspense!"

—*The New York Times*

"Strong and electric!"

—F. Lee Bailey, *The Washington Post*

Orbit

"Spellbinding . . . You'll love it!"

—*St. Louis Post-Dispatch*

"Sabotage, convincing aviation detail, nerve-jarring scenes . . . A fine thriller!"

—*Publishers Weekly*

Forced Landing

"Gripping . . . heart-pounding!"

—*Pensacola News*

"The man can write . . . *Forced Landing* builds toward a rip-snorting climax!"

—*Pittsburgh Press*

Airship Nine

"Exciting and riveting high-altitude suspense!"

—*Stephen King*

*Other books by
Thomas H. Block*

AIRSHIP NINE
FORCED LANDING
MAYDAY
ORBIT

SKYFALL

Thomas H. Block

A JOVE BOOK

SKYFALL

A Jove Book / published by arrangement with
the author

PRINTING HISTORY
Jove edition / June 1987

ISBN: 0-515-09178-2

Jove Books are published by The Berkley Publishing Group,
200 Madison Avenue, New York, NY 10016.
The words ''A JOVE BOOK'' and the ''J'' with sunburst
are trademarks belonging to Jove Publications, Inc.

PRINTED IN THE UNITED STATES OF AMERICA

It's time to acknowledge those thoughtful readers who have spurred me on with words and letters. A special heartfelt note of appreciation to EFB.

To two fathers, Ben and Hank,
who raised grateful children—
God rest their souls

"Science, freedom, beauty, adventure. What more could you ask of life? Aviation combined all the elements I loved."

—Charles A. Lindbergh

"We shall never learn to feel and respect our real calling and destiny unless we have taught ourselves to consider everything as moonshine, compared with the education of the heart."

—Sir Walter Scott

1

With the initial chords of Tchaikovsky's *Marche Slave* reverberating in the background, Mikhail Larionov wheeled his white Ford around the corner and onto the broad thoroughfare. Once safely in his lane, Larionov reached over and adjusted the tone of the treble and bass control on the tape player more to his liking, then settled back in the driver's seat.

This is worse than Moscow at spring thaw. Mikhail Larionov knew that Sepulveda Boulevard would take him most of the way to Hermosa Beach, then all he would need would be a few short back roads in order to get to the restaurant called for in the instructions. Larionov glanced at his new American wristwatch. It was ten minutes after six, which gave him enough time to deal with the madness known as Los Angeles rush hour and still make the meeting that Okun's office had arranged.

This "Lou Gehrig" person won't show, it's all a damned waste of time. Buses, trucks and cars crowded around Larionov's consulate vehicle as they all edged together toward the next traffic light. The Tchaikovsky tape picked up

1

its tempo, but the speed of the road traffic made no move to match it. At best, Larionov was averaging no more than ten kilometers an hour in forward progress. *A pointless fool's errand.* Larionov turned on the car's headlights; the sun had already sunk below the tall buildings that lined the boulevard and the shadows were growing deeper with every passing kilometer that he traveled. By the time he reached the restaurant, it would be dark. *This is a damned waste of time.*

Yet wasting time was something that Larionov didn't mind. His assignment as an English-language interpreter to the Soviet Consulate in Los Angeles was an excuse to travel, to broaden his horizons—to waste time, more or less, in all the interesting spots of the world. South Africa had been an education, South America an experience, and the United States even more so. America was an intriguing place—the decadence, the sheer wealth, and, of course, the attitudes of the people. The women, especially, displayed what to Larionov were totally amazing characteristics. Before he had gotten this assignment he had heard from his fellow interpreters at the institute about the ladies in the U.S. and, in particular, in California. Soon after his arrival, Larionov had quickly discovered that most of the rumors and stories had been true.

The women Larionov had run into had found his position as "Soviet Official" intriguing. Naturally, he had made his own consulate job appear far more exotic than the routine staff position that it really was. Larionov had, even in the short amount of time he'd been stationed in Los Angeles, found the women to be incredibly loose, both sexually and socially. After this silly and—more than likely—no-show interview tonight with an informant known only as Lou Gehrig, who had promised a vast array of priceless information, Larionov would head for the tavern in Santa Monica where that long-legged, auburn-haired beauty he had met the night before—Vicky—had promised to wait for him. The evening most certainly held the promise of something worthwhile, even if this fool's errand didn't.

Larionov stopped for a traffic light. While he waited for the signal to turn from red to green, he mulled over the significance of the obvious pseudonym Lou Gehrig. From deep in the recesses of his memory, Larionov recalled that the real

Lou Gehrig had been a famous American baseball player from the 30's—a fact which probably meant that the Lou Gehrig who telephoned was equally as old as his hero. *Just another ranting old fart.* The traffic light flashed to green, and Larionov sped away.

Once away from the traffic on Sepulveda Boulevard, Larionov made better time and was soon approaching the restaurant. The sign for Genovese's Italian Cafe was in bold red neon, and it stood out glaringly against the full evening darkness that now enveloped it. Larionov wheeled into the parking lot, found an empty space in the rear parking area as he had been instructed to do, then shut off the ignition. He looked around.

The restaurant itself appeared neat, orderly and probably quite popular, although he was too far from the front door to see the comings and goings of the patrons. Larionov, who was already hungry and would have particularly enjoyed some of this Americanized Italian food, glanced at his wristwatch again. Six fifty-two. If he could get rid of this ridiculous Lou Gehrig character soon enough—the two of them weren't supposed to go inside the restaurant, Gehrig was to approach Larionov's car in the parking lot—there would be enough time for a plate of spaghetti before he was due to meet Vicky. He'd even be able to put tonight's dinner on his expense account; a few padded American dollars for "entertaining a prospective informer" was a good way to squeeze extra rubles out of Okun's department.

"I'm Lou Gehrig."

The voice had startled Larionov, and he twisted around in his seat. Just as he had suspected, the man standing a few meters away from the opened driver's window was old enough to be Larionov's grandfather. The old man had evidently come up to the car from the darkness behind the parking lot. "Yes, Mr. Gehrig . . ." Larionov answered as he eyed the old man carefully, not wanting to say anything yet just in case this was a police setup. But as much as he didn't like to admit it, Larionov knew that he was far too insignificant a consulate employee for the police to bother setting up a complex trap. More than likely, this contact was exactly what it purported to be: someone wanting to trade information for money. "I'm responding to your telephone call."

"What time did I call?"

"Ten forty-seven this morning." That had been the agreed-upon recognition signal indicated in the note dropped at the consulate afterward, even though according to what Okun had said, the old man had actually called sometime the night before. Larionov studied the old man carefully, but could tell very little in the darkness. He was wearing a light-colored topcoat that appeared to be of good quality, and he wore no hat. Other than that, there was not much that Larionov could see.

"Ten forty-seven is correct. May I get in?" The old man gestured toward the passenger's side.

"Of course." Larionov waited while he walked around the car, then watched him slide into the front passenger's seat. In even the dim reflected light that managed to reach them from Genovese's roadside neon sign, up this close it was obvious that this man was seventy, at the very least. From the looks of the wrinkles on his face and the whiteness of his hair and trimmed mustache, Larionov had a damned good hunch who he was dealing with: just another of the dozens of old farts who did this sort of thing on a more or less regular basis—probably another retired military man who thought that his aches and pains weren't being handled properly by the Veterans' hospital. "What can I do for you?" Larionov asked as he fidgeted nervously, wanting to get this over with as soon as possible. *A crazy, senile old man. I knew this was a damned waste of time; no wonder that fucking Okun didn't come himself.*

"You seem very young."

"I've been involved in consulate work for some time. I assure you," Larionov said, "I can help you." The old man sat in silence, staring openly and directly at him. That silence, plus the old man's stare, quickly became very discomforting. "I'm authorized to speak to you," Larionov added defensively.

"Are you authorized to deal?"

"Of course," Larionov lied. "That's why we're here." Larionov had begun to perk up a bit; something in the old guy's manner hinted at the possibility that there was more here than met the eye—perhaps this wasn't a ranting old fart after all, perhaps he did indeed have some useful information to give. Okun would shit green borscht if he had sent Larionov out to do something that might become very important to Moscow.

"Are you an errand boy that some big shot sent to do his legwork, or are you really a key part of the Soviet operation?"

Larionov paused, not knowing what to say because he had been startled by the bluntness of the question. Finally, he regained his composure enough to respond in what he thought was an appropriate way. "I may not be the Premier, or the director of the KGB, but I'm up damned high enough to deal with you."

"I see." The old man nodded slowly. "Well, if you're certain that you can make a deal . . ."

"Yes, we can deal," Larionov said, in a tone that he hoped was not overly eager. He could see that the old man was now ready to go ahead with whatever he had come for.

"Then this is for you." The old man reached slowly into the pocket of his topcoat. When his hand came out, it was holding a small gun.

"What . . ." That was all Larionov managed to say as the barrel—an extended black tube around the muzzle that he instinctively knew would be the pistol's clipped-on silencer— was aimed at his chest. Larionov heard the first of the two muffled pops, but he felt nothing as the bullets ripped into his chest and through his heart. He slumped forward against the Ford's dashboard. Mikhail Larionov was dead.

Alex Caldwell sat nervously in his Fiat Spider sports car on a side road off California Highway 1, near the town limits of Laguna Beach. He was working on his fifth cigarette in the last thirty minutes, the other four less than half smoked and all of them crushed into the small dashboard ashtray in the darkened car. *That bastard is late; what the hell is keeping him?* Caldwell watched every passing headlight from the adjoining road, but none of them made the turn into the dead-end lane that overlooked the Gulf of Santa Catalina and the Pacific Ocean.

Another car sped past without turning, and then another. Caldwell vowed that he would wait no more than five additional minutes—he even went as far as setting the elapsed timer on his elaborate wristwatch—but even as he fumbled with the tiny buttons he knew that his five-minute limit would keep stretching until dawn if need be. For the first time since his arrangement with the old man had begun several weeks ago, Caldwell was now totally dependent on him—a man whose name he didn't even know. Caldwell knew that he had no choice but to keep watching. *I must've been nuts.* If the old man didn't show, Alex Caldwell had become a criminal and a fugitive for no reason, for no gain.

Maybe he's lost, maybe he can't find the right street. Caldwell checked his watch again, pushing the buttons to give proper time rather than the elapsed time from the beginning of his last five-minute ultimatum. Nine twenty-three. Caldwell had figured on having his money by this time, and being well on his way on the first leg of the prearranged route to Rio. But instead of heading south and leaving behind the imbecilic computer engineering business that he had learned to hate, Caldwell found himself still sitting in a dark car waiting for his money—and making himself an inviting target for the police, if by some chance one of the other project engineers had gone back to the laboratory in the last few hours and had somehow discovered what he had done.

Off in the distance, another set of headlights worked its way slowly down the main road. Caldwell watched the headlights intently, hanging on their every motion. As the car approached the corner, it began to slow. Then, all at once, the headlights turned directly toward him!

Within a few seconds the headlights had advanced enough to illuminate Caldwell's Fiat. If it was the police, Caldwell was planning on reciting his prepared speech about car trouble—but he knew that his nervousness would give him away. Before Caldwell could worry himself over that possibility, the car coming toward him stopped twenty yards away and blinked its headlights twice. After a short interval, the car continued forward again.

He's here—finally, goddammit! Caldwell jumped out of his Fiat and stood in the roadway, waiting for the old man to pull alongside. "You're late!" Caldwell shouted into the opened driver's window of the white Ford that the old man was driving.

"Couldn't be helped. Too much traffic." The old man parked the white Ford in front of Caldwell's Fiat, then got out of his car and walked up to where the young engineer was standing. "I'm sorry. I've never gotten used to this much traffic."

"That's a stupid fucking excuse if I ever heard one. You should have left earlier."

"You're right." The old man walked slowly up to Caldwell's Fiat in the darkness, moving carefully so as to not bump into the car before his eyes adjusted to the black landscape illuminated only by a dim moon. When he reached the vehicle, the old man rubbed his hand along the hood. "I like your car." The old man decided to get a sports car himself, tomorrow, when he got back to Las Vegas. He could afford it now.

"I'm not here to talk about cars."

"Sorry."

"Let's get this over with." Even in the bare glow from the rising half-moon above the western horizon, Caldwell could make out the old man's irritating smile—a smile that could have meant anything from self-consciousness to sarcasm. The old man was at least seventy years old, but he looked reasonably fit, and other than being a little talkative, he was nobody's fool. "Where's my money?" Caldwell asked, getting right to the point.

"It was delivered to me a few hours ago, just like they promised." The old man nodded toward the white Ford. "Your money is in the car. First, you've got to tell me how everything went."

"Fine, for chrissake. Like I told you it would." Caldwell bounced nervously from foot to foot. "Give me my money. Let's split."

"Hey, a deal's a deal. I need the details or my ass won't be worth shit. I need the full report we agreed to."

"It went just like we planned. Isn't that enough?" Caldwell kept looking around nervously, expecting to see the police, the FBI, maybe even the fucking mounted cavalry riding down that dark road at any minute. Clearly, he realized that he was not cut out for this sort of thing.

"Is that enough? For me, it's just fine." The old man gestured, palms up, to indicate that none of this made any damned difference to him. "But for the big shots who gave me the money, I don't think so. If they want a report, let's give them a fucking report. Don't make things difficult when we're close to seeing it through the way we agreed." The old man stood rigidly erect, his topcoat wrapped around him in the damp night breeze that blew inland off the empty blackness that was the ocean. He glanced to his right, through the scattered trees and toward the Pacific. He could see the ocean's wave pattern in the moonlight.

"I don't have time for this . . . ." Caldwell stepped toward the white Ford. For a brief moment he considered just opening up the car door, finding his money and leaving. He had actually taken a half step in that direction, but something in the old man's bearing convinced him not to continue. The old man was right; they should finish it out the way they agreed and be done with it. But since they were forced to talk about it, then there was still one unanswered question on his mind that Caldwell wanted to ask. "What do they intend to do with the software?"

"Sell it, I guess." The old man shrugged, showing no interest in pursuing the matter.

"To whom?"

"How old are you?"

"Can't you ever answer a simple goddamn question without asking me another one?"

"How old are you?" the old man repeated.

"Thirty-four, if that makes any difference."

"Thirty-four. You're young and that's why you ask questions that you shouldn't. It's none of your business and none of my business. I'm old enough to know not to ask. You were picked because you're good with computers. I was picked because I've learned not to ask questions I don't need answers to."

"Okay." Caldwell sighed, then took a step away from the white Ford. The old man was right again; if someone wanted the software and encoding translator out of a Defense Department war games computer, what they intended to do with it was none of his concern. Maybe they were going to franchise the damned thing and put it into video arcades so kids could realistically nuke the ruskies. "Everything went just like we planned. This morning I switched the software packages and the encoding translators between the two computers while I was supposed to be doing that predelivery hardware analysis check. The shipping company picked up the automobile assembly computer on schedule."

"What time?"

"Quarter after eleven."

"And what about the Defense Department computer? Did anyone work on it after you?"

"Sure, but like I told you would happen, it was all the scheduled hardware checks. One thing about good old Digitex, they sure as hell love to stick to their goddamned printed schedules." For just an instant, Caldwell wondered how he had learned to hate the company he worked for. It was, he guessed, more caused by him than it—a factor that he intended to give more thought to while he lay on that sunny beach in Rio. "That's why I told you that today would be the best day for the switch. The machine itself was completely tied up with hardware testing. No one will attempt one of the software routines until Monday morning, at the earliest."

"And when they do?"

"Then all hell breaks loose because the damned thing won't belch. There's a mismatch between the data inputs and the existing software."

"Speak English, okay?"

"That means that even though the physical shape of the software packages for both machines is identical—like most companies, Digitex makes everything out of the same blank stock—the languages are totally different, and so are the encoding translators. When they turn on that Defense Department machine Monday morning with what I put in it this afternoon, the software's going to be speaking about automobile fenders and axles when the keyed inputs will want to know about missile profiles and troop strengths."

"Very good. Does the delivery date of the Defense Department machine remain the same?"

"Far as I know." Caldwell took out another cigarette and fumbled for his matches. As he did, the old man laid his hand on Caldwell's arm to stop him. Caldwell looked up, annoyed. "What's wrong?"

"Don't light that thing up, you might attract attention to us." The old man nodded toward the primary road in the distance, where an occasional car passed by. "I don't want to sound melodramatic, but you might give some cop a reason to poke his nose over here."

"Sorry."

"Besides, smoking is bad for your health." The old man put on a friendly smile. He slapped Caldwell on the shoulder.

"Right." Caldwell threw the unlit cigarette on the ground. "Once I get to Rio, I'm giving up the weed for good."

"A smart choice. When are you leaving?" As he spoke, the old man took his first step toward the white Ford and motioned for Caldwell to follow him.

"I'm taking the midnight USAir flight to Pittsburgh, a rental car to Philadelphia, then another airline to Miami." Now that it was nearly over, Caldwell was feeling more confident, beginning to open up more. "The reservations are booked under different names. They're going to have a hell of a time tracing me, even if they try."

"Sounds like you've thought of everything."

"Yeah."

"Good." The old man nodded enthusiastically. "Well, I guess I've got enough information to keep the big shots happy. It's time to settle up." He opened the driver's door of the white Ford and climbed in. "Come around to the passenger's side, I've got the money under the front seat." The old man waited while Caldwell moved quickly around the front of the car, opened the passenger's door and began to get into the seat.

"I've got a little over an hour before I leave for my plane . . ." Caldwell stopped in mid-sentence when he focused on the object that the old man was holding. Even in the dim moonlight and the darkened interior of the white Ford— he realized now that for some reason, the car's interior roof light hadn't turned on when either of the front doors had been opened—the silencer-enshrouded pistol had a presence that made it appear a hundred times larger than it physically was. "What's this?"

"You telling me that you don't know what this is?" The old man waved the pistol slightly, although never enough to take the point of the barrel more than a few inches either side of Caldwell's heart.

"I . . . I don't understand . . ."

"Easy. Listen up, take notes if you like." The old man smirked. "A college graduate like you should find this pretty easy, and there won't be any test to cram for. Not this time." As the old man quickly scanned the terrain surrounding the car, he scarcely took his eyes off Caldwell. "My name is Thomas Nicholetti. I'd prefer if for the next couple minutes you stop thinking that I'm just another uneducated jerk."

"I wasn't . . ."

"I'm doing this job for a guy I met in New York," Nicholetti continued, "for only one reason. I need the money."

"I'll split my share with you." Even without saying it, Caldwell knew that any offer to split was a waste of time.

"Some of us," Nicholetti went on as if the other man hadn't said a thing, "don't have those fancy retirement plans with that annuity crap, or those IRA or Keogh things. If we wind up living a good deal longer than we figured we might, we run out of funds. Las Vegas is a great place, but it takes plenty of dough."

"What the hell are you talking about? Tell me what you want!" Caldwell was working desperately at keeping his composure, at sounding as unconcerned as humanly possible about the fact that a pistol was aimed directly at him. But even with his best efforts, his words came out rapidly, his voice high-pitched.

"You still haven't figured things out yet, huh?" Nicholetti shook his head in disbelief. "Well, since you're so interested, college boy, let me tell you about my business." Nicholetti began to indulge himself for the first time in his long career, taking an extra minute to feed his ego. "I'm retired now, understand? But for the last thirty-five years I was what the TV shows call a hit man. A paid assassin. A damned good one, too." Nicholetti watched the young man's mouth literally drop open and his eyes grow even wider. "Did anyone tell you that you do a good imitation of an owl when you screw up your face like that?''

''What are you going to do?!''

''You *still* haven't figured it out yet?''

''Oh, Christ help me . . .'' Caldwell's words were hardly distinguishable, the separate sounds ran into each other because they were distorted by the accompanying sounds of fear.

''Most of the guys in my work don't get much press coverage, if you follow what I mean. Those TV shows make us look like real jerks, like we shoot one, maybe two guys at the most, then the cops are all over us. Well, I got news.'' Nicholetti was on a roll now, really enjoying himself, saying things out loud for the first time that he'd been wanting to say most of his life. ''I got rid of people on a fairly regular basis, and I never had a cop get close to me. Cops, they ain't so smart—but one thing cops do have is a good retirement plan. If I had a fancy fund with *my* name on it, then I wouldn't be here now.''

''But what did I do?'' Caldwell couldn't decide whether to make a lunge for the old man or simply sit and keep pleading with him.

''Thanks for the good job.'' As he spoke, Nicholetti raised the pistol slightly. He gently pressed the trigger once, the hollow popping sound of the weapon's silencer filling the interior of the white Ford.

Alex Caldwell took the single bullet directly between his eyes. He, too, was dead before his body had toppled forward into the dashboard.

With that, Nicholetti took off the weapon's silencer and jammed it back into his topcoat pocket, then wiped the pistol clean with his handkerchief. He laid the pistol on the dashboard in front of the driver's seat.

What the college boy said last week was right. Nicholetti stepped out of the car and went back to the rear seat of the white Ford, where he retrieved the body of the dead Russian consulate employee that he had earlier laid beneath a blanket on the rear floor. Nicholetti dragged the dead Russian out and around, then shoved him into the driver's seat. After the dead Russian was properly positioned behind the steering wheel,

Nicholetti took the gun from the dashboard, where he had placed it a moment before, and carefully positioned it in the Russian's hand. Nicholetti then pressed the dead man's fingerprints on the trigger, butt and barrel.

Nicholetti then took another pistol from his other topcoat pocket. He wiped it clean, then carefully placed it in the hands of the dead computer engineer. *This crap is wearing me out,* Nicholetti said to himself, nearly aloud, as he grunted from exertion. Finally, he stepped back from the staged scene that he had just created.

The two men in the front seat of the white Ford were generally facing each other, their bullet wounds in the proper places for each to have inflicted the fatal gunshot wound on the other. Both weapons were in the proper hands, and the bullets and fingerprints would match up nicely for the police investigation. *Cops ain't so smart.*

Nicholetti turned around and walked quickly down the empty roadway and toward his own car, which he had parked a mile down that road a few hours earlier. All that was left for him to do was make the last telephone call to find out where the gook had put the other half of his money, then head back to Las Vegas to begin living on what he had earned for this, his last job. *Yeah, the college boy was right. I'm too old for this crap.* Thomas Nicholetti continued down the road without a backward glance at the cars and bodies he had assembled in a neat package for the police to find sometime in the next few hours. *This time, I swear, I'm going to retire. I'm an old man.*

2

Flight Attendant Kathy Davis stood in the forward galley of the jet airliner getting ready for the passengers to board, checking over the supply manifest, busying herself with final preparations for tonight's nonstop service to Japan. "Did catering get those cups to the rear galley yet?"

"Sure, I guess." Flight Attendant Claudia Novello looked up at the senior flight attendant blankly. "They must've by now, I would think."

Kathy sighed—it was going to be a long, long night for her. Besides Claudia, who had been a flight attendant with Trans Continental Airlines for seven years physically and seven minutes mentally, the other three flight attendants assigned to tonight's trip to Osaka consisted of two new-hire girls and one gay guy. Of all of them, Fred was unquestionably the most dependable—as long as he wasn't chasing some fellow in tight jeans—and Claudia, the least. "It probably would be best if you went back and looked for those cups yourself. I'd hate to have to ask the passengers in the coach section to drink straight from the bottles."

"Okay, I'll go check." Claudia ran the tip of her tongue

14

across her newly applied bright red lipstick while she thought
about what she was supposed to do next. "But what if the
cups aren't there yet?"

"Then use the data link in the rear galley. Send a message
direct to catering—the code is LAX-CTR. Tell them we can't
go without the cups."

"Oh, damn. I hate using the data link." The expression on
Claudia's face turned to a pout. "Can't I just come back here
and tell you, or maybe go inside and call them on the
telephone?"

"No. It's too close to departure time, we'll be boarding
soon. Besides, we should put the request in writing just in
case there's a delay." Kathy knew why Claudia didn't want
to use the onboard electronic data link transmitter—it required
remembering a few discrete address codes, plus the ability to
spell the words you were typing on the display screen. "The
discrete code to catering is LAX-CTR," she repeated. "Fred
knows how to work it, he'll help you."

"Okay." Claudia nodded reluctantly, then turned and walked
toward the rear of the empty airliner.

Kathy watched Claudia disappear around the drawn curtain
that separated the small first-class compartment from the
larger coach section. *Maybe that's the only way to be*. Although she knew that she was only fooling herself, Kathy
allowed herself a tinge of jealousy for Claudia and those like
her. Relatively mindless automatons who went through life
with simplistic innocence, nothing seemed to bother them—
and in many ways they got just as much out of life as anyone
else, but without all the ulcers and the heartache. It was a
position to envy. She was reminded of a line from a song
she'd heard on the car radio on her drive to the airport that
afternoon. *I wish I didn't know now what I didn't know then*.

"All set to board?"

Kathy put on her professional smile for the airline agent
who had stuck his head through the cabin door to see if they
were ready. "Sure, anytime." She watched the young man
hustle back up the jet bridge that connected the airliner to the
terminal. In another minute or two tonight's Los Angeles
customers would begin to make the trek down the jet bridge,
then step onboard and begin the ritual of stumbling over each

other as they frantically searched for their seats. It never ceased to amaze Kathy how passengers pushed, shoved and crowded themselves into the jet bridge and onto the airplane, even though it was still a half hour before the scheduled departure time of 10:00 P.M. It was as if the passengers thought that they were boarding a subway train whose doors might slam shut on them at any moment.

The galley interphone buzzed, and Kathy reached over to answer it. It was the copilot, ordering coffee for Captain Blanchard and, seemingly as an afterthought, for himself. Kathy answered that it would take a few minutes to get the coffee—until Claudia returned from the rear, she explained, since the passengers were due to board at any moment. The copilot—a pudgy-faced young man named Clancy, whose first name she had forgotten—had flown with Kathy a few times during the last several months. Tonight, he seemed far more tense and uptight than she remembered him—and Kathy already knew damned well why. *That Blanchard is such an asshole.* But before she could get herself emotionally wound up over the need to work with Captain Blanchard for the next six days as they flew various trips around the Orient, Kathy put the entire subject out of her mind. Instead, she checked over the galley one final time.

Satisfied that everything was as it should be, Kathy glanced up at the small mirror at the rear of the galley to check her own appearance before she went on stage for the airline. What she saw reflected in the mirror would be, to any casual observer, just fine. Neat, tied-back blonde hair, a thin face with a good complexion and just a touch of blush, enough lipstick to be tantalizing without being excessive. A pretty woman. Sexy, too, as she had been told by dozens of men throughout her life. But even in the small galley mirror Kathy could see something else.

First and unmistakably, she was getting older much too quickly—something that even her generally youthful appearance couldn't hide any longer. Kathy was twenty-nine, which was nearly ten years older than the youngest flight attendant working on this particular trip with her. And then there was the growing sadness, the melancholy, that Kathy's ever-present smile could hardly keep back anymore. Although an impartial observer would have looked at it differently, as far as Kathy was concerned nothing of significance had ever worked out for her. Absolutely not a blessed thing.

Kathy stepped away from the galley mirror and assumed her position at the forward edge of the entrance door. "Welcome aboard. May I see your ticket, please?" As always, an elderly couple had led the swelling procession down the jet bridge—a very natural occurrence since elderly people, more than most other passengers, seemed always to be in dire fear of being left behind. "Your seats are in the second cabin, halfway down on the right."

"Thank you."

As the couple shuffled by, Kathy went into her standard routine of checking tickets, answering questions, and pointing out where the baggage should be placed. She had worked through approximately eighty passengers when she first spotted him.

He stood twenty feet back in the jet bridge, his attention at the moment turned toward the woman standing beside him, his face looking tanned but much older than she would have imagined. For the first few seconds Kathy couldn't move, couldn't think, could hardly breathe, until a woman passenger standing in the entranceway shoved a ticket forcefully into her hand and brought Kathy back to life. "Oh, yes . . . second cabin, third row on the left." She glanced up again just in time to have her gaze meet his.

Ron Jennings stood between his wife Barbara and his teenage daughter Charlene as they worked their way down the jet bridge toward the airplane. He had been in mid-sentence at the time, explaining to his wife what he imagined they might do during their free time in Osaka, when he first saw Kathy. There were still a dozen people standing between them, yet suddenly she was all Jennings could see.

"Ron, what is it?"

"I . . . I know that stewardess," Jennings finally managed to say in answer to his wife. *God Almighty. Kathy.* He flew so seldom and Trans Continental had grown to be so large an airline in the last several years that he never once thought that she might be on one of the few flights he took. Ron moved ahead silently, his wife and daughter now in front of him. It finally became their turn to cross the threshold and board the jetliner. Barbara, who was holding their tickets, handed them to the stewardess and half-turned toward her husband while she waited for him to say something.

"Well, hello there. Do you remember me?" Jennings finally said to Kathy as he searched for some appropriate words. He realized that there were none.

"It's good to see you," Kathy answered automatically, not knowing whether it was good or not as she tried to sort out her own feelings. "Of course I remember you." *God Almighty.* She, too, had never expected to see Ron again. Kathy held the Jenningses' tickets tightly in her hand and studied them far longer than was necessary in order to give herself more time to regain her composure. But just before she had found her voice again and was ready to look up at Ron and his family, the galley interphone behind her buzzed loudly. Welcoming the diversion, Kathy reached over and grabbed for it. "Hello?"

"This is Captain Blanchard. Has the second flight attendant returned to the galley yet?" a deep and authoritative voice asked in an undisguised tone of annoyance. "I'm still waiting for my coffee."

"No sir, not yet. Very soon." Kathy slid the interphone carefully back into its cradle, then turned to the crowd in the entranceway. "Sorry for the interruption. Now, let's get you folks seated and I'll come back to talk with you as soon as I get a chance. You're in first class, the first two rows on the left." Kathy pointed to show Ron's wife toward her seat, then turned away as Ron brushed past her to follow.

Kathy resumed her post at the entranceway and continued to take tickets from those entering, all the while scrupulously keeping her eyes away from the front left side of the first-class cabin. But even without looking, she could sense Ron's presence, she could tell that he was not very far away—just as she had been able to do years before. And beyond that, she could also sense something else: a growing dread that spread through her insides like an upended vial of acid. *God, please help me get through this.* As she stood at the head of Flight 42's cabin, Senior Flight Attendant Kathy Davis suspected that tonight's trip to Japan was probably going to be the worst flight of her airline career.

• • •

Lt. Gen. Peng Ming paced back and forth in his office, stopping occasionally to peek through the side of the drawn window shade as he waited for the Ambassador to arrive. Peng glanced at his wristwatch for the tenth time in as many minutes, although he fully understood that even though it was now nearly one o'clock in the morning, it would take the Ambassador at least ten more minutes to make the trip from the reception center in Kennedy Center to the Chinese Embassy in the Georgetown section of Washington.

The Ambassador has no choice, he has to go along with me now. Peng allowed himself another moment of guarded optimism—a curious feeling for him because he was regarded as a dire pessimist who always expected and prepared for the worst. That was, he knew, why he had advanced to the rank of lieutenant general in the Chinese Air Force at the age of only forty-nine. By being prepared for the worst, Peng had been uncannily accurate in his predictions of the difficulties China had to face during the past thirty years. In almost all instances, he had been absolutely correct.

The sound of a car in the embassy's circular drive brought Peng back to the reality of the moment, and he pushed aside the window shade just in time to see the Ambassador's car wheel out of view toward the garage on the side of the building. *A few more minutes.* Peng took a deep breath to clear his mind, then sat down at his desk and looked at the machine.

Sitting on the corner of the rosewood desk was a computer screen. On it, in green letters on a black background, was a header of codes and symbols. Below it, alone in the middle of the viewing area, was a double line of text:

SIGNAL CLEAR; UPPER DEVICE ARMED
                LOWER DEVICE ARMED

Peng pressed the appropriate places on the keyboard in front of him to test the message. It vanished from the screen's display for a brief moment, then reappeared precisely as it had been written earlier. The test and verification process was complete, so Peng knew that he was getting a readout that was no more than one or two seconds behind the actual events that were occurring in California—and the same readout that Colonel Qi at the airbase in Yangzhou was seeing.

The buzzer on his desk sounded, and Peng reached for his intercom switch. "Yes?"

"Lieutenant General, the Ambassador will see you now," a disinterested voice announced out of the speaker box. "In the main conference room."

"Certainly. Please tell the Ambassador that I'm on my way." Peng released the button on his intercom and rose to his feet. Not surprisingly, his legs felt shaky and he took a moment out to glance in the mirror to determine if he would look as high-strung to others as he knew he actually was. No, the mirror showed that he appeared calm on the outside—which was quite a remarkable contradiction to the churning in his stomach and the knotted muscles of his arms and legs.

As Peng looked in the mirror, he allowed himself a moment to glance at the cloth insignia that was sewn above each shoulder of his brown officer's uniform. The small but conspicuous insignia of rank made him swell with pride because, up until a few years ago, no distinction of ranks had been permitted. It had been a policy that Peng had always been opposed to, although he had had the good sense not to have made an issue of it.

During those worst years of the rampaging Red Brigades, the Mao Ze-dong silliness of we-are-all-one had been taken to its ultimate extreme. Out of fear of reprisal, all people in China dressed alike and tried to look alike, including the members of the military. In the Air Force, since distinctions of rank were thought of as a capitalist influence, the chain of command was enforced strictly by recognition—a common soldier would obey orders only from those officers he knew personally. We-are-all-one was typical of Mao's policies: it looked good on paper but it didn't work worth a damn, which is something any child would have known, if anyone in the country had been allowed to think or speak openly. Now, thank God, Mao had finally died, the Gang of Four was discredited, and the worst of Mao's policies and influences was nearly behind them at last.

Mao would roll straight out of his tomb if he could see us now. We've got to keep moving ahead, the Ambassador has no choice. Peng left his office and walked down the hall toward the main conference suite. *He's got to go along with me, it's the only logical thing to do. It's too late for choices*.

When Peng reached the conference room door, he hesitated a moment before he went in. The problem, Peng knew, was that this was the first time in his career that he had acted on his own, that he had gone far beyond the breadth and scope of his command. But Peng knew that he had done it strictly for the good of China, and fortified with that knowledge, he finally opened the door and stepped in.

Ambassador Li Ying-teh stood at the far wall, facing the window. After a few moments of silence, he spoke without turning toward the man who had entered. "We have much to learn from the West," Li finally said.

"Pardon me?"

"For example," Li continued, still not bothering to turn away from the window that opened out onto the blackness of the embassy's side yard, "the people of the West are much better at partying than we are in the East. The people in the West have a knack of making what they call business into parties, while we have the unfortunate propensity of making what we call parties into business." Li turned around slowly and finally faced the man that he spoke with. "The party tonight was just such an example." Li kept a neutral expression on his face, even though he was dealing with a man that he basically did not think much of.

"I regret having to call you," Peng answered with a half bow. He knew that the Ambassador would be predictably displeased at being summoned and displeased at not having the slightest idea why, but Peng also knew that what he had to say would make Li forget the Kennedy Center party soon enough. "An emergency."

"I assumed so." Li reached over to pick up the pipe from a table near the lounge chair he normally sat in, but he continued to stand his ground rather than move toward it to sit.

Even in the soft yellow light that illuminated the main conference suite, Peng could see the harshness around the Ambassador's eyes. The old man—Li had celebrated his seventy-second birthday just a few weeks before—had an intimidating stature about him. The Ambassador was a full head taller than most of the Chinese in the embassy—which made him nearly two heads taller than Peng, who was somewhat on the short side.

Worse yet was Li's habit of standing rigidly erect whenever he dealt with his people, making all those around him feel as though they were being lectured to, not spoken with. In addition to all that, the features of Li's head added measurably to his intimidating nature—total baldness, an aging scalp, a deeply furrowed brow and facial lines, a thin black mustache. Peng could easily see why Li's powers of political survival were as legendary as they were—it was rumored that even Mao himself had been wary when dealing with Li. "May I ask you to please turn the embassy computer to internal channel six."

"If you like." Li strode across the room to the ornate rosewood desk on the far wall. He reached down to flip the appropriate switch on a repeater screen of the embassy's central computer. He looked up at Peng and waited silently as the screen came to life.

In short order the computer screen filled with the same message that Peng had viewed earlier, much to his relief. What he didn't need now was for the situation in California to change markedly while he was trying to explain things to the Ambassador. "Do you recall our conversation about the American presence in the East, and my concerns about our ultimate military options?"

"In spite of my advancing years, my memory remains as strong as ever."

"During the past fourteen months, I've been investigating the possibility of getting more . . . accurate . . . information on what the Americans might do in various Eastern crisis situations."

"What good is information like that?" Li asked. He was toying with the man, goading him, enjoying a brief interlude by watching him squirm. "The Americans have become our staunch allies. The Americans and the Chinese are now the best of friends and should continue to be."

"No enemy stays an enemy forever. Neither does a friend.

Knowing ahead of time what the Americans are thinking might help us make up for some of the material and scientific military disadvantages we have in comparison to them."

"I think you must be deluding yourself."

"Being prepared does no harm." Peng shifted his weight from foot to foot as he stood—he wished the two of them would sit down so he could explain things in a more relaxed atmosphere. "This may take a few minutes to explain. Would you care to sit?" Peng asked as he pointed to the grouping of sofas and chairs in the center of the room.

"No."

Reluctantly, Peng continued on, standing right where he was. "During my search for information, I came across a young man in California who could be dealt with. This young man held a minor staff position in a computer laboratory that did work for the American Defense Department."

"A weapons computer?"

"Nearly the opposite." Peng paused, hoping to give the proper effect when he announced what he had stumbled across. "A war games computer."

"Games?" The Ambassador displayed an expression of annoyance. "You call me back from an important diplomatic party for a discussion of war games?"

"What I'm telling you," Peng said in a louder voice, trying to sound more forceful, trying to sound aggravated when in fact he was frightened to death that Li might not hear him out, might dismiss him from his military-attaché post in Washington and send him back to China before he could explain, "is that the war games themselves aren't important. What *is* important is that the software of this computer has been programmed with the current American military thinking on what might happen in various war scenarios in our section of the world!"

"I see." Li nodded slowly, then laid his pipe back down on the table. He turned his eyes away from the lieutenant general while he ran over the possibilities in his mind. *Maybe this little wart hog has stumbled onto something.* Finally, he looked up again. "What about security? Certainly the Americans must know how valuable that sort of data could be?"

"Naturally there are some security aspects involved because the computer company does do work for the Defense Department—but this is where our luck was golden. Since the software information was destined for a computer used strictly for war games *training*, it was given a far lower security rating than the information itself actually deserved." Peng was excited now but he wouldn't allow himself to show it—that might be a tactical error in his overall strategy to get the Ambassador's approval and involvement in his plan.

"So what you're saying is that you've discovered the Americans in a bureaucratic foul-up. What should be potentially high-grade security information is lying relatively unguarded inside a computer that they don't seem to regard as terribly high risk."

"Exactly!" Peng slapped his hand on the desk. "That's the only reason I had any hope of gaining access. The software in the machine had enough valuable information on American military thinking and air combat plans to give us a distinct edge in our region. From what I've seen so far, our analysts will be able to accurately predict the American response to various military air actions in the East with great accuracy. You can imagine what information like that can be worth."

"And what plans do you have for getting access to this war games software?"

Peng took a deep breath, then wiped away a growing line of perspiration from his forehead. "I've already done it," he said. His voice had dropped to nearly a whisper.

"You've already done it! How?"

Peng took an involuntary step backward as Li peered down at him. "Actually, I'm doing it right now." Lt. Gen. Peng Ming gestured toward the embassy's computer screen on the desk. The text printed on it was still exactly as it had been. "I've managed to have someone place that military software and its encoding device inside another computer. That second computer is one that we will soon be able to get our hands on."

Li paused only a brief moment to gather his thoughts, and during that time he managed to somehow hide his own amazement. Finally, he smiled softly as he shook his head. "Your statements leave open more questions than they answer. Obviously, there is quite a great deal more to this than a few quick words could resolve.'' Ambassador Li Ying-teh motioned toward the grouping of chairs in the center of the room. ''Let's sit down. I want to hear everything you have to say.''

3

When Ron Jennings had moved back from seat 2B in the airliner's nonsmoking section to seat 4D in the smoking area, he did so with the deliberate motions of a man who knew that he needed maximum benefit from every one of the next passing moments. Jennings had moved back and across the aisle from his wife and daughter for three reasons: first, to have one of his two allocated en route cigarettes now that dinner was finished; second, to avoid watching the in-flight movie—a re-release of an old Robert Redford flick he had seen with Barbara once before—which had just begun in the first-class section of the darkened jetliner's cabin; third, to have a few minutes alone so that he might talk with Kathy again.

Flight Attendant Kathy Davis worked her way down the dimly lit aisle, pretending to be in no rush as she checked on each of the nine first-class passengers in the 787's forward cabin. As she approached row three, the old man and the teenage boy on the left signaled that they wanted nothing, while the bald-headed man in the window seat on the right took off his movie headphones and motioned for her to come toward him.

"I'd like an after-dinner drink. My wife, too."

"What would you like?" Kathy glanced up to look at Ron, who was sitting directly behind the man in row three, pretending not to be watching her. She desperately wanted to talk to Ron, as she had for the last three hours, and the last thing Kathy wanted now was to get embroiled in the ritual that she knew was about to begin.

"I'm not sure what I'd like."

"What do you have?" the lady sitting beside him asked in a haughty voice as she, too, removed her headphones.

Kathy turned her attention directly toward the woman, who was obviously the power to be reckoned with in this marriage. The woman was fifty or so, grossly overdressed, overjeweled and overfed. She had three big emeralds on her fingers and enough gold around her neck to guarantee that she'd never come to the surface if they ditched. "Well, we have the normal complement onboard—cream sherry, amaretto, cognac . . ."

"Not a very interesting assortment," the woman interrupted.

"I guess it's not." *Damn.* "I can mix up something a little more exotic, if you'd like."

"Such as what?"

Kathy pretended to study the woman carefully, as if she were helping her pick out a dress for a royal tea party. She went on to list the concoctions she could put together in the small airplane galley, her thoughts all the while on Ron and his family. *Seven more hours of this, God help me.* Her only consolation came from the fact that it was now nearly one o'clock in the morning, Los Angeles time, and that most of the passengers would quickly fall asleep as soon as the movie was over—in fact, a few of them had fallen asleep already.

After Kathy had listed the potential drinks, the couple in row three selected a mixture of champagne and Chambord, served over ice, for both of them. Within a few minutes Kathy had gone back to the galley, thrown together the two drinks and brought them back to row three.

"Thank you."

"My pleasure." Kathy glanced over the seat back toward

row four again. Even with the cabin lighting restricted to reading lamps only, Ron's features were strikingly visible. As she had realized during the first few moments of looking at him when he boarded, he had obviously aged—but otherwise, he seemed as attractive as ever. Seeing Ron again after all these years created a confusing array of signals for her, some pleasant, some not so pleasant. Regardless, Kathy knew that she had to deal with them, and she probably had no more than the next few minutes to do so. This was their first and, probably, their last chance to be alone together for any length of time.

"If there's nothing else, I'll leave you to enjoy the movie." Without waiting for their answer, Kathy moved on to the last row of first class. The man on the other side of the aisle in seat 4A—a blind man, his white cane propped across the empty seat beside him—was one of those already asleep although his headphones were still clamped on tightly. Kathy turned from him and toward Ron Jennings in seat 4D.

"Is everyone settled in?" Jennings asked as he fumbled with the unlit cigarette in his hand. He had been cradling that cigarette as the fragile prize that he knew it was, reluctant to light it up too early.

"They seem to be settled and happy." Kathy put on her professional smile as she stood next to his seat. "Your family, too. They're wrapped up in the movie." Kathy realized that she had never seen Ron's wife in person before, although she had seen the woman's photograph countless times in sports magazines and seen her twice on national television. Kathy used to fantasize about a confrontation with Barbara. Barbara would be crushed, her righteous indignation serving only to push Ron further away. As for herself, Kathy, of course, would be devastated. She hadn't planned to be a home-wrecker—but the natural love and passion between her and Ron were unstoppable. Ron would leave Barbara, and Kathy would take her rightful place with the man she loved.

Nice fantasy, Kathy thought. This, however, was the real world. The famous Barbara Jennings, sitting in first class with her daughter—Ron's daughter—was totally oblivious to the fact that her husband was in close proximity and having a *tête-à-tête* with a woman who had shared his heart, his mind and his bed for eight long months. Kathy had given Barbara the kind of thorough once-over reserved for rivals. She knew that Barbara must be almost fifty by now—nearly twenty years older than she was—but her legendary prowess on the golf course had kept her body looking great. Barbara wasn't a glamorous woman; her well-bred Irish features and her shoulder-length sun-streaked hair gave her an air of approachability. She was the type who, after a morning on the golf course, still looked fabulous at the check-out line in the grocery store. "How'd your wife hurt her arm?" Kathy asked as she gestured toward where Barbara sat ahead of them, her right arm wrapped in a heavy tan-colored bandage that extended from her forearm to a few inches above her elbow. "I didn't know golf was a dangerous game."

"Tennis, actually," Jennings answered, ignoring the sarcasm. "She was playing with Charlene last week. She slipped—must've landed on her arm the wrong way. It's not broken or even badly hurt, just banged up. Doctor said that she could travel if she kept it tightly wrapped."

"Oh." At the mention of his daughter's name, Kathy thought about her, also. Charlene's appearance had been something of a surprise—the girl had gone from the gawky child Kathy had once seen from a distance to nearly an adult in the past six years. Kathy knew that the girl would be about sixteen by now. She was tall and beautiful, a combination of the best features of both her mother and her father. She also had an air of unmistakable poise and confidence about her that was normally lacking in girls her age. Like her mother, she was supposed to be a pretty good golfer, too.

Kathy had watched them earlier with growing jealousy as mother and daughter shared a lipstick, giggled together over an obviously private joke and sat next to each other with the ease of two people who had spent their lives together. Kathy realized that these two women also shared Ron Jennings. The three of them were a family and always would be, no matter what had happened between her and Ron six years before.

"I've seen this movie already." Jennings gestured with his free hand toward the changing images on the screen at the front of the cabin, then used that hand to take out a pack of matches. It was time for the cigarette, he couldn't wait any longer. As he lit up, he allowed the drone from the airliner's jet engines to envelop him as he took a long and deep drag. Finally, he spoke again. "Barbara's seen the movie too, but she wanted to watch it again."

"I like Robert Redford." Kathy finally slid into thè empty seat beside Ron, careful not to stare at him too directly. His close-cropped curly auburn hair had grown measurably grey at the temples. The furrows on his forehead were deeper, the features of his face more gaunt. Still, he remained as incredibly handsome to her as he had always been. His deep tan—more red than brown—highlighted his dark eyes magnificently. Those penetrating eyes of his remained as vexing to her as they had been years before. "You look great. You've got lots of good color."

"We live in Florida now."

"I had heard that. Sonny Bellman told me so a few years ago. He had run into you somewhere."

"Yes, I remember. How's he doing?"

"Great. He's a captain now, on 727's."

"He was a good copilot." The two of them had flown at least a dozen trips with Bellman in the copilot's seat—he had become something of an unofficial ancillary to their eight-month love affair.

"He's a good captain, too. I flew with him about a year ago, just before I transferred to the international division."

"Speaking of captains, who's our captain today? I saw him when he walked back to the lavatory, but I didn't recognize him."

"Alvin Blanchard. He's very senior. He's been in the international division for years—long before the merger with Central. That's probably why you don't know him."

"Probably."

"Do you keep in touch with any of the pilots from the domestic division?"

"Not too many." Jennings had already decided not to get into a discussion about that sort of thing, about his feelings that pilots who had been run out of the company on medical technicalities had very little in common with active pilots. Even more so, he had adamantly promised himself that he would not become a nostalgic hanger-on like some of the medically grounded pilots had done.

"That's too bad." Kathy had allowed her words to come out in the same lighthearted manner that she normally used with passengers, but if anyone had been watching the two of them at that moment, then her eyes would have certainly given her away. Kathy was watching Ron's motions with intent concentration, using his gestures and mannerisms—the way he held his head, the way he looked at her—as a trigger of all the shared memories between the two of them.

"I've got other interests now. I finally bought a boat, although a little smaller than the kinds of boats I used to talk to you about. I go fishing quite a bit."

"Are you playing any golf?"

"No." Jennings shrugged; he had put down his golf clubs for the last time shortly after his medical retirement—being a pure duffer married to a lady professional golfer had drained him of what little desire he once had to play the game, especially once he had been deprived of the excuse of having insufficient practice time as the reason for his high scores. "That's Barbara's field, not mine."

"Is she playing anymore? I don't follow golf, but I don't recall seeing her in any of those ladies' golf tournaments." Kathy knew very well that Barbara had stopped playing professionally, but she didn't want to appear to know too much about what was happening in Ron's life.

"Barbara retired—shortly after the airline decided that I should." Jennings kept a neutral expression on his face.

"Oh, really? Why?"

"Ask her."

Kathy could see that very little had changed, in spite of the years they'd been apart. She could tell that, for example, right now Ron was annoyed with the turn in the conversation and didn't intend to say what he really meant—which was probably that Kathy should mind her own damn business, or perhaps that there was still trouble between him and Barbara. Either way, she knew that she wasn't about to get an immediate answer. "That's okay, I was just wondering."

"Right."

Other than being a few years older, ex-Captain Ron Jennings seemed unchanged from the man she had loved so passionately, the man who had walked out of their love affair and her life when the airline medical department discovered his disabling heart condition during one of his routine annual physicals. As he sat there with his arm bare inches from hers, Ron Jennings had become a full-fledged anachronism—a visitation out of her past, like the sequence of a meaningful and lingering dream that she had nearly forgotten but had suddenly come intruding into her life during an innocent afternoon nap. She didn't know how to treat this visitation, but she knew that she needed to try. "I'll be happy to bring you up to date on the goings-on at good old Trans Continental during the last few years."

"Fine." Jennings didn't know if he really wanted to hear it, but he knew that he couldn't simply turn away—not from his past, not from Kathy. The temptation to at least hear her out was far too great.

The two of them sat in silence for a moment. A swirl of cigarette smoke rose up between them in broad, lazy circles until it reached the height where the conditioned flow of air in the airliner's cabin swept it away. Kathy glanced over her shoulder one last time to verify that the plastic divider between first class and coach remained firmly shut. She certainly didn't want anyone eavesdropping. "It's been a long time."

"Yes." Jennings didn't know what else to add to the cliché that basically said it all.

"Someone told me about what happened to you on that physical, but then I found that note you left in my mailbox."

"I wanted you to read the note first." Jennings fidgeted in the deep-cushioned chair as he ran the fingers of his free hand nervously along the armrest, the other hand maneuvering the cigarette in and out of his mouth. Jennings studied the young stewardess for a moment, the reflected images from the movie screen dancing along the soft features of her face. Finally, he turned away. Jennings tried to remember what he had written to her in that last note but couldn't recall the exact words.

"If you wanted me to see the note sooner, you should've given it to me personally."

"You know I couldn't do that." Being a golf widower had

been Jennings's rational excuse for having the affair with Kathy, although he now realized that he could just as easily have attributed the whole thing to temporary insanity or the infamous male mid-life crisis. Yet no matter how much he had been in love with Kathy, he knew that things had changed for both of them. It had been six years since he had written that letter of explanation, put it in her company mailbox and walked out of the Trans Continental crew room for the last time. Six years had passed since he had been forced to retire from the airline because of what the doctors had labeled as his disabling heart condition. Six years had gone by since Barbara had voluntarily given up her spot on the golf tour to stay home with him.

"That note is probably not a good subject to get into, please forgive me." There was a touch of bitterness in Kathy's tone that surprised even her.

"I did what I had to. I did what I thought was right."

"I didn't mean it the way it sounded." Kathy leaned toward him. "I'm glad that you wrote me that note. It meant a great deal to me at the time."

"Do you still have it?"

"Have what?"

"The note." Jennings wondered why he had asked such a ridiculous question. He changed the subject. "How do you like flying the 787?"

Kathy ignored him as she went back to the original question. "I held on to that note for a long time. Too long, probably. I had convinced myself that it was all I had left. I finally threw it away when I moved from Chicago."

"You moved from Chicago?" Without even trying, Jennings could picture her apartment quite clearly—something he hadn't thought about for years. The two overstuffed chairs by the bay window where they would sit by the hour and watch the street traffic below, the bed crammed up against the far wall. He could hear the place, feel the place, smell the place. He wanted to tell her so, but he didn't know how. "I'm surprised."

"You won't be when I tell you why. I moved because I got married."

"Oh?" Jennings knew that he should congratulate her, but couldn't get the word out.

"I wasn't getting any younger." Kathy pushed aside a wisp of her blonde hair that framed her blue eyes and oval-shaped face. "When you wrote me that note I was twenty-three. I'm twenty-nine now."

"I understand." But Jennings didn't understand at all—he had heard her words but hadn't accepted them because none of them made any sense to him. The fact that she was married should have been no more than another point of information, yet somehow it hadn't been. He still sincerely loved his wife as much as he always had—he had, except for those years when Barbara was heavily committed to the golf tour and away from home for weeks at a time, always been extremely close to his wife; they had a good enough marriage—yet just sitting next to Kathy for a few minutes had brought back all the memories of how much he had been in love with her, too. "Who's the lucky guy?" he finally asked.

"No one from the airline. His name is Jason. We've been married four years. He's an architect. We live in Los Angeles."

Both of them lapsed into silence, regrouping their thoughts and getting their defenses ready for the next exchange. "How long did you say you've been on the international runs?" Jennings gestured around the big darkened cabin of the Consolidated 787 jetliner, working hard at changing the subject as he concentrated instead on what he had heard and read about the airplane. The long-range version of the 787 was a new airplane for Trans Continental. They had acquired the first one just slightly more than a year before. Built by a new international consortium that used financial and engineering inputs from Boeing, McDonnell Douglas and Airbus International, the Consolidated Industries 787 was the ultimate example of state-of-the-art technology. By now Trans Continental had a dozen or more of these ships, most of them flying the long-and-thin routes like this nonstop from Los Angeles to Osaka, Japan.

"I transferred to the international division eight months ago."

"How do you like it?"

"It's great," Kathy said, omitting the fact that at the

moment nothing seemed great, nothing at all was right for her. "I enjoy working the first-class service. After almost ten years I've finally got enough seniority to get the kind of flight schedules that I like."

"Do the pilots like the airplane?" Even though he hadn't touched an airplane of any kind in six years, Jennings's pilot's instincts had caused him to begin evaluating the airliner as soon as he had stepped onboard. It was a long, sleek machine with a cabin the same width as the airliners he had last flown—a single aisle with seats on either side—but this airplane was at least fifty feet longer. Yet what he had noticed first was what he already knew that it lacked: more than two engines. Back when Jennings flew the line for Trans Continental, it was illegal and considered unwise to take anything less than a three-engine airplane across vast bodies of water— most of them the wide-body jumbo jets like 747's and DC-10's. Now airlines were flying their long-haul Atlantic and Pacific flights with only one engine on each wing in equipment like the European Airbus, the Boeing 767 and, now, the Consolidated 787.

"I can tell that you're counting engines," Kathy said with a laugh.

"Is it that obvious?"

"Yes. It happens all the time. Retired pilots have the same response, that we haven't brought along enough engines."

"Are we wrong?" Jennings glanced out at the enormous power plant on the airplane's right wing. It was, he knew from his reading, a Rolls Royce engine capable of far more thrust by itself than the combined thrust of both engines on the smaller Boeing airliner that he had last flown as captain on. "Have the engines become that reliable?"

"Yes." Kathy went on to tell him what she had heard about the technical aspects of the big airliner, while Ron mentioned several factors that supported the logic of having more than two engines for overwater flights. It was nothing but small talk that both of them were happy to indulge in, all of it concentrated in the areas where they were comfortable. As he told Kathy about the simultaneous failure of all four engines that had occurred to a British Airways Boeing 747 several years before when it flew through a massive cloud of volcanic ash, she nodded as he spoke but hardly heard his words. Instead, Kathy sat back and revelled in the sensation that the two of them were still sitting in her Chicago apartment together, talking just the way they once did, feeling the way they used to.

"So do you see my point?" Jennings asked.

"I always see your point," Kathy answered. She touched him playfully on the arm and smiled, but was careful not to let her hand linger. Inside, she ached.

"Right." Jennings smiled back sincerely. He had very much enjoyed the last few minutes with Kathy—it was, in many ways, just like it had always been. But, down deep, Jennings could feel a cold rush of anxiety. Barbara was not far away, and nearly as bad as far as his own composure and peace of mind were concerned, he knew that questions about his physical condition were also not very far away. Jennings wanted to put those questions off as long as possible.

Jennings hated talking about what the doctors called his heart condition. According to their fucking machines with their endless readouts of jiggling lines and columns of numbers, his own body had deserted him in nearly every way that it could have, short of death. They said he had a diseased and weakened heart that might stop beating at any moment—or that it might possibly go on beating feebly for the next twenty or thirty years.

As far as Jennings was concerned it was a topic to be strenuously avoided. Even though he had suffered a few mild attacks of palpitations, lightheadedness and nausea over the last few years, it was the *knowledge* of his condition and not its actual manifestations that was the worst part. Jennings didn't want to dwell on any of it, didn't want to face it—and he certainly didn't want to share any of it with Kathy, Barbara or anyone else for that matter. As in that old George Romero movie, he had become one of the living dead. "If you'll excuse me for a minute, I'm going to the washroom."

"Are you okay?" Kathy asked as she let him pass by and into the aisle.

"Yes, dammit," Jennings answered abruptly. Without waiting for her to reply, he turned and stepped aft. Jennings covered the few feet between his seat and the first-class

lavatory quickly, and was glad to see that the door annuncia-
tor showed that the lavatory was unoccupied. But before he
went in, he pushed aside the curtain that separated the first
class from the coach sections and peeked past the coach
galley into the long middle cabin.

The airplane was about half full, and the flight attendants
in the back were just finishing the dinner service. Soon
the coach-class movie would begin, with probably half the
passengers watching the movie and the other half falling
asleep. Jennings glanced at his wristwatch: it was one-ten in
the morning, Los Angeles time, yet he wasn't sleepy in the
slightest. He dropped the curtain, turned toward the lavatory,
then opened the door and stepped inside.

"God Almighty . . ." What he saw in the lavatory's wash
basin caused him to back up, startled, against the bulkhead
wall.

A homemade bomb lay cradled in the stainless steel sink
bowl, the sticks of explosives wired to a small central box
wedged between them, the strips of wires held together by
wrappings of black tape, which fastened the assembly where
it lay. Above the bomb, against the mirror, was a note. The
note was composed of words and letters cut from magazines
and pasted on a sheet of paper. While Ron Jennings ran his
eyes over the note again and again, the bile rose up in his
stomach and he could feel the rapid heartbeats as they filled
his chest.

THIS IS A HIJACKING. DO NOT TOUCH
THIS RADIO CONTROLLED BOMB
OR IT WILL EXPLODE
SEVERAL HIJACKERS ONBOARD
WITH THREE MORE BOMBS.
MORE INFORMATION IN ONE HOUR.

4

After he had discovered the bomb in the washbasin of the first-class lavatory of Trans Continental Flight 42, Ron Jennings stood where he was for several seconds before deciding on his next move. *Stay calm. Think things out.* Jennings bent over and studied the compact array of wires and explosives carefully, hoping to find some obvious reason to discount this thing as nothing more than an elaborate hoax. Unfortunately, the closer he looked at the carefully constructed package, the more the damn thing appeared all too real.

The bomb itself was an elaborate affair of wires and several small boxes that looked like they were designed to contain electronics—all of it wrapped securely around two yellow cylinders the size of soft-drink cans. The impression that Jennings got was that the yellow cylinders contained the explosives while the rigging surrounding them was made up of the detonators, plus some sort of anti-tampering device.

Jennings gave up on the bomb and turned away. He opened the door of the lavatory and stepped out into the aisle of the jetliner. Jennings let his eyes adjust to the relative darkness of the cabin before he proceeded up the aisle, since the movie in the first-class section was in full swing and the few passengers who had earlier left their reading lights on had since extinguished them. Everyone in first class was engrossed in the Robert Redford movie or asleep. Jennings approached the seat where Stewardess Kathy Davis was waiting for him. "I've got to show you something."

"What?"

"In the lavatory."

"Is this some kind of joke?"

"No." Jennings didn't know what else to say, since there were far too many ears within hearing distance. "There's something back there you should see."

"Something's wrong?" There was slight annoyance in Kathy's voice, since the last thing she wanted now was to waste her few precious moments with Ron on some stupid airplane problem. "Are we out of miniature toothpastes again?"

"It's a . . . something that you should know about—a plumbing problem."

"I'm not a plumber. If memory serves me correctly, I don't believe we brought a plumber along in this particular flight crew."

"Dammit." Jennings bit into his lower lip to control himself. "It's something you could fix. A leak at the sink. I think it might be a valve that needs to be tightened down."

"A valve? Are you being serious?"

"Yes."

Kathy looked at him, puzzled. "I don't know anything about valves. If there's really a leak back there, I'll get the copilot to come back to look at it."

"No, you can do it yourself." Jennings worked hard at keeping himself from grabbing her by the arm and dragging her back with him.

"Okay, if you say so." Kathy shrugged, then rose to her feet. She still suspected that this must be some kind of dumb joke, but, then again, something in Ron's behavior told her that it was not. She followed as he led the way rearward to the door of the lavatory.

"It's here, in the first-class lavatory. Like I said, a small leak. Maybe you'll know how to fix it." Jennings spoke in a soft voice that was still slightly louder than necessary, just in case anyone else could hear him. But even though his words remained calm and collected, anyone who knew him would have seen through his pretense. "You step in first. You'll see what I mean. I'll show you where the leak is."

"Okay." Kathy edged past her ex-boyfriend cautiously because she had already picked up his unintentional anxiety signals. Unless her memory of Ron had gone off-base with time—an unlikely possibility, since he had never been gone from her thoughts for very long during the past six years—something was wrong, something was happening that was a great deal worse than a leaky sink valve. She stepped into the lavatory and looked at the sink. "Good God!"

"Be quiet," Jennings whispered tersely. He blocked the entranceway to the lavatory with his body, so that no one in the first-class cabin would be able to see Kathy's reaction to the bomb. "Keep your voice down—you don't want a damned panic in the cabin, do you?"

"Of course not." Kathy quickly regained her composure. She turned from Ron and quickly read the note pasted against the lavatory mirror before turning back to him. "Do you think this is real?"

"I don't know, I'm not sure."

"I'm not either."

"It looks like a bomb to me, but I've never seen a bomb up close before."

Kathy glanced back at the collection of wires and explosives wrapped in thin strands of black tape and placed carefully into the washbasin. "I could turn on the sink water and flood it. That might disarm it."

"Don't be ridiculous."

"You're right. Sorry." Kathy knew that she wasn't making any sense. What she really wanted to do was run as far away from this horrible thing as she could—which was nowhere near far enough to provide the slightest bit of safety from its potential destructive force, as she knew all too well. Instead, she recalled the words from the airline's emergency manual: *analyze the bomb carefully, so that accurate information can be radioed in by the flight crew. Take special note of the arrangements of wires, timing mechanisms, etc.* Kathy pointed toward the yellow cylinders. "These must be the explosives."

"That's what I thought." Jennings had already noticed the several sets of wires that went into the rear of each of the yellow cylinders. Some were probably for the normal detonators, and some were part of the anti-tampering circuits.

"And what about this?"

"That must be the antenna. This thing is supposed to be radio controlled." Jennings pointed toward the hijack note, but then noticed that Kathy wasn't following him. Her eyes were riveted to the bomb. "We've got to go on the assumption that this thing can do exactly what the note says it can."

"If the bomb detonates, the hijackers would be killed, too," Kathy said, thinking out loud.

"Yeah. Maybe they don't care. Maybe they're part of one of those fanatical groups that want to free political prisoners or some crap like that." Jennings wiped at a growing bead of perspiration on his forehead. His attempts to remain calm and cool were beginning to fray at the edges. "How the hell did they ever get this thing past airport security?"

"I don't know," Kathy answered as she looked down at the bomb. "I didn't think it was possible to get something this big through the x-ray checks."

"Neither did I."

"What should we do next?"

"We've got to think this thing out before we touch anything."

"Right." Kathy nervously played with the buttons on her tan uniform jacket for a moment as she considered the possibilities. While she did, she realized how much influence Ron's presence was having on her actions—having him next to her made things infinitely easier for her, his presence helped her keep her self-control. She had always been known as a decisive and intelligent woman, but having Ron around had added an unshakable calm to her life that she had never felt with anyone, either before or since. It was an aspect of their relationship that they had once joked about years before—his maturity rubbing off on her, her youthful enthusiasms rubbing off on him. "I think I should lock the lavatory door. We've got to keep this from the passengers."

"Good idea." Jennings restrained himself from reminding her that he was, both legally and practically, no more than just another passenger himself. "You should write a note," he added instead, "a notice to pin up on the door that this lavatory is closed because of a broken pipe or something. That might help in keeping people from getting too inquisitive."

"I'm going to take the hijack note to show to the captain." She leaned over the bomb carefully so as not to brush against it, then peeled off the small pieces of tape that held the hijacker's note to the lavatory mirror. When the note came down, she folded it and put it into her pocket. "Let's get out of here."

"Okay."

After Ron exited from the doorway, she stepped back into the aisle and pulled the lavatory door shut behind her. She took out a short screwdriver-like tool from her uniform pocket and used it to lock the lavatory door from the outside. "That's done, no one can get in. I'll write the notice later."

"What's next?"

"Tell the captain."

"Of course." Jennings cursed himself for not thinking of the obvious; the need to inform the man in charge that the routine flight under his command has just been turned into a nightmare. "I'll go up to the cockpit with you. Maybe I can help."

"Okay. First let me go up and tell him, then I'll come back for you in a minute." Kathy turned and moved quickly up the darkened aisle of the first-class section, her body briefly cutting a shadow across the movie screen as she walked in front of it. She passed the first-class galley and, a few steps later, came to the cockpit door. Using the key on her chain, she opened the cockpit door and quickly disappeared inside.

Jennings stood awkwardly in the middle of the aisle at the rear of the first-class section. He glanced around at the passengers, trying to pick up any signal that might indicate which passenger was part of the group that had planted the bomb, which one of them intended to give "more information in one hour." There was, he already knew, a total of nine passengers in first class, out of the sixteen available seats. Discounting himself and his family, that left six others. Jennings looked at each of them carefully, as best he could in the darkened cabin.

For the moment, the first row was completely empty on both sides of the aisle—Charlene had been sitting in seat 1A, but she had moved back one row when the movie had started. In the second row, Charlene now sat in the window seat on the left, with Barbara next to her on the aisle. Across from them at the right-side window was an Oriental man, middle-aged, in a three-piece suit. To the best of Jennings's memory, that man had not left his seat as yet. He could possibly be part of the hijack group, but he certainly wasn't the one who had planted the bomb and note.

Behind the Oriental man were the prosperous husband and wife that Kathy had served drinks to a short while before, occupying seats 3C and 3D. Jennings had overheard enough of their conversation after he had moved to the fourth row that he could discount the two of them completely—they were, as far as he was concerned, exactly what they appeared to be.

Across from the husband and wife were an older man in a three-piece suit and a teenage boy beside him. The boy—he looked a little younger than Charlene, probably about fourteen or fifteen—was big and powerful for his age, and sullen looking, too. But the man beside him—well dressed, about seventy years old—dispelled any notion that the two of them might be involved with the bomb.

As Jennings watched carefully, he saw that neither the man nor the boy displayed any interest beyond the movie screen—full-face shots of Robert Redford being intent-yet-vulnerable for the camera. Both of them stared straight ahead, their airline headphones clamped on, neither of them appearing involved in the cabin happenings in the slightest. Jennings decided that there was no way they could be part of a hijack scheme—or that if they were, then the two of them were the best damned actors he'd ever run across.

Behind the older man and the teenage boy, seated in the last row on the left side of the first-class cabin, was a man traveling alone, dressed in a jacket and tie. He was about sixty years old, tall, thin, and with an angular face. But

Jennings had discounted that man immediately, and for the most obvious of reasons: he was blind.

The blind man sat at the window seat, and Jennings had been close enough to him to see what he had been doing earlier in the flight—reading, in Braille. The book lay open on the empty seat beside him, the etched rows of characters visible even in the dim cabin light. Clearly, this man was in no position to make any attempt at hijacking the airliner—unless, of course, he was another great actor who was doing a convincing job of faking his blindness. Jennings let out a slow and deep sigh—he was totally disgusted at his inability to learn anything about the people in the first-class cabin, since none of them seemed to be even possible members of a hijack group. Jennings turned away.

But maybe I'm looking in the wrong place. Somebody from the coach section could have come forward while the lights were turned down for the movie. Jennings turned around in an attempt to investigate the coach cabin. The cloth partition between first class and coach remained closed, so he couldn't see into that area without moving it aside and drawing attention to himself. He wrestled with the idea of peeking around the partition, but then decided against it. There was probably nothing to be learned by doing that and he might be tipping off the hijackers in some way. Besides, he now remembered from when he had looked earlier that the area directly behind the curtain that separated the front and middle compartments was occupied by the forward coach galley—Jennings would need to walk through that galley in order to clearly see back to the passenger seats. That, alone, would draw far too much attention to him.

Jennings shook his head in disgust, then turned around again. Kathy had just come out of the cockpit, and she was carefully locking the cockpit door before she walked down the aisle toward him. As she came up to him, she had put her professional smile back on again.

"Are you ready to go forward?" Kathy asked in a pleasant voice. "Captain Blanchard tells me that he's ready for your visit." Obviously, she was putting on a show for whichever of the passengers might be watching. "I'm sure that you'll find our modern cockpit very interesting. The pilots tell me that the equipment onboard is a great deal different from what we had on the aircraft you flew before you retired,'' she added as she turned and began to lead Jennings toward the airliner's cockpit.

"I'm looking forward to it." As Jennings approached his wife's seat, he stopped and bent over so he could say something to Barbara. "I'm going to the cockpit, a short visit."

"That's nice, hon." Barbara Jennings was sitting on the aisle seat in row two, her right arm with its heavy bandage propped up on the empty meal tray in front of her. Charlene was sitting by the window, and both of the women had their headphones on. Barbara had moved her headphone only slightly off one ear to hear her husband, showing that she didn't expect too much of an interruption to her movie. "Did you say that you knew this captain?" she asked to be polite, most of her attention still on the movie screen ahead.

"No, I don't think so. I just want to see what a 787 cockpit looks like," Jennings lied. "I've heard a lot about it."

"Hey, Dad—did you say you were going to the cockpit?" Charlene asked as she leaned over to be part of the conversation. She had pushed her headphones off and they dangled around her neck. "I want to go, too."

"No way, princess. You know the rules—no civilians up front during flight."

"I'm not a civilian, I'm a pilot, too."

"I don't think your student pilot's license is going to make much of a difference as far as the rules are concerned. I'll try to get you invited up for a look at the cockpit when we're on the ground in Japan." Jennings put aside any thoughts of whether or not he was being overly optimistic about them ever reaching Japan—obviously, the hijackers, whoever they were, had other ideas.

"Those stupid rules are no fun." Charlene put on a trumped-up frown, which quickly turned into a big smile. "See ya', Dad," she said as she slid her headphones off her neck and back onto her ears.

"Have a good time." Barbara also slid the headphone back over her ear and twisted around to face the screen fully again.

Jennings lingered just a moment longer than he had to, wondering if and how he would tell Barbara about the bomb.

He considered just hiding the facts from her, but deep down he knew that it wouldn't work—once the Robert Redford distraction had played out its last reel, Barbara would quickly figure out that something was wrong.

I'll have to tell her. Soon. The two of them would be married for twenty years next week—this family vacation to Japan was actually a mutual anniversary present—and Ron had hardly ever lied to Barbara about anything of significance during their life together, a fact that was greatly influenced by her talent of usually figuring out whatever was on his mind.

But not always. Ron had intentionally lied to Barbara—and had gotten away with it—during the eight-month period while he was having the affair with Kathy. During that time, Ron had found himself lying about a great many things to his wife. Now, it was ironic how Kathy Davis was again the person who knew one more thing about Ron's life that Barbara didn't—this time, the existence of Flight 42's onboard bomb, the beginnings of a hijacking. With great reluctance, Jennings finally moved past his wife and toward the cockpit door.

Kathy, who had been waiting for him at the cockpit door, pushed the door open and stood aside. "Step right in—the flight crew is looking forward to meeting you," Kathy announced, again as part of her performance in case of onlookers. She allowed Ron to walk past her, then quickly closed the door and locked him inside the cockpit as she stayed in the cabin.

Jennings stepped into the cockpit. The overall area was illuminated even more dimly than the cabin had been, although the circles of light from the instruments on the flight panel gave him perspective and a target to step toward. When his eyes finally did adjust, Jennings was struck again by the sensation of how totally different everything was up front, how the stark realism of a darkened cockpit was completely divorced from the plastic and velour facade of the airliner's cabin. It was, in many ways, as if the cockpit and the cabin of this jetliner were totally separate and did not coexist in the same basic steel and aluminum frame—a frame that was moving through the upper reaches of the atmosphere at a high rate of speed.

"Jennings?"

"Yessir." The man in the airliner's left seat—a big man with a bullish face and thinning grey hair, from what Jennings could see from the glow of the map light above his head—had turned around in his flight chair. His demeanor left little doubt that there'd be no time taken on introductions or preliminaries.

"What the hell is happening back there? How come you're the one who happened to find this bomb?" Captain Alvin Blanchard leaned further rearward in his flight chair, as if he intended to take hold of Jennings and shake the answers he wanted out of him. Even before Jennings could open his mouth to answer, Blanchard began to ask something else. "Do you have any kind of identification?"

"Sure." From being an ex-employee who had volunteered to help, Jennings had somehow fallen into the category of unsavory character. Still fumbling in the darkness, he took out his wallet, flipped it open to his employee medical card and handed the entire thing over to the captain. "Didn't Kathy tell you who I was? She and I . . . flew together . . . a great deal. She knows me very well. I was in the domestic division, a captain on Boeing 737's, based out of Chicago . . ."

"This medical card isn't worth a shit as identification— it has no photograph or physical description on it." Blanchard waved the wallet in his hand but made no move to return it. "If you're a pilot for us, then why don't you have a regular company identification card?"

"Because I'm retired, dammit!" Jennings had answered the captain's accusation as calmly as he could—which was not calmly at all. Some of Jennings's agitation could be attributed to the bomb, but a great deal of it was a direct result of being surprised by the captain's attitude. "Didn't Kathy tell you that I was medically retired . . ."

"How long have you been retired?" Blanchard interrupted. The tone of his voice and the way in which he held the wallet left no doubt that he was now testing Jennings on the contents of his airline medical card.

"Not long enough, if you don't do something about what's in that lavatory sink." Jennings could hardly believe how the conversation had turned; incredibly, this captain seemed to consider that having the proper paper credentials was more valid than a personal verification by one of his crew members.

"Okay, never mind." Blanchard flipped the wallet back to Jennings as if he had been playing some kind of parlor game that he had suddenly gotten tired of. "You say that there's something that resembles a bomb back there?"

"Yes—plus a note. Did Kathy show you the note?"

Blanchard gave a half-nod, then waved his hand for Jennings to continue.

"It's in the first-class lavatory," Jennings added. As he spoke, he watched Blanchard closely. For a pilot to be apprehensive was one thing—Jennings had felt that way many times in his career—but carrying on with bellicose irrationality was quite another.

"Are you absolutely certain that it's a bomb—could it be a hoax?"

"No, it's a bomb all right. I wanted to think otherwise myself, but I looked at it carefully—there's no doubt about it."

"I see." Blanchard shook his head slowly as he turned away from Jennings and toward his copilot who sat on he other side of the dark Boeing cockpit. "Well, don't just sit there—give me some of that advice and assistance that they pay you so damn well for. What's your opinion on all this?"

First Officer Richard Clancy turned in his flight chair to face the two other men in the cockpit. "It's hard to say," he finally answered after a long silence.

"Oh, fucking great!" Blanchard slammed his hand down on the instrument pedestal between the two pilot seats.

"All I mean," Clancy answered hurriedly, "is that hijackers aren't very predictable, from everything that I've read. We don't have too many options. We can either play it for real and wait to see what they want, we can try to disarm the bomb or we can disregard the whole thing as a hoax."

"It's no hoax, it's a bomb—radio controlled—and it's sitting fifty feet behind us right now." Jennings said as calmly as he could. "We can disregard it, but it sure as hell isn't going away on its own."

"Then our choices are to either go along with the hijackers, or try to disarm that bomb." Even in the dim light it was obvious that Clancy was fidgeting in the copilot's seat, clearly uncomfortable with either option.

"Do either of you two know anything about disarming bombs?" Blanchard asked.

"Not me," Jennings answered, all the while praying that Blanchard wasn't going to announce that he did. Jennings looked to the copilot, but he didn't need to wait for the young man's answer to know what it would be. In the glow of the instrument lights Jennings could tell that the copilot was no more than thirty years old, with a round, pudgy face and a receding hairline. He certainly didn't look like the bomb disposal–team type.

"Before I learned to fly, I went to college for accounting," the copilot said. He waved his hand to indicate that bombs were far outside his field of expertise. "I wouldn't know where to start."

"Well, I know one damn place to start—I'm going to take a look for myself." Blanchard jumped up from the captain's flight chair, pushed past Jennings and retrieved his hat and coat from the rack at the rear of the cockpit.

"Captain, it's nearly time for me to make the next position report," Clancy said. "Do you want me to tell them about the bomb?"

"No, don't tell them. These days, nine flights out of ten come in with bombs on them anyway, so we'll treat this as a strictly routine occurrence, right?" Blanchard glared at the copilot as he pulled on his uniform jacket, its four gold stripes on each sleeve and the set of gold wings above the breast pocket reflecting in the dim light of the aft cockpit. "Don't waste my time with idiotic questions—of course you should give them a full report about the bomb!" Blanchard reached for his flight cap. "Follow all the standard procedures. Use the data link to notify dispatch in San Francisco, too."

"That's what I wanted to do; I just wanted to check with you first," the copilot answered defensively. He immediately turned back to his instrument panel and busied himself in preparation for the radio report.

Blanchard turned to Jennings. "You stay right here in the

cockpit, don't move—and don't touch anything," he said. "I'll be back in a minute." Without another word, Blanchard turned and left the cockpit, locking the door behind him.

With the captain gone from the flight deck and the first officer busy with his radio duties, Jennings let out a long sigh and tried to relax. *Calm down, stay calm. This guy's going to need help getting through this.* While he waited, Jennings looked around the cockpit to see how much he could understand about the modern airplane he was on. In some ways, the cockpit of the 787 was a repeat of the same configuration and layout of the other cockpits he had spent so many thousands and thousands of hours in. In other ways, though, this cockpit was pure Star Wars.

The flight instruments, in particular, were exotic variations of the same gauges he had known years before. He could make out everything easily enough—altimeter, airspeed, pitch and roll attitude, magnetic heading—but the presentation was completely electronic. In the place of wobbling needles in circular dials were electronic digital displays. Mechanical devices were all gone, replaced by graphic electronic visuals that made the panel look more like a video arcade than any cockpit he remembered. The navigation data displays were the most exotic, with cryptic lettering on each control panel, most of which he couldn't even begin to guess at. An electronic moving-map display in front of each pilot was jampacked with an assortment of colored symbols—green, red, amber, purple, yellow—that created an intermixture of arcs and lines. For the first time since he had medically retired, Ron Jennings began to realize how far beyond him aviation had progressed in the last six years.

"Well, it's done," the copilot announced as he turned in his flight chair to Jennings, who was still standing in the shadows behind the captain's seat. "Everyone knows."

"What did they say?"

"What do they ever say? Roger, wilco, all that kind of crap." The copilot held up his microphone as if it were some kind of nasty, vile object. "This is just a delusion, false advertising. We call for help and talk to these people like they're twenty feet away ready to rescue us, but they're not. Right now, our position is approximately three thousand miles northwest of San Francisco and at least a thousand miles from any land mass—what the hell are all these voices going to do for us?" Clancy didn't wait for an answer, he filled in the void himself. "Shit, that's what. Nothing but bullshit. I might just as well try to get my mother on the radio and see if she has any brilliant suggestions. They're sitting around right now coming up with a lot of shit to tell us—only they won't call it shit, they'll call it things like company policy and crisis avoidance procedures."

"Is that what they told you, that they would be coming up with something?"

"I did every one of the damned things in our emergency handbook. I notified air traffic control, then I sent a hijacking message to our dispatch office through the data link." Clancy pointed at the small electronic display screen on the instrument pedestal between the two pilot seats. "Everybody acknowledged the message, everybody came back with their standard *standby, we'll get back to you.* You'd think that they'd at least say good luck, or something a little more appropriate along those general lines."

"Well, I . . ."

"I call this whole thing a fucking joke," the copilot continued, rambling on out of nervousness. "Here we are with our asses strapped inside an aluminum tube screeching across the Pacific at six hundred miles an hour and who's along for the ride, maniacs with bombs, lunatics. Pretty soon some desk jockey is going to start telling us what we should do. Pure bullshit."

"I agree with you." Without even mentioning it directly, the two of them had already acknowledged how alone and vulnerable the passengers and crew on Flight 42 had suddenly become. Just as worrisome was the fact that the man who was ultimately in charge of their safety and welfare was acting strangely himself, not making a great deal of sense as far as Jennings was concerned. "Is the captain always so . . . volatile?"

"No." The copilot paused, then added, "Blanchard's never been one of my favorite people—as you've probably figured out for yourself. But normally, he's calm. I guess the news of the bombs hit him hard."

"I guess so." Jennings stood silently as he looked around at the elaborate array of panels and flight instruments in front of him. Even though he had been an airline pilot for twenty-three years, everything Jennings currently remembered about the job started and stopped with the date that the flight crew disability check was supposed to arrive every month. He asked the copilot a few questions about the flight panel and the data link screen on the center console. While Clancy was answering them, the cockpit door opened and Captain Blanchard stepped back onto the flight deck.

"You were right," Blanchard announced with a scowl as he hung up his hat and coat. "It's a bomb, all right. Looks like a radio-controlled detonator, just like the note said."

"That's what I thought," Jennings responded, resisting the urge to add more. "What do you think we should do next?"

"No choice," Blanchard said, as if he were stating the obvious. He stepped past Jennings and slipped back into the captain's seat. "We've got to go along with whatever they want. We've got to assume that the bomb is live, and that the hijackers can detonate it with the push of a button from wherever they are in the airplane."

"And if we rip the antenna or the radio receiver away from the explosives?" the copilot asked tentatively. "Wouldn't that disarm it?"

"I doubt it—and I certainly wouldn't allow that sort of impulsive action on any airplane under *my* command." Blanchard topped off his statement by shaking his finger at Clancy.

"I'd have to agree with the decision not to do that," Jennings said, mostly to lessen the tension between the two pilots. The mounting cockpit tension was a bad sign, but the first good sign was that Blanchard sounded far more rational now than he had earlier; maybe he was calming down and getting hold of himself. "That bomb looks like a pretty elaborate setup. What I've seen makes me believe that there's an internal trigger set to explode if any part of the mechanism is separated from the explosives."

"Right," Blanchard agreed. "And then there's the three other bombs still to be dealt with."

"How in God's name did these people ever get so many

bombs through the airport security checks?'' Jennings asked, although the question was posed more to himself than the other two men in the cockpit.

"Who knows?'' Blanchard shrugged. "It's an irrelevant point anyway. We're stuck with the bombs no matter how they managed to get them onboard.''

"Yeah, these guys have got us fucked for sure.'' The copilot shook his head, then turned to Jennings. "I hope those bastards want something that we can give them. We sure as hell can't get them to Cuba from the middle of the Pacific—where else could they want to go?''

"Russia, maybe?'' Jennings volunteered. Up until that moment he hadn't given the hijackers and their ultimate destination any thought, only the threat of the bomb itself.

"Russia? God Almighty! Those Russian bastards will shoot us down, just like they did with the Korean airliner.''

"I don't think so. The Korean airliner situation was a great deal different than ours,'' Jennings said, hoping that he sounded more convinced about it than he felt. "I would guess that the Russians would escort us to a landing, especially now that all the proper authorities have been notified of the hijacking.''

"It's a waste of time keeping up this guessing game.'' Blanchard turned back to his flight instruments and scanned them quickly. "We'll have to wait and see what the hijackers want.'' Without even looking up at the other two men, Blanchard resumed his checking of the flight panels. "We're supposed to be getting more information in one hour, which obviously means that the hijackers are watching us. They know when we found the bomb. We've got to be careful from this point on.''

"What about the passengers?'' Jennings asked. "Are you planning to tell them, or keep them out of it for the time being?''

"I've already told the senior flight attendant not to tell anyone—not even the other flight attendants—until I give her the word. I want to wait until we get the hijackers' demands before we involve more people.'' Blanchard turned in his flight chair and stared directly at Jennings. "And I expect complete cooperation from you. Not a word to anyone—do you understand?''

"Yes." Jennings nodded his agreement. "I'll go back to the cabin now."

Blanchard ignored Jennings and turned his attention back to his flight panel.

Jennings let himself out of the cockpit and back into the cabin, making sure that the cockpit door had locked behind him. The first-class section was still darkened for the movie, and Jennings nodded to both his wife and daughter as he approached their row. He could see that they had hardly noticed him, that their eyes were still locked on the screen; Charlene had ignored him completely, while Barbara gave him no more than a cursory wave.

Jennings continued on past his family. *Can't tell them anyway, not yet.* Ron Jennings walked down the remainder of the first-class aisle toward the last row on the right. There, Flight Attendant Kathy Davis was waiting for him.

5

Kao Wei closed his eyes for a brief moment, put his head back against his seat and allowed his thoughts to drift back to West Lake, in the city of Hangzhou. He knew that it was with the deepest of ironies that with every passing kilometer that this American airliner headed west, Kao's longing for his native city welled up in him more powerfully. Even though he was more than halfway to Hangzhou already—and if things continued according to plan, he could be sitting in the Lou-Wai-Lou by tomorrow evening—the need to experience the beauty and serenity of the place of his birth, his childhood, his life's work, was nearly more than he could contain. *Soon*.

Kao squeezed his eyes shut even more tightly and began to again recite the menu from Lou-Wai-Lou from memory, picking and choosing selections as if the waiter were hovering over him at that very moment. Instead of another plastic tray of nearly inedible Western food, the vinegar fish would probably be his first choice tomorrow night—although the sautéed freshwater eel or the fragrant crispy duck also made his

mouth water. *There will be time for all of them. Peng is good
for his promise.*

Kao opened his eyes. To his relief, nothing had changed in
the rear cabin of the airliner. The in-flight movie with its
foreign images continued to play at the front and mid-section
screens that had been pulled down from the ceiling, and Kao
noted again that most of the passengers in the coach section
continued to watch the movie. The movie itself was apparently an adventure story of some sort in which a sport was
taking place, with one very American-looking man swinging
a long and rounded piece of wood whenever a small white
ball was thrown toward him—the name *baseball* came to
Kao's mind as the sport that they were playing. To Kao, the
scenes in the movie that he had noticed so far—the sports
moments, the interludes of violence and shouting, the explicit
relationships between this man and two different women—
seemed incredibly barbaric and embarrassing. Peng was right,
there was no long-term future in dealing with Westerners and
their strange, violent culture.

Kao looked around the cabin once more. Some of the
passengers slept. One baby could be heard whimpering lightly,
apparently on the verge of sleep—just the way his brother's
two children would sometimes do. Whenever he heard that
sort of thing, Kao would sometimes wish that he had taken a
wife, that he had fathered a child of his own. Instead, he had
devoted his life to his work, to his government service as the
minister of distribution for the Hangzhou region—a decision
that he was, other than being childless, quite satisfied with.

Kao knew very well that as a middle-aged bureaucrat holding an excellent government position, he was living a life
more privileged and comfortable than most. When his old
boyhood friend Peng Ming had indicated that he might need
assistance with a plan that could be very beneficial to China,
Kao naturally could not refuse. A request from a higher-up in
the government of China, a person that Kao knew well enough
to be nearly family, was no different than a request from his
father or his brother. Peng's request for assistance was an
immediate obligation to be carried out as best and as quickly
as possible.

Kao leaned forward in his seat and peered straight ahead.

Out of curiosity he was attempting to locate where in the cabin the whimpering child was lying. Unfortunately, he could see very little in the darkness. *Don't worry, little child, everything will go well. There is no need to worry.*

The portable computer lay on the empty seat beside Kao, and he reached over to pick it up. Again, he began the pretense of working on fictitious reports for some make-believe importing company. As Peng had suggested, Kao had been careful not to appear too concerned about the computer and its crucial readout and interlink with its companion unit in the airliner's baggage compartment. Instead, he treated the device as just another work tool for the busy executive from Taiwan that he was supposed to be.

Yet Kao also knew that he hadn't carried the charade of nonconcern too far; he had been careful enough when checking in for the flight at Los Angeles to take a seat at the rear of the airliner, row thirty-eight—and in a row where all three seats on his side were empty. A row of three seats, all to himself, was another indication that the dragon of misfortune was firmly at bay and would remain so.

After glancing around to be certain that no one was about to interrupt him—he had discovered that the American stewardesses were particularly adept at bothering passengers when they would rather be left alone and, seemingly, ignoring them completely whenever they wanted something—Kao turned up the portable computer's tiny display screen. There, in small English letters in the center of the darkened rectangle where the messages could be read, was the current one being sent:

SIGNAL CLEAR; UPPER DEVICE ARMED
LOWER DEVICE ARMED

Kao let out a slow and measured sigh. It was nearly time for his involvement. He glanced at his wristwatch, which was still set to Los Angeles time. It was ten minutes past two o'clock in the morning. From what he had been told, the movie in the coach section would be over within thirty minutes. Shortly after that, while other passengers began to settle themselves down for sleep, Kao would make his move. In forty-five more minutes, Kao Wei would begin his contribu-

tion to what Peng Ming had told him was the most important
of the Four Modernizations for China.

"Look."

Ron Jennings turned in his seat and faced in the direction
that Flight Attendant Kathy Davis had indicated. "What?"

"The credits. The movie's over." Kathy unfastened her
seat belt and began to move out from the window seat in row
four of the airliner's first-class section. "I've got to get back
to work. Some of them will want drinks, and if I'm not
around they might figure out that something is wrong."

"Okay." Reluctantly, Jennings moved back to allow Kathy
past him and out into the aisle. "I guess there's nothing we can do
now anyway. Not until the hijackers make themselves known."

"Right." Kathy stood up and straightened her skirt as the
last of the movie credits played on the screen at the front of
the cabin. "All we can do is wait," she said.

"I'll keep my eyes open."

"One more thing," Kathy continued, her voice low. "When
I first told Captain Blanchard about the bomb, he got so
frantic that I forgot to give him the hijack note. Here," she
said as she slipped the note out of her pocket and handed it
inconspicuously to Jennings, "you hold on to it."

"Okay." Jennings took the note and shoved it into his
pocket. "I wish these bastards would at least come out and
make themselves known, tell us what they want. It's already
been more than an hour."

"I've got to go," Kathy said as she glanced back at the
movie screen. The credits had ended, and while she watched,
the automatic camera shut itself off and the first-class cabin
got even darker. "I've got to turn on some lights."

Jennings watched as she walked quickly toward the galley
in the front. A few seconds after she disappeared around the
corner a scattering of overhead lights came on and some of
the people in the cabin began to stir back to life. Others,
including the blind man across the aisle from Jennings, continued to sleep—or pretended to be asleep, Jennings could not
tell for sure. After watching the people in the cabin for a
while, Jennings turned and looked out the window.

The scene outside, partially lit by a nearly full moon high

in the cloudless sky, was a picture of pure serenity. From the window of row four, Jennings had a good view of the big right-side engine and the leading edge of the massive wing that it was attached to, most of the illumination coming from the lights that poured out through the cabin windows. The lines and curves of the aluminum wing skin gleamed. The 787's wingtip—the glow from its green wingtip light providing a distinct visual point that made it clearly visible against the ink-black horizon—was slightly raised upward by the aerodynamic forces that played against it.

The wing itself appeared as if it were cemented to an invisible line that separated what Jennings knew was the ocean from the sky above. Everything looked and felt absolutely motionless, even though Jennings knew that the airliner was moving toward Japan at a speed of nearly six hundred miles an hour, and at an altitude of forty-three thousand feet. After a few more moments of emotional reprieve while he watched the placid world outside, Jennings finally turned back to the cabin.

"Too bad you didn't watch the movie with me, it was great." Barbara Jennings, standing next to him, motioned for her husband to move over to the empty window seat so she could slide into the seat on the aisle. She waited while he moved over, then spoke as she sat down. "I really like Robert Redford."

"I don't." Jennings shrugged and attempted to look nonchalant. He fumbled for something appropriate to say. "Did Charlene enjoy it?"

"Yes. She loved it, too. I'm glad she caught it this time around; she somehow missed this movie when it was first released a few years ago." Barbara tossed back her shoulder length hair and smiled. "How about buying me a drink, big boy?"

"Sure thing, lady." Jennings fidgeted, not knowing what to do next. He desperately wanted to tell Barbara about the bomb, for any one of a dozen reasons—not the least of which was that she always seemed to say the right thing to make him feel better, always seemed to give him another way, a more upbeat way, of looking at things. He wondered for a moment what kind of positive aspects Barbara might be able to find about having a gang of maniac hijackers onboard. "Have I told you lately how much I love you?"

"Oh, oh. I'm in trouble now." Barbara put on one of her big, toothy grins. "I read in *Cosmo* that whenever a fifty-year-old woman gets an unsolicited pronouncement of affection from her long-standing husband, then it's time to batten down the hatches and stand by for the big blow. Where's the gale coming from, Commander?"

Jennings quickly suppressed the urge to tell her the truth. "I read in *Playboy* that gorgeous blondes that just turned fifty . . ."

"I'm a brunette, you must be thinking of someone else."

". . . just turned fifty are the best in the sack there ever was. I was just buttering you up for when we get to the hotel." *If we ever get to the hotel.*

"Buttering me up?" Barbara laughed. "For the last ten years I'm the one that's been chasing *you* around the bed." She made her eyelids appear heavy and affected a Romanian countess accent. "You know how flying in the first-class section makes me feel—very sexy, *dahlink.* Matter of fact," she said as she put her hand on her husband's thigh and let her voice slide back to her normal tone, "I was just going to have you tell the captain to pick up the pace so we could get to the hotel a little sooner, before my glow wears off."

"I guess I could ask him to make the jump to light speed." Jennings worked hard at keeping up his smile and his end of their familiar banter. When he looked at Barbara, she appeared exactly the same to him as she had twenty-one years ago when they first met. She was tall, broad-shouldered, and had an eye-pleasing shape—a solid appearance, but with the proper feminine curves in all the right places. The healthy, wealthy look, as one of his friends had once commented. Barbara was always upbeat and positive, except for a few odd hours here and there when she slid into more average behavior—and from Barbara, displays of average behavior made her seem like a monster compared to her normal disposition. For the ten thousandth time since his affair with Kathy, he wondered why he had done it. Loneliness, boredom, ego, all the middle-aged standards. "I wish I'd known you ten years earlier."

"As I've told you, you wouldn't have liked me. All I wanted to do back then was play golf—I was the only twenty-year-old virgin in captivity. No time for jumping on bones when my five wood was beckoning."

Jennings nodded absently as his eyes followed a man down the aisle and toward the first-class lavatory. When the man—the Oriental from seat 2D, still neatly dressed in his pin-striped three-piece suit—reached the lavatory door, he grabbed the knob and pulled. He had pulled on the knob twice before he noticed the note that Kathy had pinned on the locked door. The man shrugged, looked around, then pushed aside the curtain and walked aft into the darkened coach section where the movie was still playing.

"What's the matter, do you have to go to the washroom?" Barbara asked when she finally got her husband's attention back.

"Huh, no." Jennings ran a few lines through his mind before he settled on one. "I just thought that I recognized that man, that's all."

"Sure, me too."

"Really?" Now it was Jennings's turn to ask questions.

"Yes, don't you remember? He did our laundry when we lived in Chicago—Mister Ah-much-starch." Barbara good naturedly poked her husband in the side as punctuation to her ridiculous joke. Ron was, she could tell, worried about something. There was no need to push him, he would tell her soon enough. He always did, one way or another. "Hey, whatever happened to that drink you promised me?"

"Here comes the stewardess." Jennings raised his hand in a hesitant gesture to attract Kathy's attention, another one of the things that he really didn't want to do.

Kathy pushed the cart of after-dinner drinks down the aisle and made her last stop adjacent to Ron's wife. Kathy had exchanged a few words with the woman during the initial boarding while embarrassed introductions were being made, but all of it had come too suddenly and ended too abruptly for Kathy to be anything but totally on the defensive. Now, she had been watching this older woman for the past five hours, listening to her speak, seeing her exercise those little wifely prerogatives that women in reasonable marriages enjoy with their husband's time and attention. "What can I get for you two?"

"I'll have a scotch on the rocks." Jennings's face had flushed slightly; this was the first time that the two women in his life had ever dealt directly with each other. He hoped to hell it would be the last.

"I think I'll have a vodka and tonic." Barbara smiled up at the stewardess as she looked her over. Younger than herself by nearly half, she was thinner too. She didn't have a beautiful appearance, but she had a penetrating one. She looked like an intense, sincere person—probably far too intense and sincere; Barbara had met that type of young woman far too often in the past. "How many years has it been since you and Ron flew together?"

"We were talking about that very thing a little while ago," Kathy said lightly. She reached for a glass, put ice in it, then reached for the scotch. She was making Ron's drink first. "Probably seven or eight years, neither one of us could remember exactly."

"It was out of Chicago," Jennings volunteered as he reached for his drink. He knew he had to add something to the conversation or his unnatural silence might raise Barbara's suspicions. On the other hand, he definitely didn't want to say too much. Without waiting for his wife to get her drink, Jennings took one big gulp from the glass that brimmed with scotch, then quickly took another.

"Well, it certainly is a nice coincidence that you're on this flight with us."

Ron remained expressionless and mute, unable to deal with the fact that his wife and his ex-mistress were engaged in idle conversation. He forced himself to glance up at both of them, and the direct comparison caused him for the first time to realize how markedly younger Kathy was than Barbara. Incredibly, his ex-girlfriend now seemed far closer to the age of his daughter than his wife—which, in reality, Ron had all along known that she was. He shivered once, then turned away.

"It certainly is a pleasant coincidence having you folks onboard," Kathy said. "Over the years a lot of people have asked about Ron. I'll be sure to tell them that I saw him, tell them what he's doing.''

"Which is not much." Jennings turned back to them, put the scotch to his lips and pretended to take another long sip. This time he was using the motion of drinking to avoid looking directly at either of the women.

"That's not exactly true, Ron does plenty of things."

"Oh, really?" Kathy didn't want to show too much interest, but it was difficult not to. "Like what?"

"He putters and fixes—although quite often the things he fixes are broken because he was puttering with them the day before." Barbara laughed as she glanced over at her husband.

"Is that so?" Kathy could see that this subject was some kind of recurring shared joke between the two of them. It was another annoying example of how far on the outside she really was.

"Actually, I'm only kidding. Most of his time is spent on our boat, either working on it or using it."

"Oh, really? He didn't tell me about a boat," Kathy lied. *What your husband didn't tell me was that he was going to spoil me for anyone else.* "What kind of boat is it?" she asked as she watched Barbara casually lay her hand on Ron's arm. That little gesture of hers had said it all.

"A twenty-eight-foot Bertram flybridge cruiser," Jennings answered. "I like to fish and it's a good boat for it. It's also got a nice platform at the rear to swim from that Charlene and Barbara enjoy using." Jennings had purposely thrown his daughter's name into the conversation as if it were a magic amulet to protect him from what was happening, but he could see now that nothing would help. The small-talk act was killing him—in some ways, Jennings would have preferred dealing with the bomb in the lavatory than the inane pack of fabrications and pretenses that the three of them were engaged in. "I guess it's a nice boat, but it's probably more trouble than it's worth," Jennings added. He waved his hand in a gesture of dismissal.

"'Oh, I wouldn't say that." Kathy allowed her eyes to lock with Ron's. "Everyone's got to do something to keep themselves off the streets. We all need something to keep busy.

If we don't have that, then we can easily get ourselves into trouble."

"I guess." Jennings wanted to crawl under the seat; he had gotten what he assumed was Kathy's pointed barb toward him, and he prayed that Barbara hadn't. The three of them lapsed into silence for a moment, and that gave Jennings a chance to regroup his thoughts.

"Are you the one who arranged for Ron's trip to the cockpit?" Barbara asked as she reached for her drink that the stewardess had finally gotten around to making. She took a sip; the tonic was slightly flat. "I know that he's been looking forward to it, that he's been wondering how much things have changed in the cockpit during the last few years."

"It was my pleasure." Kathy allowed her smile to linger a moment longer than necessary. "In fact, Captain Blanchard asked me a few moments ago if Ron would care to come up again."

"Really?" As much as Jennings didn't care to participate in any conspiracy against Barbara, he cared for this three-way conversation even less. He would go anywhere, even back up to deal with Blanchard again, to end this insanity. "I'd really enjoy that."

"It was something about a special navigation instrument he was going to show you."

"Yes, it was a question I had asked him. He couldn't show me at the time," Jennings said as he added to the lie. "I'll go up right now."

"Go ahead." Barbara reached for her magazine, which she had put into the seat back when she had sat down. "I'll read what else *Cosmo* has to say that pertains to us." She winked at her husband.

Jennings nodded, then edged past his wife and out into the aisle. Kathy had already begun to push the liquor cart back and was halfway to the galley when Jennings started up the aisle. He quickly caught up to her.

"What do you and your wife read in *Cosmo* that interests you so much?" Kathy asked when Ron stepped into the galley.

"Never mind that. What is it you want?"

"You." She had said it; now it was too late to back off.

"Is that so? What about your husband?" Jennings answered harshly. He glanced around the small first-class galley, making certain that no one could see them where they stood. With the cabin lights on low and the galley curtain partially drawn, they were safely out of sight from Barbara and Charlene.

"We're separated, we've been separated for a long time. That's why I moved from Chicago."

"I thought you said that your husband was in Los Angeles."

"I lied." Kathy could feel the tears in her eyes; her emotional dam had burst, there was no holding it back. "I never should've married him. You're the reason that I did, a classic case of rebound. You can read about that kind of thing in *Cosmo*."

"Goddammit, don't give me that."

"Then don't listen." Kathy took an involuntary step backward and pressed herself against the galley bulkhead. She shook her head slowly from side to side. "I was too much in love with you." The first of her tears began to slide down her cheek. "Then you walked out on me. I figured that since you were such a bastard about it, that would help me get over it."

"What else could I do?" Jennings wondered if he looked as helpless and bewildered as he felt.

"But do you know what?" Kathy continued as she began to cry more openly. "I didn't get over it. Not at all. Not for a minute."

"Stop crying."

"Don't tell me what to do, damn you."

It was time. Kao Wei laid the portable detonation computer on his lap and carefully pushed the appropriate buttons. Within a few seconds the readout on the tiny display screen disappeared, to be replaced a few moments later by another message:

SIGNAL CLEAR; UPPER DEVICE COUNTDOWN IN
PROGRESS—30
LOWER DEVICE COUNTDOWN IN
PROGRESS—30

As soon as the new message was displayed, Kao put the computer down on the empty middle seat, unhooked his seat belt and stood up. There were only a few scattered lights on in the airliner's rear cabin; most of the passengers had quickly settled down to sleep after the movie. A few continued to read, three or four chatted, but otherwise it appeared that the timing was perfect for stage two of Peng's plan.

Thirty minutes from now as absolute maximum, Kao reminded himself as he consulted his wristwatch. It was exactly three o'clock in the morning, Los Angeles time. By three-thirty at the latest, the code would need to be changed or the automatic sequencer in the cargo compartment would irrevocably take over. *There is more than enough time, things will work out,* Kao said to himself as he stepped into the deserted aisle and began to work his way forward. *Stay calm, there should be no problems.*

The coach section of the airliner was no more than half full, which left many open seats for the sleeping passengers to stretch out in. Kao moved quietly row after row, quickly reaching the rear coach galley, which he stepped through without looking up at the two flight attendants—one male, one female—who stood in there cleaning up from the last of the drink service.

The next group of seats was the no-smoking section of coach, and the situation there was identical to what Kao had seen around his seat at the rear of the airliner. None of the few passengers who sat with their reading lights on had bothered to glance up at Kao as he walked past.

The forward coach galley was next—and if there was anyplace where Kao had expected a premature confrontation, this was it. Much to his pleasant surprise, the galley itself was empty. He continued forward, pushing aside the drawn curtain that separated the coach section from first class.

Kao rapidly surveyed the spacious first-class cabin. Just as in the rear, the overhead lights were set dimly—although more people in first class seemed to still be awake. Yet observing no reason to hold himself back, Kao continued forward directly toward his target: the cockpit door.

Flight Attendant Kathy Davis was still standing with her back to the galley bulkhead when the Oriental man walked past her, brushing the galley curtain with his shoulder as he did. Kathy quickly wiped her eyes and stepped out of the galley toward him, leaving Ron standing in the galley alone. "Sir—can I help you?"

Kao Wei continued forward for another step, stopping just short of the cockpit door. "Yes." His English was quite good, and besides, he was now using lines that he had rehearsed hundreds of time. "I believe that the pilot wishes to see me. I have the information that he has been waiting more than one hour to hear."

Kathy stood in disbelief, her mouth open. Even though she had been waiting for the hijackers to make their appearance, the actual moment had stunned her more than she would have thought possible. From an abstract problem that was now literally locked away behind the lavatory door, the hijacking had suddenly manifested itself into a flesh and blood reality in the presence of this anonymous-looking Chinese man. "You can't go up to the cockpit."

Kao said nothing—he had been briefed to expect exactly that sort of response. After a long silence, he pointed toward the first-class galley, its curtain partially drawn. "Perhaps it would be more discreet if we spoke privately."

"Yes." Kathy moved back into the galley, with the hijacker following her.

When he entered, Kao was surprised to see the man standing at the rear. He was very large, very American in appearance, with reddish skin and red, curly hair. "There are many bombs onboard," Kao announced hurriedly in a low but firm voice. "They will go off in thirty minutes unless I indicate to the others in my group that our plan is being followed. These bombs will go off immediately if anyone attempts to overpower me."

"What is it you want?" Jennings took a half step backward, as a graphic display that he intended no confrontation with the hijacker. The man himself—a small, thin, middle-aged Oriental with nondescript features—seemed ill-suited for the roll he was in. "Where do you want us to go?"

"Are you the pilot?"

"No."

"I must speak directly with the pilot—with the captain,"

Kao added, recalling the expression for the pilot who was in command of the aircraft.

"Use this telephone." Kathy's hand shook as she released the interphone from its cradle and buzzed the cockpit. Captain Blanchard answered; she quickly explained the situation to him, then handed the phone to the hijacker.

Jennings watched carefully and also attempted to listen, but could only hear small snatches of the conversation because of the way the hijacker had turned. For the most part, the hijacker seemed to repeat what he had already told the two of them. Something about a destination was said, followed by instructions of some sort. Finally, the hijacker handed the interphone back to Kathy.

"Yes?" Kathy said as she pressed the interphone to her ear.

"Let that man up to the cockpit." Blanchard had spoken tersely, without preamble.

"But that's not . . . we're not . . ." Kathy was dumb-founded by the captain's instructions because they went against the basic tenets of dealing with hostile situations. "We're not supposed to . . ."

"Listen to me," Blanchard interrupted, cutting her off, "I'm the captain here and I'll decide what we're supposed to do, period." He paused just long enough to allow his words to sink in. "There is an entire group of hijackers back there, with enough bombs onboard to blow us into orbit, for chrissake. This one hijacker has relayed their demand, which is simple enough: they want to be taken to the interior of Communist China. The man standing next to you has the exact coordinates of where they want to go, and he's familiar with the airport where they want us to land—which he assures me is large enough for our airplane. I don't intend to jeopardize the safety of everyone onboard just to make some bravado stand in order to comply with recommended guidelines in a printed handbook. None of that means a crock of shit when you're up here holding the bag. Let that man up to the cockpit *right now.*"

"Yessir." Kathy hung up the interphone, her hands shaking so badly that she needed to use both of them to get the black plastic handset into its cradle. "Follow me." Without turning back to Ron, she led the hijacker out of the galley and up to the cockpit door. Kathy took out her key, hesitated for a brief moment, but then slid the key into the lock and turned the handle.

The cockpit door swung open, revealing a darkened interior with an array of instrument lights on the large flight panel in front of both pilots. Kao Wei stepped into the cockpit and quickly closed the door behind him.

"I can't believe it." Jennings had come up behind Kathy; the two of them stood facing the closed cockpit door. Jennings's face was ashen white. "I don't think I would've done that," he whispered. "At least not so quickly."

"Me, neither."

Jennings glanced over his shoulder. No one in the cabin seemed to have noticed what had happened. He pointed to the galley, and followed Kathy as she stepped back behind the curtain.

The two of them stood in silence in the forward galley for quite a while. She was the one who finally broke the silence. "Maybe it'll work out, maybe this is the best way."

"Maybe."

"What about the other hijackers? What about the other bombs?"

"I don't know." Slowly, they began to talk about the possibilities, the number of hijackers, the places where on-board bombs might be hidden. But before either one of them could say very much, Jennings was stopped in mid-sentence by a startling noise, a shout, that had come from the cockpit. "What in God's name . . ."

Kathy didn't have time to make any kind of a reply because of the exploding sound of a gunshot that suddenly shattered the silence. It was followed rapidly by three other loud shots.

"Oh, my God!" As Jennings took his first step forward, the aircraft lurched violently beneath his feet. "Hold on!"

"I can't!" Kathy was thrown to the floor of the galley; the airliner had lurched left, then dropped suddenly—like an elevator in an office building suddenly out of control, its cable snapped, its steel car flung downward toward the con-crete below. Kathy screamed, her own panic adding to the chorus of screams and shouts that had all at once erupted from the cabin.

Out of control. Jennings was now lying on the galley floor, struggling to get himself up, to find a handhold, to get himself toward the cockpit door. Yet the enormous weight of the rapidly building aerodynamic forces held him a virtual prisoner, making it nearly impossible for him to do more than raise his arms in his futile attempt to crawl toward the cockpit.

Spinning, we're spinning. God help us. From the corner of his eye Jennings saw that the forward galley had begun to spew out its contents all around him—glasses, bottles, trays, bits of food, sprays of water and coffee. The debris smashed repeatedly into the walls, the floor, the ceiling. Several times Jennings was hit directly by a bottle, glass or tray, the objects ricocheting painfully off the arm that he had raised in order to protect his head and face.

But Jennings knew that injuries from the hurtling debris would mean nothing compared to what lay just moments ahead for them. Flight 42 was falling, spinning at an incalculable rate, the aerodynamic forces building far too rapidly, far beyond what the designers could have expected or prepared for. Ron Jennings knew that if someone didn't get them back under control, then the airliner would follow those immutable laws of physics and, within a few moments, begin a massive in-flight disintegration. The Pacific Ocean below them was the least of their problems—they'd all be long dead before the first pieces of the airliner's remains hit the surface of the sea.

6

Wally Poel tugged at the knot of his tie as he looked absently around the room. From his seat on the elevated platform in the center of the Trans Continental Airlines dispatch office in San Francisco, Poel had an excellent overview of the dozens of dispatcher work desks, the weather charts and satellite photos to his right, and the large flight status board directly ahead. Yet none of that data told Poel a single thing more than he already knew from the earlier Teletype message: Flight 42 had a bomb onboard and was in the process of being hijacked to an unknown destination. "Whoever these bastards are, they sure as hell can't tell time—it's already been almost two hours."

"Maybe that's part of their plan." Assistant Dispatcher Tom Labitzke put a fresh cup of black coffee on Poel's desk, then turned and looked toward the status board at the front of the room. The status board, with its long horizontal strips of colored paper that represented the progress of each of the airline's en route flights, was always the visual focal point of any conversation in the dispatch office, even though it provided very little real data. "I remember reading something about hijackers trying to keep people off balance by being late with their deadlines. That 'more information in one hour' crap could be something like that."

"Could be."

"It might even be a good sign. It might mean that the hijackers have backed out, that they've had second thoughts about it."

"I doubt that."

"Me, too, actually." Labitzke shrugged. "Wishful thinking, I guess."

Poel gestured toward the large wall clock mounted above the center of the flight board. It was set to California time, and it read 3:05 A.M. "Keep in mind that the flight crew started from Los Angeles over five hours ago. According to what I've read, that means that their bodies are now at the lowest point, that their resistance will be the least. That might be what this delay is about."

"Yeah. I never thought of that."

"On the other hand, maybe it's something else. Maybe the hijackers fell asleep, or maybe their watches have stopped." Poel fumbled in the pocket of his black suit jacket and took out a deck of playing cards. Without consciously realizing it, he began to shuffle blindly through the marked deck of cards while his fingers picked out the coded patterns for the Ace of Spades, the Queen of Hearts, the Jack of Diamonds. "Are data link communications still normal?"

"Absolutely. I've got 42 connected to the alert light." Labitzke gestured toward a red monitor light at the front of the room. The light was, at the moment, on. "We're sending a continuous data link loop message, to sample circuit continuity. If the data link fails on either end, the monitor light will go off within five seconds."

"Good." Poel fingered the Ace of Hearts and turned it, face up, on his desk. His hand rummaged through the deck until he felt the mark for the King of Hearts; he laid that card, face down, beneath the Ace. "Captain Blanchard's last data link message said it all—that whatever's going on, it seems to be very well planned, very well controlled."

"It's better if the crew can deal with an organized group rather than a wild gang of terrorists. If their demands aren't too absurd, maybe Blanchard can go along with them without the passengers knowing about it until the very end."

"That's almost too good to hope for." Poel laid down the stack of playing cards, closed his eyes and began to rub his temples.

"How are you feeling?" Labitzke asked. He glanced over at Poel, trying not to make his concern too obvious. When the man hadn't taken time to spruce himself up—which he hadn't tonight— the combination of Poel's dark hair, mustache and trim beard could appear scraggly, even sinister looking. "The coffee any help?"

"I'm okay now." Poel wasn't lying either. He knew that he had already sobered up completely—a combination of the countless cups of black coffee, the passing of two full hours since he had been called away from the *'Frisco Magicians'* quarterly meeting, and the level of general stress caused by the hijacking situation. Poel had come directly from the downtown Holiday Inn after the club treasurer volunteered to take Alice home, and he was still dressed in the black suit and tie that he wore for his magic performances.

"Stark called."

"When?"

"A few minutes ago." Labitzke tried to sound neutral, even though his preference was overwhelmingly for Wally Poel in this ongoing battle of office politics. "I guess someone finally found Stark and got him the message about 42's status."

"Did you tell him that I was already here?" Even without asking, Poel knew that his presence wouldn't make any difference, that the other senior duty manager wouldn't let an opportunity like this get past him. To Byron Stark, a hijacking or a crash was nothing more than another opportunity to continue his climb through the flight management hierarchy.

"I sure did tell him that you were here, that you had already signed in and taken control of the situation. He said that he would come anyway, that you might want help."

"Right." Poel shook his head in disgust—he was tired enough not to be able to hide his true feelings as well as he should have. "How soon is he expected?"

"Right now." Labitzke gestured toward the door on the

left, which had just opened to reveal an impeccably dressed Byron Stark. The man stood in the doorway for several seconds, obviously sizing up the situation before walking in.

"Christ help us," Poel mumbled. He pulled at his black suit jacket to straighten it as he stood up in order to look a little more formidable. It was, Poel knew, a comparatively futile gesture since Stark always appeared as if he had just stepped off the page of an advertisement for expensive men's clothes. *How the hell can he look like that at three o'clock in the fucking morning.* Poel stood his ground at the duty manager's elevated platform while he waited for Stark to step up to him.

"Wally, what's the situation?" Byron Stark climbed the four steps that led to the platform of the command desk with just the proper blend of assurance and concern. Stark had already managed to convey, through his movements and bearing, the impression that his arrival on the scene was the next necessary step to whatever would be the ultimate solution to the current problem.

"What have you heard so far?" Poel didn't enjoy being evasive, but he had learned the hard way that it was best not to volunteer too much to Stark.

"That 42 was hijacked, that it's still five hours east of the coast of Japan, that Captain Blanchard feels the hijackers are a well-organized group who intend to play the situation very carefully." There was a slight trace of a smile on Stark's face, although not enough to accuse him of being anything other than properly serious. Stark was on stage now, displaying to his opponent that he had already arranged to get all the information that he needed. "I understand that, other than the initial discovery of the bomb and the hijack note, there's been no further communication from the hijackers."

Poel groaned inside. "That's everything," he said through clenched teeth as he glanced over the dozen men working on the dispatch floor. One or more of them were part of Stark's army; they had obviously been the ones to call him, to brief him thoroughly. "Now we wait. That's all we can do."

"Did you notify corporate, public affairs and legal?"

"Does a bear shit in the woods?"

"Fine." Stark refused to allow Poel's conversational patterns to grate on him—the man's lower-class upbringing was never far below that thin veneer of respectability he had managed to feign. "And government involvement? Where are we in that arena?"

"We're at the standard bullshit phase. FAA, FBI, CIA, and a hundred other alphabet outfits have notified us that they're in full swing—whatever the hell that means." Poel knew damn well what it meant in the ultimate sense, that each of those agencies would generate enough paperwork at the conclusion of this incident to easily exceed the gross weight of the airliner.

"Excellent." Stark clapped his hands together, a gesture of approval that he had once seen on television and adopted for his own. "And search and rescue?"

"The Air Force, Navy, Boy Scouts and Campfire Girls have been notified." Poel worked hard at controlling himself; what he really wanted to do was toss his cup of stale coffee across Stark's grey suit, Countess Mara tie and starched Van Heusen shirt to give the man the kind of look he really deserved. Instead, Poel glanced down at the paperwork in front of him. "The Japanese have been alerted. So have the Russians, since we don't know yet where these bastards want 42 to go."

"That's good," Stark said reluctantly, wishing that he had been the first one to take the call so he could have implemented these obvious procedures. "We certainly don't want another Korean airliner on our hands."

"I'm glad you agree," Poel answered coolly.

"But is there any way we can verify that the proper channels in the Soviet Union have indeed been notified? Can we get some positive feedback from their people on that point?" Stark was speaking loud enough so several of the dispatchers at their work stations could overhear.

"The CIA—or was it the State Department, I don't remember—assures me that it's all been taken care of." Poel shifted his weight uncomfortably, noticing that he had somehow already been put on the defensive regarding the Russians. Stark had done it to him again, forcing him into the position of nearly guaranteeing what the goddamn Russians might do. "I don't know what else you could expect us to accomplish from here."

"How about calling them? How about verifying for ourselves?" Stark pushed back a few strands of his carefully groomed hair as he waited for an answer.

"Calling them? The Russians? Are you kidding me? How the hell am I supposed to do that?" Poel looked at the man in disbelief.

Stark waited until he saw that several of the dispatchers were watching them, providing the audience that he wanted. "I beg your pardon?" he said in mock puzzlement in order to draw the conversation out.

"Unless you've got Moscow's area code somewhere, I don't know how the hell I'm supposed to get in touch with them. Who am I supposed to call anyway, the Minister of Hijackings?"

"Now, Wally, don't get sarcastic on us—this is a serious matter."

"Serious! What am I supposed to say to Moscow, that this is Trans Continental Airlines calling and we're offering you fifty thousand free bonus miles if you don't shoot down our airliner!" As he rambled on, wound up far more than he should have been, Poel suddenly realized that he was being suckered in once again, that his fatigue and tension were causing him to be much too easy a target. This competition between him and Stark to fill Rick Dunlap's position as department director had been getting in the way of the normal routine since Dunlap's impending retirement had been announced five months before.

"Call Moscow?" Stark laughed curtly. "Of course not. I only meant that perhaps you should call the Soviet Embassy in Washington, or the Soviet Consulate in San Francisco." He glanced down at the dispatchers to see if he had made the impression he intended when, annoyed, Stark realized that none of the dispatchers were watching him—they had all turned to Tom Labitzke, who was rushing toward them with a new message from the data link communications printer in the adjacent room.

"Trouble," Labitzke said as he vaulted up the steps to the

command desk and slapped the message down in front of the two duty managers. "An automatic status printout."

"Christ." Wally Poel scanned the short message on the data sheet twice before he glanced up at Stark. His rival's eyes remained passive but fixed on the printed words. Poel turned back to read the automatic signal one more time, the signal that had just been sent via satellite link from midway across the Pacific because of the programming in Flight 42's data link communications equipment that resulted in a readout of any abnormal flight characteristics being instantly radioed to the San Francisco dispatch center.

> FLIGHT 42: DESCENT IN PROGRESS AT MAXIMUM RATE
> HEADING PARAMETERS UNSTABLE
> ALTITUDE PARAMETERS UNSTABLE
> BANK ANGLE IN EXCESS OF AUTHORIZED LIMITS
> AIRSPEED IN EXCESS OF AUTHORIZED LIMITS

* * *

Li Ying-teh turned away while the meal was being served. He glanced out the window. Through the partially opened draperies that otherwise shrouded the view in and out of the second-floor conference room in the Chinese Embassy in Washington—the drapes being a precaution that the visiting security officials from Beijing had insisted on a few months before—Li could see just a bare hint of the morning sky. "A cloudless day," he commented as the last of the meal was being laid on the table in front of them.

"A good omen." Lt. Gen. Peng Ming sat at the other side of the carved mahogany table. He waited until the two servants had left the conference room and closed the door behind them before he said more. "All is going well, and all signs are positive. Good fortune is smiling on our project. By the time we can lay ourselves down for our much deserved rest, another important key to the defense of China will be firmly in our hands."

"Perhaps." Li turned in his seat and raised an eyebrow just enough to show that he had caught Peng in the act of taking liberties: they both knew that it was *our* project only as long as things went perfectly, that at the first sign of trouble the lieutenant general would be alone. "I can only hope that you have not given yourself tight shoes to wear."

"The plan goes perfectly," Peng said as he dismissed the Ambassador's allegory that it was he who might become the ultimate victim. "The West will learn that we are no longer a nation to be trifled with—something they have seemingly forgotten. It was their very own Napoleon who said many years ago: 'When China wakes, the world will tremble.' We are waking now, finally. They will tremble soon enough."

"Perhaps."

"And the meal you ordered for us has a delicious aroma," Peng said, pretending not to be consumed by what was happening on the computer display, by what was going on at that very moment over the Pacific. The last thing in the world he wanted to do now was to sit down to a meal, but there was no way past the Ambassador's wishes on this, or any other point, for that matter. "Shall I pour the tea?"

"Certainly." Li watched as his small, ornate cup was filled with the hot amber liquid. As he had instructed, the chef had sent up the special blend of tea leaves that Li had brought back with him on his last trip to Chengdu. Even before he raised the cup to his lips, Li knew that the taste would be as satisfying as he remembered it.

Then Li picked up the pair of bone-white chopsticks that had been given to him as a gift by Chairman Mao himself, slightly more than a dozen years before. Li began to carefully sample the food on the small plate. The pieces of steamed duck combined with mushrooms, bamboo shoots and spring onions were, of course, delicious. Even though it was now six-fifteen in the morning, Washington time, Li had selected this particular meal as a morning snack for them because of the nutritional value and stabilizing influence it would have on their behavior. If they were, as Peng suggested, still faced with several more hours of waiting, then it was best to eat well and often, in small quantities.

"No wonder the people in the West are having a difficult time thinking clearly," Peng volunteered as he quickly finished off his own plate of food, discovering that he was far more hungry than he had imagined. "Look at what they eat. Giant pastries, enormous cups of sweetened coffee, the eggs from chickens, meat from pigs—and all of it hardly cooked."

Li nodded but said nothing. He finished the last bites of his own small meal, then put his chopsticks down. "Very well," he announced as he rose and walked toward the table that held the computer screen, "what is your current analysis?"

Peng stepped up beside Li and looked at the readout again. The two lines of text remained the same as they had since this phase of the operation began sixteen minutes before, just before the servants had arrived with the food.

SIGNAL CLEAR; UPPER DEVICE COUNTDOWN IN
            PROGRESS—14
            LOWER DEVICE
            COUNTDOWN IN PROGRESS—14

"To refresh my memory, those numbers on the right are the minutes remaining?" Li asked, even though he already knew the answer. It had always been a ploy of his to ask the same basic questions over and over—especially after sleep or after a meal, since he suspected that the chemical alterations in the body could well trigger a different response if the person's first answers were intentionally devious. It was a theory that he had seen bear fruit on more than one occasion.

"Correct. Both the upper device that was planted in the aircraft's lavatory and the lower device that was sent as checked luggage will detonate at precisely the same moment."

"Your method of getting the lavatory bomb onboard was indeed quite clever," Li interrupted, making reference to the startling details that the lieutenant general had recited to him less than a half hour before. "But how could you be so certain that the bomb sent along as checked baggage—the lower device, as you are calling it—would escape detection by airport security procedures?"

Peng allowed himself a small and inconspicuous smile as he revelled in this opportunity to explain yet another aspect of his brilliant plan. "Our success was guaranteed by thorough research into the airline's security procedures, and a proper choice of materials."

"Please explain."

"Baggage which is not carried onboard by the passengers is shipped inside a lower compartment. That lower compartment is inaccessible en route, so it is naturally of secondary concern to security personnel."

"Naturally." Li listened intently.

"That lessening of concern toward checked baggage traveling in the lower compartment is even more prevalent on a segment where the potential for terrorist activity is considered remote."

"Such as the segment from the United States to Japan?"

"Precisely."

"And the choice of proper materials?" Li asked. "What about that factor? What sort of materials are more proper than others?"

"A new variation of plastic explosives, which our army has recently produced in very limited quantities. It is highly refined, exceedingly expensive, and far outside the detectable profile of what the airline security procedures and machines are targeted to detect. This is especially true when a more casual inspection is being done, as they would be doing for checked baggage en route to Japan."

"I see." Li nodded affirmatively.

Peng smiled again, this time more broadly. In front of him, the right-hand numbers in both columns of the embassy computer suddenly changed. "Thirteen," Peng announced as the old numbers were replaced by new ones.

"So that is how many minutes remain before the aircraft is totally destroyed by the two bombs?"

"Yes, but it won't come to that," Peng hurriedly added. "Kao Wei will return from the cockpit at any moment now, retrieve the portable detonation computer from his seat and type in the countdown-reversal code. The portable computer will send the reversal codes to the auto-sequencer inside the checked luggage, and that information will be transmitted to us simultaneously."

Li turned his head toward the lieutenant general and scowled slightly. "You are certain that nothing else can happen, that there are no other possibilities, that success of the plan or total destruction of the airliner and all its evidence against China are the only alternatives?"

"Absolutely."

"And you are certain that these bombs are enough to bring the airliner down?"

"Without question." Peng spoke with confidence because he, along with Colonel Qi, had supervised the assembling of those bombs. He knew that the explosives that had been put in the lavatory probably weren't enough to do the job alone, but the large suitcase that Kao had checked as baggage would. That suitcase not only contained the battery-operated transmitter whose signal the Chinese satellite was at that moment receiving to make these computer messages possible, but also contained enough explosives to instantly scatter the pieces of the airliner over many miles of ocean, making any investigation into the accident meaningless. Just as had once happened to the Air India Boeing 747 airliner, a massive explosion over the open sea left no clues—Peng had researched all of this quite thoroughly. "If Kao Wei were to fail, all evidence of our involvement would be erased forever by the explosions. We have nothing to lose. We have everything to gain."

Li bent over slightly and peered at the computer screen. Although he never would have admitted it to anyone, the age of the computer was one that he felt totally unprepared for. The Long March, the Great Leap Forward, the Cultural Revolution were different times, but ones that he had adapted successfully to. Not so with computers; Li felt as if the gods themselves were inside that black box, writing their whims on fluorescent letters that danced across a screen—and that these gods were foreign gods to him. "What signal will we see when Kao Wei returns from the cockpit and enters the code to terminate the explosives countdown?"

"The computer will read *signal clear, upper and lower devices armed.*"

"And what signal will we see if the countdown continues and the bombs actually explode?"

"That won't happen," Peng answered.

"So you say. But I request that you indulge a silly old man with his foolish questions. What will be the indication to us of the airliner's destruction?"

Peng paused a moment, then pointed to the screen. "After the countdown numbers have reached one, they will then begin to count down from sixty. That indicates the number of seconds remaining. At zero the explosions take place.''

''And then?'' Li continued to stare at the light green message written on the cathode tube in front of him; as he watched, the numbers for both explosive devices changed to twelve.

Peng let out a slow breath. ''Remember, in addition to the larger bomb, there is also the radio transmitter inside that piece of checked luggage. That transmitter is the sole linkup with our orbiting satellite, and that radio link through the satellite is what is providing us with these computer messages. At the instant that the lower device explodes, the transmitter in the aircraft will be destroyed. That will be displayed on our screen as *signal terminated*.''

''I see.'' Li remained expressionless, only a few growing beads of perspiration across his bald scalp giving evidence that he felt anything special about the next few minutes.

''But that signal won't occur—Kao Wei will deactivate the bombs any moment now.''

''We will see.''

''Yes. Now we wait.'' Yet even though he had said otherwise, Peng had begun to wonder himself if anything had gone wrong. Their hundreds of carefully orchestrated run-throughs had indicated that Kao Wei should have been back from the cockpit by now, that the countdown-reversal code should have already been placed into the portable detonation computer and that the bombs should have already reverted back to their armed-but-safe status. Lt. Gen. Peng Ming had, in the last few minutes, become quite concerned himself. *What could be happening out there?*

7

Ron Jennings crawled along the floor of the airliner's forward galley as he attempted to resist the aerodynamic forces and make his way to the cockpit door. *Spinning to the left, tightening, falling faster, God help us.*

Flight Attendant Kathy Davis lay at the opposite end of the galley and covered her face in a futile attempt to protect herself from the debris that flew at them from every angle. She glanced up just in time to see the heaviest, most lethal article yet—the number two coffeepot—as it was violently lurched from its rack and began to tumble backward toward the open galley. "Ron, look out!"

"Christ!" The coffeepot—bright aluminum, with a long rooster tail of hot liquid trailing behind it—seemed to hover in space above the two of them for several moments as if it were deciding which way to go. Jennings, who had been struggling toward the cockpit door, let go with his handhold and allowed the acceleration forces to roll him backward, across his stomach, toward the rear galley bulkhead. Jennings slammed into the rear panel of fiber glass just as the coffee maker hit the floor bare inches from his feet. The hot coffee spilled in the opposite direction, taking the boiling liquid away from where he and Kathy lay.

Jennings wasted no time in his attempt to move forward again toward the cockpit door because he knew that he had no time to waste. He could feel the pulsing vibrations of the high-velocity air that was buffeting the aircraft—the 787 was already going far too fast, falling far too rapidly—and yet the airliner continued in what seemed to be unbridled acceleration, its gyrating spiral taking them quickly toward the ocean below.

"Ron, hurry!" Kathy had stood up as best she could, both her arms wrapped tightly around the protruding shelf that she had used during dinner service and had left partially extended. "Get to the cockpit!"

Jennings didn't answer. Instead, he rose from the floor quickly, and in one fluid motion meant to overcome the forces that were attempting to knock him back down and aft, he threw himself toward the cockpit door.

Grab it, now. Jennings focused all his efforts, all his thoughts, on the single task of grabbing the cockpit doorknob because he knew that without a firm hold on it he would be thrown toward the sidewall again. As he lunged forward, both hands managed to grab the doorknob for a fleeting moment— only to have his left hand slip off again as the aircraft lurched violently the other way. *Coming apart, God help us.*

With only his right hand on the doorknob, still holding tightly to it with its death grip, the reversal of the aircraft's direction caught Jennings off balance and he was slammed around and backward, his body pivoting the opposite way as he stumbled over his own feet. Even though he tried to stop himself, he couldn't—Jennings's head, shoulders and back smacked hard into the fiber glass bulkhead, nearly hard enough to knock the wind out of him. For a fleeting moment he realized that he might well black out. *Don't let go—shake it off.*

Jennings shook his head to clear it, then opened his eyes. *We're holding together.* Whatever had caused the change of motion in the airliner, it was not the beginnings of its in-flight breakup as Jennings had thought—the 787 was still shaking violently, but it now seemed to be on a trend of less oscillations and random motions, not more. *Blanchard's regaining control.*

Jennings allowed himself a brief moment to glance aft, toward the first-class cabin. Unlike the bright fluorescent illumination that surrounded the area adjacent to the galley, the overhead lights in the cabin were mostly off and only a few random reading lamps were on to provide scattered pin-points of light. For just an instant in that dim and shadowy glow he thought that he caught sight of Charlene's face, then Barbara's. The scene of hysteria and disarray in the dimly lit cabin danced in front of him for one blurred moment, as if those faces in the darkness—their screams, their pleas for help—were apparitions on some ghostly, deadly carnival ride.

What brought Jennings back to reality again was a sudden jolt, another change of motion, as the airliner pitched its nose rapidly downward and he was nearly lifted off his feet as the altering forces made the occupants in the jetliner nearly weight-less for a moment; Jennings knew that he could allow himself no time to think about the cabin, that whatever semblance of flight control had been regained was now, for whatever rea-son, lost again.

"Ron!" Kathy had stumbled forward, although her posi-tion in the galley had better allowed her to break her momen-tum, and she hit against the fiber glass bulkhead beside Jennings far more gently than he had when he was slammed into it a short while before. Kathy twisted her body as she reached the wall and grabbed hold of Ron to steady herself, one hand around his shoulder and the other around his waist. "Open the door, get up to the cockpit!"

Jennings had regained his balance well enough to turn around and face the closed door again. He grabbed the knob and tugged with both hands. As he pulled, the sensation in his hands told him that he discovered yet another problem in this never-ending nightmare of theirs. "It's locked!"

"Break it down!"

"Can't!" Jennings pulled with the savage strength of a struggling animal who knew that the only alternative was certain death—and even though he felt that the door was giving way slightly against its hinges—he could also tell that he was still a long way from pulling the door apart to gain entry to the flight deck, to the controls. By then it would be far too late. "The key—get me the key!"

"What?" The young stewardess looked at him, uncomprehending. All she wanted at that moment was for Ron to get up into the cockpit, for him to make things right again, to stop the howl of the wind, the pitching and oscillating of the airplane; her mind was not tuned to any other change in direction, any other idea.

"The key, dammit!" Even as he shouted at her, Jennings continued to yank harder and harder on the locked door—yet it still remained steadfastly impassable.

"Key, I've got it here . . . no . . ." Kathy fumbled through her uniform pocket, but where the key usually was, she was surprised to find nothing. Empty. "I . . . don't know . . ."

"Find it!"

Kathy looked down on the galley floor, thinking for an instant that she might have dropped it out of her pocket when she was flung to the floor at the beginning of their wild ride. The galley was totally covered with debris, with food trays, liquor bottles and napkins piled everywhere. "Can't find it . . ." she started to say, when suddenly she realized where the key was—she remembered now having placed the cockpit key inside one of the liquor drawers, as a precaution, once the hijacking had begun. "Wait . . ."

"Hurry."

Kathy let go of Ron, and as soon as she did, she regretted her action. The aircraft, which was diving, had begun a sudden bank to the left just as Kathy took her first step toward the liquor drawer to retrieve the cockpit key; the floor literally fell away from her feet and she pitched forward helplessly. She screamed, but only a short burst of sound managed to come out of her throat before her forehead caught the corner of the extended galley shelf. Flight Attendant Kathy Davis was unconscious before her body fell the remaining distance to the galley floor, and she began to roll through the mound of debris while blood poured from the deep gash in her head.

Flight Attendant Fred Lyle sat facing rearward in the aft coach galley, the crew seat hastily pulled out and the shoulder harness quickly buckled when the Consolidated jet began its first pitch downward. *Oh, God—here we go.* To Fred, it seemed hours since that first jolt had nearly thrown him out of the galley—he had no idea what was wrong, he only knew that they were in grave danger, that the airliner now seemed to be falling more than flying. He also knew that it had been no more than a minute or two at the most since the ordeal had begun. *This is how it happens, this is where I die.*

Fortunately for Fred, most of the debris that spilled out of the galley bins had been flung in the opposite direction, toward the aft partition. Some of it had, however, gone beyond the rear limits of the galley, and Fred could see that a number of passengers in the rear coach compartment had been bombarded by the bottles, glasses and trays. Even in the dim light in the mostly darkened cabin area, Fred could see that a few of those passengers had been hurt.

A sudden beam of bright moonlight flashed through the porthole in the starboard galley door, and Fred twisted around in his crew seat to focus on it; the nearly full moon provided the only external reference to the airplane's rapid motion, and Fred wished that there had been no moon at all because what it was showing him was far too frightening to be believed. As he watched, the view of the moon moved quickly past his field of vision and disappeared toward the rear of the aircraft—as if it were nothing more than a stage prop on a rope that had been yanked away too quickly.

Fred turned toward the galley on the opposite side of the companionway. Flight Attendant Claudia Novello was over there, strapped into that galley crew seat as she also attempted to ride out the gyrations. But Claudia had not been as lucky as Fred, because an entire stack of meal trays had come down on her.

"My hair, my hair . . ." Claudia heard herself repeating, as if it were someone else's voice and not her own. *Calm down, you're bleeding, put something on the cut . . .* But as much as she attempted to focus on the small cut in her cheek where something too sharp—a bent tray corner, a wine opener, a piece of broken glass perhaps, any one of those things from the pile of debris on the galley floor—had ricochetted against her, the food that had been dumped all over her and into her carefully styled hair seemed to be all that her voice and her physical efforts were concerned about.

"Claudia—we're leveling out!" Fred shouted, his voice barely carrying even as far as the adjacent galley because of the howling noises of the airplane and the constant, maddening screams from the people in the cabin.

"Help me!" Claudia took a swipe at the globs of food that lay all over her, pushing them away as if they represented the most immediate kind of danger in themselves. "Help me!"

"We're steadying, flying level—look!" Fred pointed out the porthole toward the moon, which was now framed dead center and remained motionless in reference to the aircraft. Although the 787 was still pitched too far downward, at least the spiraling motion was now gone.

"Help me!" Yet even as she pleaded, a part of Claudia's mind was able to comprehend what Fred had meant. Though she had never really understood the mechanics of flying, Claudia now knew from sheer instinct that Fred was right, that the violent motions had ended. Without realizing what she had done, Claudia reached for the release mechanism on her shoulder straps as she strained to get up from the pile of debris on the rubbish-laden section of the rear galley. More than anything else, she wanted to be where Fred was on the cleaner side of the galley.

"No!"

But it was already too late, because Fred had shouted a moment after Claudia had pressed the button to release her shoulder straps. As the grey straps retracted into their holder above the crew seat, Claudia had hardly moved more than a few inches when another massive change in direction caused the cabin of the airliner to slide away from anything that was not securely tied to it.

"Look out!"

Claudia screamed savagely as she realized that she was now momentarily suspended in midair, the cabin floor falling away, the ceiling coming toward her. "Fred!"

"Here!" Fred leaned toward her as far as his own cinched-up shoulder harness would allow, yet he knew that it would not be far enough to grab hold. Claudia was flung beyond his reach as her body began to comply with the complex forces of

motion that were toying with it, accelerating her body toward
an inevitable collision with the frame of the machine that she
was riding in.

Yet what Claudia hit first was not the ceiling but rather the
corner of the galley bulkhead, since she was accelerating both
upward and aft. Her leg was whipped into the corner of the
bulkhead and she took the full-force strike squarely with her
right ankle. Even through her own screams of terror she could
hear the snap of her ankle bone as it broke just above the
strap of her uniform shoe.

"Claudia!"

A small change of aircraft motion tumbled her over and
dropped her to the floor. She hit hard on her right ankle
again, shattering it even further. As she rolled backward
through the debris and into the first row of passenger seats in
the aft-most coach section of the jet airliner, Flight Attendant
Claudia Novello mercifully lost consciousness when the pain
from her mangled right ankle became too much for her to
bear.

At the front of the first-class cabin, still holding on to the
locked cockpit door, Ron Jennings had watched in horror as
Flight Attendant Kathy Davis was pitched forward and thrown
into the galley. "Kathy!" But even before he had seen the
blood that was spurting from the gash on the young stewardess's forehead, he had already forced himself to think along
another line, one that was far more timely and necessary if
any of them were to survive. *Find the cockpit key, our only
chance.*

Jennings already knew from what she had said that Kathy
didn't have the key in her pocket, that it was somewhere else.
She dropped it. Without releasing his grip on the cockpit
doorknob, Jennings allowed his eyes to frantically search the
pile of shifting debris around his feet. *Useless, it's gone,
never find it.* But then as his eyes passed over Kathy's
unconscious body where she lay in an awkward position
against the far corner of the galley, Jennings realized something else: Kathy was too careful, too meticulous, too organized to lose the cockpit key— in fact, she was far too careful
to even keep it on her once the hijacking had begun!

Without hesitating in the slightest, Jennings dove for the galley, grabbed a good handhold on the extended serving tray with his left arm and began to rummage quickly through the drawers with his right. *Key. Under something. Hidden but accessible. Weighted down, unable to bounce out.* Jennings let his intuitions about where Kathy would've hidden the key run through his mind unbridled, and as he did his free hand darted from one drawer to the next, moving things aside, omitting drawers or places where he suspected that she wouldn't have hidden the cockpit key for one reason or another.

Key. There it was, beneath a tray of miniature vodka bottles. Jennings grabbed the key and spun around toward the locked cockpit door. He hesitated a moment to let one tremor of motion subside, then he dashed back to the door, grabbed the knob for balance and shoved the key into the lock.

The cockpit door sprung open, knocking Jennings backward slightly as he shifted his weight to keep his balance. Ahead of him was the eerie glow of the instruments, the red floodlights of the center panel and a vision of the bright full moon in the distance as the aircraft's turning motion slowly edged the moon across the windshield from left to right.

Get control. As he entered the 787's cockpit, Jennings could see now what the problem had been: the explosions he had heard had been gunshots, and everyone in the cockpit had apparently been hit.

The Chinese hijacker lay sprawled across the base of the cockpit pedestal, his arm reaching out toward the captain's seat, the back half of his head totally blown away as if it had been chopped apart by a meat cleaver. There was blood and brain tissue everywhere.

To the hijacker's right was the copilot, his body draped forward and over the control column, a huge red spot in the middle of his back to show where the bullet had entered through his uniform shirt. Jennings could see shattered glass on the face of one of the instruments on the copilot's panel marking, undoubtedly, where the exiting bullet had lodged. *He's dead.*

Jennings turned toward the captain, whose white uniform shirt was also soaked with blood across the shoulder and down the right side. *He's dead, too,* Jennings thought, but just then he saw Blanchard open his eyes and move slightly to the rear of his flight chair as the captain attempted to sit upright. Blanchard's arms were wrapped around the control column in front of him, and it was now apparent that he was pulling the wheel backward with all his remaining strength—a delicate balancing act between his diminishing efforts and the dead weight of the copilot's body as it pushed forward on the control column on the other side of the airliner's cockpit.

"Can't hold it." The captain's words were muffled and strained, and the expression on his face—pain, total exertion, fear—showed that he was about to lose control of the airliner once again.

"I've got him." Jennings pushed the hijacker's body aside and reached across the cockpit for the copilot. He grabbed the man's inert body by the shoulders and pulled him backward in his seat. As he did, the control wheel beneath the copilot's arm was suddenly set free of its weighted downward influence, and Blanchard's constant pulling on the other wheel was suddenly without any resistance against it in the opposite direction.

"Let go!" Jennings shouted toward Blanchard, but even as the words came out it was already too late to stop what was happening; the captain involuntarily yanked the control wheel far back in his lap, and the big jet altered its direction drastically a split second later—from far too much nose down to now far too much nose up.

"Can't stop it!" Blanchard shouted as his body fell backward in the captain's seat. He released his grip on the control wheel, but it seemed to make no difference in the airliner's flight path. "Help me—pitch it down," Blanchard said in a weak and barely audible voice as he slumped lower in his seat and allowed the building aerodynamic forces to drain him of what little strength he still possessed.

Jennings had tumbled backward when the airliner lurched from nose down to nose up. He struggled back to his knees, and with his shoulder pressed against the mangled body of the hijacker and his right hand latched tightly to the rear of the copilot's flight chair, Jennings desperately attempted to get forward to the copilot's control wheel. *Going to stall. Get the nose down. Last chance.*

Jennings shot a quick glance at the airspeed indicator on the copilot's flight panel, and it clearly showed him what his instincts already damn well knew. Although the numbers themselves were nothing but a blur, the position of the needle against the face of the electronic gauge said it all: it was pegged in the bottom third of the airspeed scale, and it was still decreasing. When stalling speed was finally reached—any moment now, if this hellish climb angle continued—then the airliner would give up altogether, snap-roll over on its back and spin uncontrollably into the ocean below.

"Grab the wheel!"

"Christ!" The hijacker's mangled, bleeding body had rolled across the cockpit center pedestal and was now jammed in the space between Jennings and the copilot's flight chair. Jennings, still on his knees as the airplane continued to pitch upward, tried to muscle his way past the inert body that was blocking him—but there was no empty place left in which to push the hijacker. *Get him out, now.* Jennings reached forward and grabbed the Chinese man's body at the only place he could get a handhold—around the man's blood-soaked shoulders and neck. As he maneuvered the hijacker's body upward and then shoved the man aside, he could feel the eerie warmth from the globs of tissue that had been torn away by the gunshots—pieces of brain, muscle, scalp—as they rolled across his hands.

Jennings then leaped forward, springing up from his knees and lying across the copilot's body as he pushed forward on the airliner's control wheel. *Nothing's happening, we're in a deep stall, we're dead.*

"Trim!" Blanchard shouted as he tried to pick himself up and reach his own control column. Yet even though the captain's wheel was no more than ten inches in front of him, the captain found that his arms would no longer respond no matter how hard he attempted to raise them. "Pitch trim . . . full up . . ."

"Pitch trim?" Jennings looked around for a moment, bewildered, before he finally understood what Blanchard was saying. Evidently the captain had run the airplane's electric pitch trim to full nose up while he was struggling to get the airplane out of its earlier dive, and now the airliner was responding to that influence with nearly as much authority as Jennings's meager efforts with the copilot's control wheel. "Electric pitch—here?" Jennings asked as he grabbed at what he remembered from so many years before from the different airplanes he had flown.

"Yes!"

Jennings laid against the electric switch on the upper left corner of the control column, and while he did he could feel the pressures in the control wheel begin to change. At first the 787 did not respond very quickly, but finally the airliner did begin to level itself out and stop its suicidal climb that would have lead to an irretrievable stall and spin in just a few more moments. "I've got it under control!" Jennings shouted, as the airliner's nose pitched down and the forces that he held in the control wheel began to feel normal again.

"Ron, I'm here—what can I do?"

Barbara's voice was strong and clear, and Jennings could tell that she was now standing just a few feet behind him. Without moving from his precarious position which was somehow providing him with just the proper amount of leverage—he was draped over the copilot's body, both his hands locked tightly to the control wheel—Jennings kept his eyes on the bright moon in the otherwise black sky and used its brilliant silvery glow as the target to level the aircraft's nose and then its wings. "Help the captain."

"He's unconscious."

"Get him out of the seat. Be careful."

"Okay."

Jennings glanced to his left and saw that Barbara was unfastening Blanchard's seat belt while at the same time she was being careful to keep the man's arms away from the controls. While she did that, several other passengers rushed into the cockpit behind them. After the news that they had nearly been hijacked was told to everyone in the cockpit and a few words were exchanged, a group of them helped lift Blanchard out of the captain's flight chair and carry him aft.

"Daddy, I'm here too."

Charlene was now on Jennings's right side, standing close to him. Her voice was hollow and it trembled with fear, and she was obviously forcing herself to try to be helpful. Jen-

nings could see that Charlene's left arm was already braced
against the copilot's upper torso to keep him from leaning
forward into the flight controls again. "Can you grab the
wheel?" he asked his daughter.

"I think so." Her voice was tenuous; holding the control
wheel was clearly something that she would have preferred
not to do.

"You can do it. Just hold the wheel steady with your other
hand—it'll fly like the Cessnas at home. Keep the airplane
pointed in the same angle to the moon that we're at right
now. I need just a few seconds to get into the captain's
chair."

"Okay." Reluctantly, she reached forward with her right
hand and grabbed the control wheel.

"Ready?"

"Yes."

Jennings relinquished the copilot's control column to his
daughter, then watched her for just an instant. She continued
to hold the wheel firm and steady, giving slight inputs to keep
the ship straight and level. Satisfied, Jennings edged himself
backward across the copilot's body, then rolled into the space
between the flight chair and the center pedestal where the
hijacker's body had been. Someone had already dragged the
Chinese man's body to the rear of the cockpit, so it took
Jennings only a few more seconds to move to his left and
slide into the vacant captain's flight chair.

"Daddy, do you have it?"

"Yes, you can let go." Ron Jennings put both hands on
the captain's control wheel and scanned the flight panel in
front of him. The airliner was straight and level at seventeen
thousand feet, with an indicated airspeed of two hundred and
eighty knots. Jennings made an adjustment to the two engine
throttles to maintain that speed and altitude. While he looked
over the instruments to get his bearings, Barbara led another
group of passengers up front to take the copilot out of his
flight chair and to help move his body aft.

"Are we in bad trouble?" Barbara asked in a hushed voice
after the others had moved aft with the copilot's body. "Is
there a lot of damage to the airplane?"

"Not that I can see." Jennings glanced over the electronic

flight instruments one more time. From what he could tell—which was not much, he had to admit—the engines, the instruments, the aircraft systems all seemed to be working normally. "How are things in the back?"

"Some injuries. A few people didn't have their seat belts on, and several others were hit by debris."

"How about the cabin attendants?" Jennings thought about Kathy and how she had been thrown into the galley shelf, how she had been bleeding all over the galley floor.

"I don't know yet; I'll find out as soon as I can."

"Right." Jennings paused, then turned slightly in the captain's flight chair and faced his wife in the darkened cockpit. "How are Blanchard and the copilot?"

"The hijacker is dead," Barbara began as she laid her hand on her husband's shoulder.

"I already know that." An involuntary shiver passed through Jennings as he thought about holding the man's brains in his hands as he had lifted the body and pushed it aside.

"And the copilot's dead also." Barbara stopped speaking and stood silently, her eyes locked on her husband.

"And Blanchard?" Jennings turned away from her and looked out the windshield toward the bright moon ahead. In the distance, on the horizon, he could see reflective lines created by the streaks of moonlight against the black ocean surface below. "How is he?"

"Still unconscious. I think he must have lost a great deal of blood. There's still a bullet in him, too—either in his shoulder or his upper chest."

"Do you think he'll be all right?" Jennings nervously rubbed his hands along the control column while he made minor inputs to the wheel to keep the airliner straight and level. "What do you think?"

"I think it's too soon to know." Barbara squeezed her husband's shoulder as she edged a little bit nearer to him. The heavy bandage on her right arm rubbed against the metal rungs of the flight chair's shoulder straps. "I'll let you know as soon as anything changes. But I think that, in the meantime at least, you're going to have to stay in charge."

"Right."

"What about the radios? Can we call someone?"

Jennings glanced down at the radio panel between the pilots' seats. It was covered with blood and gore, and for the first time, he could see that at least one bullet had been blasted into it and that several of the panels had been badly damaged. "I don't know how these radios work or what frequencies I should use. I don't know which ones have been damaged. If Blanchard comes out of it soon, he'll know how to set them up—and I'm reluctant to change things if I don't have to."

"Okay." Barbara Jennings glanced down at the mess that lay on the radios. "Should we clean this mess up? Maybe the blood and stuff can do more damage if we leave it lying there."

"Yeah, okay, I guess so." Jennings turned away and concentrated on the flight panel in front of him. *Stay straight and level. Maintain this altitude and airspeed. Hold the westerly heading.* Other than those thoughts, Ron Jennings blocked everything else out of his mind.

8

The three men at the command desk of the Trans Continental Airlines dispatch office in San Francisco huddled around the readout of Flight 42's data link transmitter, as they had since the first message of the jet upset had come through. The automatic messages, which were now being relayed continuously to the command console, had shown for the past several minutes that the airliner was apparently out of control. The 787 jet had climbed and dived so many times that the men in the dispatch room had lost count.

"There he goes again."

"Damn." Senior Duty Manager Wally Poel shook his head as he watched the readouts of altitude, airspeed, bank angle all change rapidly from one wild extreme to another. Since the aberrations had begun eight minutes ago, the aircraft's performance had gone back and forth between and even beyond its published limitations more often than he had imagined was possible. "They're not going to hold together much longer at this rate."

"Consolidated builds tough airplanes," Tom Labitzke said. He, as assistant dispatcher assigned to the command desk, stood a respectful distance behind the two senior duty managers and watched the screen over their shoulders.

"One of these times he's going to stall and spin into the ocean." Byron Stark glanced up at the other two men, but noticed that neither one of them had bothered to look back at him. "He's going to stall it out this time, I'd bet on it."

You wouldn't know a stall from a fart, you asshole. "Okay, you're on—five bucks says he don't." Poel didn't bother to look at Stark; instead he kept his eyes glued to the readout on the screen. He wasn't sure what had happened to Flight 42 several minutes earlier to begin this incredible series of maneuvers—they had begun without any sort of warning message from the airliner—but Poel was certain that whatever Stark said might be the cause was bound to be dead wrong. Or was it only his fatigue that was making him think like that? All of them, Poel knew, were looking at this with a strange detachment—as if it weren't really happening, as if it were nothing to them beyond a TV show. No matter how hard any of them tried, Poel realized, it was a sensation they couldn't completely shake.

"Now, Wally, I was only using that expression about a bet as a figure of speech . . ."

"Look!" Poel jabbed his hand at the screen, his fingers pressed under the numbers that showed that Flight 42 was leveling out. "Seventeen thousand feet, straight and level, at a good airspeed! Blanchard's getting it back under control!"

"Christ." Labitzke wiped the sweat from his forehead. "It's about time."

"You owe me five bucks." Poel turned from Stark and back to the screen. "Still holding steady. He's got it under control."

"Right."

"You know, it's almost as if someone just got into the pilot's seat to fly it," Poel said, thinking out loud as he studied the numbers on the data link display. He was trying to put himself in that cockpit, trying to figure out what was happening.

"How could that be?" Labitzke asked.

"Who knows?"

"I was only kidding about that bet." Stark had spoken in

an uncustomary low voice. "Anyway," he continued, resuming his normal tone so that everyone within twenty feet could hear him, "I'm happy to see that the situation is finally stable."

"Stable? Are you kidding? The only thing that's stable about this situation is that I'm five bucks ahead."

"I don't follow you." Stark ignored the part about the money.

"Forty-two is still in deep shit. Don't you let yourself believe otherwise."

Stark read the parameters on the display screen once again. Everything was normal, a complete reversal of what had been going on during the wild acrobatic excursions that had lasted for nearly ten minutes. "What are you talking about?"

Poel looked at the man standing next to him. Stark was, in his designer clothes, picture-perfect. He knew all the right words and all the social graces. But, deep down, the man didn't have any understanding of anything that was real; he had no feel for any situation beyond the environment that his political world revolved in. Without being able to express exactly why, Wally Poel knew that Flight 42 was at that moment taking no more than a brief pause in the flight for its life. "Forget it."

At the very end, it had felt to Flight Attendant Fred Lyle as if he were on a roller coaster that was just about to go over the top of a sheer incline. The jet had hung at what had seemed to be a nearly full nose-up attitude—and with Fred strapped into the rear-facing galley crew seat, his view toward the rear of the passenger compartment was straight down the aluminum tube that they had suddenly become unwilling prisoners in. In all the years that he had worked for Trans Continental, Fred had never felt this afraid or this helpless before. *Dear God, protect me.*

But then, all at once, it had ended. The airliner flattened out its climb at the very last possible instant, sank back to straight and level, then held that constant, familiar and reassuring flight attitude for several long seconds. Fred held his breath and waited to see if the nightmare would begin again. Finally, after half a minute, he allowed himself to reach for

the release button for his shoulder straps. He punched the
button, watched as the shoulder straps retracted into their
holder above the crew seat, then carefully stood up in the
galley.

It's over. Fred looked around the cabin, which was in total
shambles. In place of the customary order that he always
strove for in the cabin, there were odd bits and pieces lying
everywhere: dinner trays, cups, napkins, newspapers, magazines, shreds of food, broken shards of glass, shattered sections of plastic. The wild maneuvering of the airplane had
caused many of the overhead bins to pop open, and they in
turn had disgorged their random contents in every direction.
Coats, hats, blankets, small suitcases, valet bags were scattered across the rows and in the aisle.

But what amazed Fred more than the sights in the cabin
were the sounds. After having shouted and screamed continuously while they were being thrown around, the passengers
now sat silently, almost in a trance. Hardly any of them
moved or spoke. From behind Fred he could hear the sobs of
one woman and, from another section of the cabin, what
sounded like the cries of a small child. Other than that,
everyone now sat frozen, in total shock and amazement,
overwhelmed by the fact that the horror that had started so
suddenly could have ended just as quickly.

Fred took two steps aft, reached for the cabin light switch.
A scattering of ceiling fluorescents blinked on, and that seemed
to act as the signal for the passengers to come back to life.
The sounds of voices, of sobbing and crying, of whimperings
and pleas, began to build like a symphonic crescendo.

Fred grabbed the public address microphone from its galley
cradle and pressed the button. "Attention, everyone . . ." He
didn't know what to say next. ". . . try to control yourselves,
stay calm, don't shout, stay in your seats if you can, help
those around you . . ." More than his words, it was the
simple sound of his voice that was reassuring to the more than
one hundred people who all thought for sure that they were
about to die. "It's over now, everything's going to be all
right, but we've still got to remain calm . . . help those
around you . . ."

Slowly, the scene in the cabin changed. First a few men,

then a few women got up to help those who were injured. Fred stepped back to where Claudia lay in the aisle just aft of the galley bulkhead—she was being cradled in the arms of an older woman, another woman carefully dealing with the stewardess's deformed ankle, which had already swelled to twice its normal size. Claudia's eyes were shut, but she was beginning to move her head and arms. "How is she?"

"Just coming around," the first woman said as she held Claudia's head and gently stroked her face. "Looks like a bad break—do you have anything to help with the pain? I think she's going to need it when she regains consciousness."

"I'll get out the first-aid kits. I'll see what I can come up with." As much as he wanted to stand there with Claudia, Fred knew that he had to keep moving, had to check on the passengers and the rest of the crew.

Most of the people remained in their seats, obviously shook up but otherwise apparently unhurt. "No, I don't know what happened yet . . . we'll be okay . . . please stay in your seats . . . the captain will talk to us shortly . . ." Fred said in an ongoing patter as he worked his way to the very back of the airliner, stopping for a moment here and there to move some debris from the aisle or lay a hand on someone in order to help calm them.

Call the cockpit? No, don't bother them—the captain will get to us as soon as he can. Pass out the first-aid kits, get some of the debris put away, get everyone seated and strapped in, make a list of the injuries, deal with the worst cases first. As Fred ran his plan through his mind, he noticed something out of the corner of his eye: it was on the floor, in front of an empty row of seats toward the back half of the aft coach compartment. A glint of reflected fluorescent light shone off the small computer screen, and that was what had caught his attention. Fred reached over to retrieve what he saw.

It was a portable computer, still turned on, a series of electronic words etched across its rectangular grey screen.

SIGNAL CLEAR; UPPER DEVICE COUNTDOWN IN
                    PROGRESS—8
                  LOWER DEVICE COUNTDOWN IN
                    PROGRESS—8

The words meant nothing to Fred, and besides, his thoughts were racing ahead to what he should do next. He laid the portable computer down on the empty row of seats, turned around and began to walk briskly up the aisle to check out the center of the airplane and, after that, the first-class compartment. Fred was somewhat surprised that Kathy hadn't come aft or at least called on the galley interphone, but then he decided that she was probably too busy up front. With the potential for hysteria among the passengers now markedly lessened, it was time for the cabin attendants to become organized into the efficient working force that they had to be in order to deal with whatever problems still lay ahead.

"Seven minutes remain."

"Yes."

"Do you have any idea why this might be happening?" Ambassador Li Ying-teh was pacing nervously now, moving back and forth in a well-laid pattern between the view out the embassy's conference room window and the ornate rosewood desk where the computer screen was kept.

"No." Lt. Gen. Peng Ming placidly stood his ground beside the rosewood desk, his eyes locked on the computer's screen as he attempted to appear much calmer than he actually felt. "At this point, I have no idea. There must be trouble onboard."

"To say the least." Li allowed a small measure of his anger and concern to vent out at the man who was basically responsible for it. He knew that Peng's only chance to personally escape unscathed from the potential repercussions of his plan was for it to end successfully. Yet with every passing moment, the chance of a positive outcome was becoming less a possibility.

"But even if the countdown does reach its conclusion, we would be no worse off than if we had done nothing," Peng said, as if he had been reading the Ambassador's thoughts.

"Well, perhaps."

"When the countdown reaches zero, the two bombs will explode. That will do away with all evidence that China was in any way involved."

"For your sake, I would hope so." Like most Chinese—

especially those who had risen quite far in the hierarchy of social control—Li and Peng knew that they shared the same attitude toward the people onboard the airliner: an attitude of noninvolvement. It was an accepted superstition in China that to come to the aid of strangers would invariably bring great misfortune to one's self and one's family.

Peng pointed at the computer screen soon after the number had changed to six. "Once the countdown reaches zero, China's involvement will cease. So will mine." Peng looked up at the Ambassador, but stopped himself short of asking the direct question about whether Li Ying-teh would press for Peng's dismissal. The old man had, they both knew, more than enough power to do so if he cared to.

The Ambassador stepped toward the computer screen again, then stood silently for a long while. He was deep in thought. His head nodded slowly a few times, but his face remained completely expressionless. Finally, he reached out and tapped the cathode ray tube with the bowl of his long-stemmed pipe. "Now that I have considered it carefully, I believe that all of this is nothing but moon on the water."

"Yes, in one manner of speaking, it is most certainly unreal." Peng then waited cautiously. While he did, the countdown number on the screen changed to five.

"So what should my proper concerns be?" Li stayed stone-faced and rigidly erect. "These tiny specks of light that dance randomly across a tinted glass—are those electronic symbols ultimately my greatest concern?"

Peng waited for more, but no elaboration was going to come voluntarily. "Please excuse my ignorance," Peng finally added with a slight bow, knowing full well that he would have to ask directly in order to hear what he desperately needed to know. "I fail to understand."

"And so do I," Li responded. The computer screen number suddenly changed to four, and both men glanced at it before they turned to face each other again. "We are watching a predictable sequence of numbers being displayed in front of us, and quite frankly, I feel that this electronic exhibition is more properly suited for small children."

"A good point." Peng fidgeted nervously.

The Ambassador, who had just come to his own conclusion

about what to do about Peng, was nearly smiling now—although nothing on earth would have made him tip his hand so blatantly. He had decided a short while before that he had misjudged the lieutenant general somewhat—that China now needed more men of action just like him, men who were willing to make bold advances while taking nothing more than carefully guarded risks. If the alternative plan of Peng's went precisely according to the predictions he had earlier announced, then nothing that occurred to a group of foreigners—a group of strangers—on the other side of the globe was of any concern to the Ambassador.

"Yes, perhaps this is nothing but moon on the water," Peng said as he finally began to get the idea. He tapped the computer screen with his finger, and as he did, the countdown number changed to three. "And when the figure on the screen changes to two, then one, then zero, we will have watched an interesting but inconsequential experiment that has finally been taken to its full conclusion."

"We will have done so, as long as the ultimate summary is appropriate."

"How is that?"

"I am an old man," Li said in an authoritative voice that left no doubt that he was still firmly in charge of Peng's destiny, "but I remind you that my memory is sound. When the number on the right side of the screen reaches zero," Li continued as he gestured toward the computer screen, "then the message on the left must alter also."

"And it will, as long as . . ."

Li put up his hand to stop the lieutenant general. "I have made my decision. Only when the message on the left of the screen changes into *signal terminated* will your alternative plan have reached its full and acceptable conclusion. At that time—and that time only—can my concerns about this matter between us then be ended."

"But surely . . ."

Ambassador Li Ying-teh interrupted Peng again. "Your future role in the leadership of China depends solely on our receiving a computer message that the signal from that airliner has been abruptly terminated."

The computer screen countdown changed to two.

• • •

After he had walked most of the length of the cabin, going from the rear to the front, Flight Attendant Fred Lyle was pleased to find only a few of the passengers had suffered any injuries during the airliner's wild excursions. Basically there was nothing beyond a few dozen cuts and bruises among those he had checked as he moved up the aisle, most of them from hurtling debris.

The few passengers who didn't have their seat belts on had been held down by those who did, and what could have been a very serious group of injuries had turned out to be nothing worth looking at. "Everything will be all right . . . please try to stay calm . . . please remain seated . . . no, I don't know what happened, I'll find out . . . the captain will speak to us shortly . . ." he repeated over and over as he spent a few quick moments with the groups of passengers that he walked past.

But Fred was shocked to see what had happened to most of the cabin crew. As he worked his way up the aisle from where Stewardess Claudia Novello was being cared for at the rear coach galley, Fred had to make a lengthy stop to calm down the two young stewardesses who had ridden out the nightmare flight at their forward coach galley positions. Both Debbie and Pam were still strapped to their galley crew seats when he arrived, and they released their seat belts and made a tentative effort to stand up only on Fred's direct order to do so.

"Are you sure we're safe?" Debbie Biederman pushed back her auburn hair and blinked nervously as she glanced over at her girlfriend.

"How could this have happened?" Pam Jansen said. Her dark eyes were filled with tears, and her beige uniform was covered with stains from the food and beverage barrage that had occurred during the worst of the wild maneuvering. "They told me in training that nothing like this was possible . . ."

Kids. "I guess anything's possible. Whatever it was, it's all over now."

"Are you sure?"

How the hell would I know? "Absolutely." Fred reached

out and touched the arms of both of the young stewardesses in a reassuring gesture. "We'll be all right, I promise you." He looked at the two of them—they were barely in their twenties, scared shitless, totally without a clue as to how to regain their composure—and Fred knew instinctively that what they needed now was something to do, something concrete and manageable to occupy their hands and minds. "Since everything's back to normal, I'd like you two to get this galley straightened up, to take inventory of the damage, to make a listing of what food and beverages are still useable for the remainder of the flight."

"Are we still going on to Osaka?" Pam asked as she looked around the galley. She frowned—there would be at least an hour's work ahead of them before they could even begin to take an accounting of what remained.

"Well, we're sure as hell not going to land out here." Fred motioned at the galley window toward the ocean below. The surface of the sea was brightly lit by the glow of the nearly full moon.

"Oh. Right."

"I'll be back soon." Fred turned and left the galley, satisfied that he had given them enough of a make-work assignment to keep them busy and keep them at their stations. He figured that by the time he got back to them, both girls should be relaxed enough to begin doing something useful.

Fred pushed aside the draped partition, stepped past the first-class lavatory and into the first-class compartment. Up there, he discovered even more disorder than he had found in the rear. Unlike the coach end of the airplane where most everyone had remained seated, the few passengers in the first-class compartment were milling around in the fluorescent-lit galley area—or even walking in and out of the cockpit.

Fred was taken back by the sight of it, the passengers wandering around indiscriminately through the comparative darkness of the cabin area and the offensive-white brilliance that poured out of the galley. There was, quite obviously, a total lack of supervision and control. As he stepped forward, Fred now realized that a few of the passengers were kneeling down to help others who lay on the floor just aft of the opened cockpit door. "What's going on here?"

"We're having a Sunday picnic." An Oriental man in a three-piece grey suit glanced up as he spoke, the only one of the people within hearing distance who had even bothered to answer. "Instead of asking idiotic questions, how about giving me a hand, sport?"

"What happened?" Fred had wanted to turn on more of the overhead cabin lights first, but instead he immediately dropped to his knees beside the man. As he did, Fred realized that the person lying on the floor next to him was the senior flight attendant, Kathy Davis. Her eyes were tightly shut, there was blood across her face and her beige tunic was covered with big smears of red. "Oh, God."

"What happened, you wanna know? You tell me, ace." Ken Komura glanced at the man kneeling beside him and eyed the uniform—a flight attendant's silver wings and name tag were pinned to his chest, and he remembered now having seen this guy earlier, during the dinner service. "I'm just a paying passenger, buddy. You're the one who's getting paid to know the answers here."

"I mean with her." Fred propped his arm under Kathy's shoulder and helped raise her. Kathy was beginning to move, and her eyes were starting to open. The Oriental man had already wrapped a bandage of sorts around a cut in her forehead, but the makeshift bandage was coming loose. "Let me get to that."

"Sure thing, ace." Komura had experienced a great many emotions during the past ten minutes—fright, panic, despair, guarded optimism, euphoria—and now he was experiencing yet another: anger. Somehow, his first-class ticket to Osaka had been turned into a first-class ride to hell and back. "Quite an airline that you people run here."

"We didn't do this on purpose."

"Don't get flippant with me, you asshole."

"Sorry, you're right." Fred resisted the urge to argue with the man and he concentrated instead on rewrapping the bandage—which was, in actuality, a white linen dinner napkin. As he worked with the bandage, he saw that Kathy was beginning to come out of it. By the time he was finished and he had propped her up to lie against the bulkhead, she was groggy but conscious. "What happened to you?" Fred brushed his hand gently against Kathy's face.

"Must've hit the galley . . . yes . . ." Kathy Davis, sitting partially upright, spoke in a thin, weak voice that left little doubt that she had just regained consciousness a few moments before. "Are we flying okay?"

"Yes, we seem to be."

Kathy closed her eyes again for a moment, then opened them. She turned her head slightly to the right and saw that the cockpit door was open. "He got in . . . thank God."

"What?" Fred glanced around, uncertain as to what she meant. Something good, he assumed. "How are you feeling?"

"Better." Kathy touched her forehead, then recoiled slightly from the throbbing pain. She looked up at Fred, then gestured weakly toward the galley on her left. ". . . always said . . . galley shelves . . . are dangerous . . ." Kathy tried to smile, but found that she couldn't.

"Sit still, get your strength back." Fred touched her again, then stood up. He faced the Oriental man, who was still kneeling beside Kathy. "It looks like we've finally gotten everything under control."

"Yeah? I'm impressed." Komura, a second-generation Japanese-American who owned a large string of gift shops in California, had enough good sense to realize that his momentary sense of rage would pass once he gave himself a little time. "Tell you what, ace. You attend to your duties and I'll take care of her." Komura had spoken the words tersely, but there was enough of a conciliatory tone in them to indicate that he was getting himself under control again.

"Thank you." Fred turned and faced the open cockpit door. Beyond it, silhouetted against the surreal background of a moonlit horizon that separated the view of the shimmering sea from a black sky, Fred could see the glow of the dozens of flight panel lights from where he stood. The hues of red, blue, green, amber, purple, magenta conspired to give an unusual dimension to the darkened front end of the cockpit.

As Fred's eyes adjusted to the relative darkness of the area he was looking toward—the major source of light in the forward part of the airliner was, at the moment, coming from the one large fluorescent fixture in the first-class galley just a

few feet to his right—Fred suddenly realized that the man in
the airliner's left seat was obviously not Captain Blanchard!

"Attempted hijacking," Kathy said in a loud voice as she
turned from her hurried conversation with the Oriental man.
Kathy had just learned for herself what had happened while
she was unconscious, and she wanted to get Fred's attention
so she could tell him, too.

"A hijacking!" Fred took one step forward, hesitated, then
turned around and knelt down beside Kathy again, his shoulder brushing into the arm of the Oriental man. "Who's that in
the pilot's seat—the hijacker?!"

"No, the hijacker's dead," Ken Komura volunteered before Kathy could speak. He gestured toward a body lying a
few feet away from them in the deep shadows, rolled up in a
nearly fetal position at the lower edge of the main entrance
door.

"Oh." Fred looked at the hijacker's body for several seconds before he realized that there was another body beside it,
too. "Who's that?"

"The copilot."

First Officer Richard Clancy's body was lying only a few
feet away from the hijacker's; Fred shivered as he realized
who it was and that he was indeed dead, too. "What about
Captain Blanchard?"

"A gunshot wound." Komura looked first at the male
flight attendant, then at the injured stewardess. Since she had
been unconscious until just a short while ago, he hadn't yet
had a chance to tell her anything about the captain's condition. "But they tell me that he's doing okay."

"Thank God." Kathy sat further upright—she was beginning to feel better, beginning to think that she was just about
ready to get to her feet and take control of the cabin again.
"That explains what happened."

"I don't understand." Fred looked around blankly—from
the very beginning of this nightmare, he had assumed that it
was some kind of equipment problem with the airplane. The
possibility of a hijacking had, for some reason, never entered
his thoughts.

"Blanchard and Clancy must've struggled with the hijacker,'' Kathy said, "and those were the shots that he heard.''

"I never heard any shots."

"You were too far back."

"Take it from me, sport," Komura said, "there were shots fired. We sure as hell heard them up here."

"Anyway, I guess the flying problems started when Blanchard was trying to regain control even though he'd been wounded."

"They told me just a little while ago that the captain is still unconscious, although he seems to be improving," Komura added. He pointed toward the group of three passengers hovering over where Blanchard lay sprawled on the cockpit floor just aft of the empty copilot's seat.

"But who's doing the flying?" Fred looked back at the cockpit, astonished. Somehow, when he had looked up earlier, his eyes had focused on the panel lights and on the pilots' seats, and he had simply looked right over the top of the closed knot of people kneeling in the shadows behind the copilot's flight chair.

"Ron Jennings is flying."

"Who?"

"Jennings. He's the retired pilot that I told you about." Kathy had cryptically mentioned his presence to Fred shortly after everyone had boarded.

"Oh, your . . . friend."

"Yes." Even though she had said very little, Kathy knew that she had told Fred—who was pretty perceptive—too much, given him too many hints about her and Ron. "Like I told you, Ron was medically retired—some kind of technicality. He should have no trouble flying this ship," she said, although Kathy had no real idea whether that was true or not.

"Oh, right, I see." Fred blinked a few times, not knowing what to make of it. "Then he's in command?"

"Well, I guess so . . . but not after Blanchard regains consciousness. Then he'll be able to take command again."

"I can tell you right now," Komura interrupted, "that this captain of yours isn't going to do any of the steering, no matter how much of a recovery he makes."

"What do you mean?"

"I went up there a little while ago and they showed me," Komura said. "The captain took a bullet up here," he added as he tapped his right shoulder, "and it's lodged somewhere in that area. No way that he'll be able to use that arm—and I suspect that he's lost enough blood that he'd be too weak anyway. This retired pilot can do the steering, and if the regular captain comes around, then he can be the brains and make the decisions. As far as this retired pilot is concerned, I assume it's like riding a bicycle, that you never forget. Am I right?"

"Absolutely." Fred glanced over his shoulder at the cockpit, having no idea if a retired pilot would have any difficulty remembering what to do. It was certainly not a point that he cared to dwell on at the moment, and in any event, the airliner seemed to be flying straight and level.

"At least that's one break for us—that one of your grounded pilots was bumming a free ride." Komura saw that Kathy was trying to stand up, so he rose to his feet and helped her on one side while the male flight attendant helped her on the other. "You okay?"

"I'll be fine." Kathy shook her head to clear it, but that made her feel even more lightheaded. "Maybe I should sit for a few minutes."

"Good idea. Here." Fred steered her to the first row in first class, where he gestured toward the aisle seat. "How about if you take care of the front cabin and the coordination with the cockpit, and I'll take care of everything in the back?"

"Sounds good." Kathy smiled weakly; it would still be awhile before she would be doing much, although at the moment, it seemed as if not much needed to be done. Ron was at the controls, the airplane was apparently working okay and the hijacker was dead. "I'm not bleeding, am I? Do I still need this silly napkin around my head?"

"No, bleeding's stopped," Komura said as he took off the makeshift bandage. "But your forehead looks like the American flag, you know? Red, white and blue."

"Should I tell the passengers about the attempted hijacking?" Fred interrupted. He now realized that the passengers in first class already knew what happened to them because they had witnessed some of it and been told about the rest, while everyone in the coach sections was still totally in the dark as to what had happened to the airliner.

"Do you think we really should?" Kathy glanced over her shoulder at the first-class lavatory where, behind the locked door, the hijacker's bomb was. Only she, Ron and Captain Blanchard knew that there was still a bomb onboard—and Blanchard's last order was that the hijacking was to remain a secret. Then there was also the possibility of more hijackers and more bombs, as the hijack note had indicated. Yet that additional threat now seemed more of a bluff, since no other hijackers had come forward during the shoot-out or the struggle for control. Maybe it was over after all.

"We should tell the passengers something," Fred said. "We have to give them a reason for what happened. If we don't, they're going to start thinking that whatever it was could just start happening again."

Ken Komura nodded. "I agree with him. The passengers should be told that there was an attempted hijacking and that the hijacking was thwarted—that was the reason behind all the wild flying. The important point is that the problems are all behind us now, so there's nothing to be worried about. That should calm them a bit."

"That might be a good idea." If there still were more hijackers onboard, Kathy now thought that announcing that a hijacking had been attempted but had been unsuccessful could help convince the others to do nothing further, to accept their defeat and remain anonymous so that they could get away after the airliner landed. She looked up at Fred. "You take care of it—use the PA system from the rear galley station for the announcement."

"Okay." Fred turned to leave.

"And I'll give the stewardess a hand here," Komura chimed in. He brushed some of the food stains and dried blood off his three-piece suit. "If she needs any help or if that pilot does, I'll come back to get you."

"Very good. Thank you." Fred looked down at the Oriental man's clothes. His pants were more dirty red than grey, and his vest was streaked and stained with every imaginable color. "Don't worry about your suit—I'm sure the airline will replace it."

Komura laughed. "Don't *you* worry about my suit—when my attorney gets done with this, I'm sure that I'll be able to have several dozen new suits made—to say the very least."

"Oh. Right." Fred gave a curt nod, then turned and walked down the aisle toward the rear of the airliner. He stopped for a moment to supervise Debbie and Pam, who were still working at cleaning up the mess in the forward coach galley, then resumed his walk to the rear. Fred moved quickly, stopping for no one, saying the same thing: ". . . a public address message will be coming in just a few minutes . . . everything's okay . . ." to any of the passengers who looked up at him.

When he reached the rear coach galley, Fred stepped a few feet further aft to check on Claudia. She was conscious now, obviously in a stable condition but in great pain. She moaned loudly from where she had been laid across a row of seats, the two middle-aged women who were treating her looking down with the helpless expressions of good Samaritans who had done everything they possibly could. "Claudia, everything's going to be all right."

She didn't answer coherently, but moaned once more instead. As Fred turned, something caught his eye again. He stepped a few rows aft. Lying on the aisle seat of row thirty-seven was the portable computer that he had looked at earlier. For some reason that he wasn't quite sure of himself, Fred reached down and picked the unit up.

The display was still on, just as Fred had left it, the black electronic letters etched against the grey screen. *Something's wrong here.* Fred studied the words, which were just about what they had been when he had picked up the computer on his earlier trip back.

SIGNAL CLEAR; UPPER DEVICE COUNTDOWN IN
        PROGRESS — 28
        LOWER DEVICE COUNTDOWN IN
        PROGRESS — 28

Device? But before Fred could think anymore about that

word, he suddenly noticed something else that was different
from the last time he had picked the unit up. The numbers on
the far right were now changing rapidly, getting progressively
lower, counting down. *Counting down in seconds.*

Twenty. Fred looked around at the row where he was
standing. There was something special about this row, yet he
couldn't put his finger on it, couldn't figure out why he felt
strange about this computer, the cryptic words on the screen,
the place where he was standing. *Back here. It was something
bad. I'm sure of it.*

Fifteen. Fred strained to remember. He looked around at
the passengers in the rear coach section—there were just a
few of them, and none seemed to be paying any attention to
him at the moment. Yet that didn't dissuade him, because he
had always been a strong believer that hunches, subliminal
clues, little rumblings of peripheral knowledge inside a perceptive person's head, if given free reign, would ultimately
put the whole picture together. Fred closed his eyes and
allowed his mind to go quiet, to see if the hidden message
inside his own thoughts would come to the surface if he
stopped pushing it so hard.

All at once the vision of the man who had sat in this row
filled his memory! Even before he glanced around to verify
his absence Fred knew without a question that this was the
man who had done the hijacking!

Ten. Now he remembered more, remembered distinctly the
sight of that man—short, Oriental—walking briskly past him
up the aisle not more than fifteen minutes before the nightmare of the wild flight had suddenly begun! *The hijacker—a
portable computer making a countdown! This thing is connected to a bomb!*

Five. Fred stood where he was, frozen. The small portable
computer seemed to weigh a thousand pounds in his hands.
He thought about smashing it, but he instantly realized that it
was too late for that option, that it would take far too long for
the few seconds they had remaining.

Three. The electronic words indicated that some kind of
signal was "clear." That might mean that this was the primary control panel for a radio-operated bomb. *Shut it off.*

Two. Fred flipped the unit frantically to its side. Nothing.

He twisted it over the other way, nearly dropping it from his hands as he did. There, at the edge, was a small plastic slide switch marked with the labels on/off.

One. He grabbed for the switch, missed it once with his sweaty hand, then found it. Fred pushed the small switch backward nearly hard enough to lift it right out of the unit itself.

Zero.

9

Zero. Lt. Gen. Peng Ming blinked when the number on the computer screen changed to the one that he'd been waiting for so desperately for the last ten minutes. He kept his sweaty hands motionless on the embassy's rosewood desk while he held his breath and waited for the next change in the signal, the final indication that he needed in order to know for certain that he had gotten away with whatever was responsible for this colossal mistake.

"How long . . ." Ambassador Li Ying-teh stood behind the lieutenant general, his own body hovering over the smaller man as they both remained totally focused on the computer screen.

"Any moment now." Peng nervously ran his tongue across his dry lips. "Remember that the message has to go from the airliner up to our orbiting satellite, then down to the embassy receiving station and finally into our computer." Peng was talking slowly now, in what he realized was a fanciful attempt to get the last of his words to coincide with the expected alterations on the computer screen in front of them. But even after he had finished, nothing had happened, there had been no change in the display.

Li took a half step backward from the rosewood desk, as if he were trying to distance himself from the screen. "This is ominous." The Ambassador's words were solemn.

"No, a slight delay is expected." Peng stole a quick glance at the Ambassador, then back at the computer screen. "There are electronic relays that must change position—and there is a built-in time delay to prevent the circuits from giving nuisance alarms caused by signal interference or a momentary signal lapse."

"Then how much longer?"

"Within seconds." Yet in spite of his own words, Peng was losing heart himself, beginning to think that something else, something horrid had happened once again to his elaborate plan. "I don't know what could . . ."

"Look!"

Peng turned back to the screen. The electronic words had erased themselves and the computer display was blank at the instant that he looked at it. A blank screen was, he knew, the precursor of a complete change in signal, a completely updated message. "I knew it would work!"

"Yes." Li let out a measured breath himself. "Here it comes," he said as the new words began to be displayed on the computer screen.

"What?"

"How can this be?"

"I . . . I have no idea."

"You have lied to me." Ambassador Li Ying-teh took another step backward, distancing himself even further from the rosewood desk and its computer screen. "This was not a possible message, not from what you told me before."

"This can't be happening."

"I need a complete explanation. *Now.*"

But Lt. Gen. Peng Ming did not answer the Ambassador. Instead, he sat with his eyes wide, his attention mesmerized by the new words being displayed on the electronic computer screen. *None of this is possible, this cannot be happening,* was all he could think of while he reread the message over and over.

SIGNAL CLEAR; AUTO-SEQUENCER DISARMED

•   •   •

Zero. As the final number displayed itself on the portable computer screen being carried at the rear of the airliner's cabin, a rapid sequence of preprogrammed events was set in motion. A short-range radio signal was immediately sent from the portable detonation computer and was recognized by two separate receiving devices that had also been planted onboard Flight 42. Both radio receivers—one attached to the small bomb in the first-class lavatory, one attached to the larger explosive device being carried in a piece of checked luggage in the airliner's aft cargo bay—took in the complex signal and began the process of executing its command.

At precisely the instant that the process began, the portable computer in the cabin had been manually shut down by its on/off switch. Because of that, the radio signal to execute the command was then abruptly terminated. The elaborate series of relays that made up the larger suitcase bomb in the aft cargo compartment instantly lost their impulse power to remain closed, and as an immediate result, enough of the sequence relays reopened to render the unit temporarily inoperative. The larger suitcase bomb had been within one-quarter second of final detonation when the interruption of the execute signal from the portable computer sent the unit back to its armed-but-safe status.

The operation of the lavatory bomb was different. Because it had been designed to be small and portable, there were no parallel circuits to assure that the entire detonation package would explode at precisely the same instant—the compactness of that bomb allowed it to utilize a single initiator. Rather than a series of complex relays which had to close in sequence to carry the detonation signal to a massive explosives package, the small lavatory bomb needed only one on/off radio trigger to make it work.

When the initial signal to detonate was sent by the portable computer at the rear of the airliner, the receiver on the small lavatory bomb instantly took the message and closed its single relay just as it had been designed to. Even though the execute signal then totally ceased a microsecond after it had begun because the portable computer had been shut down, it was already too late to prevent detonation. The small bomb in the airliner's first-class lavatory exploded.

Flight Attendant Debbie Biederman was working her way across the forward coach galley, right to left, as she rummaged through the mounds of debris from Flight 42's jet upset in order to salvage what she could. "What a damn mess. I hate this."

Pam Jansen looked up from her own position at the aft end of the galley. "This isn't my idea of fun, either." Pam retrieved two more unbroken liquor miniatures from the mass of food, papers and plastic that had piled against the rear bulkhead. She wiped down the two bottles, then laid them in a plastic tray near to where she knelt. "I noticed that our senior queer didn't offer to get down and dirty with us," she added as she reached into the mess to get out another bottle.

"Right. Well, fuck him."

"Really? Would you like to?" Pam turned and looked at her friend.

"Don't be silly. I've seen vibrators with dead batteries that were more interesting than he is. Probably more capable, too." Debbie giggled at her own joke.

"Do you think he's a switch hitter, or just a queer?" Pam rose to her feet and stepped toward the galley shelf, the tray of salvaged liquor bottles in her hands.

"I'm not sure. I've heard a little of both about dear Freddy."

"What's your guess?"

"Why?" Debbie looked coyly at her friend. "Don't tell me that you're getting that desperate. What happened with that cute guy that I saw you talking to in the parking lot last week?"

"Mark. He's okay, just not my type."

"Oh. He's married?"

"He says he's separated from his wife." Pam let her eyes drop down to the galley shelf as she pretended to be cleaning.

"Yeah, he's separated from his wife. By about ten miles, I'd say."

"Anyway, he's not my type."

"And queer Fred is?"

"Absolutely not. I'm just curious, that's all."

"I bet."

"I'm being serious."

"Tell it to your chaplain."

"You're not being . . ." Pam Jansen never got to finish her sentence because, at that instant, the explosion of the bomb occurred less than ten feet to her left behind the thin fiber glass partition of the first-class lavatory. The heftier center section brace of that bulkhead was snapped off and propelled laterally outward across the aisle and into the forward coach galley.

Before either of the flight attendants had so much as felt the first reflex of fear, the section of razor-sharp metal bracing—pushing its way horizontally through the air as it accelerated—cut both of them neatly in half. Pam's body was severed just below her breasts, while Debbie's body was split at approximately her hip joint. For just an instant, the girls saw the lower halves of their bodies being violently carried away before the effects of the explosion and their injuries caused them to close their eyes forever.

The explosive force that erupted in the lavatory pushed out in all directions from where it had begun in the sink bowl. The thin structural components that made up the lavatory itself were the first to go, the sections of fiber glass, bracing, plumbing, sheet metal, interior components. As the debris moved out, some of it began to break apart into smaller components—thin slivers of fiber glass and metal shot in all directions at enormous speed.

The passengers sitting in the forward part of the coach section were the first to receive the full-force brunt of the initial explosion; the battering from the sound itself—a shock wave intense enough to knock down most things in its path—created a wall of sudden and violent energy that was so abusive it ruptured eardrums among many of those who were seated anywhere within fifty feet of the explosion.

At the same time a dozen passengers grouped in the forwardmost section of coach were mutilated by the flying shards of fiber glass as they impacted against their faces, necks and shoulders. Every passenger forward of row nineteen died instantly from the massive traumatic injuries they suffered.

Because the bomb was small, its energy was spent relatively fast as it traveled further aft in the cabin—but not fast enough to prevent substantial injuries from row twenty and beyond. One young woman in row twenty-one was instantly blinded in her left eye as a chopped-off metal rivet hit her squarely and pushed her eyeball deep into her skull. She mercifully passed out from the enormous pain.

An infant riding in row twenty-three, who had been laid down in the aisle seat by her mother not a minute before, was swept up by the force of the explosion and carried aft. The female child, still strapped to the infant's chair that she was being carried in, bounded off several seat backs before weight and inertia caused her to drop heavily into the aisle and roll between two seats. The child's mother—who had managed earlier to hold on tightly to her child all the while that the wild flying of the jet upset was going on, did get out one short scream. The woman was then killed a brief moment later by a heavier piece of molding that crashed across her shoulders and cracked her spine.

A good many of the passengers seated ahead of the aft coach galley, in rows twenty-three through thirty-one, were slammed into each other, into the seat backs or into the sidewalls by the force of the explosion. Those impacts caused several of them to break bones, and a few of them to be knocked unconscious.

By the time the force of the explosion traveled past the aft coach galley and into the rear coach section, it had dissipated greatly. Those sitting in rows thirty-two through forty were roughed up by the force of the shock wave and the scattered pieces of flying debris, but for the most part they remained relatively untouched by the immediate effects of the bomb.

Flight Attendant Fred Lyle, who was still standing in the aisle with the portable computer in his hands when the bomb exploded, was shoved backward. He tumbled head over heels until he smacked hard into the airliner's aft pressure bulkhead—a collision which fortunately occurred at such an angle that all it did was knock the wind out of him. Fred lay gasping for breath on the floor of the rear aisle, the portable computer still held in a death grip in his hands.

Up in the first-class section, the effects of the bomb were

markedly less than they had been in the rear because of the
way the explosives had been set and laid. Still, there was
considerable damage throughout most of first class.

The blind man sitting in the last row of the airliner's
forward section was pushed violently into the seat row' ahead
of him by the collapsing lavatory wall as it broke from its
ceiling mount—an occurrence that actually protected the
blind man from further injury by providing a fiber glass shield
over which most of the effects of the bomb then traveled.
Once that lavatory bulkhead wall had been pushed down, the
lethal projectiles of metal and fiber glass being launched in
that direction now had nothing in front to slow them down.

Ken Komura had been standing adjacent to his seat in row
two when the explosion took place, and he had managed to
turn a quarter step around by the time the blast reached him.
His three-piece grey suit was shredded by a barrage of fiber
glass fragments, the larger of them tearing holes big enough
in his body to cause a sudden eruption of blood from his arms
and chest. Komura tumbled backward and slammed hard into
the edge of the galley, breaking his neck as he did.

Flight Attendant Kathy Davis had been slumped down in
the first row, seat 1B, still trying to get her strength back
from her previous injuries in the galley. When the explosion
occurred, a shower of debris ricochetted off the panels directly above her. One of the heftier pieces of hurtling metal
smacked against the side of her head, knocking her unconscious, and causing her body to slump forward as far as her
seat belt would allow.

The husband and wife sitting in row three—they had just
returned to their seats after giving some help in the cockpit—
were pummeled by shards of sharpened metal that had been
blasted off the polished-aluminum trimwork in the lavatory.
The man's upper back was punctured several times by the
long spears of metal, one of which reached far enough forward to penetrate his heart. His wife suffered two hits from
the metal shards, with one of them slicing through her jugular
vein just above the neckline. She slumped in her seat, the
bright red blood from her neck pouring out across the broad
chains of gold jewelry that she wore. The woman's body then

draped awkwardly across her husband's, the blood from her lethal neck wound puddling into his lifeless lap.

The teenage boy in row three, who had also been slumped down low in his seat when the bomb exploded, took only one direct hit: a random piece of metal smacking into the left side of his face. But most of the force of that blow had already been taken up as the twisted, charred metal careened harmlessly off the set of stereo earphones that he had put on a short while before.

The boy spun to his right, just in time to see his grandfather being hit from behind by countless fragments of fiber glass and metal that penetrated the old man's neck and shoulders. The teenage boy grabbed his grandfather before he pitched forward, and he managed to pull the old man close to him and keep both of them down low in their seats as mounds of debris began to fall all around them.

The shape of the charge in the lavatory basin had caused most of the force of the explosion to be directed aft, although a great deal of the energy was also aimed straight up. That meant that the forces acting against the interior roof line of the airliner were far greater than what was being sent toward the front of the aircraft, and that would ultimately result in far more damage in the aft and up directions. As a result of that, the panels along the ceiling of the lavatory soon began to fail.

A tunnel of electrical circuits occupied the roof-line area above the lavatory, and the gangs of color-coded wire were ripped apart as if they were no more than thin pieces of yarn stretched across a knitting board. A few of those wires fell against twisted pieces of the wreckage, and that caused varying amounts of voltage to be carried across the dislodged metal framework. Several sections of the cable then began to arc wildly, causing nearly all of the lights in the cabin to go out and vivid blue and white sparks to jump erratically across various components of the structure.

As the energy from the explosion began to finally expend itself, the remnants of the force still continued to push upward and out. In a spot directly above the initial blast point, the aluminum skin of the airliner's fuselage was finally weakened to a point far beyond what the designers could have reasonably built it to withstand. It was only a small section of the skin that finally gave way, but even a small break in the pressure hull was all that was needed in order to have happen what would occur next.

The rip in the upper fuselage skin expanded quickly. As it did, the pressure of the cabin air—even at the airliner's low flight altitude of seventeen thousand feet the automatic pressure regulator had already pumped up the internal cabin pressure to well over six pounds per square inch—added its own muscle to the attempt to push the fuselage outward.

Within moments the crack to the outside atmosphere had gone from a fraction of an inch to nearly four feet across before it stopped abruptly at a reinforced cross member that had been designed for just such a purpose. The fuselage would rip open no more, but the effects of a sudden four-foot gaping hole would cause damage enough.

The air inside the cabin acted like any fluid under pressure and immediately attempted to rush through the opening to equalize itself with the lesser atmospheric forces outside. Not only was the pressure differential significant—at the airliner's current cruising altitude, the ambient atmosphere outside was approximately one half of what was being carried inside the cabin—but another significant factor was the large volume of internal air inside the big 787. Thousands of cubic feet of pressurized cabin air began to rush toward the sudden and unexpected opening in the airliner's skin.

The wind inside the cabin of Flight 42 went from calm to nearly hurricane force in just a handful of seconds. As it gathered speed, it swept along with it more and more of the contents of the cabin—blankets, pillows, magazines, newspapers, cups, trays, luggage—everything that had not yet been securely put away after the jet upset.

The contents of all three galleys emptied out again, only this time the assortment of debris was being carried purposely in a specific direction rather than being flung around randomly by the changing forces of abrupt maneuvering. A number of passengers were struck by objects that hurtled past them in the predominantly darkened cabin, but none of those injuries were anything beyond minor cuts and bruises.

Most passengers who had not been injured sat rigidly in their seats in a frightened stupor, hardly believing what they saw. The long tube of the coach cabin was pitch-dark everywhere aft of the damaged area, excepting what eerie light was cast by the intermittent sparking of the shorted electrical circuits in the wreckage around the first-class lavatory and what dim light came in the right-side cabin windows from the quartering position of the nearly full moon. Those few passengers who had the courage to look saw either pain, unconsciousness or stark terror in those around them.

The movements of the aircraft itself were now being felt again, as it apparently pitched down and began a dive toward the ocean below. Someone from the rear shouted, "We're going down!" but no one else responded—either because the aircraft's aggressive maneuvering now seemed mild compared to what they had experienced a short while before or, more likely, because the conscious and uninjured passengers had become mentally prepared to die.

The motion of the expelling cabin air reached its peak a few seconds after the gash in the fuselage had ripped to full size, the mountain of internal pressure having reached its maximum velocity by that time. Now even strapped-down objects were being moved, and the bodies of the passengers—conscious and unconscious alike—were buffeted in their seats, saved from being dragged toward the gaping hole in the ceiling by the tensile strength of their seat belts.

Only three in the coach section didn't have their seat belts securely fastened when the explosion occurred: the infant, still strapped to its baby seat, and the two flight attendants at the very back, Claudia Novello and Fred Lyle.

The infant, who had been thrown backward by the initial blast of the bomb and had glanced off a seat back and then dropped into an empty row, was still relatively uninjured because the initial impact had been taken up by the hard plastic baby seat that she was strapped to. The four-month-old baby girl howled a frenzied and primordial scream of sheer terror.

The rush of pressurized air then began to pick the infant's chair up as it pushed it toward the gaping hole in the roof. As the baby moved forward, prodded by the unseen wind from behind, the outer plastic edge of the infant's seat wedged itself against a frame of the seat row ahead of it. The baby seat, with the infant firmly strapped to it, stopped moving no more than a quarter-inch from where it would have broken free and been swept away to certain oblivion by the howling pressure.

Fred Lyle, who had been pushed back against the airliner's aft-most bulkhead by the explosion, was lying in the aisle when the pressurized air began its rush to escape. Fred had been totally disoriented by the sudden blackout in the cabin, and he was still very much dazed from his fall. He would have been completely at the mercy of the unnatural wind, were it not for the fact that by being at the very aft end of the airliner there was not very much air behind him—the volume of pressurized forces that pushed against Fred were simply too small to quickly move an object his size and weight. As soon as he began to involuntarily slide forward, Fred grabbed for an adjacent seat frame and managed to hold on.

Claudia Novello was not quite as lucky. She had been lying stretched out across a row of three seats just behind the aft coach galley, her badly broken ankle propped up on a mound of pillows and blankets. Even though she was hardly more than half conscious in her delirium of pain, the explosion and the subsequent loss of the cabin lights caused her to sit bolt-upright and scream hysterically.

Had she remained in her prone position with her body well below the top of the seat backs, Claudia would have been able to resist the surge of pressurized air by being below a chair line that would have shielded her. But when she began to scream, she sat further upright into the wind and, worse, caused the blankets around her injured leg to be partially kicked out into the windswept aisle.

The force of the pressurized air took the blankets like a sail and spread them full out in the direction of the gaping hole in the fuselage some sixty-five feet ahead of where Claudia had been lying; the injured flight attendant was then yanked off the seat by the furl of blankets around her leg as they billowed out and carried her along. She was dragged nearly twenty feet forward—through the aft coach galley and into the forward coach compartment—like a horseman being pulled along the ground behind a stampeding animal.

Claudia's left arm, which had been flailing wildly in an attempt to catch hold of something to stop her, was suddenly snagged beneath the luggage-restraint bar of an aisle seat. In one jarring motion Claudia's left arm was yanked from its socket, and because the blankets were still pulling incessantly against her leg, her badly broken ankle was twisted and smashed even further.

Once again, Claudia Novello passed out from a new wave of incredible, intolerable pain. But—at least for the moment—by having her left arm pinned beneath the luggage-restraint bar she was no longer capable of being dragged along by the escaping torrent of cabin air.

Yet even though no person was at that moment being pulled toward the fuselage hole by the outward rush of air, other things were still headed that way. The fiber glass panels surrounding the first-class lavatory, the structural members and the various sections of plumbing, electrical and airframe components had all been violently jarred from their fixed positions by the explosion of the bomb, and hardly any of them were still firmly attached to the airframe in any significant way.

Over on the other side of the aisle, the hold-down clips of the forward coach galley itself—a hefty array of cabinets, shelving, ovens, cooler chests, bins and miscellaneous fixtures that were, in fact, portable units—had also given way under the force of the explosion. Now with the pressurized air pressing against the galley units from the other direction, they easily broke away from the few hold-down clips that still restrained them. The entire galley unit then began to come apart—in sections big and small—as it was pushed along in the relentless rush of the escaping air.

Within seconds the structural debris from the explosion began to collapse in the same direction, as all of it came together like so many logs being carried down the rapids of a swollen river. The bodies of the two dismembered female flight attendants were also swept up and carried along in the grotesque carnage that folded in on itself as the forward coach galley and the remnants of the first-class lavatory jumbled together into an impenetrable wall of debris.

Before any of the passengers or crew even recognized what was happening, a mountain of twisted metal and fragmented fiber glass had completely covered the single aisle between first-class and coach sections of the airliner. All that could be heard now were the overwhelming howls from the cabin air as it continued to rush around the tangled debris and out the ragged hole in the fuselage; all that could be seen were the erratic electrical sparkings that gave warning as to how much high voltage was being injected into that area—an area that had now become a jungle of human flesh and fresh blood.

Up in the cockpit, Ron Jennings struggled with the flight controls of the wildly lurching airliner as it reacted to the explosion. Right after the shattering explosion, Jennings heard the screams of both his daughter—who was still in the copilot's seat—and his wife as the 787 yawed violently left, then right. He put their screaming out of his thoughts as he concentrated totally on the flight panel, the attitude instruments, the altimeter and airspeed, the engine power gauges.

"Ron, we're on fire!" Barbara struggled back to her feet from where she'd been thrown to the cockpit floor directly behind the captain's seat by the force of the explosion. She held onto the seat back with both hands and looked aft toward the carnage in the dimly lit cabin. As she peered back there, things started to look differently to her than what she had first thought.

"What?!"

"No, wait . . ." Barbara glanced quickly at her husband, who was struggling with the control wheel. The airliner's nose, she could now see, was level and being held in generally the direction that it had been—several degrees to the left of the full moon that lit up the blackness of the night sky. *We're still under control, still flying straight and level.*

"Are we on fire? Dammit, talk to me!" Like most pilots, the thought of an uncontrollable in-flight fire was just about the worst thing that Jennings could imagine, something that he knew there would be absolutely no reprieve from. If there was even a small fire in the cabin, it had to be dealt with right now, before it could get out of hand.

"No, I was wrong." Barbara turned back to the cabin, determined more than ever to give her husband as much information as she could—she knew that the last thing he needed now were hysterical or inaccurate reports about their condition. "Not a fire . . . sparks . . . electrical sparks . . . partway back . . ."

Before he could answer, Jennings heard and felt the cabin pressure surge as it began. *Losing cabin pressure, God Almighty.*

At that very instant, everything in the cockpit that was not firmly tied down began to blow aft as the air surrounding them was suddenly sucked toward the point of the pressure loss. Maps, pencils, aircraft manuals, torn flight plans, sheets of computerized weather and data messages all were pulled from their holders and sent out in a literal snowstorm of debris.

"Ron, help me!"

"Grab on!" Jennings wanted to reach back and hold onto his wife, but he couldn't spare a hand from the control wheel. Out of the corner of his eye, he suddenly saw a handbook of company procedures lifted up from beside the copilot's flight chair, suspended in midair for a brief instant, then carried away behind him. The air in the cockpit was swirling all around, yet he now saw that there wasn't enough of it to endanger Barbara—Ron could feel her arms wrapped tightly around his shoulders, the roughness of her right arm bandage rubbing abrasively against his neck as she managed to keep her position behind his flight chair. Charlene was still safely strapped into the copilot's seat.

"Look out!"

A large packet of flight charts smacked Jennings in the side of the head as it was sucked out of its holder near the left-side window, but it was lightweight enough for him to have hardly even noticed. What Jennings did notice was the dirt and dust from the floors, the corners, and the out-of-the-way places in the cockpit that was being sucked up by the wind and swirled around him. Dirt flew into his eyes, and Jennings squinted hard as his tears flowed heavily in an attempt to wash away the foreign objects that threatened to cut off his vision of the flight panel.

Then, almost as quickly as it had started, the rushing air died away. Jennings took one hand off the control wheel to rub the dirt and tears out of his eyes, then looked up at the cabin pressure gauge to verify what he already knew—that the internal air had been vented overboard by some kind of damage to the airframe itself, some sort of hole in the skin. Now, they no longer had any artificial atmosphere in the cabin—outside had become inside. "Hang on—we've got to go down!"

Jennings pushed forward on the control wheel and snapped back on the twin throttles to decrease engine power. He didn't know how much damage the explosion had done, but if it was critical to the flight controls, then there was nothing he could do anyway. Regardless, they had to get the airplane to descend, to get everyone onboard to a more breathable altitude.

Jennings toyed carefully with the flight controls in his hands, then let out a small sigh of relief—the explosion had evidently left the controls in full functioning order. That, and the fact that the airliner had made its final recovery from the previous jet upset at a relatively low altitude, were the only two breaks they had gotten since this nightmare of a flight had begun. They only had to descend a few thousand feet more and . . .

"Sixteen thousand feet."

His daughter's voice brought Jennings back to the moment, and he could tell that Charlene was trying to force herself to be calm even though she was on the verge of losing control of herself. "Keep reading me the altitudes," Jennings called out. It was obvious to him that she wanted to be of help, wanted to do something positive rather than watching helplessly as the problems kept piling up—and he welcomed the help. "Watch the engine gauges, too—tell me if they're okay."

"Which ones?"

"Center panel." Jennings couldn't afford the time to remove either hand from the control wheel, or to take his eyes away from the flight instruments in front of him. The 787 was descending in a ten-degree nose-down attitude, the wings were level, the airspeed needle was in the middle of its range, the vertical speed was reasonable—parameters that he intended to keep that way, no matter what.

"Engines look . . . fine." Charlene gazed at the stack of electronic instruments, none of them making any more than just the slightest bit of sense to her. She forced herself to look at each of them carefully, taking in their readings, looking at the needle positions, watching for the kinds of erratic indications that her flight instructors had taught her might mean some hint of mechanical trouble. "Everything looks okay."

"There's smoke in the cabin—definitely."

Jennings glanced over his shoulder, past where Barbara was pointing. If they were on fire, then they were all as good as dead—unless someone could get that fire out before it spread. But as Jennings looked into the darkness of the cabin area, he could see that the billowy clouds of white that rolled along the ceiling were not the indication of a fire. Just the opposite, in fact. "Condensation, water vapor. Nothing to worry about. From the rapid loss of air pressure."

"Oh."

"Keep your eyes open. What's happening back there?"

"Don't know. Can't tell, too dark. I still see some sparks, but everything else is black. Do you want me to go back?"

"No." The last thing he wanted now was for Barbara to leave him; her hands were still clasped firmly around his neck and shoulders, and her touch was reassuring.

"Daddy, twelve thousand feet."

"Right." Jennings looked back at the flight panel. "I'll go down to eight thousand," he said aloud, more to himself than to his family. "That'll be a good altitude."

"No fire back there—I'm sure of it," Barbara said as she studied the view to the rear.

"Thank God."

"There's still some electrical sparking, but otherwise I don't see anything. No one seems to be moving. Are you sure that you don't want me to go back?" Barbara had her hands on the top of Ron's flight chair, and as he moved in the seat, she could feel the warmth of his body and the drenching sweat of his skin through his shirt. She prayed that he wanted her to stay up front with him, but she knew that it was an offer she had to make.

"No. Wait until I level out." Jennings couldn't think of any rational reason for his wife to keep standing behind him, he just knew that he wanted her to. Once he had gotten the airplane thoroughly under control, then he could worry about what was happening in the cabin—for right now he wanted to keep his entire concern centered here; he would keep his family, the flight instruments, the flight controls right where he could see them at every moment.

"Okay."

"Daddy, we're descending through nine thousand feet."

"Right." Jennings nodded toward his daughter, and as he did he realized how he had begun to feel. Rather than the numbed reaction of terror and pure survival that he had initially climbed into the pilot's seat with, his old senses toward flying were beginning to come back. Feelings of having things in a semblance of control, rather than being dragged along by the incredible events of a nightmare, were beginning to take hold of him. "Keep your eyes open—tell me if anything looks wrong."

"Okay."

Charlene was being a big help, and Jennings was glad that she was up here with him; he appreciated her assistance more than he would have thought. "Leveling out." Jennings pushed up the 787's twin throttles, and the big engines responded quickly as the airliner stopped its descent. Altitude was eight thousand; airspeed was two-sixty; pitch attitude, vertical speed and heading were all stable.

"Daddy, look."

"What?"

"This gauge." Charlene leaned forward in the copilot's flight chair and pointed to one of the needles in the long row. "It's coming up."

"Damn."

"What is it?" Barbara took a half a step forward and peered at the gauge, but it made little sense to her. "What does it mean?"

"Nothing, maybe." Jennings glanced again at the indication on the panel, and as he did, he could feel a vague sensation in the flight controls that was confirming what the needle was saying.

"And that means that it might be something, right?"

"Yeah." Ron Jennings avoided looking at either Barbara or Charlene. "Vibration, left engine. Increasing, I think I can feel it. We must've taken some of the debris from the explosion through the left engine."

"What happens next?"

"I might have to shut the left engine down."

"Is that bad?"

"Not really." Jennings swore to himself as he glanced over the flight panel—he could feel his heart racing even faster as he looked over at the engine vibration needle again. It was, unquestionably, far above normal. The pulsations through the flight controls seemed to be getting stronger, also. "This airplane is made to fly with only one engine running," he said to reassure the two of them.

"If you say so."

"I do." Jennings squirmed in his flight chair and stared straight ahead while he steered the airliner toward the invisible line of the black horizon. Technically, Jennings knew that the airliner could be successfully flown on either one of its two engines—but he also knew that he was bullshitting, that he was omitting the most important part.

As quickly as the sensation of gaining control over the damaged airliner had welled up in him, it had now disappeared. Since he hadn't touched any airplane in over six years, Jennings realized that flying the crippled airliner on only one engine was far outside the level of his current skills. Ron Jennings knew that he would be damned lucky to keep them from crashing even if everything onboard continued to work normally.

Which, apparently, it wouldn't.

10

SIGNAL CLEAR; AUTO-SEQUENCER DISARMED

The message on the computer screen in the Chinese Embassy in Washington had not changed, and at that point, Ambassador Li Ying-teh did not expect it to. Even though he had little understanding of the workings of computers, he had come to the reluctant but obvious conclusion that the airliner was still flying and that there was very little that they could do to change that.

"There is the possibility that this message is an error, that the bombs have exploded as they were supposed to." Lt. Gen. Peng Ming sat in front of the computer console, although his eyes were aimed slightly to the side of the screen as he stared blankly at the ornate patterns in the rosewood desk. His last words had been hollow and shaken—evidence that he, too, hardly believed in the statement he had just made.

"Don't be a fool." Li stood where he was behind the desk while his mind raced in every direction. "And do not, for even a brief moment, consider me as one." He took a half step backward toward the conference room door, then hesitated and turned back to Peng. "We both understand that the bombs have not exploded. That much is obvious. The question is, why?"

"For the simplest of reasons." Peng closed his eyes, shook his head and allowed his voice to drop even lower. A short while before, after agonizing over the meaning of the unexpected computer message for several minutes, it had suddenly become painfully clear to him what must have actually happened. "We had tested the bombs, the suitcase transmitter, the computer link and satellite connections very thoroughly for quite some time. We were absolutely certain that there could be no failure that would render the system inoperative."

"I am not interested in history. I am interested only in the future—and the repercussions that this future will certainly bring if that airliner and its damaging evidence manages to survive."

"Let me explain." Peng rose and faced the Ambassador. The heavy draperies that covered the far window were still closed, but they had been separated just enough to allow a penetrating slice of the bright morning sunlight to overpower the soft yellow glow from the conference room lamps. "We engineered for every mechanical and technical possibility; Colonel Qi and I worked on this project for many months. But what we failed to provide for, I must now assume, was a human possibility."

"Which was?" Li was getting impatient; he had two or three thoughts that might be of help, but none of them offered any more than a glimmer of hope that China could avoid even a small measure of blame. This entire affair would make the Chinese-CIA spy scandal from a few years back— the incredible Larry Wu-Tai Chin blunder, his arrest, trial and eventual suicide—seem like an afternoon stroll through the Peking Gardens.

"The automatic sequencer was set to detonate thirty minutes after it was armed . . ."

"We already know as much."

But Peng was not to be put off—he needed to tell the entire story as he now had it pieced together because he needed to hear it himself, to hear those incredible words being spoken out loud. "The countdown could only be suspended by a code typed into the portable computer's keyboard. That's what we thought." Peng stopped speaking, then shook his head slowly as if he were lost in his own thoughts.

"Yes?" Li said to fill the silence. "Go on."

"But what we failed to realize," Peng continued reluctantly, "was that the countdown clock itself was physically a part of the circuitry inside the portable unit. I now see that the countdown clock should have been constructed independently— as a totally separate circuit attached to the radio unit itself and, thus, located inside the suitcase bomb."

"And if this countdown clock had been part of the suitcase bomb, what would have been the advantage?" Li was having increasing difficulty following the explanation, although the complexity of it was giving him some hope that inside this maze of technocratic words and contradictions might be a solution that they could use to extract themselves from their critical problem. He had always felt that, in many ways, technology was a very close cousin to magic, and as such, the right words would always be helpful in prodding the spirits in a proper direction.

Peng found himself standing silently again, unable to even say the simple sentence that was the next phrase being generated by his thoughts. Finally, he managed to formulate the words and push them up through his throat. "If we had designed the system the way I just mentioned—the proper way—then no one could have done what they did to disarm it."

"Which was?"

"Someone must have found the portable computer at the last moment. They simply shut it off. That stopped the countdown clock, and because of that, the relays for the bombs were automatically reset."

"What?!" Li could hardly believe his ears.

"Someone shut down the portable unit." Peng shrugged, but avoided looking up at the Ambassador.

"And that would be it? That was all that was necessary to throw this elaborate plan of yours aside—the movement of a single switch?"

"Unfortunately, yes."

Li stepped toward the doorway where the switch for a nearby table lamp was located. "Do you mean, like this?" he said as he reached up and flipped off the wall switch. The lamp extinguished, and the conference room grew somewhat darker. "Is that the sort of action you spoke of?"

"In a manner of speaking." Peng fidgeted where he stood, knowing too well the sort of criticism that the unfortunate turn of events had opened him up for.

The Ambassador solemnly turned the wall switch on, then back off again. "This small action was all that it took? This one movement was the one that could lead a nation of over one billion people into embarrassment and potential political ruin?"

Peng said nothing in reply

"Did I not remind you at the outset," Li continued, "how dependent China has become on favorable foreign trade— especially with the United States?"

Peng's eyes remained fixed on the Ambassador. The lieutenant general finally opened his mouth as if to speak, but after a quarter-minute of continued silence he closed his mouth and turned away. Peng could say nothing because he realized too well that there was nothing left to say, that there was no way to lessen the impact of what he had done—or, more accurately, what he and Colonel Qi had left undone.

"Incredible." Li flipped up the wall switch and watched the lamp relight again. He then turned back to the lieutenant general. "But I suppose that there's always the chance that you are mistaken, that it is something else that has caused the problem that we now find ourselves in."

"No." Peng had finally found the strength to speak up again, although he realized that he was beginning with yet another confirmation of his own errors and oversights. "There is absolutely no chance that anything else could have happened—this is the only way that the computer message we've received can make any sense at all. It is the only thing that I have overlooked in the initial design. I'm certain of it."

"Just as certain as you had been of everything else?" But Li didn't pursue the point any further because it was obvious that Peng clearly understood what would happen next—that he would be paying a grave price for what he had allowed to happen. The ultimate price, more than likely.

"Everything else in our system is functioning perfectly." Peng turned back to the computer screen. "That's why the satellite signal is still being received clearly—because the suitcase transmitter and its bomb are ready and capable of destroying the airliner. Only the timer itself has been taken out of the loop."

Li looked at the smaller man standing in front of him with marked annoyance. He was supposed to be a technical expert, but in reality, he was a technical fool. All of these modern technocrats were nothing but fools, really, because none of them understood much of anything beyond their own specialty. "Let me understand this completely. One switch was moved to turn the unit off, but everything else remains exactly as it was?"

"Yes."

"Is there any way that we can explode the bombs from here?" Li asked as he pointed to the computer screen on the rosewood desk. "Is there any way we can send a signal down through our satellite to execute that command?"

"I only wish that there were." Peng reluctantly shook his head from side to side. "But executing from here is absolutely impossible. Only a close-range transmitter of the proper frequency and coded sequences could execute the detonation commands."

"I see." The Ambassador stood silently for a short while, his eyes staring straight ahead toward a colorful painting on a distant wall even though he was obviously seeing nothing beyond his own thoughts. "What about a military solution?" Li suddenly asked as he turned toward the lieutenant general again.

Peng squirmed. "Do you mean a fighter intercept?"

"Certainly."

Again, Peng shook his head negatively. "I've already considered that."

"And?"

"Too risky."

"Why?" Li demanded.

"Because of the delay. By the time we would mount a

proper fighter intercept, the airliner would long be under
protection of fighter jets from other countries. Japan, perhaps—
although more than likely the escorts would be American jets
from their Japanese land bases or from their naval carriers if
there are any in the area.''

Li nodded in agreement; he could see the point. "We
would have a difficult time explaining the arrival of an armed
formation of our own fighter jets after that airliner is already
being escorted by American military aircraft.''

"Very difficult, to say the least.''

"But are we possibly overlooking the simplest solution of
all—that everything is going exactly as you had planned,
with the exception of an equipment failure?'' That was a line of
reasoning that Li had often used and had often found successful in the past: that it was the equipment, not the men, whose
failure was the least expected and predictable and, because of
that, the most disastrous. Modern men were inclined to
depend far too much on their machines—which Li basically
distrusted anyway—and not enough on themselves or their
intuitions.

"Are you saying that the bombs may have exploded anyway, in spite of the message?'' Peng asked. He glanced over
at the computer screen. The *signal clear* message was still
there, still etched on the screen in bright green letters, still
haunting him.

"Absolutely not. Do not get absurd with me,'' Li snapped
angrily.''I understand enough of your technocratic explanations
to see that we are receiving an *active* signal that is telling us
that the onboard bombs have not yet exploded. It is not a
passive signal, so the possibility of that signal being in error is
almost nil.''

"I agree,'' Peng answered in a low voice. "The bombs
have not yet exploded.'' He glanced at the computer screen,
then back at the Ambassador. "Then what sort of equipment
failure are you considering?''

"The most obvious kind. Perhaps it was *your own man*
who shut off the portable detonation unit. It is possible that
this man attempted to shut off the countdown process as he
was supposed to, that the unit itself failed to respond and out

of desperation he then shut down the entire unit as his only way to prevent detonation.''

"Exactly!'' In the back of his mind, Peng wondered for a moment if Kao Wei could have possibly been clever enough to figure all of that out, especially with only a few moments remaining before a massive explosion. Peng pushed that disquieting thought aside. "I am an idiot for not having considered it—that must be what happened!''

"It is a possibility.'' Li nodded. He looked at the computer screen; the message on it remained the same. *A very good possibility*.

"So if everything is still going according to the plan, the hijackers still have complete control and the airliner is still headed for Yangzhou!''

"Yes.''

"So nothing has changed.''

"Perhaps. Although the lack of control over the onboard bombs might well be a further complication for your people.''

"How?''

"You told me before that your people have only one pistol between them, in addition to the bombs. If the other passengers and crew somehow discover that the bombs cannot be detonated, then they might very well begin thinking of an uprising when their confidence is bolstered by . . .''

"The American fighter jets! Of course!'' Peng slapped his hand down on the rosewood desk.

"Precisely. When the fighters join up in escort, the mood of those onboard will swing dramatically.'' Li knew what he was talking about—he had seen it happen, firsthand, during those grim battles of the Long March. Whenever he managed to mount even one thin column of uniformed soldiers throughout the ranks of his ragtag army, even the most demoralized of his men would fight far more fiercely when surrounded by those graphic symbols of their invincibility and prowess. It was human nature to believe, especially when they so badly wanted to.

"So where does that leave us?''

The Ambassador turned and strode toward a telephone on the far side of the conference room. "We must do what we can to keep the onboard mood correct, to keep the remainder of the passengers and crew feeling helpless and overwhelmed so that they don't mount a counterattack. The balance of fear, hope and respect onboard the airliner must remain proper, or there is no chance for the success of your people." Li now had the beginnings of an idea, a workable plan, to solve at least that part of the mysterious equation that they were seeing only the barest fractions of.

"Do you have a particular course of action for us?" Peng knew that it was an unwise question to ask, but he couldn't wait a moment longer.

"I will know very soon."

"Can I be of any assistance?"

"The predictable answer is that you have already been far too helpful." Li glanced up quickly at the lieutenant general, an unmasked expression of dislike on the old man's aged and weathered face. He had suffered from an association with far too many fools during the decades he had spent in political life, and at this point, he had no tolerance left for yet another. "But you will remain close by, on the chance that you might be needed to provide information."

"Of course." Peng's voice was slightly upbeat; from what the Ambassador said, there might still be an opportunity to redeem himself.

Li quickly picked up the change in Peng's tone. "Remember, however, that you and your cohorts—this Colonel Qi that you have mentioned, and I assume others—have already proven yourselves quite thoroughly. The best explanation so far is that the equipment you have designed has proven to be inadequate, the worst explanation is that you have failed completely. You are a gang of idiots." Li turned away and began to hurriedly leaf through his notepad.

"I'm certain that we can find a way out of this," Peng said, not wanting to allow the slight hint of optimism he had sensed to fade from their conversation.

"You have found the way in—*I* will find a way out." Li turned another few pages in his notepad before he found the private telephone number of the person he was looking for, the one person whom he thought might be able to help him lessen the consequences of fighter aircraft involvement if he was correct about the problem being electronics only. If the problems were greater, the developing situation would require some rather elaborate fabrications from Li in order to lessen the inevitable damage to China that would grow out of this colossal political error.

Ambassador Li Ying-teh dialed the private number of the American Secretary of State.

"It's running rough, but at least it's still running. I'm going to leave it run," Ron Jennings said as he gestured toward the instruments for the airliner's left engine.

"Whatever you say," Barbara Jennings replied. She kept her position behind him, looking over her husband's shoulder at the complex array of flight instruments on the panel. As much as she tried, Barbara wasn't even able to figure out their current altitude and speed—never mind the more complex things like the condition of the throbbing left engine. Barbara had just begun to feel the existence of the engine problem for herself because the irregular vibrations had begun to pass up through the airliner's floorboards.

Ron Jennings turned from his wife and toward the 787's copilot seat where his daughter sat. "Anything on the radios yet—anything at all?" he asked Charlene, although he could tell from her expression what the answer would be.

"No."

"Keep trying."

"Okay." Charlene slid the headphones back over her ears, put the microphone up to her lips and began to transmit again. Every few moments she would stop to wait for a reply—which had yet to come—before she would twist the radio tuning knobs on the center control panel to the next frequency, just as her father had instructed her. "Nothing. Not a sound."

"Damn." Jennings bit into his lower lip as he continued to steer the airliner on its steady course across the endless surface of moonlit sea beneath them. Heading was two nine-zero, airspeed was two-eighty, altitude was eight thousand feet. It had been three or four minutes since he had leveled the airliner out and began the futile attempt to get one of the radios to work. Now that it was more than obvious that the radios had somehow been damaged by the explosion—the cables to the antennas or, more than likely, the electrical circuits or the control heads themselves—there was nothing else for him to do but go on to whatever alternative plan he could come up with. "We've got to check out the situation in the cabin."

"Do you want me to go back now?" Barbara had released her death grip on her husband's shoulders, but her hands were still resting lightly against his sweat-soaked shirt, her bandaged arm lying across the top of his flight chair.

"Yes. You go alone. I'll take care of the flying. I want Charlene to stay with me to work the radios." Jennings avoided saying anything about how he felt, his continuing shortness of breath, the incessant pounding in his chest; Charlene would stay up in the cockpit to work the radios and—as much as he didn't want to admit it even to himself—to work the flight controls, too, if he were to suddenly pass out. That horrible possibility now seemed to be getting far too likely, and getting to be more so with every passing minute. Jennings had begun to feel the onset of one of his attacks, and at this point, he had no idea if it would simply go away or if it might begin to increase severely. "Check on Captain Blanchard first."

"I already did." Blanchard was lying flat on his back at the rear of the cockpit, only six feet from where Barbara stood. While Ron had been instructing Charlene on the radios after they had leveled out, Barbara had knelt down beside the unconscious pilot and checked on his condition once again: no change. "He's breathing, but he's still out cold."

"Did his bleeding stop?"

"Yes. The bandages are on, everything is as good as we can make it."

"Okay."

"Can you turn on some cabin lights for me so I can see back there?"

"No, I don't know how. Too many of the circuit breakers are popped," Jennings said as he glanced over his shoulder at the electrical panels that made up most of the interior roof line behind the pilots' seats. Dozens of the small black circuit breakers were extended out from their casings, an indication that each of those particular circuits had shorted itself out.

"I'm afraid to touch anything, because if I screw it up then we're in real trouble."

"I understand."

"As long as we've got enough electrical power to get along, I should leave things the way they are."

"That makes sense," Barbara agreed.

"I don't know what the hell is working in this mess and what isn't," Jennings continued. He didn't want to turn the ship's autopilot on because he wasn't exactly sure how to go about it, and even if the damn thing was successfully engaged, it might eventually fail in such a way as to jeopardize their straight and level stability. The only reasonable thing to do right now was for Jennings to leave things alone, to hand fly the airplane until Captain Blanchard regained consciousness—something that he prayed would occur pretty damn soon.

"Whatever you think." Barbara looked over her shoulder, into the darkness of the cabin where she was about to go. Partway back, she could see an occasional sparking of electricity from a mass of twisted shapes where the aisle that lead to the rear should have been. "There's still electrical sparking back there."

"I know, I saw it. Some of the severed cables must be shorting out against the frame. I don't know which circuits are live and which aren't—and I don't stand a chance of locating the proper circuit breakers. You've just got to be careful."

"Don't worry about that. I'm going to deal with this like it was a twenty-foot birdie putt." Barbara was scared to death, yet she desperately wanted to act calm—with her husband in the pilot's seat, she did have faith that he'd somehow be able to get them out of this. Besides, if her teenage daughter could stay calm, then she could, too.

"Okay, good," Jennings answered absently, trying to sound positive. While he did, he attempted to take a deep breath to steady himself—which he found that he couldn't. A lightheaded sensation came over him instead, and now he felt a slight wave of nausea begin to engulf him. He fought it off, and soon it passed. Had it passed for good? He had no idea.

"Do you have a flashlight up here—that would help me in the back."

"Here, Mom." Charlene reached over to the side pocket of the copilot's seat and pulled out a flashlight that she had seen when she first sat down.

"Thank you." Barbara took the flashlight, clicked it on, then reluctantly stepped aft into the darkness behind her.

As she passed where Captain Blanchard lay at the rear cockpit bulkhead, she shone the flashlight on his face. His eyes were shut tight, although he was breathing regularly and his face seemed to have more color to it now than it did a short while before. Barbara suspected that Blanchard would be waking up shortly, although she had no idea what sort of condition he might be in when he did.

Without hesitating further, Barbara stepped out of the cockpit and into the cabin. The flashlight she was carrying was small and the batteries were weak, but with it she could see plenty of evidence of the overwhelming disarray and carnage all around her. Even though the moon was still high enough in the sky and nearly full, Ron had turned the airliner directly toward it, so very little moonlight was now able to be reflected into the cabin windows.

No moon, no lights—it's dark as hell in here. What had been the ordered, high-technology interior of a modern jet airliner less than a half hour before had become a dark and shadowy pit of horror. Barbara shivered once, then swept the flashlight around.

To her right, the narrow beam of light passed over the bodies of the hijacker and the dead copilot. To her left was the first-class galley and, at the rear edge of it, the body of another man—the Oriental passenger who had initially been seated across the aisle from her and Charlene. Barbara knelt down and turned the man over.

Oh, God. As soon as she did, Barbara was sorry that she had. The man was obviously dead, and his chest and legs were completely riddled with holes—hundreds of punctures from slivers of fiber glass, many of them with the shards of plastic still sticking into his cold skin. Barbara felt a reflex to gag. She allowed the man's inert body to slump back to the floor, then she jumped to her feet.

Keep going, don't think about it. She took another step aft, the thin yellow beam from the flashlight sweeping back and forth across the cabin. What she also noticed as she continued to move rearward was that the noise level in the cabin seemed to increase markedly—a loud whistling, whining sound—with every step she took. Also, it seemed much colder back here than it had been up in the cockpit, although she couldn't be certain of that because she was now shivering too much from the adrenaline of her fear.

Within a few steps aft Barbara had reached another person, this one strapped into the aisle seat of the first row. A woman. Barbara carefully removed the scattered debris from the explosion that lay all around her, then pushed the woman upright against the seat back to look her over. She was the young stewardess, Kathy, who had been working in the first-class section—and she was definitely alive. Barbara bent down to unbuckle the fastened seat belt, and as she did, the stewardess's eyes opened.

"Can you hear me?"

"Yes . . ." Kathy nodded slightly, hardly aware of where she was or what had happened—all she knew for certain was that everything in her body ached, that she was on the verge of vomiting and that she was very cold. "What . . . where . . ."

"Don't talk. Everything's okay." Barbara finished unclasping the seat belt, then got the stewardess to sit further upright. "Are you all right—does anything hurt?"

"Everything hurts." Kathy Davis looked around her at the darkened cabin, and she then began to remember what had happened: the gunshots, Ron trying to get into the cockpit, her fall into the galley shelf, her taking the seat she was sitting in just before the explosion. Although she didn't remember the explosion itself, she remembered enough events leading up to it to assume that the bomb in the lavatory was what had caused all of this. "Is Ron flying?"

"Yes."

"Is the airplane okay?"

"Ron says it is." Barbara glanced over her shoulder toward the cockpit, but all she could see from this distance was a glow from the panel lights.

"Is anyone hurt?"

"That man is dead," Barbara said as she aimed the flashlight at the mutilated body near the aft edge of the galley. "I haven't gotten any further yet."

"I'll go with you." Kathy attempted to get up, but as she did, a sharp pain in her shoulder caused her to groan loudly.

"Is anything broken?"

"I don't think so." Kathy Davis moved slightly in the chair to test herself. Her shoulder ached and her whole body shivered, but she was able to move her arm in all directions in spite of the pain. Other than the soreness, and the constant throbbing from the cut on her forehead, she seemed to be relatively uninjured. "My forehead's not bleeding, is it?"

Barbara aimed the weakening flashlight at the stewardess's face. "No, it isn't." The two-inch cut and bruise was jagged and swollen, but it posed no immediate threat. "It doesn't look too bad."

"Okay, then I'm fine. Help me up."

"Don't rush it."

"Help me up."

"Do you want a blanket?"

For a brief moment Kathy considered taking a blanket to wrap around her shoulders to try to keep warm, but she then decided that it would just get in the way. "No."

"Take my hand." Barbara grabbed the stewardess with one hand while she held the flashlight with the other.

"Your batteries are dying," Kathy said as she struggled to her feet. She stood in the aisle, her body leaning heavily against the seat back beside her, Ron's wife steadying her on the other side. "We need new batteries."

"We need the ones with nine lives." Barbara swept the flashlight around them. Across the aisle were the bodies of the well-to-do couple—they were also obviously dead, the seats and carpeting around them soaked with their blood. "God, this is awful." The loud whistling noise in the cabin had gotten loud enough to cause Barbara to raise her voice to be heard.

"What's happening up front—are you sure Ron doesn't need any help?" Kathy asked as she glanced toward the cockpit lights. She could see the outlines of people in the pilots' seats, but it was too far away in the darkness to tell who they were.

"He says everything is under control. Charlene is in the copilot's seat, trying to work the radios."

"Where's Captain Blanchard?" Kathy asked. She remembered that the copilot had been killed, and the hijacker, too.

"He's still unconscious, although he's starting to look better and . . . wait . . ." Barbara swept the weak flashlight beam in the direction of a muted sound that she had just heard above the incessant whining noise that filled the cabin. Two rows behind them was a dark and huddled shape—and it suddenly began to move. "Look!"

"Hurry." Kathy had already gotten much of her strength back, and she was the first to reach the row where the people were. She began to pull the debris off them—panels of roofing material, torn fiber glass sections, twisted sections of tubing and sheet metal—as quickly as her sore arm and shoulder would allow. "Here, give me a hand!"

Barbara came alongside and helped move the last piece. As she did, she saw that it was the older man and the teenage boy, still sitting in the seats they had been assigned to.

"Help me—help my grandfather."

Kathy knelt down beside the old man, who was seated in the aisle chair. The back of his neck and shoulders were a bloody pulp, with a portion of the upper half of his shirt ripped away by the violence of the explosion that had come from behind him. "He doesn't look good," Kathy said, thinking out loud, knowing that none of the others could hear her in the continual low roar of what she guessed must be the sound of the wind through a hole in the fuselage somewhat further aft. Kathy released the old man's seat belt and pulled him forward into the aisle where she could lay him flat.

"Is he breathing?" Barbara kept the dimming flashlight pointed on the old man, who, from the rear, looked far beyond hope while, from the front, he appeared reasonably normal. "What do you think?"

"He's breathing." By now the teenage boy had come out of his seat and was kneeling down beside Kathy and the old man. "Are you hurt?" Kathy asked as she looked over at the boy.

"I'm okay. Help my grandfather." Steven Stidham brushed the dust, fiber glass shards and dried blood off his face—he had a few cuts and bruises, but had otherwise been quite fortunate. Because of their seat positions, his grandfather had taken the full brunt of the explosion. "Is he going to live?"

"He's alive," Kathy said, avoiding the direct question so that she wouldn't have to say that the old man didn't look like he'd be able to stay alive much longer.

"Do something *right now*. If you don't, you'll be sorry," Steven said loudly and belligerently. More than anything in the world, he had to do whatever he could to protect his grandfather, a man he loved and respected far more than anyone else, far more than his own parents.

Kathy looked at the boy. He was big and powerful, and he was on the verge of either tears or rage—or both. "Let's get your grandfather toward the galley where you can lay him out and stop his bleeding." There was still a moderate flow of blood oozing out the area of sheared skin at the back of his neck and shoulders. "That's the first priority. You can use napkins and tablecloths from the galley for temporary bandages, until I can find a first-aid kit."

"Okay. I'll take him." Doing something, anything, suited Steven. He stepped around the stewardess and began to maneuver his grandfather as carefully as he could in a dark and narrow aisle scattered with debris. He half picked up and half dragged the old man toward the open area around the galley, using the lights from the cockpit flight panel in the distance as a guide to head for.

"Be careful," Barbara called to him, wondering if he heard her above the cabin noise.

"Hurry up with the first-aid kit. Get some ceiling lights on," Steven called back frantically, angrily over his shoulder as he stepped in the blackness outside the beam of the flashlight.

"Right away," Kathy answered toward the retreating figure as the boy maneuvered his grandfather forward.

"There's nothing we can do for him," Barbara said in a loud voice that was still too low for anyone beyond the young stewardess beside her to hear. Barbara swung the flashlight further aft and took a partial step in that direction.

"I know. That man will be dead before we get back

there.'' Kathy stood up. The beam from the flashlight had
diminished to hardly more than an amber glow, and anything
more than just a few feet beyond them was hardly distinguishable. ''We've got to find out what's going on in the back,
that's our first priority.''

''That's where the sparking was from, although I haven't
seen any in a while. Ron says there are live wires back here,
somewhere. We've got to be careful.'' Barbara was leaning
close to the stewardess to make herself heard above the noise
that surrounded them.

''I wish we had better batteries.''

''Me, too.''

''It's colder back here.''

''Too much of a breeze.''

''There must be a hole somewhere in the fuselage, that's
where all this wind is headed toward. That's the reason for
the noise,'' Kathy shouted.

''Yes, I remember now that we lost the cabin pressure
when the bomb exploded—it must have made the hole. That's
why Ron dove us down to a safe altitude.''

''I see.'' Both women stepped aft carefully, toward the
dark shape that they assumed was the cloth curtain covering
the passageway between the airliner's first-class and coach
sections. The noise, the cold and the wind this far back in the
aisle were far greater than they had been up front, and both
women were shivering violently by the time they stopped.
Barbara could feel Kathy's arm on her, both for balance and
security. She was thankful it was there, too.

As they maneuvered further aft, Kathy was the first to
realize that the object in front of them in the darkness had
somehow become a solid, impenetrable mass. Blocking their
path, she now saw, was a pile of twisted wreckage—solid
sheets of aluminum, damaged galley shelving, ragged sections of fiber glass partitions, bundles of blankets and linens,
food trays, tubing, hoses, braces and clamps—that stretched
from floor to ceiling, from wall to wall. ''Oh, God, no.''

''Don't touch anything.'' Barbara saw one small spark out
of the corner of her eye. ''There might be electricity inside
this thing,'' she shouted above the wailing wind that whirled
around them.

"I'm not touching anything—where do you see the sparks?"

"Over here." As she pointed, Barbara aimed the dim bulb in the proper direction and slapped her free hand against the casing of the flashlight. The jarring motion moved the batteries inside the dying flashlight just enough to provide one last surge of voltage to the tiny bulb, and for just a few seconds a far more powerful beam of light shone out toward the mountain of twisted debris that lay across their path.

Barbara was the first to scream, and Kathy's scream was longer and far more hysterical—although even it was mostly drowned out by the cacophony of overwhelming sounds created by the escaping air through the mountainous maze of debris. As the sight of what was ahead registered to each of them, both women bolted backward from the scene that the flashlight had illuminated.

No more than four feet from where they stood, propped ludicrously inside the electrified cage of debris and twisted cross members, was the severed head and upper torso of Stewardess Pam Jansen. The dead flight attendant's eyes were opened wide, and her mouth—now held in a rigid, sneering expression, several of her front teeth snapped backward at their roots—was dribbling out a small but continuous flow of bright red blood.

11

When the red light at the front of the Trans Continental Airlines dispatch office in San Francisco blinked off, Wally Poel groaned inside. "Dammit. Look," was all he could manage to say out loud as he pointed toward the front wall where the light was.

Assistant Dispatcher Tom Labitzke followed his boss's gesture and turned around. "Oh, no."

"What does that mean?" Byron Stark asked as he vaulted up the few steps that lead to the center command desk. Stark had just returned from the men's room, where he had been combing his hair and straightening his tie once he had learned that Senior Vice President Chuck Reckson was due to arrive at the dispatch office at any moment. Stark was glad to see that he had gotten back just in time for this crucial turn of events, whatever it was.

"Any chance that it's strictly in our circuits?" Poel asked as he ignored Stark's question.

"Maybe. I'll check on it." Labitzke jumped down from the slightly elevated center platform, then ran around the desks and toward the equipment room entrance at the side of the main dispatch area.

"What does that red light mean?" Stark asked again, this time in a firmer voice as he stepped up to Poel. Even though they shared the same official status in the structuring of the dispatch organization, Stark knew that there was no official way that he could order Poel to tell him what was going on. "What does it mean?"

"Leave me alone, I'm thinking."

He's leaving me out of it, I've got to do something. Since Poel had been the senior dispatcher to sign in first as emergency duty manager, that meant that he was solely in charge until the vice president arrived. Still, there was no way in hell that Stark was going to allow Poel—a buffoon of a man, as far as he was concerned—from knowing something that he didn't. "I can see that you're under a strain, but I don't think it's smart for you to get temperamental on us. I might be able to help if you just let me know what's happened while I was gone," Stark said in a deceptively calm voice.

Poel wheeled around, angry. "The fucking red light means that things have turned a darker shade of shit."

"Give me a straight answer," Stark said, keeping his composure. "Two heads are better than one. Besides, I have a right to know."

"Yeah, you've got lots of rights." Poel stared hard at Stark. While he did, he suppressed the urge to drag the man back to the men's room and shove his face into a toilet bowl. *The prick wants me to hit him, that's what he wants me to do. Then he'll say that I fell apart under the pressure of 42's emergency.*

"Yes, I do indeed have rights," Stark said with a touch of vehemence as he sensed that this was the proper moment. "Exactly the same rights as yours, matter of fact. Just in case you've forgotten, let me remind you that we're both senior duty managers. It's only a matter of chance that you happened to get up to the office before me, to take command. Don't make too damned much of a big deal about those few minutes that you beat me here by."

But you sure as hell would, if you had gotten up here first. Poel stewed in his anger for another moment, before it began to subside on its own. *But, honest to God, I really wish that you'd been the first up here. Then I wouldn't have to be doing this. Then I could be home with Alice right now, or be drunk, or maybe both.* "The red light," Poel answered in a flat voice now that he had finally gotten himself under control again, "was temporarily hooked to 42's data link transmitter, as I'm sure that you remember. Since it's out now, that might mean that the linkup with 42 is gone."

"Oh." Stark blinked a few times while he sorted out the possibilities. This was a new wrinkle. If 42 was no longer communicating via the data link, there was no way that any of them in San Francisco could be held responsible. Unfortunately, that also meant that there was no way of getting a shot at taking any credit for whatever might happen, if somehow it turned out to be positive. "What do you think?" Stark asked, simply to get a better feel for what he might do next.

"There's no sense speculating on it—here comes Labitzke." But even as he pointed toward the young man rushing toward them, Poel could see from his expression that the news was not good. "The data link signal has been broken?" Poel guessed out loud.

"Yes. An absolute zero on their signal return status."

"And our equipment?"

"Our end is working perfectly—it's them, for sure." Labitzke slowed his pace as he stepped up to the command console; there was very little he could say, very little he could add that would make any damned difference now. "Just to be sure, I ran a test link to flights 188 and 93—both of those flights are over the Pacific in different sectors. The tests came out positive to both of them, our equipment is okay."

"Anything on the recorder, any last messages from them or from the automatic upset monitors?"

"No, it was a clean break-of-signal. It occurred approximately two minutes ago." Labitzke glanced at the wall clock. It was three-fifty in the morning in San Francisco, which meant that it was around midnight or so local time where 42 was flying. "It's dark out there," Labitzke said, appropriate of nothing beyond his own thoughts.

"Yeah. Middle of the fucking night." Poel shuddered. It was the middle of the night for those people, somewhere over the Pacific. Search and rescue would be damned lucky to find even a single piece of the wreckage. For a moment Poel thought about how long it had taken NASA and the Navy to find the major parts of the space shuttle *Challenger*—and that accident had occurred within twenty miles of the shore, with more cameras, recording devices and witnesses than anyone had even bothered to tally.

"So you think she went down." Stark said, making his question sound more like a statement. He glanced back up at the wall-mounted red light, but it was still extinguished. Flight 42 had crashed, that now seemed obvious enough—the real question was what his own position on this development should be.

"I'm not sure." Poel looked around the room, although he was careful to avoid the faces of the dozen dispatchers who sat at their own work stations, each of them pretending not to watch, every one of them straining to hear every word that he said as they continued with their own tasks and assignments for the dozens of other Trans Continental flights. "Hell, I guess they must have gone down," Poel finally said. "There's no other reason why the data link . . ."

"Yes, that would be my evaluation also," Stark added, addressing his comment mostly to the room at large rather than to the man who stood beside him on the command platform. "I'll coordinate the notification of the FAA, air traffic control and search and rescue. I'll tell them that we're certain that 42 has crashed at sea."

"Wait." While Stark was talking, something else had occurred to Poel, a hint of a chance that 42 wasn't in the water yet. Poel looked up at the red light on the wall, and even though it was still out, it seemed—in his mind's eye, at least—that the light was glowing faintly, showing everyone who would look closely enough that 42 was hanging in there, still struggling to get home. "Wait a second."

"Wait? For what?"

Poel wasn't seeing any optical illusions because he knew, in reality, that the red light on the far wall was still out. But now it suddenly *seemed* to him as if the light were back on again. "We could be jumping to conclusions. Maybe all that wild acrobatic flying somehow pulled off the data link antenna. Maybe the unit itself broke, or they had an electrical failure, or . . .''

"Or maybe they've crashed. More than likely. Certainly.'' Once Stark had made up his mind on something, he didn't want to have to change it again. "Just like you said before.''

"Maybe. But not certainly.''

"Come on.'' Stark took a step forward, so he could lower his voice to hardly more than a whisper. "Don't be foolish. We should accept the obvious and carry on from there.'' Stark had already figured out that if 42 had crashed, then he could probably talk Poel into going home and turning over command to him. That was, as he now realized, a necessary step—to get his own name on the official reports and summaries, reports that everyone from the airline's president on down would be reading over and over during the next few months.

"No.'' Poel glanced up at the red light. It was still out, but now he could *feel* its unmistakable presence. Was it an illusion—like a magician's trick—or was it an intuitive signal? Poel paused for a moment and allowed his thoughts to go blank while he weighed the variables on a subconscious level.

"You're wasting our time.''

"No.'' At that instant Poel shrugged off his skepticism, since he knew in his heart that the best magicians were the ones who basically believed in their own magic. "I don't think they're down, not yet.''

"Ridiculous.''

"Maybe.'' He turned to Labitzke. "Contact the proper people and tell them that we've lost data link capability for the moment, although we still think that they might be flying. If they ask why we think so, tell them we're not sure.''

"I understand.'' Labitzke nodded in agreement, although he wasn't sure why.

"Also, get hold of our people in maintenance and engineering and tell them that I want an immediate rundown on what could have caused the data link transmitter to cut itself off so abruptly—other than a crash at sea. Let's find out if we've got any place to turn on that one.''

"Yessir.'' Labitzke grabbed the telephone and began to dial.

"You're wasting your time. You're wasting everyone's time," Byron Stark said. He tried to keep his expression neutral, but it had turned unmistakably sour; if he didn't get Poel out of here pretty soon, he might not be able to get his own name on the final reports. "You're going to make yourself look like a real ass."

Wally Poel turned and looked at the red light one last time. It was still extinguished, but for a million different reasons, he felt good, damned good, about what he had decided to do. "That's an excellent point, Byron," Poel said as he continued to face the front wall. "But since I'm in charge and I say that we're going to keep things going this way a little longer, you might as well climb on our bandwagon."

"There's nothing else we can do," Stark answered.

"Wrong. There's something else that *you* can do. Something for all of us."

"Yes? What is it?"

Poel didn't reply. Instead, he brushed past Stark and stepped down from the command platform in the center of the room. He was headed toward the data link machinery in the adjacent office, to see the printouts of the last signals from Flight 42 for himself.

"Wait. What is it that you want me to do?" Byron Stark called out to the retreating figure of his rival. He had to find something, anything, to get himself involved in before Senior Vice President Reckson arrived.

Wally Poel continued in the direction that he was headed, although he did turn his head half around to answer Stark. "Byron, go comb your hair again."

When Captain Alvin Blanchard began to wake up from his unnatural sleep, the very first input to his conscious mind was that of the steady, predictable noises that surrounded him—the familiar undercurrent of sound that marked an airliner during cruise flight. *Fallen asleep* was Blanchard's first thought as he began to open his eyes.

What he expected to see, of course, was his flight panel in front of him, his copilot to his right, the needles and gauges of the instruments etched at their customary spots. What he saw instead as he forced his eyelids open was the face of another person staring directly at him.

"He's awake—yes!" Barbara Jennings shouted toward her husband as she continued to assist the injured pilot. She slid one hand behind his neck and the other hand against his left side as she simultaneously steadied and braced him as best she could considering the awkwardness caused by her bandaged right arm.

"What . . ." Blanchard had hardly gotten that one word out before he winced in excruciating pain. His entire right side seemed as if he were on fire, and he could feel his heartbeats as they pulsed incessantly through the damaged muscles and tissue in his right shoulder and arm.

"Don't try to move."

Blanchard didn't. He was still disoriented, although his blurred view of the cockpit flight panel a dozen feet away from where he lay was beginning to clear rapidly. He was also beginning to remember where he was—and why. "Flying . . . who is . . ."

"Don't try to speak yet—sit still."

Blanchard tried to sit further upright, but realized that he couldn't, so he allowed himself to sag backward into the woman's firm grip.

Flight Attendant Kathy Davis knelt down from where she had been hovering near the two of them at the rear of the cockpit as she moved to the other side of the injured pilot. "Don't move. You'll be all right."

"Is . . . the autopilot on?" Blanchard tried to see beyond the two women who were helping him, trying to get a view of the instruments that would give him the information that he needed to know. But even though his blurred vision had just about totally cleared, he still couldn't see quite that far in the dark cockpit. "Autopilot . . ." he said again, closing his eyes as a new wave of pain from his shattered right shoulder covered over him like a blanket of thorns.

"No. A pilot is flying—the retired pilot who originally found the bomb. The one who had gone up to the cockpit to tell you about it," Kathy said. She was speaking slowly and carefully, realizing that Blanchard couldn't possibly be recovered enough to be completely up to speed yet, couldn't possibly be following everything she was saying. "The pilot's name is Ron Jennings, you'll remember him. He got into the cockpit just as you must've passed out. He leveled us off. He's the one who's flying now."

"Ron found the bomb?" Barbara kept her constant and steady grip on the injured captain, although she managed to twist her body sideways to face the young stewardess kneeling beside her. "You mean that Ron knew about the bomb before it exploded?"

"Yes." Kathy had forgotten that, other than those who had been in the cockpit, only she and Ron knew about the existence of the bomb in the lavatory before it went off. As she glanced over at Ron's wife she could see, even in the shadowy interior of the rear section for the cockpit, the bewilderment on her face. For just an instant, Kathy found herself nearly enjoying a feeling of superiority—a feeling that she had known something about their critical situation that Ron's wife hadn't. At this point it was a mixed feeling at best, a feeling jumbled up in the conflicting emotions of fear, hope, terror, and a growing sense of shared destiny that she had with those immediately around her. "It was Captain Blanchard's orders, that's why he didn't tell you. No one was to know."

"Oh." Barbara glanced over her shoulder at the silhouette of her husband. He was in the airliner's left seat, his hands on the flight controls. "I see," she said, although she didn't, not exactly. There had been a bomb in the cabin—a bomb very near to where she and Charlene had been sitting—and Ron hadn't told her.

"The bomb exploded?" Blanchard sat upright, his back now resting awkwardly against the cockpit sidewall. He looked first to the front of the cockpit—where everything appeared relatively normal—and then to the rear. Even though the cockpit door was wide open, the cabin area just a few feet aft of it was pitch-black. Also, there was a great deal of wind noise coming from back there. "What kind of damage?"

"We're still flying, but there's been a lot." Kathy shivered at the memory of what they had discovered: the bomb had created an electrified barricade out of what had been the forward sections of the coach compartment and galley, and the first-class lavatory.

"What kind of damage?" Blanchard asked again, this time in a more demanding tone. His voice was firmer now, although his face still showed the effects of the constant pain that he was in.

"We're blocked off from the rear. Totally. We have no idea of what's going on back there."

"How about the intercom?"

"Dead."

"Can you see anything through the debris? Can you hear anyone?"

"No, can't see a thing—and it's so damned noisy that there's no way to hear anything either." Kathy omitted mentioning what they *had* seen, because she didn't want to remember it herself. Yet there was little doubt in her mind that the vision of Pam Jansen's severed head would haunt her for the rest of her life—however long that might be.

"Anything damaged in the structure?" Blanchard asked. He was gaining back his strength with every passing moment, although the pain, too, seemed to be increasing. By using all his willpower and sitting perfectly still, he found that he could block out the pain just enough to be functional. "That wind noise has got to be coming from somewhere."

"Right. There seems to be a hole in the ceiling near where the bomb went off. We're unpressurized."

"We're flying at eight thousand feet," Barbara said, adding something that she remembered from what Ron had told them. "The left engine, which was acting up before, seems to have settled down. It's running normal."

Blanchard nodded absently as his thoughts raced in a thousand directions at once. Every few seconds, a passing jolt of pain caused him to tense up measurably. *Got to get back in the seat, got to get back in command.* Yet he knew instinctively that he wouldn't be able to handle the controls himself. Blanchard turned and looked toward the pilots' flight chairs. "Who's in the copilot's seat," he said.

"Charlene, our daughter. She's an amateur pilot. She's helping Ron," Barbara answered in quick defense of her family—although she had no idea why she felt the need to defend them.

"Get her out of there."

"Ron wants her there—she could still be of help."

"Get her out of there *right now*," Blanchard said in a raised voice. "Then you two help me into that seat."

"You can't fly, your arm . . ."

"You listen to me, goddammit. Since I'm still breathing, that means that I'm still in command around here. This retired pilot of yours can do the flying for the time being, but I'm going to be giving the orders." Blanchard stopped talking because a wave of pain had just begun to pass through him like an increasing pulse of electric current. He clenched his teeth and dropped his chin to his chest, in an attempt to help himself ride out the worst of it.

"You okay?"

After a second the pain had passed enough to be barely tolerable. He was able to look back up at the two women again. "Yes," Captain Alvin Blanchard said as soon as he had taken a few deep breaths to steady himself. "Now get me into the copilot's seat."

"Have you ever been here before?"

"No."

"Top of the stairs, first door on the right, wasn't it?"

"That's what he said." Eleanor Cameron followed her assistant up the wide staircase that led to the second floor of the Chinese Embassy. While she walked, her gaze drifted from one ornately carved baluster to the next as she took in its details.

"Some woodwork, huh?" Wagner Vanweele commented as he glanced over his shoulder and noticed what his boss was looking at. He had made it a point, from that very first moment that he had sat down for his job interview and constantly for the seven months since then, to anticipate what was going on in the lady's mind. Most times, he had been quite successful. "I've never seen a staircase done so elaborately."

"Very interesting," Eleanor answered dryly as she resisted the urge to say what she really thought.

"And did you see all that gilded lily just inside the portico?" Vanweele added in a conspiratorial whisper. "Some digs for an appointment secretary and a couple of guards, huh?"

"I'll tell the President that you were favorably impressed. Perhaps he'll then he inclined to do the same kind of decorating for White House security."

"Not his style."

"Really? How would you know?" Eleanor enjoyed being able to remind her young aide that *she* was the closest he was likely to get to the political hierarchy—and then, only at her discretion.

"A very good point." Vanweele nodded solemnly—he, too, understood the barb quite well. He had developed enough of a sense of self-preservation, even at the young age of twenty-nine, to not take exception to it or even comment on it for that matter. "Then it's a firm no to redoing the West Wing in Chinese modern?"

"Right." As she neared the top of the stairs, Eleanor looked around again. From her position high above the main entrance hall of the embassy, she had an overview of what the Chinese decorators had done—and, with that, her mind had quickly deciphered the intention behind it all: visitors were supposed to be powerfully and continually reminded that they had entered the inner sanctum of a culture that was alien to their own.

It was a good plan. It might even be helpful in intimidating the weak willed who entered here, but what the designers hadn't realized, Eleanor found herself speculating, was that the overall effect of all this wood, ivory, jade and tapestry etched in vivid pastels was a finished product that was more humorous than startling. The entrance hall had been made to look more like a cheap Chinese restaurant than a house of state. These people needed a consultant. Badly.

"This must be the conference room we're looking for," Vanweele said as he stepped up to a wide double door. As Eleanor had taught him to do, he knocked lightly once, then opened the door without waiting for anyone inside to respond. Vanweele stepped aside, to allow Mrs. Cameron to enter the room first. As she strode by him, he caught just a whiff of her familiar perfume.

"Ambassador Li, I've come as quickly as I could."

Vanweele watched as Eleanor walked straight ahead without the slightest hint of hesitation in her step. She was easy to watch. Her lean dancer's body and dark-haired beauty were the perfect backdrop to her emerald green eyes. Her stare could melt the resolve of the most hardened Capitol Hill politician or instill terror into fellow negotiators at a conference. Eleanor Cameron was fast approaching her fiftieth birthday but the years had been friendly to her. She seemed to age with grace and style. She knew how to instantly become a commanding presence in any room that she entered. She went straight toward the only person in the room—an elderly man standing on the far side of a center grouping of a couch and several upholstered chairs around a low table. Even in the dim light that permeated the conference room, its sole and elderly occupant was easily recognizable as the legendary Li Ying-teh. Vanweele stepped inside the conference room and carefully closed the doors behind him.

"It was so good of you to come, especially on such very short notice," Ambassador Li Ying-teh said as he first bowed slightly, then shook hands with the American Secretary of State.

"Not at all," Eleanor answered as she took the Ambassador's outstretched hand. His fingers were cold and clammy, as they usually were, and his eyes had that penetrating and calculating stare that she had seen from him dozens of times before. Eleanor knew how to read other people's eyes as well as she knew how to manipulate her own persona. Intriguing. Something was definitely up, although Eleanor had already decided that the early morning summoning was nothing beyond planned theatrics by the Ambassador and his staff. It was a trait that the Chinese were particularly prone to. "Although I do confess that I did have to do some powerful juggling of schedules to get here."

"Nothing too pressing, I hope," Li said as he gestured toward the couch where he wanted them to sit.

"An Arab delegation, a South American diplomat—nothing

that couldn't wait.'' Eleanor smiled expansively, in the gesture that her husband had years before labeled as *giving notice*. ''Nothing that wouldn't wait until I could properly respond to this undefined emergency that you spoke of,'' she added, omitting the fact that she had desperately wanted to get out of the scheduled morning meeting that the President had insisted on with those camel jockeys because her briefing papers weren't yet done to her satisfaction.

''Yes. An undefined emergency—indeed, an apt choice of words.'' Li smiled back, then paused just a moment before he added the proper facial punctuation to his words by allowing his smile to melt like so much butter tossed into a hot pan. ''Naturally, you understand that I would never have used the private telephone number that you had so graciously given me a few months ago if it wasn't a matter of gravest concern.''

''That's why I gave you the number.'' Eleanor squirmed in her seat because, as usual, she was finding this predictable verbal warming-up exercise a rather aggravating distraction. *Get to the fucking point already*. It was one of the things that Alex was so fond of doing whenever he ran one of those absurd company board meetings of his—which was another reason why she couldn't stand the sight of her husband. ''I'm here to help you, if I can.''

''I'm certain you'll be able to.'' Li moved his eyes slowly from the lady politician who sat across from him and over to the young man she had come in with. He was standing near the double doors, obviously taking in the conversation. ''What I have to tell you is, of course, necessarily confidential.''

''Let me introduce my personal aide, Wagner Vanweele.'' Eleanor knew right away what Li was getting at, and—if for no other reason than to make the Ambassador uncomfortable— she was going to keep Wagner right where he was. Tactical advantage, as those clowns in the Pentagon were apt to say. ''He works strictly for me. There's no need to be concerned.'' She looked back at Vanweele, who, she noticed, had the good sense to remain standing at the same place he had been. He was learning fast.

''Certainly. If that is your preference,'' Li answered as he gauged her response.

"Don't be concerned," Eleanor repeated as she continued to look back at Vanweele. He stood motionless near the door, like a statue. Adonis—with a Harvard MBA and a burning, overwhelming desire to succeed in politics. A great combination, as far as she was concerned, and one that she had exploited to the fullest in every possible sense.

In the dim light of the conference room, Vanweele now looked even younger than his twenty-nine years, and more handsome than ever to her. The yellow glow of a nearby lamp warmed his features and softened the lines and angles of his face. Even the wire-rimmed glasses that he wore somehow added to his overall appeal—he was a deft cross between male-as-pure-hunk and the best features of masculine intellect.

Eleanor had realized months earlier, soon after her forty-eighth birthday—the dreaded fiftieth was closing in on her from all sides, and far too rapidly—that she could no longer control the disquieting urges that ran through her. For forty-eight years she had been in total control of herself, and now she discovered—to either her dismay or pleasure, depending on her mood—that the company of males just about half her age could be a perfect evening's diversion from her tension-filled days.

They were especially perfect diversions when they knew when to talk and when to keep quiet—which Wagner certainly did. For just an instant Eleanor indulged herself and made a mental note to tell Wagner how damned good he looked to her that moment—no small feat at eight in the morning, after only one cup of coffee.

"Very well." Since Li had no choice but to accept the young man's presence in the room—he certainly didn't want to do anything to jeopardize his relationship with the Secretary of State—Li turned directly toward the woman seated in front of him as if nothing had been said about her assistant. "Tea?"

"No, thank you." Eleanor waited, purposely looking impatient.

The Ambassador picked up his pipe from the low table in front of him, rubbed it gently a few times, then laid it back down. He slowly turned back to Mrs. Cameron. "We have blundered grievously."

"Oh?" This was, she assumed, more inane preamble that
would basically lead to nowhere. The main event was, she
imagined, still several verbal sparring rounds away.

"Yes. I'm afraid that a certain faction of our military has—
without the slightest hint of authorization from above—
committed an act that I must apologize for." Li had, of
course, precisely calculated what he would be saying to her—
but he hadn't arrived at the final version of his request until
just a short while before. It had been less than fifteen minutes
earlier that Li had been thunderstruck by the notion of what
an incredible opportunity this was; the whims of good fortune
had presented him with an opportunity he could not ignore.

"Apologize?" Eleanor sat forward in her chair. She had
expected something relatively ordinary out of this "emergency" summoning—a flowery invitation for the President to
come to Peking or an announcement of a minor political
change in China or the death of some Chinese VIP that none
of them had ever heard of but whose burial required the
attendance of a high emissary from the United States. In other
words, political bullshit. What she hadn't expected was anything of substance. *Apologize?* Out of the corner of her eye,
Eleanor noticed that Wagner had taken a few discreet steps
closer to the conversation after the Ambassador's first remarks.

"But before I can say more about the act itself, I care to
make a direct proposal to you." Li allowed a softening
expression to cross his face as he prepared himself to take in
the nuances of her response. As he and Mao often agreed, the
first few seconds of a person's reaction to unexpected news
were the only true ones, the natural weather vanes that would
point which way the person would ultimately be drifted by the
winds of their inclinations. Within moments after first hearing, a mask of calculations would invariably hide what was
basically recognized by that individual as the best course of
action for them to take.

"Proposal?" Eleanor sat back on the couch, attempting to
look nonchalant. "I'm all ears."

"Simply and most directly, I offer you this." While he
reached down to pick up his pipe, Li used the gesture to
glance around the conference room one final time. Peng Ming

was still in the adjacent anteroom with the door firmly closed—
and since there was no other exit out of that room, Li knew
that the fool would stay put. The embassy computer screen on
the rosewood desk, carefully positioned to make it barely
visible to Li and not at all visible from the spot where he had
asked the American Secretary of State to sit, was still turned
on and still displaying its infuriating message. There had been
no change in the airliner's condition—according to the computer, the suitcase bomb had not exploded. The die was cast,
Li had no choice but to go ahead with his plan. "The trade
issues. All settled in one package. All in accordance with
your country's last proposal of two months ago."

"What?" Eleanor was shocked, to say the very least. Open
trade with China? She had considered their last bargaining
position as almost insulting; it had been so one-sided toward
her own country and so contrary to what the Chinese could be
reasonably expected to accept. "Are you kidding? Is this
some kind of joke?"

"The free market that you insist on will be opened to you.
Not just major cities, either. All provinces. An open market."
What Li was failing to say was what he had realized less than
fifteen minutes before—that through the blundering of Peng
Ming and his band of idiots, Li now held the tools in his
hands to force the dissidents in the Party to go along with the
Deng Xiaoping strategy.

I can control the Central Committee with this. In one grand
gesture of collusion with the Americans, Li could force those
on the Central Committee who were attempting to keep China
shackled to its outmoded ways to finally allow their glorious
nation to jump into the next century—and even beyond! The
historical legacy of Li Ying-teh would be in how he had
craftily used the threat of American sanctions and world-
wide political embarrassment to get his country headed firmly
in the direction that it ultimately must go anyway. This affair, if
handled properly, would be the ultimate in good fortune for
him and for his country.

"I can't believe this." Eleanor Cameron shook her head.
She resisted the urge to look over at Wagner, although she
didn't know what else to do right then and there. She was

nearly speechless. "But why?" she finally asked as she leaned forward. As she did, she noticed that the Ambassador's face remained placid, but that his forehead and scalp were glistening with sweat. *He's fucking serious.* "This is . . . wonderful," she said. "But what is it that you want from us?"

"One quick task," Li answered. "One that you will not find too difficult, but one that—if accomplished quickly and efficiently—will tie our two great nations together. Nations with well over a billion people who will then be steadfastly locked together in a mutual embrace of free and open trade for decades to come." Li smiled, now that he was about to deliver the portion of the proposal that he figured would be the most compelling if he had judged things correctly.

"Open trade is what we've always wanted," Eleanor said, mostly to hear the sound of her own voice as she tried to anticipate what would be coming next.

"Furthermore," Li continued, "these trade agreements will be credited solely to *you,* because of the strength of your individual leadership. You are a great friend of China, and you have reasoned with us until we have reached a point at which all of this is finally possible."

"For God's sake, man, tell me what it is!" Eleanor could resist no longer; she glanced over her shoulder at Wagner before turning back to the Ambassador. "Please—get to the bottom line," she said, her voice louder and higher pitched than she had wanted it to be.

"Certainly. To be blunt, all of the benefits I have mentioned will hinge on the flight path of one airplane."

"The flight path of an airplane?" Eleanor blinked in disbelief.

"Yes. I have information from our security personnel that an American airliner—Trans Continental Flight 42—is right now in the process of being hijacked. The hijacker's destination is Yangzhou, China."

"A hijacking to China! Incredible!" Eleanor sat forward in her chair. "I assume then that you'll want military cooperation from us, correct?"

"Almost the opposite. What I need from you is your immediate influence to keep your military from intervening, from becoming involved at all."

"What?!"

"I need some assurance that nothing will upset the temperament and mood of those onboard the hijacked airliner, that no outside influence will complicate the plans of the hijackers to bring the airliner to Yangzhou." As he had always preached, Li had decided to keep his story as absolutely close to the truth as possible, omitting or distorting the facts as he related them to the American Secretary of State only when it was clearly in his best interest to do so. The best lie was the one that was only a shade removed from the absolute truth.

"You're asking me to aid a gang of hijackers?!" Eleanor slouched in her seat, her shoulders hunched forward as she heard the incredible price for these equally incredible trade benefits. "Impossible," she said. "I can't do that."

"I understand your reluctance, although I'm certain that you'll change your mind when you hear the full story."

"Which is?"

"That our military had preknowledge of this hijacking and they allowed it to occur anyway . . ."

"That's despicable," Eleanor interrupted, her voice full of bitterness. If there was any single issue that instantly boiled the nation's blood—and hers, too—it was the impotence of the United States in dealing with the issues of terrorism and aerial hijackings.

"Very correct. I agree," Li said. "Despicable. However, the intentions of our people were good. The military, in cooperation with our secret police, have set a trap for this gang of political extremists and contraband merchants—a trap that will close on them irrevocably once they land at Yangzhou. With one move we can break the back of one of the largest criminal organizations in China. We will do that by capturing their key people and discrediting their organization."

"Oh. I see." Eleanor didn't quite see, not yet, but she was more than willing to listen to more—she was more than willing to listen to *anything* that might open up free trade with China. The hell with a single hijacking, the political ramifications of free trade were incalculable. "Go on."

Ambassador Li Ying-teh sat further back on his side of the couch. While the message from the computer screen on the rosewood table had continued to be bad, he had observed that the message coming from the face of the American Secretary of State had been good. Quite good. "Give me your general assurance to secrecy and that you agree, in principle, to give my proposal a fair hearing. That is all I ask before I will most willingly provide you with all the details."

12

It was with more effort than he ever would have imagined necessary for Captain Alvin Blanchard to strap himself into the copilot's seat of the jet airliner. Even with the two women helping him across the short distance from the rear of the cockpit, it was a slow and agonizing journey. Once they had gotten him adjacent to the copilot seat itself, the large control pedestal that jutted out between the two pilot flight chairs meant that there wasn't enough room for the women to keep assisting Blanchard; he was on his own as he began to maneuver into the seat.

"Watch it!" Kathy shouted.

Blanchard staggered once, then began to fall toward the airliner's center control pedestal after a slight yawing motion caused his weakened leg muscles to give way. The throttles, the levers for the engine fuel controls, the primary switches for the pitch-trim devices were all in front of him as Blanchard began to lose his balance—and pushing any one of those controls in the wrong direction could lead to immediate disaster.

"Christ!" Watching the entire maneuver out of the corner of his eye, Ron Jennings had seen what would happen next.

171

He reacted swiftly and out of an immediate reflex to protect the controls as he flung his right arm away from the control wheel and into Blanchard's descending left shoulder. The glancing blow that Jennings managed to give was enough to tip the scales in Blanchard's favor. Shoved backward, the off-balance captain partially regained his footing. "Grab him, quick."

"I've got him." Barbara Jennings reached forward as far as she could and took a tentative hold of Blanchard by the collar of his blood-stained white uniform shirt as she tried to keep him from falling again. As soon as she saw that she wouldn't be able to get a good grip on Blanchard where he stood in the narrow space between the copilot's flight chair and the center control pedestal, she did the next best thing she could: Barbara pushed Blanchard toward the copilot's seat and away from the controls that Ron was obviously attempting to protect.

Blanchard half fell and half sat in the copilot's chair, his body dropping heavily, his legs and body twisted away from a proper seating position. He was positioned in the copilot's flight chair awkwardly, but at least now his bulk was no longer a threat to any of the flight controls around him.

"I told you to stay in the back, dammit!" Jennings said as he allowed himself to lose his temper. He then turned his total attention back to flying the airliner, and he discovered that even in the brief time that he had allowed his attention to be distracted, the aircraft's heading had drifted, and so had its altitude. Jennings worked quickly to bring both of those values back to the ones that he wanted.

Blanchard spent a few seconds catching his breath, then several more seconds in deep silence as he rode out a new wave of pain, this time triggered by the motions of his move to the copilot's seat. After what seemed like nearly an eternity, he managed to speak. "Fuck you." Blanchard held his head rigidly still, his eyes averted from all of them, until the remainder of his pain had subsided. Finally, he looked up. "Don't you start telling me what to do, goddammit. None of you." Blanchard abruptly turned away again.

Since he was sitting sideways in the copilot's seat, the copilot's flight panel was directly off Blanchard's right shoul-

der. He examined that panel first—it was an exact duplicate
of the captain's flight panel that he had spent so many thousands of flight hours looking at—to determine their current
status. He immediately saw that airspeed, altitude and heading were all in order. Blanchard turned slightly to his left.

The center instrument panel was next. Here were the gauges
for the aircraft systems and engine parameters, and another
quick glance at the myriad of instruments told him that everything was basically as it should be—with a few exceptions.

The first and most obvious abnormality was that the airliner's cabin was unpressurized, even though the pressurization
system itself seemed to be operating normally. "We're
unpressurized?"

"Yes. We lost all the cabin pressure, right after the bomb
went off. Must be a hole in the cabin," Jennings said,
without looking over at Blanchard. "You can hear the wind
noise back there."

"Right." Blanchard now remembered that one of the women
had told him that there was a hole in the cabin roof just above
where the bomb had gone off. The airplane was evidently
leaking its pressurized air out a great deal faster than the
pressurization system could bring the air in—that would account for their unpressurized condition, and the noise, too. It
was no big problem, although it did mean that they'd have to
remain at a very low altitude for the remainder of the flight so
they'd be able to breathe. The only bad part of flying at a low
altitude was that fuel consumption would increase markedly—
but hopefully not to the point where they would run short.
Blanchard figured that they'd have enough for what he still
had to do, although he decided to do exact calculations of
their fuel condition as soon as he got a free moment.

Yet there was one other gauge whose needle was away
from its normal position, and that discrepancy bothered him
more. The left engine vibration monitor—another thing that
he vaguely recalled one of the women having told him about—
showed a steady array of low-amplitude pulsations, with occasional excursions much further up the scale. Definitely bad
news. "How long have we had these vibrations in the left
engine?"

"Continuously, from right after the explosion." Jennings didn't take his eyes off the flight panel in front of him as he continued to steer.

"Have they gotten any worse?"

"No. Holding steady, just about the way you see it. Maybe even a little less." Jennings was going to say more—about the feel of the vibration in the airframe, about what might be a grating pulse of metal-on-metal that he thought he might be picking up through his hands on the control wheel. Instead, he said nothing.

"Have all the other engine indications stayed steady?"

"Yes." Jennings wasn't sure what any of this vibration business might mean—it could be a normal feeling in this type of airplane, for all he knew, and he didn't want to unnecessarily alarm Barbara and Kathy who were right behind him, listening to every word. Besides, Blanchard was the captain, this was his ship, and he would know what was important and what wasn't. He would also know what to do next—a point he had already made more than clear to all of them. Jennings couldn't blame the man for his outburst before, not really. *It's his ballgame.* Jennings continued to steer the airliner westbound, his eyes locked straight ahead on the flight panel.

"Well, we might have picked up a little debris through the left engine fan section. Bent things a little," Blanchard said as he pointed to the vibration gauge. He wasn't ready to deal with the thought of losing an engine, not with everything else on his mind. "It shouldn't get any worse."

"Whatever you say."

"These are tough engines, they'll keep going." As he finished speaking, the captain twisted around in the copilot's flight chair and positioned himself normally, his legs straddling the big control column with its black plastic wheel, both of his feet resting lightly on the copilot's rudder pedals. Still, he was hardly ready to fly himself; his entire right side felt as if it were doing a good imitation of a fifty-pound sack of chopped meat that some sadistic butcher was working over at that very moment. Blanchard stared straight ahead into the moonlit night sky, trying to ignore his pain, as he began to analyze their situation.

For nearly two minutes they were all silent, the two pilots in the flight chairs, Barbara and Kathy standing behind them and, a little further back, Charlene Jennings. All of them remained perfectly still. Behind Charlene, kneeling on the floor just aft of the opened cockpit door, was the teenage boy who continued to work on his grandfather's wounds—he, too, worked in silence. That was all that was left of the passengers and crew from the front end of the airplane who had survived the jet upset and the bomb blast, and none of them could bring themselves to say a single word for quite some time. Ron Jennings was the first one among them to speak. "What do we do now?"

"I'll tell you in a minute," Blanchard answered after another slight pause. He took his eyes off the moon in the distance and turned back toward the flight panel. Reluctantly, he began a methodical check of all the instruments, the radios and the electrical components around him. During that entire time, he did not say a word to any of them.

"By the way, I found the hijacker's gun," Barbara said to break the silence and to add more information to what the captain already knew.

"Oh, yeah?" Blanchard turned around and looked at her, obviously interested. "Where is it?"

"Behind the observer's seat, against the far cockpit side-wall." Barbara gestured to her left. "It must have rolled back there during the wild maneuvering. You were still unconscious when I found the gun."

"Where is it now?"

"I stuffed it in this seat pocket so that it couldn't bounce around anymore." Barbara pointed at the cloth pocket on the back side of the copilot's flight chair.

"Here?"

"Yes."

"That was a damned good idea." Blanchard reached over his seat back and into the pocket. "We sure as hell didn't need this thing bouncing around the cockpit," he added as he took the weapon out from where it had been placed. Blanchard held the small gun in his hand, turning it over carefully, studying it.

"How did that guy ever get a gun through the security

checks?'' Jennings asked as he glanced over at the weapon for a moment before he turned back to concentrate on the flight panel.

''Who knows?'' Blanchard held the pistol in his hands a few more moments before he shrugged, then laid the weapon down on the floor beside him. ''But that's not our problem now, we've already got enough things to think about. Give me some more time to check over the instrument panel, okay?''

''Whatever you say,'' Jennings answered as he continued to steer the airliner.

''I'll check on the boy and his grandfather,'' Barbara whispered to Kathy, not wanting to bother the captain or her husband any further. She turned and looked aft, toward the cleared area just outside the opened cockpit door where the teenage boy and his grandfather were. Even in the dim light, she could see that the boy was still dabbing at the old man's wounds with the linen napkins he had found in the galley. It was, they all knew, a pointless gesture since the old man would be dead all too soon no matter who did what for him. ''I'll take Charlene with me.''

''Okay.'' Kathy reached out and touched Barbara on the arm, their eyes locking on each other for several long seconds of mutual sympathy. Finally, Kathy forced a small smile—one prodded more by hope and prayer than any other discernible reason. ''I'll tell you as soon as they decide something. Call me if you need any help back there with him.''

''We'll be all right.'' Barbara smiled at the young stewardess, then stepped back into the deepening shadows. She gestured for Charlene to follow her.

Blanchard ignored the activity behind him. He continued to check out the instruments for a while longer, before he looked up at Jennings. ''Why aren't you using the autopilot?''

Jennings almost laughed out loud; Blanchard's tone had made him feel like something he hadn't been for nearly thirty years—a new copilot, caught in an apparent oversight and forced into trying to explain his way out of some obvious technical error. ''Not for the fun of it, I assure you.''

''Answer the damn question, I don't have time for bullshit.''

Jennings could feel the nub of a building anger in him, but he kept it out of both his voice and thoughts. In just a few seconds, after he had thought about it, he was glad that he had controlled himself—Blanchard was completely right, they were still in deep trouble, this was no time to play verbal games. "I haven't turned on the autopilot because I'm not sure that I know how to do it. What I do know for certain is that if I turned the autopilot on and if it were to jam or something, I sure wouldn't know what to do then."

"I'm turning on the autopilot." Blanchard reached for a switch on the flight panel in front of him. As he pushed the switch up, a loud cockpit horn began to blow and several red panel lights began to flash. Quickly, Blanchard punched a button which shut down all the horns and warning lights. "Shit."

"What do the horns and lights mean?"

Blanchard shook his head. "An internal autopilot malfunction, the safety circuit won't let the autopilot engage. Maybe I can figure out why later on."

"Maybe."

"Is there anything I can do to help?" Kathy asked from behind the pilot's seat where Jennings sat. She looked over at Blanchard, although in her mind she was actually speaking to Ron.

"No," Blanchard answered without looking back at her.

"Not right now," Jennings added. He glanced at Kathy for just a brief instant, then turned back to the flight instruments.

"In that case, I'll go back to help Barbara and Charlene. It looks like they might need help with the boy and the old man." Kathy gestured over her shoulder toward the shadows behind her where the four others were gathered, in the semi-darkness, near the entrance to the first-class galley.

"Fine." Jennings looked over his shoulder and watched her as she walked away. He then turned and continued to steer the airliner westbound, directly at the bright moon that sat high above the black horizon. After a few more seconds he spoke to Blanchard. "It seems to me that having a working autopilot would be a nice addition," Jennings continued, picking up on what they had talked about before, "but I think it's a pure luxury."

"I suppose it is."

"Yes. I'm sure I can fly the ship okay, until your arm feels better," Jennings said in a positive voice. From what the women had already told him and what he had seen himself, Jennings knew that there was no way on earth Blanchard would be able to successfully manipulate the flight controls anytime during the next few days, never mind the next few hours.

"Okay, you fly for now, I'll take it later."

"Right." Jennings knew damn well that he'd have to do all the flying himself, that much he had already accepted. But things didn't seem as bad to him now because Blanchard was next to him, giving the kind of guidance he'd need. From the copilot's seat, Blanchard could tell him how to operate the essential equipment, what sort of power settings and airspeeds to use during the approach and landing, all the necessary kinds of technical instructions he'd been worried about. Even better than that, Blanchard would be the one who would make the decisions and keep an eye out for trouble—all Jennings would have to do was steer. With that kind of help, Jennings was sure that they'd be able to make it back safely.

"So we'll forget the autopilot for now," Blanchard said, speaking mostly to himself. He glanced at the radio controls between the two pilots' seats. "Have you tried any of the radios yet?"

"Damn right. I've done everything but try to sing on them. Not a sound from any of the sets."

"What frequencies?"

"Every frequency we could tune in. I had Charlene dial through each set where she could get the tuning knobs to work and call on every frequency, just to be sure."

"I see." Blanchard looked over the radio gear carefully, fingering the holes in the faces of the equipment where three separate bullets had penetrated during the first moments of the cockpit shootout. Most of the tuning knobs were bent over or smashed in, and the frequency display windows were nearly all shattered. The once neat and orderly center console looked, at close inspection, as if someone had taken a hammer to it. On top of that, in spite of an obvious effort by someone to clean the mess up, there was still ample evidence of dried blood and tiny fragments of human tissue wedged at the corners of the console. "I would've figured this stuff wouldn't be working anymore. It's shot up pretty bad."

"Right."

"What about navigating? Have you checked out any of that equipment?" Blanchard attempted to look at a panel directly over him, but as he did a sharp pain caused him to drop his head and sit motionless.

"Let me help. What are you trying to look at?"

"The internal navigation equipment." Blanchard's voice was low, he was still struggling to accommodate the tremendous pain in his right side and shoulder, to somehow function in spite of it. "The primary displays are on the overhead panel."

Jennings scanned the panel above him. "I see it. A lighted window, and some selector switches." This sort of equipment was new to him; he had never operated anything even vaguely resembling it in all his years of flying.

"That's it. What does the display window say?"

"Nothing, it's blank."

"Son of a bitch." Blanchard tried to raise his head to look for himself, but he couldn't. "There's a three-position selector beneath the window. Which way is it pointed?"

"Far right." After each peek at the overhead panel, Jennings turned back to the flight instruments to make certain that the jet was still flying straight and level. It was.

"Okay. Turn the selector to the center position, then tell me what it says."

"Here goes." Whatever it was, Jennings knew that it was important. He turned the selector to the center; the screen remained a dull, blank grey. He waited, hoping something would appear on it, hoping it would be whatever was the message that Blanchard wanted to see.

"What does it say?"

"Nothing. Blank like the first one." Jennings looked over at the captain. "Does this mean that we've got one last inertial unit to check—that this is the last chance we'll have

to know where we are?'' Jennings had already figured out
that without a good idea as to their position, they'd never be
able to find land before they ran out of fuel.

"Something like that.'' Blanchard shook his head in total
discouragement, a combination of his extreme physical discomfort and his feelings toward their chances with the last
navigation readout. *This is my last chance. I'll never be able
to pull this off without something to navigate with.*

"Here goes.'' Jennings flipped the switch to the last position. Suddenly, the viewing window filled with bright, luminescent figures. "God Almighty, we've got numbers!''

"What do they say?''

"It's a position readout, latitude and longitude." Jennings
read off the coordinates. "But how do we know if they're
accurate?''

"They sound reasonable enough, and besides, this hot-shit
equipment does constant self-checks. Anytime it begins to
doubt what it sees, it shuts itself down. That must be what
happened to the first two sets.''

"Yeah." Jennings didn't quite understand, but that made
no difference. Their nightmare flight had turned into what
was now nothing more than an elaborate array of technical
problems—that was what he wanted, because that was what
he and Blanchard could cope with. Technical problems, technical solutions. In the end, they'd walk away from this. "Is
there any chance that the other two sets popped their circuit
breakers, maybe during the wild maneuvering or because of
the electrical shorting after the bomb? Maybe if they're out,
we could put the circuit breakers back in and get all three
navigation sets back?'' He was acting just like a pilot, Jennings thought—a minute ago he would've given three fingers
off his left hand just to get one set working, now he wanted
all three. *Pilots are greedy bastards.* Jennings almost laughed.

"No way." Blanchard turned slightly in his seat to watch
Jennings; he watched the man fly the airplane for a few
moments before he added any more. "We can't reset those
inertial navigation units in flight anyway—the airplane has
to be completely motionless for thirty minutes for a reset—so
it doesn't make any difference why they shut down. Once
they're gone, they're gone for the duration.''

"Okay, but what about the other circuit breakers? How about the circuit breakers for the radios, or for this thing? What did you call this?"

"Data link," Blanchard answered with a frown.

"Right. Data link." Jennings patted his hand on the center console data link screen, which had also remained totally blank ever since he had climbed into the pilot's seat. It was the display screen that the now-dead copilot had shown Jennings during his first visit to the cockpit, the screen that connected the airliner with the airline's dispatch headquarters in San Francisco. "Maybe some of the circuit breakers for these things can be reset."

"Let me look." Blanchard cursed himself for not thinking clearly, for not considering the radio circuit breakers on his own. *Got to get sharp, got to start thinking.* He turned toward the circuit breakers at the right rear of the copilot's seat, as quickly as his injured shoulder would allow. It was dark back there, and Blanchard couldn't be certain of what he was seeing. He sure as hell didn't want Jennings or the stewardess to be rummaging around the circuit breaker panel; he would need to find out for sure what the situation was himself. Then Blanchard remembered something. "I think I've got a penlight on the side pouch of my flight case. The case is on the floor, to the left of your seat. If you can find that penlight, pass it over to me."

"I thought you said that you didn't have any other flashlights?"

"This one isn't much, even if it works. I forgot about it until just now."

"We sent Barbara into the cabin before with an almost-dead flashlight. If we had known about a penlight, it would've made things a lot easier for her." Jennings quickly found the penlight in the captain's flight case and handed it over to him.

"This thing might not even work." Blanchard fiddled with the penlight using only his left hand since his right arm hung uselessly at his side. When he first pressed the button nothing happened, but after a few times he managed to get the light to glow weakly. "Like I said, it's sure as hell not much." Blanchard turned in his flight chair and aimed the penlight at the circuit breaker panel behind him.

"How's it look?"

The weak and narrow beam of the penlight scanned back and forth across the rows of circuit breakers for the communications equipment. All of those circuit breakers were popped out abnormally, the extended white collars on the internal shaft of each circuit breaker sticking far out from the flush face of the black plastic panel itself. "Hey, give me a chance to look it over, okay?"

"Sorry."

Blanchard pretended to study the circuit breaker panel carefully; he was deep in thought about other things. The condition of the panel was an obvious enough indication that each piece of communications equipment had tripped off sometime earlier because of a surging overload or an electrical short. That could have been a temporary condition. For the moment at least, none of the communications equipment was getting any electrical power—which was the most immediate reason why none of it was working.

"Well?"

"All the circuit breakers are still pushed in," Blanchard said. He hurriedly clicked off the penlight and turned back to Jennings. "Everything on the power panel appears to be normal. They're getting power, it must be something else."

"Damn."

"Yeah, well, no big deal. Communications are the least of our problems," Blanchard volunteered. "At least we can navigate—and that means that we can get ourselves out of this."

"Right." Jennings nodded enthusiastically; Blanchard was correct, it was unimportant whether the people on the ground knew what was happening, as long as they knew which way to go to find land. "Okay, which way do we head?"

Blanchard leaned forward and began to make keystrokes on a display screen by his left knee. After several inputs and a few additional checks, the captain gestured toward a navigation display needle on the flight panel in front of Jennings. "That's the new heading, see? About fifteen degrees right of the heading that you're on."

"I got it." Jennings maneuvered the airliner smoothly

toward the new heading, then rolled the wings level. "Where are we headed for?"

"The airfield at Yangzhou, China."

"What?" Jennings couldn't believe what he had just heard. "But . . . why?" was all he could think to say.

"Because we have no choice," Blanchard snapped. His voice was now firm, and quite belligerent. "Maybe you forgot, but there are still more hijackers aboard. Even though they're trapped in the back end of the airplane, they still have us by the balls. They've got more bombs back there with them, and they'll set those bombs off at the first hint that we're not taking them where we're supposed to. That's our only way . . ."

"No. I don't believe it." Jennings had raised his own voice in response, and out of the corner of his eye he could see that Barbara and Kathy were coming forward again and were nearly adjacent to the pilots' seats by the time he turned directly toward Blanchard. Jennings didn't care anymore what the women heard; there was no way that he could accept this, that he could believe that they were still in grave danger. He had already thought about the threat of more hijackers and more onboard bombs, but had dismissed that as nothing but a bluff by a single hijacker who was now dead. Besides, they had managed to live through too many dangerous situations already. He just couldn't accept any more of them, period. "No, hell no, this whole thing is ridiculous. You don't have any *proof* about any more hijackers or bombs, for chrissake—you're just guessing!"

"And so are you!" Captain Alvin Blanchard was shouting back, his body raised slightly in the copilot's flight chair as he waved his left arm menacingly toward Jennings. "More bombs is what the note said and what the hijacker told me just before the shootout, and that's what I'm going to believe until someone shows me a clear reason to believe otherwise. The additional hijackers are still in the back of the airplane—and for all they know, the first bomb went off by mistake and their buddy is still up here in the cockpit, still directing us to their destination. They'll blow us apart like a goddamn Roman candle on the Fourth of July if we don't do what they told us. Now center that fucking navigation needle and fly this airplane exactly the way I tell you—directly to Yangzhou!''

The back end of the airliner was pitch black, save for the glow of the moon through the cabin side windows and the single wand of dim illumination from Flight Attendant Fred Lyle's flashlight. ''I've got to shut it off. I've got to save the batteries.''

''No, I need it. I can't work these bandages properly without some light.'' The woman passenger looked up at Fred with pleading eyes as she hovered over her injured husband and tried to stop the bleeding from the severed artery in his shoulder. ''I need the light. Please,'' the woman said in a voice loud enough to carry over the incessant wind noise that permeated the front end of the coach cabin.

''Damn.'' Fred kept the flashlight pointed at the man's wounds, even though he could already see that the batteries were beginning to deplete. He had one other large-cell flashlight in his pocket—Claudia's; she was barely conscious and in far too much pain to function—plus the small penlight that he always carried on his key ring. Other than that, there was not a single working light in the coach section of the airplane where they were trapped.

As he held the flashlight and waited, Fred glanced around the coach cabin. In the darkness, his ears told him more than his eyes did; even above the high-pitched noises of the air that was rushing through the mound of wreckage, he heard an undercurrent of excited, nervous voices and, above that, the moans and cries, the whimperings of pain, even an occasional panicked scream that would instantly shatter the illusion of orderliness in the cabin, until one of the uninjured came to the aid of that terror-stricken passenger and tried to calm them down.

Yet for all that sound, Fred could hardly see a soul. Just as well. From the first rounds he had made as soon as he was able to get up after the explosion, the human carnage that had been illuminated by the beam of his flashlight was more than he could take. Fred had already vomited once, after he had stumbled across the body of a woman lying near the front of the coach cabin whose face had been nearly chopped in half. From that point on, nothing he saw seemed to be quite as shocking or revolting. "Come on, hurry up."

"Just another minute."

The sight of the wreckage, too, was the most incredible thing he had ever seen. What had been the forward coach galley and the first-class lavatory had been transformed in one split second into an impenetrable mass of twisted wreckage that covered the entire passageway and blocked any sight of the first-class section and the cockpit area in front of it. By probing gently with a piece of metal trim wrapped in a torn section of fiber glass while he held the flashlight in his other hand, Fred had quickly discovered that the mass of debris was electrified, too. There was no chance of trying to dismantle the barricade, since anyone who tried would be instantly electrocuted. There was no way to shout through it either, since the howling of the wind in that area thoroughly blanketed every other sound.

"I'm done."

"Okay, keep him quiet, he'll be all right."

"Do you really think so?"

"Yes." Fred turned away from the woman and aimed the flashlight aft, before she could see from his eyes that he was lying. Still, a good many of the passengers were a great deal worse off than this woman's husband was, so, for all he knew, his prognosis was correct: he'd be all right, *if* they got him to a hospital soon, *if* they landed at a suitable airport in the not too distant future, *if* the airplane continued to hold together, *if* there was still a functioning flight crew up front . . .

Forget that shit, just do the best you can, that's all you can do. Fred pushed the other thoughts out of his mind as he moved down the aisle, using his flashlight to check on those survivors lying across the unbroken seat rows, everyone having moved aft in the cabin to get as far as possible from the source of the noise and the windswept mound of debris. As Fred walked past them, he ran the numbers through his mind again. There had been eighty-seven adults, six children, two infants, plus four flight attendants in the coach section of the flight before the explosion. As best he could tell, the survivors in the back totaled fifty-four adults, three children, one infant and two flight attendants—and a good many of them were injured, some barely, some much more so.

The two younger stewardesses in the crew had died where Fred had left them, at the forward coach galley. Fred shivered as he thought about the fact that he was the one who had ordered them stationed there. He had also pushed aside the memory of what he had seen when he first poked around the edges of the electrified barricade that the forward coach galley had been transformed into; Fred had caught sight of a bloody stump of a leg and, soon after that, a severed hand. Each time, he had moved the light away quickly, before he could be completely certain of what he was witnessing.

Fred stepped into the aft galley, shut off his flashlight, then picked up the ship's interphone. "Hello, hello . . ." he shouted several times into the dead microphone as he listened for a reply from the equally dead earpiece. Not a sound, no voices, no static, nothing. The line had been cut by the explosion, he was sure of it now.

"Anything on it?"

In the dim reflected moonlight, Fred could barely make out the features of the man who had come up beside him in the galley. Big, middle-aged or older, seemingly unhurt—Fred had a slight recollection of seeing him seated in the very rear, toward the aft end of the smoking section, when the bomb went off. "I guess smoking's not bad for your health after all."

"What?"

"Never mind." Fred slid the interphone handset back into its cradle. "This thing's dead, I think it's completely broken. I don't think it's going to start working anytime soon."

"That'd be my guess, too. I tried it a little while ago—I got nothing either."

"Right." Normally, Fred wouldn't have tolerated a passenger touching a piece of equipment that was meant strictly for the crew. Things were different now, that was for sure.

"So what do you think? Are we headed back home? Do the pilots finally have this thing under control?"

Fred shook his head slowly, wondering how much of his expression the man could see. Hopefully, not much. "Listen, I'll be honest. I don't know. I wish I could get hold of the cockpit to find out," he said as he pointed to the dead interphone handset, "but I can't."

"What's your guess?" The man was calm and matter-of-fact, as if he were asking what time they intended to serve dinner or show a movie.

"Well, we do seem to be under control, that much I can see. A little while ago the airplane did a gentle turn that changed our heading. It's been flying steady ever since."

"How could you tell that we did a gentle turn? I can't tell nothing back here."

"The moon." Fred had already thanked God more than once for that outside reference—without the nearly full moon and cloudless sky, it would have been like being trapped inside a closet. "It was directly on the nose for a while, now it's steady on the left-front of the airplane."

"Okay, sounds good. I'll keep an eye on the moon from now on."

"But don't tell anyone, I don't want a panic in the cabin when the moon begins to get lower in the sky—they'll think we're diving or something."

"Don't worry, I don't tell nobody nothing." The man stepped a few inches closer and dropped his voice even lower. "Call me if you need anything, any kind of help. I'm a pretty calm kind of guy, and I know that you're under a lot of pressure. Some of these people might start to get pretty ugly, once the initial shock wears off them, if you know what I mean."

"Yes." Fred didn't know what he meant, not exactly, although he more than welcomed whatever help he could get. He also knew that he instantly liked this guy, that he was glad as hell that the man had decided to step forward and make himself known. "What's your name?"

"Max."

"I'm Fred. Where are you seated, Max?"

"First row behind this galley, on the left."

"Got it. I'll call you later, you can depend on it."

"Okay." The man nodded and left, disappearing totally before he had stepped more than a few feet away from where they had stood in the pitch darkness of the rear galley.

Fred stood where he was for quite some time, mulling things over. He had done all he could for the passengers, which wasn't very much, and he had attempted to contact the cockpit but had found out that communications were impossible. All that remained was for him to go over in his mind the things that had happened, and to think about what still remained undone.

And to pray.

13

The American Secretary of State Eleanor Cameron stood beside her desk in the Chinese Embassy, telephone pressed against her ear, while she stared blankly ahead. She was waiting for a response from the other end—she had been put on hold once again, as the Pentagon operator routed her secure-line call through the various stages of satellite relays that would ultimately connect her with the United States Air Force installation at Sasebo, Japan.

"Anything yet?" Ambassador Li Ying-teh asked. He had begun to fidget where he stood beside the American Secretary of State, in a mild display of nervousness that was a highly unusual behavior pattern from him.

"Nothing. But very soon—at least that's what these military clowns on the line keep telling me."

"I understand." Li nodded knowingly, then glanced over at where Lt. Gen. Peng Ming sat in front of the computer screen on the rosewood desk. Peng looked discernibly uncomfortable—a predictable emotion, considering the situation he was in. "Regardless of which country's uniform they wear, the people in the military establishments share the same basic value toward time—their time is valuable, yours is not.''

"True." Eleanor spent a few additional moments listening to the incessant scratching and hissing on the phone line, then motioned for her assistant. "Here, take this damn thing. Let me know if this colonel whatever the hell his name is can get the right general to answer his goddamned phone."

Wagner Vanweele stepped around the desk and took the telephone without comment. His own thoughts were racing ahead in every direction—as they had continually since the completion of the Ambassador's incredible explanation to them—in an attempt to predict what would happen next so he could plan properly. "Still nothing but static," Vanweele said as he held the telephone to his ear.

"He should be back on the line soon, unless they've disconnected us. I wouldn't be surprised by that, either."

"Nor I." Vanweele didn't share Eleanor's dislike of the military—something that had gotten her in hot water with the President more than once in the last few months—but he knew enough not to contradict her. Besides, all that mattered now was that he come up with a recommendation that would enable them to maximize the potential of the pure-gold situation that they'd been handed. Free trade with China would be the ultimate coup for the State Department—and it certainly wouldn't hurt either of their careers. The thought of giving assistance to a group of hijackers was unnerving, but Vanweele pushed that notion aside with the idea that they'd be doing it for all the right reasons.

As Eleanor had pointed out, any opening of trade with China would be wonderful for the country—and it also meant that the potential possibilities for personal gain would be nearly unlimited. There would be new government agencies to run, there would be consulting fees from industry and there would be high-level management positions available in major exporting corporations in the United States for anyone who had an inside track on what was happening in China. People like himself and, of course, Eleanor. The events of the next few hours would, Wagner knew, have an incalculable effect on their futures. "Wait, here's someone . . . hello? Yes, I can hear you—a little scratchy, but understandable. She's right here.''

Eleanor took the telephone without comment. After she had identified herself, she continued to stand close to Wagner, her face a total blank as she listened to what the general on the other end of the telephone-to-satellite linkup to Japan had begun to explain.

Peng Ming got up from where he was sitting by the computer screen and joined the three others by the telephone. He silently moved himself into a position adjacent to the Ambassador and intently watched the woman's face as he attempted to get some indications about the news she was hearing. He, too, obviously realized that he had a great stake in what would be happening in the next few hours.

"Okay, let me run this by you so I'm sure that I've got it." Eleanor paused, eyed the three men around her, then continued. "The airliner is still totally out of communications with everyone, although you've just identified it on the long-range Japanese defense radar. They're flying at a low altitude, and on a heading that's coincidental with the direct course to what had earlier been radioed in as their hijack destination—Yangzhou, China."

"One hundred and fifty kilometers northwest of Shanghai," Peng volunteered in English, in a low voice, to the two Americans. "Approximately one hundred kilometers inland from the coast." Peng desperately wanted to become involved, to become a participant in the Ambassador's plan to salvage this situation for them. Obviously, the trend of events had shown that the Ambassador had been correct, that the hijacking to Yangzhou was still going ahead as planned. *Kao Wei must have been the one who shut off the portable unit—he is still in total control.* Yet even with that knowledge, Peng was still having difficulty understanding what Ambassador Li's ultimate intentions were. Unfortunately for him, at that moment he was certainly in no position to ask.

"The assumption your experts have made," Eleanor continued on the telephone, "is that the hijackers have taken total control of the aircraft and they're not allowing the flight crew to use the radios. That's logical, that accounts for the lack of communications even though they're still flying."

"Yes, that makes sense," Peng commented in a hushed voice in the background. In his mind, he could imagine Kao Wei onboard the airliner, still in complete control of the situation, but now concerned that the bombs were no longer under his absolute direction after he had been forced to shut down the portable detonation device. *Kao is an intelligent man. He will improvise correctly, he will do fine.*

Peng then put those thoughts out of his mind and concentrated instead on his own situation. He had been told by the Ambassador to carefully explain to the Americans how he and his men had "discovered" the hijackers' plan weeks ago, yet had elected to allow the hijacking to occur anyway—all of it a giant, elaborate lie that Peng had been carefully briefed on before he had been brought into the conference room to meet the American Secretary of State. "The hijackers are ruthless men, capable of great violence," Peng added as an embellishment to his own fabricated story.

"Be still." Li put up his hand to indicate that he wanted the lieutenant general to be quiet. Li was still fearful that Peng would say too much too soon—that he would inadvertently tip the Americans off that they were being duped.

"Sorry." Without wanting to, Peng found himself looking to the Americans for support and encouragement, anything to indicate a change in their attitude. What he got instead was a hostile stare from the young assistant, and nothing whatsoever from the woman Secretary of State—they continued to treat him disdainfully, just as they had since soon after Peng had come into the conference room and been introduced by the Ambassador as the military man who had "allowed" the supposedly "criminal elements" onboard the airliner to go ahead with their hijack plan.

"All right, I understand," Eleanor was saying into the telephone. While she spoke, she looked at Wagner and gestured in an inquisitive way, as if she were asking him for an opinion of what they should do next.

"Are they sending out search and rescue, and intercept aircraft?" Vanweele whispered.

Eleanor repeated the question into the telephone, then listened to the answer. "Okay, you've already sent three interceptors with instructions to remain out of sight to the rear of the airliner so the hijackers don't get alarmed. Very good, yes, as I suggested, we feel that it's the best tactic at this point. Simply escort the airliner to the Chinese border, without anyone onboard being able to spot the escorts. The Chinese can continue the job the rest of the way to the hijackers' destination. The operative concept here is that we remain out of sight, so none of the hijackers get the idea that both governments are on to them.''

"Get an estimated time for border crossing,'' Vanweele said.

"Approximately five hours from now,'' Eleanor repeated, after she had asked the question. She glanced at her wristwatch— a gold and diamond Rolex that her wealthy husband had given her a few years before. It was 8:54 A.M., Washington time. "That'll be approximately 2:00 P.M. here in Washington,'' she said into the telephone.

"That will be approximately six o'clock in the morning, local time, at the China coast,'' Peng volunteered.

"Will you be quiet!'' Li said through clenched teeth at the lieutenant general. It was still too soon for the next stage of his plan to begin, and Li was still living in dread that this little warthog of a military man next to him would now jeopardize the brilliant finishing touches to Li's scheme by opening up his big mouth.

"And, incidentally, as I explained to the colonel I spoke with first,'' Eleanor continued on the telephone as she ignored the comments in the room, "I'm here at the Chinese Embassy in Washington with the Chinese Ambassador beside me. We'll take care of the notifications to the Chinese from this end. You can go on the assumption that they'll rendezvous with the airliner shortly after it reaches their airspace. I'm happy to report that, naturally, the Chinese Ambassador has pledged his country's complete cooperation.'' After a few more words and a promise to call back shortly, Eleanor hung up.

"I assume that all is going the way we had hoped,'' Li said.

"Yes. I've convinced the Air Force to let everything happen just that way—which wasn't too difficult, since no one is quite sure who should be in charge and what should be done.

Anyway, the United States Air Force will send jets out from their bases in Japan to intercept and follow the airliner to the Chinese coast. The Japanese have already given us approval to do the shadowing ourselves, and they've also given assurances that they won't get involved as long as the airliner doesn't stray over Japanese soil.''

"Excellent.''

"Another break in our favor is that the United States Navy doesn't have any carriers in the area. That means that I don't have any in-service rivalries to try to smooth over.''

"Very good.''

"Once the hijacked airliner reaches Chinese airspace, your own aircraft can provide the most proper type of in-trail escort." Eleanor stopped and stared directly at the Ambassador, not wanting to add any more quite yet. Even in the dim yellow light of the conference room, she could easily see the rivulets of perspiration on the Ambassador's forehead and scalp—indications that he was concerned about China's culpability in this affair. As far as Eleanor was concerned, all that mattered now was the issue of free trade—that's what she wanted to talk about now, not this stupid hijacking.

"So once the airliner has crossed into Chinese airspace, the American jets will turn back. We will then be the sole escort. That will give us total control of the situation so that we can be assured of successfully springing our trap.''

"That's our hope. The ball, as they say, will then be in your court.''

"Very well." Li took a deep breath, glanced at the lieutenant general, then back at the Americans. It was time to go on to the final step of his plan, the final variation. "Then I confess that I must admit to one more thing. I have systematically lied to you.''

"What?" Eleanor took a half step backward. She glanced at Vanweele. He, clearly, was as shocked as she was. "Lied? How?''

"By giving you half the truth. A hijacking is indeed in process on Flight 42, and it is indeed taking the airliner to Yangzhou. But what we told you about criminals and contraband is not strictly the truth. The criminal involved is Lieutenant General Peng Ming, the prize is a military one—a top-secret United States war games computer that had been stolen and is now riding in the airliner's cargo compartment.''

Peng jumped up, grabbed the Ambassador by the shoulders and began to shake him. "Are you crazy! Have you lost your mind! What are you doing!"

"Let go of me, you little toad!" As old as he was, the Ambassador still had all his vigor and strength, and was able to easily brush the lieutenant general away. He turned to the Americans, who were standing with their mouths open, their eyes wide. "What I tell you is now the absolute truth. It also opens up an incredible opportunity for all of us."

"Eleanor, we've got to get out of here. Right now!" Vanweele instinctively knew that the situation—whatever the hell it was—was going too far, becoming too complex and dangerous. He took a step toward the conference room door, but then saw that Eleanor was not following him.

"Wagner, be quiet." Eleanor's voice was calm, her stare unrelenting. "I can tell that this is something that I'll want to hear. That much I can tell for sure."

"Yes. You are very wise, very capable of understanding how we must sometimes do disdainful things for the ultimate betterment of all." Without further preamble the Ambassador began to fill in the details of the hijacking, explaining completely what had happened and why. Several times during the lengthy explanation he glanced over at Peng, who glared back at him with a mixture of hate and fear. Still, the Ambassador continued until the full story was out, without any of the others saying a single word.

"So the free trade issues are for real?" Eleanor said after a full minute of silence had gone by after the end of the Ambassador's explanation.

"Yes. That is the real point. Those of us in this room understand completely that free and open trade between China and the United States is the best thing that could happen to all of us."

"But why don't we just . . ."

"Impossible!" Li interrupted. "The internal factions in China could drag this evolution out across *centuries* if we cannot find a forceful way to make them speed up the process."

"And the potential exposure of this hijacking plot would be

your weapon to force the various factions in your government
to go along with free trade?''

"Yes, yes." Li was speaking quickly now, his words
tumbling out in a nonstop barrage of attempted persuasion.
He *had to* get the Americans to believe him, to cooperate. It
was for *everyone's good!* "You and I must work in collusion
against the Chinese Central Committee, against a gang of
relics whose bones are as old as mine but whose minds are
hundreds of years older! They are anachronistic fossils from a
dark age who will voluntarily give up no vestige of control.
We must force them to do so—humiliate them, threaten
them!''

"Then what you're proposing is that it'll be you and me
against the world, so to speak," Eleanor said. She was
obviously deep in thought; there was a small but noticeable
smile at the corners of her mouth.

"In a manner of speaking, yes."

"Now I understand." Eleanor nodded her head positively.
"But I have one more question, if I may."

"Of course."

Eleanor pointed at Peng Ming, who was standing beside
the rosewood table. "I realize that our countries will benefit
enormously, and our personal benefits will come from our
belief in free and open trade and potential fallout from that.
But what will this man be getting from this arrangement?"

Li paused for a moment before he answered. "His life,"
he finally said. "I could have had Lieutenant General Peng
Ming summarily executed for what he has done, for the
unauthorized initiatives that he has taken. But instead of
doing that, I now offer him the possibility of a pardon, a
reprieve. That, in exchange for his complete cooperation." Li
knew that the time was now right for a small display of his
immense personal power. "Peng, shall I summon downstairs
to have you removed and eliminated at this very moment, or
do you vow to cooperate, to support my intentions, to maintain our much needed secrecy if our goals are to be reached?"

Peng looked at the Ambassador, then at the two Americans. He was shocked and bewildered, but he understood
quite well that he had little choice. "I will cooperate," he
finally said.

"You pledge it?"

"I do."

"But will the Central Committee go along with that?" Eleanor asked as she watched the lieutenant general squirm.

"That will be easy enough to fix. Remember, I am a member of the Central Committee myself and have many friends who feel as I do. What I am saying is that we can use the threat of exposure and censure to tip the political scales in our favor, to clean house, to make the sweeping changes that are necessary. The spirits are in harmony and all is ready for this change—all we need do now is act courageously."

"Much along the lines of what happened when the Gang of Four was removed," Eleanor volunteered, remembering the State Department briefing bulletins that she had read. Eleanor shivered slightly as the thought of their personal exposure crossed her mind, but then put that thought aside as she realized that she was witnessing a turning point in history, the ending of one era and the beginning of another. It was one of those micro-moments in history that Wagner was always babbling on about—only this time she would be participating in it, not merely observing it. "I see what you're saying. I think it might work."

"It will work, I assure you. But it can only work with your assitance."

"What sort of assistance. Be specific," Eleanor said.

"We will arrange a private audience between you and the Central Committee within the next forty-eight hours. I will tell them of our arrangement of ignoring our incredible military blunder in exchange for complete and open trade. The votes are ordained, the dissenters will be removed and the country will be opened. Once that happens, of course, there will be no turning back." Li smiled and nodded; he could see that this personal journey of many miles that he had been attempting to accomplish for the last twenty years had suddenly covered a great deal of ground in just the last few minutes. As his impish grandson from Beijing might have observed, the old man's ox cart had suddenly become jet-propelled. Li smiled.

"And I see something else, too. That we can't allow the airliner to land in Yangzhou." Eleanor looked over at

Vanweele, who appeared dazed, spaced-out. She turned back
to the Ambassador. "You do understand that point, don't
you? Are you ready to accept that part, too?"

"That option is entirely yours," Li answered before Eleanor could add any more; he had anticipated that she would
say something along those lines. "I will at this moment give
you my solemn oath that we will return the secret war games
computer to you, or destroy it. My only concern in this
situation is the ultimate appearance of our embarrassment, our
jeopardy, our exposure to an unfriendly act committed against
a nation whose cooperative relationship is correctly perceived
as critical to our ongoing growth and ultimate survival. It is
with that weapon of culpability that I can force the dissenters
on the Central Committee to step aside and allow complete
and free trade arrangements between China and the United
States to occur all at once, rather than slowly over a period of
decades."

"Eleanor, we've got to stop this," Vanweele said, his
voice hollow and shaken even though he had finally found
enough courage to speak. "On top of everything else, now
we're talking about *classified* data here—top-secret material.
For God's sake, that's the kind of thing that goes into the
definition of *espionage!*"

"True," Eleanor answered coolly. "A good point, Wagner.
We certainly can't afford any hint of impropriety on our part;
we can't tolerate any thought that we didn't do absolutely
everything to prevent a top-secret machine from falling into
the wrong hands."

"Exactly." Vanweele took another half step toward the
conference room door, expecting her to follow. She didn't.

"And there's something else, too." Eleanor stood with her
hands on her hips, her legs widely apart, her face beaming.
She had regained her composure completely, and anyone who
knew her would realize that she had assumed her customary
negotiating posture, that she was back in control. "I'm certainly not a traitor . . ."

"I have already made a vow to turn the secret material over
to you," Li said somewhat indignantly.

"Bullshit." Eleanor waved her hand accusingly. "Let's
not take this trust-and-brotherhood thing too far. It's great for

press releases, but here in this room we can call it like it really is. I realize now that the only way I can go along with this program is if you completely destroy that airplane and its stolen top-secret equipment.''

"Eleanor!"

"Wagner, shut up." Eleanor turned back to the Ambassador. "There's a second advantage to destroying the airliner.''

"What is that advantage?" Li asked, although he already knew what it would be. He also knew that it would mean much more if the idea came from her, not from him.

"Blood. By allowing you to destroy the airliner, we're signing our pact with the Central Committee in blood.'' Eleanor cringed slightly at the mention of that word and all it implied, but she was experienced enough not to show it. All that mattered to her now were the trade issues; they overshadowed everything else completely. One airliner more or less didn't mean a damn thing. "It's American blood we're talking about, too—the red, white and blue variety. I don't know how certain you are about your votes and political clout, but once you've shot that airplane out of the sky, there's no way that the Central Committee can back out of your deal without their house falling down.''

"Very well, the choice is yours. The airliner will be destroyed.''

"It must be destroyed in-flight, too," Eleanor added.

"Why?" Again, Li already knew the answer—but he also knew that verbalizing the question and hearing the spoken answer would do far more to cement their relationship than mere subtle or implied agreements.

"The airliner has to be destroyed in-flight to assure complete destruction of the stolen top-secret machinery. This equipment must be destroyed well before you ever could have gotten your hands on it to see what makes it tick.''

"I see." Li nodded, pretending that he hadn't thought of that point himself.

"Then I will *personally* accompany the investigating team that sifts through the wreckage. I'm telling you here and now that we better not find a salvageable piece any bigger than the junk heap we were left with when our space shuttle exploded. If we do, all hell will break loose—I can guarantee that. What

I'm looking for, obviously, is for the classified data to be completely destroyed in a way that we can easily verify.''

"And a way that you can easily prove to your own security people," Li added.

"Yes. Easily proven from our point of view." Eleanor nodded at the Ambassador. "That is a non-negotiable item between us."

"Very well, I agree." Ambassador Li Ying-teh smacked his hands together and turned to Peng. "Instruct a suitable unit of our Air Force to expect the airliner to enter Chinese airspace in approximately five hours. Instruct those jet fighters to destroy the airliner as soon as it is out of sight of the escorting American jets."

"Hold on a second," Eleanor said. Even though this operation was being totally conducted by the Chinese, it still obviously had the downside potential of being far bigger than Watergate. "Ambassador Li, just how do you propose to keep the discussions we've had here from leaking out? Obviously, we have taken far more liberties than any government could possibly allow. Even though I am no more than a reluctant observer here, one interpretation of what I'm doing could possibly be that I'm a conspirator in mass murder."

"You are familiar with the term 'vested interest,' I would believe," Li answered quickly in response.

Eleanor did not reply; she simply stood her ground and waited for the old man to continue.

"On the negative side, we each would pay quite a price for divulging the truth. On the positive side, we can salve our consciences with the knowledge that the close alliance of our countries is the best possible deterrent to a nuclear confrontation—either among ourselves, or with our common enemy. One might say that we are sacrificing a few to save many millions—and one would be literally correct in saying that."

"That is one interpretation," Eleanor said, her voice upbeat; clearly, she wanted to be convinced, she wanted to go along with what the old man had proposed.

"Let me finish," Li said as he raised his hand to indicate that he had more to add. "The actual bottom line, as you Americans are so fond of saying, is that the subject will never come up. No interpretation of you being a conspirator in mass murder is possible. Crazy hijackers blew up an airplane, period. By next week that news will be relegated to the back of the newspaper. Madame, you are still quite young. In your heart you may still believe that important decisions are made during open and rational debates at conference tables or on the floor of congresses.''

"I'm not so young anymore," Eleanor said, fidgeting. "Anyway, I don't think that I've ever been that young."

"When it comes to these lofty concepts, we are all that young, we are all potentially naive," Ambassador Li Ying-teh answered. "Even myself. But what we are seeing here is how the world has always worked, and how it will continue to work as long as men inhabit the earth.''

"Get the body back as far as you can."

For several seconds Steven Stidham looked at the stewardess who knelt beside his grandfather, then finally nodded his consent. "Okay." He stood up, then reluctantly stepped over to the body sprawled on the floor several feet behind the group. Steven pulled the covering blanket aside, then took hold of the dead man's bloody shirt by its partially shredded collar as he began to drag the man aft from where he lay near the first-class galley. The front and side of the man's neck were in the same pulverized condition that his grandfather's shoulders were in, and it caused a steady flow of blood and bodily fluids to trickle across Steven's fingers.

"Be careful of dangling wires, and don't get too close to the wreckage," Kathy Davis called out as she watched the teenage boy disappear down the dark aisle.

"I will." As Steven had been instructed, he was going to make more room for them by taking the body of the Oriental passenger as far aft as possible. But what he understood—as they all did—was that the real reason for dragging this mutilated body aft was simply to get it out of sight. None of them could tolerate another moment of having that shrouded reminder of their situation only a few feet away from where they were working to save the life of Steven's grandfather. "You stay with my grandfather. I'll be right back."

Steven dragged the body backward, moving slowly and cautiously, glancing over his shoulder toward the blackness behind him, then looking forward at the dim cockpit lights in the distance to get his bearings. When he reached the third row of first-class seats—that was the last row still intact, according to the stewardess—his intention was to put the body in there, then get back to his grandfather.

The further aft Steven had gone, the noisier the cabin had gotten—and the colder it had gotten, too. He stopped, shivered, then looked around him. The pilot had already explained to them about the rupture in the fuselage, the air leak and what the roaring, howling noise was. The pilot had also explained why he had decided to keep the airliner headed toward the mainland of China as the hijackers had demanded.

The other pilot had said that going to China was a bad idea, but the real pilot—Blanchard was his name, as Steven remembered—had said that they needed to do exactly what the hijackers had told them in order to be absolutely safe. That made sense.

There certainly could be more bombs and more hijackers in the rear, and Steven was glad that Captain Blanchard had regained consciousness and been able to get back to his cockpit duties. Even though they all could see that Captain Blanchard's arm and shoulder had been badly injured, it was a good thing that he was in the cockpit now because he obviously knew what he was talking about and he could tell the other pilot what to do. As Blanchard had said before, once they landed in China the authorities would be able to take excellent care of the injured—Steven's grandfather in particular—since they had wonderful medical facilities there.

The wind whistled by Steven's ear, and from the change in pitch and tone he could tell that he was very near to the pile of wreckage that blocked the front from the rear of the airliner. He wished again that they had a flashlight to use, but there was only one still in working condition and it was working dimly. Captain Blanchard had insisted, very logically, that their one working flashlight remain up in the cockpit where they might need it the most, that the people in the cabin would just have to do the best they could in the darkness since none of the cabin lights would work.

Steven began to move aft again. After another few steps he bumped into the armrest of seat 3C with his right hip—he had come back far enough. Steven began to push the bulk of the dead man's body into the narrow space between the rows, working at trying to keep the man's blood off him, but knowing that he was getting it all over his hands, his pants, his shirt. That was one small advantage of the cabin's darkness, that at least he didn't have to see the blood and the gore that he was working with.

Over the howling noises of the rushing air, Steven suddenly heard something else. The new sound was abrupt and nearly overshadowed by the wind, but it was noticeable. Steven laid the body down between the seats, then stood motionless in the aisle and listened for more.

At first there was nothing beyond the ambient roar of cabin air being sucked through the wreckage and overboard. He glanced around, away from the few lights that shone back from the cockpit. Steven's eyes had already gotten as accustomed to the dark cabin interior as they could. Coupled with the small measure of moonlight that edged through the cabin windows, Steven could now see the outlines of the debris.

It was a skeleton-like collection of twisted metal bunched up with irregular sheets of fiber glass panels that rose from floor to ceiling and from wall to wall. He couldn't see much else, and what he did see seemed to take on a constantly changing pattern of absurd sizes and shapes—a platoon of miniature headless horsemen galloping through the woods, a flurry of giant aberrations of all kinds rising from a smoldering mass grave. Steven knew that none of that was real, that it was all an optical illusion, a mind-trick, but that didn't stop him from shivering again—this time more from the haunting images than the cold. Still, Steven managed to keep his resolve; he stood quietly and waited.

Again, the sound came to him—and unmistakably from the direction of the mound of wreckage very close to where he stood. It could have been words, or a shout, or both. Or, possibly, it could have been nothing, the wind, the creaking of the wreckage itself or just another illusion, this one from his ears not his eyes. Steven wasn't sure. He took another step into the aisle, then bent over and listened carefully.

This time, the sound was unmistakable in both location and quality: a human voice had shouted out to him from beneath the sheets of torn fiber glass that were piled only a foot or two to his left. "Someone's back here!" Steven shouted toward the front of the cabin before he moved further aft. "Hurry."

Steven could see two of the other people from the forward galley area coming back toward him, their shadowy outlines moving as slowly toward the rear as he had needed to just a short while before. Without waiting for them to reach him, he took another step aft and laid his hand on the wreckage.

The sudden surge of electric current was enough that it would have cemented his fingers irrevocably to the aluminum piece he had touched, if it were not for the angle that he had grabbed the debris at. Literally knocked off his feet by the high-voltage charge from the severed cables that were mingled with the debris, Steven fell backward, his body weight yanking his hand away from the electrified structure.

"Don't touch anything!" Kathy had shouted toward the boy, already knowing that it was too late to remind him, to warn him. She could see a sparking of current ahead of her, the grey-blue flash that lit a section of the cabin for an instant, the vague figure of the boy tumbling backward in the momentary flash of light. She reached him just a few seconds later, dropping down beside him on the floor of the aisle.

"Be careful, don't *you* touch anything!" Barbara Jennings was working her way down the aisle also, having left Charlene near the galley to stay with the grandfather. She had seen and heard the commotion in front of her and had realized what had happened. "Don't touch him!"

Kathy already had her hands on the boy when she realized that she should have been more careful, that the boy's body could still have the electric charge running through it. But he didn't—thank God—and the boy was breathing, too. Kathy could feel the heaves of his chest and stomach as they moved rapidly in and out. "Can you hear me?"

It took Steven several seconds to answer, but he finally did—more with a loud groan than any recognizable word. Steven was dazed, but being young and very strong he had already begun to sit upright. As he did, he felt the stewardess's arms around him, helping him to sit up, even though he couldn't quite see her in the blackness of the cabin.

"Are you okay?" Kathy shouted to make herself heard over the wind.

". . . think so." Steven shook his head, then took a few more deep breaths to steady himself. As he did, he began to feel the pain in his left hand—a searing, throbbing pain. "I burnt myself."

"Bad?"

"Not too bad, I don't think." Steven wasn't sure, but he didn't want to believe anything else. "I'll be okay."

"Tell me what you heard back here." Kathy could sense Barbara's presence beside her. "Where was this sound coming from?"

"Inside the wreckage," Steven pointed, but soon realized that the women couldn't see him in the darkness. "On the left."

"What is it?"

"I told you. A voice. A shout. There's a person in there."

"Are you sure?"

"Yeah."

"Okay, you sit still." Kathy turned toward the spot where she assumed the boy thought he had heard something from. "If you can hear me, say something," Kathy called out in as loud a voice as she could. "But don't move—there's electricity in the metal parts of the wreckage around you. Don't know how to shut it off."

It took awhile, but a voice finally responded, a man's voice. ". . . help me . . ." was all he said.

Both women stood up, helping the teenage boy as they did. "We hear you," Barbara yelled back, the first one to reply. "Don't move."

"Can't move . . . help . . ." the voice trailed off as it mixed with the ambient sounds of the rushing air around them.

"Can you see us?" Kathy had shouted her question, then glanced over her shoulder at the cockpit lights in the distance. Since they were standing between the cockpit and the wreckage, it might be possible, she reasoned, for whoever was trapped in the debris to see them against the lit background, to make it easier for them to be directed to exactly the spot where the person was trapped. She had to know at least that much, because there was no way for them to rummage indiscriminately through that pile of electrified debris.

Again, there was no reply for a long time. When the voice finally called back, it was even more forced then it had been the times before. "Blind . . ." was the only word spoken, and it was followed by a loud and agonized moan that left little doubt as to how badly injured the man trapped in the wreckage was.

"I don't understand," Barbara said.

But Kathy had understood at once. "The blind man."

"What?"

"He's the blind man. He was seated in the last row. He must've somehow survived the bomb, and now he's trapped beneath the collapsed fiber glass wall panels."

"God."

"He's trapped inside that electrified debris that Captain Blanchard says we can't turn off. That's going to be the biggest problem." Kathy cursed herself for not thinking about the man earlier, although she wondered if it would ultimately make any difference.

"What can we do?" Barbara Jennings asked, her own voice now strained and trembling as she began to lose some of her carefully erected composure.

Flight Attendant Kathy Davis stood in the dark aisle of the damaged airliner, her one hand on the arm of the injured teenage boy, her other hand tightly gripping Barbara's shoulder. After a delay of far too much time, she finally said the only thing that she could think of, the only response that entered her mind that seemed even the slightest bit realistic. "I don't know."

Gerald Marks had been totally blind since an untreated childhood disease took away his sight at the age of seven; he was two weeks short of his fifty-first birthday when he bought the ticket for the Trans Continental flight to Japan and stepped aboard the airliner in Los Angeles. During most of the flight he had been working on the income projections for his wholly owned company he had established years before to commercially market the skills of blind workers. Marks had fallen asleep just a short while before the initial jet upset, and had been sitting attentively in the last row of first class when the bomb exploded a short distance behind him.

The blast had been structured in such a way that its least effective direction had been down and forward. That, coupled with the double bulkhead wall of sheet metal and fiber glass that the lavatory plumbing ran through, provided just enough protection to prevent the bomb's destructive forces from reaching Marks in those first moments. The man's back and neck had been peppered repeatedly with metal shards and he had already lost a great deal of blood, but at least most of the blast's momentum had been deflected away from the collapsing walls that he was now trapped beneath.

"Blind . . ." Marks managed to say, in response to the muffled voice that was calling out to him above the noises from the wind that swirled around him. Marks was doubled over on the floor, his legs twisted painfully behind him and each caught by pieces of the wreckage that were pressing in from all sides. Marks had been unconscious for quite some time after the blast—the result of his head banging hard against the floor, a large black-and-blue knot raised on his forehead where he had hit. After that, he had been no more than semiconscious at best, his rational thoughts floating through his mind like water running through a sieve, unable to keep his attention focused for more than a few seconds at a time. It was like a horrible nightmare that he couldn't seem to shake, couldn't wake himself out of.

Finally, Marks managed to clear his head enough to understand what had happened to him and why. It had taken all that while since the explosion for his hearing to clear enough to be able to perceive first the incessant sounds of the wind, then the muffled shouts from outside the pile of debris that he was trapped beneath. Marks could easily tell that he had suffered hearing damage from being too close to the explosion. That was, he knew, the least of his problems.

Marks groaned loudly and continuously, the involuntary sounds coming out of him in spite of his attempts to control himself, to listen closely to what the voice in the distance was telling him. The pain—from his back and neck, his legs, his left arm, several of his fingers—welled in on all sides and made it nearly impossible to think of anything else. But

Marks knew that he'd have to think about something beyond his pain, if he was going to survive. *Move, show them where I am, they'll find me if I can help them.* Marks took a deep breath, then selectively attempted to move each of his arms and legs.

Both his legs were completely immobile, and his left arm was caught in some kind of vicelike array of tubing that Marks couldn't find a release for. His right arm was the least trapped, and in just a few moments of effort he managed to break it away from whatever had been gripping it at his shoulder.

There's something here—someone else. Marks was using his facial vision—an extra sensitivity that some blind people possessed, a heightening of their remaining senses that enabled those who had it to somehow detect the presence of obstacles in front of them—to map out the area directly ahead. Even in the cramped confines of the small hole of debris that Marks had been shoved into, his facial vision had begun to work well enough to sense a flesh-and-blood obstacle not far from where he lay. This was one instance where Marks was not at a disadvantage compared to those around him—the ink-bottle darkness inside the airliner was of no concern to him because he had lived in perpetual darkness most of his life.

Another person. Maybe they're alive. Even if the person Marks sensed in front of him wasn't alive, he realized that by pushing against that body he might be able to move enough debris to attract the attention of the rescuers who were calling him. Marks couldn't understand most of their words, but he knew that they were there, knew that they were trying to find him, to help him.

After a great effort that nearly exhausted him to the point of giving up, Marks managed to get his right arm in toward his body and then out toward the object that he sensed was not far away. His fingers moved around the jumbled piles of interceding fiber glass, fabric and vinyl from the demolished seats and serving trays until his fingers had gone a few inches past the front of his face. Sensing that the object he was after was only slightly further, Marks shoved his hand forward to get it past the last of the debris.

The blind man's fingers went directly into the mound of gore that was the severed torso of Stewardess Debbie Biederman. With his sensitive touch it took him just a few moments to realize what he had grabbed and to act accordingly. Unable to contain his horror and revulsion, Marks howled in terror and yanked his arm back. As he did, his movements raised his body slightly against the pile of debris.

The high-voltage electric current, which was flowing through a piece of distended metal trimwork lying inches above him, found a new source of less resistance as the sweat and blood on the area of bare human skin beneath the torn shirt brushed against it. In less than a second, several hundred volts arched through Gerald Marks's body, torching the skin at the entry and exit points, stopping his heart and searing his brain cells. Long before his body had stopped its involuntary muscle convulsions, the blind man was dead.

The blue arcing light from the surge of high voltage made more of an impression on the three witnesses to the blind man's death than the man's howls of terror; those had been muffled by the debris surrounding the victim and further obscured by the noise of the wind that rushed through the wreckage and out the overhead hole in the fuselage. The light itself lasted for just a few seconds, although it was long enough for all three of them in the aisle to understand completely what was happening.

"Oh, my God!"

"Don't move!" Flight Attendant Kathy Davis shouted as she tightened her grip on the other two. Kathy, Barbara Jennings and Steven Stidham were frozen in position, their eyes locked onto the agonizing scene of death not more than ten feet away. "Stay here, there's nothing we can do."

"I know." Barbara shivered, then laid her hand on top of Kathy's, which was locked to her own arm. "There was nothing we could do."

"Right." Complete darkness had once again enveloped the cabin, and what with that sudden burst of electric-arc light to ruin their night vision, they were totally out of visual contact with their surroundings. "Be careful, turn around slowly, keep your hands on me," Kathy shouted to the others. "We'll work our way toward the galley again." Kathy led the way up the aisle, and with every passing step in the proper direction, the ambient noise around them lessened and she could also make out slightly more from the reflected light from the cockpit in the distance.

Just before they reached the first-class galley, Steven bolted ahead to his grandfather. He knelt beside Charlene Jennings, who had stayed with the dying old man, took a linen napkin from the young girl's hands and began to wipe his grandfather's forehead himself. "Did he say anything?"

"Sort of." Charlene glanced up at her mother; even in the dim reflected light from the cockpit, the tears that streaked down her face were more than obvious. "He said . . . he knows that he's dying. He wants to talk to his grandson."

None of the others moved as Steven bent down closer to his grandfather. "Please don't die," the teenage boy said in a flat voice that was surprisingly void of emotion. "Don't die. I need you not to die." More than anything else in the whole world, Steven needed this man to live.

"Steven . . ." The old man opened his eyes; his vision was blurred from the pain, from the sweat and the blood that ran along his face. Yet he could see his grandson just as he always had—those strong, purposeful eyes of his, his determined stare, his basic understanding of far more than his few years of age should have allowed. Edward Stidham's own son had said on far too many occasions that his son Steven was just no damned good, just too wild, too misbehaved, too disobedient—but the grandfather knew better. Steven had always responded to his grandfather, too—as he had responded to no other person. He was closer to the old man than he was to either of his parents, or to his older sister or younger brother.

"Please don't die," Steven said again. He held his face very close to his grandfather's, close enough to feel the old man's breathing, those shallow breaths coming and going more irregularly now. "Please."

"Don't believe anything except what I tell you now." The old man had sat up slightly as he looked directly into his grandson's eyes.

"Please, stay quiet. Don't try to sit up."

"Listen to me. Your father loves you, but he's wrong about you . . . you're a good boy . . . the best . . ."

"Stop. Don't . . ."

"Basics are good. Yours." The old man's attention was wandering, he was weakening quickly. But he also knew what he wanted to say, what still had to be said. "Don't doubt yourself . . . go with your basic instincts . . . your gut reactions . . . you are a damned good boy, a damned good person, if you let yourself be one," the old man said in a faltering voice. He paused a moment, his eyes got wide in pain, but he tried to ignore it, to continue with what he felt that he had to tell his only son's troubled child. "Steven . . . you . . . are . . ."

"No!" Steven had grabbed the old man's head before it fell back to the floor, but even as he cradled his grandfather in his arms, he knew what had happened. The old man had died in his arms. "No, please." Steven held his grandfather's face against his own as he began to cry uncontrollably. "Not fair," the teenage boy kept saying through his sobs as he rubbed the old man's cheek against his, the boy's tears mixing with the residue of perspiration and tears of his grandfather. "God, it's not fair, oh, God."

Kathy, Barbara and Charlene took an involuntary step backward from the scene they were witnessing. There was nothing they could do, no way they could help, no words that would make a damned bit of difference. They had known for certain, from that very first moment they had seen him, that the old man was going to die. Yet that knowledge hadn't lessened the shock or the sense of incredible loss that they were now feeling. In no more than a handful of minutes, two of the survivors in the forward compartment of Flight 42 were dead. For all they knew, everyone in the back of the airplane was dead too.

Barbara Jennings was cradling her daughter in her arms as she turned toward the young stewardess, leaned on her shoulder and began to cry openly herself. "Not fair, none of it," Barbara said in a choked-off voice, automatically repeating what the boy was saying because it was an indisputable truth—a truth that they all recognized.

Kathy Davis wrapped her arms around Barbara and began

to hug her tightly. She began to cry also. Kathy was crying
for each of them, herself included. *Not fair, none of it.*
"No," she whispered, not able to bring herself to find even
one positive word, unable to find any way to bring to them
even the slightest bit of encouragement. "No." With every
passing moment, the fate of those onboard Flight 42 seemed
increasingly doomed.

14

Flight Attendant Fred Lyle glanced out the cabin window of the dark airliner for the hundredth time in the past twenty minutes. Other than the fact that the nearly full moon had tracked lower in the sky in the two hours since he'd been watching it, there was nothing else visible except the stars. The silvery glow of the ocean below had been replaced by a dull grey blanket of low overcast clouds.

"Still nothin', huh?" Max Berger asked from his seat beside Fred's in the last row of the rear cabin.

"No," Fred shrugged. "The cloud cover is solid." He looked at the luminescent dial on his wristwatch, which was still set to Los Angeles time. 8:10 A.M. "We were originally scheduled to land at Osaka at 9:55 A.M., Los Angeles time, which is little less than two hours from now. We should be seeing the ground lights of northern Japan in the next fifty minutes or so," Fred said. He had flown this trip dozens of times the past summer, so he knew what to expect.

"We'll see the lights only if the clouds break and only if we're still headed to Osaka. Maybe the pilots are taking us somewhere else." Berger's tone was dry and matter-of-fact, as if he were describing a purely routine operation. "Besides, it's no big deal if we don't see any ground lights until we get to wherever we're headed. I'm beginning to think that it's not such a good idea to introduce something new—like waiting for ground lights to appear—at this stage. That might be enough to upset our little apple cart."

"I don't follow you."

"The last two hours we've had—I've almost lost count already—about seven or eight outbursts of hysteria, plus three episodes of pure rage. When that last guy came at you, that older gent in the torn jacket, I almost didn't get hold of him in time to save your skull from the piece of hard plastic he was swinging."

"Thanks again for that." Fred had spun around in the dark aisle just in time to see the two shadowy figures—Max and the old man—come together a few feet behind him. The struggle only lasted a few seconds, before Max pushed the old man back in his seat and took the makeshift weapon from him.

"I don't know how long we're going to keep being that lucky. That piece of plastic wouldn't have killed you, but it sure would have given you a damned good headache."

"At the very least." Fred shivered at the memory of what had almost occurred—which was right along the lines of what Max had predicted. Some of the survivors in the rear cabin were irrational and hostile, and they were beginning to identify Fred as an authority figure to strike out against. He had thought about taking off his uniform jacket and airline emblems, but had decided against it—everyone knew who he was by now. If they were out to get him they'd find him, even in the darkness.

"This kind of thing is a type of retribution for death and destruction. It's not very rational, but watching your loved ones turned into chopped meat tends to suspend a person's rational judgment."

"I've heard of things like this in combat situations, but never at the scene of an accident."

"Bombs ain't no accident."

"True."

"And you're the only available authority figure."

"It ought to be pretty obvious to everyone that I didn't plant the damned bomb."

"It's only obvious if you think about it. It's obvious to me that none of this is your fault, but these people," Berger said with a wave of his hand toward the dark cabin ahead of him, "ain't doing too much clear thinking. Can't say that I blame them, either."

"Maybe." Fred turned toward the window and looked at the moon. It was very close to the horizon line ahead of them, and it had transformed itself into a large yellowish-red disk—the usual visual prelude that meant that the moon was about to drop out of sight below the horizon. "We're going to lose the moon pretty soon."

"Yeah. It'll get considerably darker back here when it does go down."

"Darker? This place is like an ink bottle already."

"No it isn't, I can see things—for example, I can see you. I can tell that you've got one hand raised, the other down and in your lap."

"Correct." Fred turned slightly in his seat.

"We're all going to be surprised at how much reflected moonlight we were getting."

"I don't think anything would surprise me. Not at this point."

"I guess you're right on that score." Berger took out another of his cigarettes, and as he did, he noticed that he had already gone through nearly the full pack. Up until tonight, he'd been trying to quit, or, more accurately, at least trying to cut down. *What the hell, cigarettes might not matter much anymore.* Berger took out a match—he only had a few matches left; he had used far too many trying to see things in the cabin—cupped the match in his hands and lit up. The cabin was so dark that the light from one match was enough to be quite startling so Berger was purposely careful with it, purposely discreet.

Fred watched out of the corner of his eye as Max lit his cigarette. In the glow, he could make out the man's handsome features, the black mane of hair with just a touch of grey in it, the strong muscles in his neck, his alert, inquisitive eyes. He was, Fred had learned during their on-and-off conversations for the past two hours, a forty-seven-year-old plumbing contractor from San Diego, a man who had turned an inherited father-and-son storefront business into a small but thriving company with nearly a hundred employees. "What did your wife die of?"

"Cancer. Too much smoking." Berger took one more drag on his cigarette, looked at it disdainfully for a long moment, then reluctantly snubbed it out in the ashtray. "With no kids, we spent most of our time working. Her office desk looked like a cigarette factory. Her desk at home looked even worse."

"How long ago did she die?"

"Be two years in June. That was her name, too. June."

"Miss her?"

"Yeah."

Fred couldn't think of anything else to say, although there was plenty on his mind. He sat back in the darkness and thought about it all for a moment. He was surrounded by death, yet he had found more inner strength and courage than he ever would have dreamt possible. He was sitting beside a man who was a hundred times what any of his past male lovers had been, yet he felt differently than he ever had. Fred felt admiration and camaraderie, he felt friendship and sincerity, he felt *simpatico*—but he felt nothing that even vaguely resembled lust toward the shadowy figure of Max Berger. Was Fred changing, or was it just the situation? Was this a temporary reaction to the death and destruction and horror around him? Fred didn't know for sure, but he did know that he liked how he felt at that moment. "I must be in shock."

"How's that?"

"Nothing. I'm rambling, that's all."

"Go ahead, you're entitled."

"Thanks." Fred found himself smiling for the first time since the nightmare had begun. "When we get out of this, I'm going to personally take you out for the best dinner we can find to show my appreciation for all your help."

"Hell, when we get out of this, I'm going to take you up to Tahoe to go skiing for a week, then we're both going down to Vegas to get laid."

"You're on." Fred was amazed at how quickly the words had come out of him. He had been to bed with three girls in his life, more as a dare from his boyfriends than for any other reason. With Max along, maybe it would actually be fun. "I'm looking forward to it."

"Plan on it." Berger squirmed in his seat, glanced up the deserted aisle, then turned back to Fred. "All's quiet. That's a good sign."

"We could use a few good signs right about now."

"Yeah. Maybe that means that everything's working out, that nothing we can't handle will go wrong."

"Something we can't handle? Like what?" Fred didn't want to pursue this line of reasoning, but he knew that it was necessary, that it was his job to plan ahead, to anticipate problems.

"I dunno. Something catastrophic—like a flash fire or another bomb exploding."

Another bomb. The words hit Fred's thoughts with incredible impact. *Another bomb onboard*. His mind whirled as the memory of something he had seen, something he had not really focused on so far but had stored away to deal with at a later moment, suddenly slid into full view in his mind's eye. Pushed into the background by the need for continual emergency activity since the detonation had occurred, the electronic words that Fred had seen on the second line of the portable computer now possessed a new and frightful clarity to him. *LOWER DEVICE COUNTDOWN IN PROGRESS*. "Oh, my God."

"What is it?"

Flight Attendant Fred Lyle put his trembling hand on his friend's arm. "Pick up that portable computer, it's on the seat next to you."

"Why?" Max Berger reached over the aisle and retrieved the small electronic unit from where they had placed it a short while before, after they had both examined it to be certain that it was still shut down.

"Let me have it, I've got to look at it again. I think the message I remember from the second line of the screen readout might mean there's still another bomb onboard."

Ron Jennings's neck and shoulders ached as he sat in the captain's seat of the Consolidated jet and continued to steer westbound, directly toward Yangzhou, China. The single navigation needle on the flight panel remained centered, as Captain Blanchard had ordered, which meant that they were taking a direct path to the hijacker's destination. "You were right about the autopilot, we sure as hell could've used it."

"I've tried everything. I can't get the damned thing to work." Alvin Blanchard laid his hand against the autopilot controls as if he were going to try again, but then a few seconds later allowed his hand to slide into his lap. "It's screwed up bad. You'll have to keep flying."

"I know." The moon had slipped below the horizon an hour before, which made the exterior visual conditions even darker than they had been earlier. Other than the sky full of stars above them, there was not a single source of visible reference in the blackness that they flew through. Jennings concentrated on the flight panel instruments which, because of eyestrain, had become something of a blur to him.

Over an hour before, when they were crossing the northern coastline of Japan, the pretense that Blanchard would be doing some of the flying soon was put to rest when the captain admitted that he was stiffening up badly, that his arm and shoulder hurt like hell. Shortly after that, Jennings also began to admit to his own deteriorating condition—that his heart was racing; he was occasionally lightheaded, slightly nauseous; his vision was blurred and his fingers and hands had begun to tingle. But Jennings continued to fly because Blanchard insisted that he wasn't able to himself.

"Can you take it, can you steer with your left hand?" Jennings suddenly said as he leaned forward in his flight chair. "I need a break. I need one bad," he said in a hollow, shaken voice.

"I told you before, I don't know if I can."

"You're going to have to try." Jennings felt faint, as if he might pass out any minute, and he knew that—even in the dim glow from the cockpit emergency panel lights—he must look like hell right now. He was glad that the other four were sitting in the cabin, and that the last time Barbara and Kathy had come up, he had looked a lot better.

"Okay, I'll try." Blanchard sat upright in his flight chair, took the copilot's control wheel in his functioning left hand

and nodded over to Jennings that he was ready for him to let go. As he did, the jet airliner bobbled slightly nose down and then up, but then steadied out again. "I'll be okay, I think I can handle the controls for a while. What's happening to you?"

"I'm not sure." But Jennings knew damn well what was wrong with him—his heart. This nightmare would have been enough strain on a man with normal health, but with a weakened heart it was getting to be far too much. "Strain, that's all. I'll be all right if I can rest, if I can just sit here and relax while you do the flying."

"Will you be okay for the landing?"

"Sure." Jennings tried to sound positive, but he found that he couldn't. He dropped his head to his lap and began to gently massage his temples. By doing that, at least his lightheadedness began to go away. "I'll be okay, I'm sure of it. You just fly for a while."

"Right."

Another fifteen minutes went by in silence. The airliner wallowed slightly but stayed generally on course, with Blanchard at the controls and Jennings slumped down in his flight chair, his eyes closed, his head resting against his arms as if he were taking a short nap. The scene would have been, to any casual observer, a picture of technocratic serenity as the jet plodded westward, the banks of colored lights and panel gauges indicating that all was going as it should. What was missing from a picture of the scene, of course, was the frenzied terror in the minds of the two men in the pilots' chairs. Both of the pilots sat stoically, giving no visual reference whatsoever to what was going on in their thoughts.

After a few more minutes, Jennings finally sat up again. By now he felt far better—fine, actually, which was something of a surprise to him. A complete recovery, or so it seemed. Jennings looked around the cockpit and saw that everything was just as it had been, that all the needles and gauges were sitting right where they were supposed to. The airliner was directly on course, with all the systems operating normally—even the left engine's vibrations were holding steady, and far below the maximum allowable digression—and the fuel consumption was staying slightly better than Blanchard's predictions, which was that they would have more than enough to complete the trip. "How's everything going?"

"Okay. How are you feeling?"

"Much better. I told you, all I needed was a rest, a break."

"Good." Blanchard turned slightly in his flight chair and nodded at the navigation chart they had earlier spread out on top of the inoperative radio controls on the central pedestal. "We're almost across the Sea of Japan, although the overcast makes it impossible to see anything. South Korea is off the right wing a couple hundred miles, the northern coastline of Japan is sixty miles to the left. We'll be in the East China Sea shortly."

"Good. What do you figure for arrival time at Yangzhou?" Jennings glanced at his wristwatch, which was set to Los Angeles time. It was 10:04 A.M. mid-morning in California, probably another sunny and temperate day. At the surface of the sea below them, it was dark and cold.

"The inertial navigation equipment does all the predicting. One hour and forty minutes from now."

"That'll be eleven forty-five in California."

"If you say so."

Jennings looked at the flight instruments, then back at Blanchard. "I'm going to have someone from the back get me a glass of water, then I'll be ready to fly again. Then you can begin briefing me for the landing."

"Right."

"You want anything from the back?"

"A glass of water, too. Maybe some food, if they can salvage anything out of the galley."

"I'll ask." Jennings picked up the penlight from the pedestal and aimed it toward the dark cabin. He pressed the button twice, their prearranged signal for one of the women to come up to the cockpit. They had stopped making periodic trips to the cockpit after Blanchard had told them not to—he had ordered them to sit quietly, telling them that their unnecessary movements through the cabin were causing complications, that moving fore and aft made it more difficult to keep the aircraft manually trimmed at its proper airspeed.

Several seconds after Jennings had flashed the light aft, he saw a single figure emerging toward him from the shadows. It was Kathy.

Flight Attendant Kathy Davis walked up to the cockpit quickly, something she could do because the lights from the panel gauges at the front of the cockpit were guiding her. It would, she knew, take her far more time to walk back into the complete blackness of the cabin since they still hadn't managed to get any of the lights in the rear to work and there was no other working flashlight. Kathy had finally found her own flashlight in the pile of cabin debris, but it had been smashed to bits when it had evidently been tossed around the galley during the aircraft's wild maneuvering. "What's up?"

"We each need a glass of water. The captain wants something to eat, too, if you can find it."

"Probably can, although the menu might be a little limited."

"Anything at all, anything except cheese. I don't like cheese."

"No problem, I should be able to find some fruit or something like that." Kathy turned to Ron. "What can I tell them in the back, how are things going up here?"

"The airplane's flying fine, we've got more than enough fuel and we're flying on schedule. One hour and forty minutes until we land in China."

"Okay, good." Kathy laid her hand on Ron's shoulder. "How are you feeling?" To her, Ron appeared even paler now than he had before, although, possibly, that was just an illusion caused by the glow of the panel lights. She hoped so. Kathy and Barbara had talked about Ron's health an hour before, and Kathy was startled to find out how sick Ron had really been, how potentially critical his condition continued to be.

"Better. What I'll need after this is a week's worth of sleep." Jennings laid his own hand on top of hers. Even with his wife no more than twenty feet away, Ron felt no desire to remove his hand—they had all been through far too much together to even think about that sort of thing.

"That'll teach you to take vacations."

"I guess." Jennings nodded—he remembered all the times Kathy had asked for the two of them to go away, to take a vacation together—and all the excuses he had made as to why he couldn't. His entire affair with Kathy had been, he realized, one of reluctance on his part, of being dragged into something that he wouldn't promote. But it was also something that he didn't have the courage to prevent, either. "How's Barbara and Charlene. How's the boy?"

"Your family's quite a group. Barbara is an exceptional person. I can see why you love her."

"I do."

"I know that." Kathy paused. She gently removed her hand from Ron's arm. "Charlene, too. Hard to believe that she's only sixteen. Very mature, very smart."

"The boy?" Jennings had seen the teenage boy for just a moment after his grandfather had died, had seen the look of agony and bewilderment on his face. "How's he taking things?"

"Hard to tell. He's sitting by himself in the second row. He's not crying anymore, but he doesn't want to talk. I tried a few times, but I can't get him to respond."

"There's nothing else you can do. Take it from me, when a person doesn't want to talk you should just leave them alone."

"I know." Kathy stood beside Ron for another few moments without saying a word, before she finally turned and walked away.

Jennings watched her disappear into the darkness of the cabin. He turned back to Blanchard. "I'm ready to fly."

"You got it." Blanchard released the copilot's control wheel, observed that Jennings had the airplane going steady, then sat back in his flight chair. His injuries, plus the short spell of flying, had exhausted him. "I hope she doesn't come up with cheese, I hate cheese."

"Some kinds of cheeses aren't too bad."

"Cheese sucks."

"If you say so."

They flew on in silence for a few more minutes until Kathy returned. She handed out the glasses of water, some fruit, a few slices of rolled-up ham. Even Ron found himself eating, he was hungrier than he had imagined. While she waited for them to finish, Kathy looked around the sky.

Above them was an awning of stars, some in heavy clusters, others in small arrays. A few of the stars were much brighter than the others, but for all their brilliance against the black background above, none of them added the slightest bit of illumination of what was below the airliner. The sight of the overcast had disappeared when the moon did, and the only tip-off that a solid deck of clouds was beneath them was that none of the coastal lights of Japan were visible as they paralleled the shoreline—something that Kathy had seen repeatedly on her past flights along this route. "When we get to China for the landing, will it be daylight yet?"

"By my calculations, just barely," Blanchard answered. "The morning sun should be just above the horizon as we touch down."

"Good. That'll make things a lot easier for me." Jennings spoke without looking at them, as he played with the airliner's control wheel to keep them exactly on course.

"Easier for all of us," Kathy said. "By the way, something else we were wondering about—it was Charlene's question, actually. If we're this close to Japan—how far did you say?"

"The city of Kitakyushu is approximately a hundred miles to our left," Blanchard answered as he pointed to the chart.

"Okay, a hundred miles. Then how come no fighter jets have come up to rendezvous with us? Surely they know that we're here, surely the Japanese see us on their radar."

"We were talking about that before," Jennings answered. "We figure that it's because we lost all communications after the explosion and the ground facilities had already been told that we were being hijacked. Remember, the transmission about us being hijacked had been made by the copilot long before the bomb exploded."

"Yes, I remember."

"The copilot also made one other transmission, giving the hijacker's destination of Yangzhou, China," Blanchard added. "That was just before he made a grab for the hijacker's gun."

"Oh."

"Those fighters you're asking about are probably out there right now, more than likely trailing behind us by several miles. They just don't want to take any chances by getting too close.''

"So they don't scare the hijackers?"

"Exactly."

"And that's an excellent idea, too," Blanchard said. He sat up slightly in his seat. "Also remember that we don't know what the hell is going on in the back," the captain said emphatically as he gestured toward the rear cabin, "or what it'll take for those madmen in the rear to detonate another bomb. I'm sure I don't have to tell you what shape we'd be in if another bomb—even one that was smaller than the first— went off."

"I wouldn't want to think about it."

"Neither would I. So it's best that we don't do anything to excite those people, and that certainly includes a formation of jet fighters sitting on our wingtip. The last thing we want now is for one of those three other bombs to go off."

"Two other bombs," Kathy said in a matter-of-fact voice as she glanced out the cockpit window. "The third bomb is the one that already exploded." Everything was pitch black along the horizon line; she couldn't see anything that even resembled a hint of a jet fighter in any direction that she looked. Kathy wondered where the jet fighters were.

"Three," Blanchard said automatically. "There are three other bombs onboard, plus the one that's already exploded."

Kathy took a backward half step in the cockpit and looked at the captain. "Do you guys know something that I don't? The hijack note said that there was a total of three bombs to begin with, including the bomb that was in the first-class lavatory—the one that exploded. That leaves two additional bombs still onboard. That's what I told you when I first came up to the cockpit. Where did you hear differently?"

"Well . . ." Blanchard looked around the cockpit. Jennings was looking at him, and so was the stewardess. "You must have told me that there were three additional bombs. I got the number from what you told me."

"No, I didn't tell you that," Kathy said vehemently. "I told you *two* additional bombs because that's what I remember, that's what I thought all along. I wouldn't have told you *three* because I thought there were *two*. That's the only number I had in my mind, that's the only number I could have possibly told you.''

''It doesn't matter.'' Blanchard shrugged. ''One, two, three, a dozen—we'd be just as dead anyway, if any of them exploded.''

''Wait a minute.'' Jennings reached into his pocket and took out the folded hijack note, which Kathy had handed him for safekeeping hours before. ''I never did remember to take this out to show it to you,'' Jennings said to Blanchard as he laid the note on the pedestal between the pilots' seats. ''And Kathy told me that she hadn't shown it to you either. Look at this.''

''So what?'' Blanchard looked down at the hijack note. Clearly, it said that there were still *three* more bombs onboard. ''It says exactly what I was telling you.''

THIS IS A HIJACKING. DO NOT TOUCH THIS RADIO CONTROLLED BOMB OR IT WILL EXPLODE. SEVERAL HIJACKERS ONBOARD WITH THREE MORE BOMBS. MORE INFORMATION IN ONE HOUR.

''I'm sorry.'' Kathy shook her head, embarrassed. ''I was nervous, I read the hijack note wrong, that's all. I only saw it once, in the lavatory, and I guess I overlooked the word *more* and focused on the word *three*. That's why I thought there was a *total* of three bombs, which meant that there were two additional bombs on the airplane after the bomb in the first-class lavatory had exploded. That's why I had the number *two* in my mind, because that's what I believed. Sorry.''

''No problem.'' Blanchard waved his hand in a gesture of dismissal, then reached for the hijack note.

Jennings grabbed the captain's arm with his free right hand, his left hand still gripping the control wheel as he continued to steer the airliner. ''Hold on.''

''What?''

''You're lying.'' Jennings didn't know if he should be saying that, but he was too tired to think clearly—he wasn't acting anymore, he was reacting.

''What the hell are you talking about?'' Blanchard looked down at where Jennings's hand was wrapped around his wrist, but he made no move to extract it. "You're not making any damned sense."

"I'm making too much sense." Jennings glanced over his shoulder at Kathy. "I don't know why it took me so long to figure this out, but it's all clear to me now. Pick up the flashlight."

Without questioning him, Kathy picked up the penlight from where it lay on the center control pedestal. "Now what?"

"Aim the light at the row of circuit breakers behind the copilot's seat. Tell me what you see."

Kathy pushed the switch. The penlight hardly glowed at all; its batteries, too, were nearly exhausted. But it did provide just enough light to see the nearby panel. "All the circuit breakers are popped out."

"Are you sure?"

"Yes. I can see the white rings around each of them—the circuits are definitely open. What does that mean?"

"They could have just now popped out," Blanchard said. He was sitting bolt-upright now, looking nervous, his body leaning toward the center pedestal where Jennings still had a tight grip on his left wrist. Blanchard's injured right arm hung uselessly at his side.

"Horseshit. You knew the circuit breakers were out all along, but you didn't want any communications—that might be too much of a complication for you."

"Let go of my arm, goddammit."

Jennings continued to steer the airliner, which had begun to bob and weave slightly whenever he turned toward the other two people in the cockpit. "Kathy made a mistake and told you there were *two* more bombs onboard because she misread the hijack note . . ."

"I must've seen the note in the lavatory when I went back to look at the bomb," Blanchard said. "Yes, that's it. I remember now."

"That's a lie, too, goddammit," Jennings said, spitting out the words. "Kathy had the hijack note in her pocket when you went back, when you left me here with the copilot. Yet somehow you knew the correct number even though she had the note in her pocket by then. Kathy was the only one who had spoken to you about it, too—that hijacking information had been withheld from the rest of the cabin crew on *your* express orders.''

"That's not true, it's . . .''

"I also remember that you had come back to the cabin just before the movie—you went back to the lavatory—but I didn't add that in. Now I can figure out when you did it, but I still can't figure out why.''

"Ron, what are you talking about?!'' Kathy looked back and forth between the two pilots in amazement; none of what was happening made the slightest bit of sense to her.

Jennings tightened his grip on Blanchard's wrist. "The reason that Blanchard knew what was in the hijack note was that it was *him* who had planted the note and the bomb in the lavatory—this captain of yours was hijacking his own airplane!''

Blanchard lunged forward, dragging Jennings's arm with him, as he suddenly maneuvered his body as far as he could against the restraints of the seat belt and the man who was trying to hold him. At the angle that the two men were locked together—each had only one arm to spare. Jennings's left hand was on the airplane's control wheel, Blanchard's right arm hung immobile at his side—the captain managed to reach far enough to his left to hit one of the throttles backward to its stop, reducing power on the left side of the airliner to nearly zero, causing a sudden violent yawing motion that threw Kathy to the floor and both men toward the opposite sidewall.

The sudden motion caused Jennings to lose his grip on Blanchard's arm. Because he was also wrestling with the flight controls to regain control of the airliner, Jennings couldn't prevent Blanchard from grabbing for the pistol that he had earlier laid near the copilot's flight chair.

The small black revolver that Blanchard picked up from the floor gleamed in the reflected light from the instrument panel, and that caused the barrel and cocked hammer of the weapon to look even larger than their actual size. "Don't move a goddamn inch,'' Captain Alvin Blanchard said as he waved the gun at the two people in front of him. "Either one of you. If you do, I'll blow your fucking heads off.''

15

Captain Alvin Blanchard had the handgun held low against his left side, the fingers of his left hand wrapped tightly around the pistol's butt, his index finger lying heavily against the small silver trigger. "Stand right where you are, both hands on top of the seat back," Blanchard said. "Don't move."

Flight Attendant Kathy Davis had picked herself up from the cockpit floor and stood where she was told, her hands lying on top of the captain's flight chair, her fingers brushing against the back of Ron Jennings's sweat-soaked shirt. "But why?" she said, her voice pleading, as she looked down at the gun. The barrel was pointed at a spot halfway between her and Ron, and a motion of just a few degrees in either direction was all that was needed for the captain to be able to shoot either of them. "This is insane."

"None of this would have happened," Blanchard said. His voice was strained and cracking as he waved the pistol slightly from side to side. "It wouldn't have happened if that fucking copilot had done what I told him. That bastard." Blanchard didn't know exactly what he would do next, but he realized well enough that none of these people could survive, that he had to kill all of them now that the truth had been discovered.

"Clancy figured it out," Ron Jennings said from the captain's seat as he continued to fly the airliner jet westbound, his attention focused completely on the flight panel in front of him. Jennings's body was trembling and his hands were shaking, but his mind was clear and he had been able to understand the situation for what it really was: Captain Blanchard had arranged to hijack his own airplane, although for reasons that were still unknown to Jennings. Blanchard must have been working together with the Oriental man—the one who had presented himself at the cockpit door so many hours before—which explained why he had allowed the man such quick entry to the cockpit, among other things. "Clancy was smarter than you—and sure as hell smarter than us. He figured it out hours ago."

"Bullshit!" Blanchard had begun to rant, his voice raised, his face contorted with hate. "Your smart-ass friend Clancy was a fucking *moron*. He didn't figure out a damned thing! All he managed to do was to screw things up, to get us in too goddamn deep!"

"Really? How?" Kathy still didn't have a complete idea of what was happening, but she knew enough to want to calm Blanchard down, to stop him from waving the pistol back and forth. "I don't understand what you're saying about Clancy. How did he manage to do those things?"

"That fucking moron decided to be a hero, period. When he realized that the gook wasn't armed, he got the jump on him and started to choke him. He would've killed the little bastard if I hadn't taken out my pistol . . ." Blanchard was saying more than he wanted to, but he didn't know what else to do. He didn't want to take over the flying yet because his right arm was in terrific pain, yet he knew that he had to, that he had to kill everyone in the first-class section and then make it look as if the hijacker had done it, just as they believed that the hijacker shot the copilot.

"It was your pistol too, right? Yes, of course," Jennings said. "That's how it got through the security check at Los Angeles—you brought the gun with you inside your flight bag. That's how you brought the bomb aboard, too."

"You're right." Blanchard waved the pistol menacingly. "This is my gun. That should tell you that I know how to use it."

"But why? None of this makes any sense." Kathy was looking at the captain with pleading eyes, trying to understand exactly how and why he was involved in this, why he was pointing the gun at them and what he intended to do next. As incredible as it seemed, she could accept the fact that Blanchard was apparently the man behind the hijacking—but she couldn't accept the notion that he intended to kill them.

"They paid you pretty well, huh? What was it, some kind of smuggling—a big drug move, something like that?" Jennings glanced sideways at Blanchard but was careful to keep his hands on the flight controls and his body as motionless as he could, so as not to provoke the man.

"Shut the fuck up." Blanchard moved the pistol slightly, to aim it more toward Jennings.

Jennings ignored the pistol. "No one was supposed to get hurt, right?" Blanchard would, Jennings now realized, kill all of them the first instant that he thought it would benefit him. Jennings decided that they had to keep Blanchard talking, that they had to play for more time. "I see why you were so rattled when we first discovered the bomb. You were play-acting, right? The only thing is that you're not much of an actor, so you overplayed your part."

"That's right. I'm not much of an actor—and I'm sure as hell not acting now." Blanchard had calmed down, had begun to think clearly again, to weigh his options. He glanced at the flight panel to his right. The airliner was still on course, still flying directly toward the hijack destination in China. *If only the goddamned autopilot were still working.*

That he needed to kill everyone in the first-class section was a certainty, the only question was when. If Blanchard killed them now, he would have to fly the airplane himself for nearly two hours until they landed. He doubted if his body would hold out for that long. "Clancy made all of this happen to us by going after that gook, even though I had told the asshole to leave things alone, to cooperate completely with the hijackers. I had to take my gun out to stop him from killing

the gook because I didn't know exactly how the onboard
bomb was controlled—when they delivered the bomb to me
yesterday, they told me that the explosives were fake and that
all the radio gear strapped to it was fake, too. I didn't believe
them.''

"You were right, the bomb was damned real." Jennings
kept his voice low and moved his eyes slowly around the
cockpit. He was looking for something, anything, that he
could use as a weapon against Blanchard. He had already
resolved to try to overpower this madman at the first
opportunity—it was their only chance. "And you brought
the bomb onboard yourself, since that was the only way for the
hijackers to be guaranteed of getting a bomb through the
security checks.''

"Yeah." There was a steady flow of perspiration from
Blanchard's forehead, a cold sweat, that ran down his face.
"But it was all a *show,* for chrissake," Blanchard added.
"None of it was *necessary;* it was just a fancy, elaborate
excuse for me to take the airplane to China. That fucking
Clancy . . .''

"And when he grabbed the gook . . .''

"Yeah, then I had to stop him. But then the goddamned
gook grabbed the gun from *me,* and we were all struggling,
and the autopilot kicked off and the airplane started to dive,
and the gun went off and the gook got killed and I got hit,
then I managed to turn the gun on that fucking Clancy just
before the airplane stalled and started to spin . . .''

Just then, out of the shadows of the right rear of the
cockpit, another figure appeared. Jennings saw the outline
first, although Blanchard was sitting just at enough of an
angle to the shadow to also pick up movement of that figure
in his peripheral vision. The figure had rapidly moved across
most of the distance between them before Jennings realized
who it was: the teenage boy.

Steven Stidham had jumped out of his seat in row two of
the darkened first-class cabin moments after the airplane had
lurched violently to the left. He had told the two women with
him in the cabin—Barbara Jennings and her daughter, Charlene—
to remain where they were, then he moved as quickly as he
could toward the cockpit. When he first saw the people ahead

of him—the stewardess standing on the left, the two pilots in their flight chairs—Steven assumed that whatever had gone wrong had been made right again and that everything was now okay. But before he walked up to ask, he allowed himself the liberty of standing quietly for a moment because he had a sudden bad feeling about the scene, although he didn't quite know why.

Don't doubt yourself, go with your basic instincts, your gut reactions. His grandfather's last words echoed in his thoughts as he stood at the rear of the darkened cockpit and watched. The two pilots and the stewardess were talking, although Steven could hardly make out any of the words. Still, he could make out enough to tell that there was anger in the captain's voice—and the captain was the one person onboard who Steven respected. The captain obviously knew what he was doing, knew what he was talking about. *The captain's angry because the other pilot wasn't doing what he was supposed to and that's probably what made the airplane jump to the left. No wonder he's mad.*

Steven was just about to walk forward into the group when something else—a gesture from the captain, the look of intense anger on the man's face, the way he rigidly held his body, the look of sheer terror on the faces of the stewardess and the other pilot—told him that something else was wrong, something far more threatening. At just about that time, Steven first spotted the pistol in the captain's hand as a slight change in the viewing angle caused the panel lights to glimmer off the steel casing of the hand-held gun.

Go with your gut reactions. Without another pause, Steven lunged at the group. He dove headlong to his right, directly at the captain, vaulting over the back of the man's flight chair as he did, pouncing on the man with all his weight.

Blanchard had spun around and raised the pistol toward the moving shadow, but it was already too late. The powerful teenage boy was all over him and, within a few seconds, had managed to twist Blanchard's left hand backward until the pistol had nearly dropped from it. But Blanchard didn't let go of the pistol because he knew that holding on to it was his last chance, his only chance. He yanked back on his left arm with all his remaining strength.

The pistol went off once, then twice. Both bullets cleared the teenage boy's shoulder by a fraction of an inch as the loud explosive noises filled the small cockpit. Both bullets impacted into the center control pedestal between the pilots' chairs, one going into the communications radios that had previously been damaged, the other bullet shattering the keyboard of the data link machinery. Fragments of plastic and metal were hurtled around the cockpit as Blanchard and the boy continued to struggle for control of the pistol.

"Help him!" Jennings was too far away himself and at the wrong angle to give any assistance to the boy, but he saw that Kathy might be able to. "Hurry!"

Kathy reached forward and tried to lay her hands on Blanchard, but each time she was knocked back by the violent kicking from both Blanchard and the boy. "I can't reach him!"

"Grab the gun!" Jennings almost let go of the flight controls to get into the fight himself, but he stopped himself at the last moment because he knew that if the airliner were to begin a dive they probably didn't have enough altitude to pull out again. Also, the weights of Blanchard and the boy were pushing repeatedly into the copilot's control column, making it necessary for Jennings to pull back with all his strength to stop the wheel from going full nose down. Jennings had to stay with the flight controls, regardless. "Get around his chair! Try from the other side!"

Kathy moved to her right and reached around the side of the copilot's flight chair. Even though the airplane was pitching and rolling continuously, she managed to get hold of a shirt sleeve. But since both Blanchard and the boy were sprawled across the seat and in constant and violent motion— Blanchard was on the bottom, the boy was on the top—she couldn't tell whose sleeve she had grabbed. Kathy prayed that it was Blanchard's and not the boy's. She yanked down hard.

Blanchard was just about to pull the trigger again because he had managed to raise the weapon slightly, and it was now more or less aimed at the boy's head. At that moment his injured right shoulder was jammed into the base of the copilot's instrument panel by the force of whoever was reaching around the flight chair to pull on his shirt sleeve.

The sudden wave of incredible, intolerable pain swept over Blanchard, and that caused him to allow his grip on the weapon to slacken. With the boy still on him and still fighting hard, Blanchard was no longer in control of the situation. The weapon moved in his hand and was now pointed down and aft, the barrel aimed at Blanchard's chest.

As Blanchard attempted to pull away one last time, the angles suddenly changed again and Blanchard's finger involuntarily tightened on the trigger. The pistol went off a third time, the loud explosive sound reverberating off the walls of the small cockpit. The bullet hit Blanchard squarely in the chest, ripping straight through his heart and then his spine as it exited through his back and impacted harmlessly into the floorboards. Blanchard was already dead before the fingers of his left hand uncurled to release his grip on the weapon.

None of the others moved for several seconds, as if they were waiting to see what else might happen. Kathy was the one who finally broke the spell. "He's dead. Get up." She helped the boy up off the copilot's flight chair.

"Are you sure?" Jennings asked. From where he sat, he could see Blanchard's sprawled-out body, but not his face.

"Yes."

"Okay. Get him out of there, away from the flight controls." The last thing Jennings needed now was the weight of Blanchard's body jammed against the copilot's control column. "Don't push on anything, stay away from the center pedestal controls," Jennings said as he concentrated on regaining the proper altitude and heading. Jennings watched out of the corner of his eye, most of his attention still focused on the flight instruments, as Kathy and the boy carefully maneuvered Blanchard's body out of the copilot's seat.

"My God, what happened?" Barbara asked as she rushed up behind where her husband was sitting in the pilot's seat. Charlene was directly behind her, and both mother and daughter stood with their mouths open as they looked at this unexpected scene of violence.

"Blanchard was the hijacker—that bastard was hijacking his own airplane."

"What?!"

While Ron explained exactly what had happened and what

they had heard and figured out, Kathy and the boy had moved Blanchard's body to the cabin, then returned to the cockpit. The four of them huddled behind where Jennings sat in the pilot's chair.

"Charlene, get in the copilot's seat," Jennings suddenly ordered.

"Ron, are you okay?" Barbara asked as she watched her daughter climb into the blood-stained seat where Captain Blanchard had died just a few minutes before. Even in the dim light of the cockpit, she could tell from looking at Ron that he was not well.

"Yes, I'm okay. Just tired." Jennings's heart was racing, and once again, he felt nauseous and lightheaded—but this time he was sure that it would pass if he took a few minutes to put his head back and rest. Pretty sure, anyway. "Are you ready to hold it straight and level for me?" Jennings asked his daughter after he saw that she was comfortable in the copilot's seat. "Just like you did before. Keep us at this altitude and heading."

"Yes, I'm ready." Charlene took hold of the controls and began the relatively simple task of keeping the airplane on the course and altitude that her father had told her to.

"You're doing fine." Satisfied, Jennings leaned back in his flight chair, closed his eyes and began to rub his temples. This time, to his surprise, the rubbing motion provided little or no relief. In fact, it seemed to make his condition worse.

"Ron, are you sure you're all right?" Kathy asked. She, too, could see the pasty, colorless look on his face, the glistening of sweat on his forehead.

"I'll be okay, just leave me alone."

Barbara glanced over at Kathy, although neither woman said a word. After a suitable time, she cleared her throat and spoke again. "Are we still going on to China?" Barbara asked in a gentle voice, not wanting to prod her husband but desperately wanting to know what would happen to them next.

Jennings paused for a long time before he answered. "Yes," he finally replied, opening his eyes and sitting up in the flight chair. His headache was measurably worse, his arms still tingled and he was on the verge of vomiting—but he knew that he had to do something to save them, that he was the only one who could. Jennings prayed that his condition would pass soon, before they reached the China coast.

"Why are we still going to China, if that's where the hijackers wanted us to go?"

"Three reasons." Jennings took a deep breath, which helped to steady him some. "The first is that maybe there really are more hijackers in the back and that this is the only way to stop them from exploding more bombs. Maybe Blanchard wasn't lying about that part."

"What's number two?" Kathy asked. She was standing behind Ron, with the teenage boy beside her. Barbara stood behind where Charlene was sitting in the copilot's chair.

"The second reason is that Blanchard set up the navigation equipment for China, and I don't know how to work it. As it stands now, all I've got to do is follow this needle to find the airport at Yangzhou, which we were told was big enough for our airplane. But if I screw around with things, I might lose everything. We've got only one of the inertial navigation units working, so trying to change it in any way could leave us with absolutely nothing left to navigate with."

"That's not good." Barbara took a half step in Ron's direction and put her hand on his shoulder. "We're better off playing it safe."

"Just like in golf, right?"

"Yes, just like in golf. You don't shoot for a birdie when all you need is a par to win." Barbara was glad to see that Ron was talking like that, maybe it meant that he was feeling better.

"And you thought that you never taught me anything about golf, didn't you?" Jennings said as he laid his own hand on top of his wife's. In spite of his headache, he managed a small smile.

"Guess I was wrong about that."

"Guess you were."

"And what's the number three reason for going on to China?" Kathy asked. She allowed her eyes to wander over to where Barbara's hand lay on Ron's shoulder.

"The third reason is a strong one, too—that we're totally out of communication. I can't raise anyone on the radios, and going straight to China is probably what everyone on the ground expects from us by now. In order to get maximum help from the people on the ground, we should probably stick to the plan that everyone is expecting.''

"But if we land where the hijackers wanted us to, won't that mean more trouble for us?''

"I don't think so. Blanchard's involvement was a ruse of some sort, a coverup that was intended to make one thing look like another—that's the only plausible explanation for it. I don't exactly know what or why, but I'd be willing to bet that if things had gone according to his plan then after we landed in China and let out the hijackers, we would have taken off again for Japan. That's why he was involved, to make that sort of thing possible.''

"Then Blanchard was right, it was the copilot who screwed things up.''

"In a manner of speaking, yes.''

"Makes sense.''

"So all we've got to do now is stay on course.'' Jennings leaned forward in his flight chair and tapped the electronic display for the navigation instrument, the needle of which was still sitting dead center and indicating that they were on course. Although he was still slightly lightheaded, his nausea and headache seemed to be diminishing. "The good news,'' Ron Jennings said as he turned around and attempted to sound far more upbeat to the four others in the cockpit than he actually felt about the thing he was saying, "is that we'll be crossing the China coastline in less than one hour. Then we'll be over solid ground again, and only a short distance from the airport at Yangzhou.''

No one in the group commented on what they had just been told. Instead, they all stood where they were and watched in silence as the airliner continued plodding its way westbound. For some reason, the idea of crossing the coastline of China did not at that moment seem like particularly good news to any of them.

"The airliner will cross into Chinese airspace in twenty-five minutes,'' Lt. Gen. Peng Ming said to the group assembled on the far side of the rosewood desk in the Chinese

Embassy in Washington. He glanced down at the computer screen to verify the news that had just been flashed to them on a separate channel, updated news on the position and course of Flight 42. "We must decide now, we can wait no longer."

American Secretary of State Eleanor Cameron laid both her hands on the conference table and turned her head toward her young assistant. "Then I assume that you're still opposed?"

"God Almighty, yes." Wagner Vanweele spoke in a hoarse whisper, fidgeted, then turned away. "This is *criminal*, we can't be any part of it. I can see nothing but trouble for us," he continued, pleading, trying to find some way to change Eleanor's mind.

"Then narrow your vision." Ambassador Li Ying-teh had grown impatient with the young American assistant, who had more problems than he had solutions, more questions than answers. He was, Li imagined, a perfect example of an American attorney. "Then if we cannot come to a consensus, perhaps we should take a binding vote—the sort of thing that you and your government are so fond of."

"That's a reasonable idea, a vote." Eleanor smiled at her young assistant. "Generous of the Chinese to teach us democracy, isn't it?"

"Eleanor, please!" Vanweele was not amused; he was frightened to death at the prospect of what they were doing, frightened by the thought of disobeying Eleanor and, simultaneously, of leaving the situation on his own.

Eleanor took hold of Wagner's arm, stepped away from the rosewood desk and steered the young assistant toward a distant corner. She didn't begin to speak until they were clearly out of earshot of the Chinese. "Wagner, where the hell are your balls?"

"This is *crazy*, a damned *nightmare* . . ."

"I had my hand on your balls the other night," Eleanor whispered tersely, "so I know damn well that you've got a set."

"It's inhuman, it's *murder* . . ."

"Did I squeeze your balls too hard back then, is that the problem?" she continued in a taunting voice. "Is that why you can't find any goddamned courage to do the things that need to be done?''

"Please, we must make an immediate decision," the Ambassador called out from across the room. "Or we will lose our options.''

"Okay." Eleanor stepped back across the room toward the rosewood desk, bringing Wagner with her. "Let's outline these two options again so we all clearly understand what we're involved with." Eleanor took another step toward the computer screen on the table, although she didn't bother to look at it. "The plan you first explained was simply for us to help keep American and Japanese military aircraft away from the airliner. That was to be something of an insurance plan to guarantee that the hijacking itself wouldn't be jeopardized.''

"Exactly," Li answered.

"What you intended to do after that point is an area we have no information about," Eleanor said with a wave of her hand to indicate her dismissal of the issue—even though she knew damn well that the Chinese would shoot down the airliner soon after it crossed the border.

While he listened to the American, Li reached for the recently warmed cup of tea on the table, took a sip, then gently placed the cup back down. He was more than willing to allow her to pretend that she knew nothing about the ultimate disposition of the airliner since that acknowledgment was actually counterproductive to his overall intentions. "Even though we are not officially having this discussion, please allow me to say that Peng's suggestion of using the original plan for destruction of the airliner has great merit to it.''

"Eleanor, for the love of Christ, we can't keep getting ourselves in deeper like this," Vanweele interrupted. He nervously wiped a growing bead of perspiration off his forehead.

"Wagner, please try to stay calm. Please try to keep the big picture in mind," Eleanor said solicitously.

"What I'm trying to tell you is that the big picture is coming out the same no matter how we try to disguise it! We're on the brink of becoming willing witnesses to a mass murder!" *If I had any brains I would leave—I would walk out that goddamned door and not come back.* But instead Vanweele stood where he was, knowing full well that he didn't have it in him to do that, that he wasn't able to turn away from this opportunity to guarantee for himself a successful future.

"Bullshit!" Eleanor slammed her hand down on the rosewood table, then looked up at Vanweele with contempt in her eyes. "What we are witnesses to is the building of a *historic monument!* What we are witnesses to is the first meaningful act to establish an irrevocable tie between two factions that control the destiny of nearly one and a half billion people!" That was far too much of an opportunity, and Eleanor knew in her heart that nothing could allow her to be dissuaded, that there was no room for timidity of any sort or for any concern other than the ultimate goal of free and open trade with China. From this point on, that was all that mattered to her. Period.

Li watched in silence as the two Americans glared at each other; he was not concerned about the outcome of this confrontation because the lady obviously remained in complete control of the situation and Li instinctively knew what her ultimate decision would be.

After a few more moments of staring at Vanweele, Eleanor turned and faced the Ambassador. "Please go on with what you were telling me."

"Certainly." Li picked up the thread of his previous conversation where he had left it off, as if nothing at all had occurred between the two Americans. "Since we have verified that at least one of the onboard bombs on the airliner is still in an active status, then all we require is one coded signal from the correct radio-frequency detonator to blow them up in-flight. Now that Peng has woken from his apparent mental sleep and realized that there is a second radio available that we can use for this task," Li added as he glanced disdainfully at Peng, "it is the natural choice."

"For many reasons," Peng said. He intended to ignore the barbs and insults from the Ambassador at all costs, to concentrate his total attention on getting the Americans to agree to this revision in the plan.

"Yes, many reasons," Li agreed. "Remember, this portable radio detonator has a range of approximately three kilometers, and we have verified independently that this duplicate detonator to the one onboard the airliner . . ."

"The original version of which was simply shut off," Eleanor interrupted.

"Yes, shut off," Li agreed. He looked at Peng again before he turned back to the American Secretary of State. "In any event, the duplicate detonator is at Yangzhou Airport, in the hands of one of the lieutenant general's men, Colonel Qi Shui. He reports that this unit—it was their backup unit, their spare—is completely functional. If we wait until the airliner gets to within three kilometers of Yangzhou . . ."

"Then we can detonate the onboard bomb, exactly as the original plan would have done it!" Peng was talking quickly now, unable to contain himself. He was close to pulling off his own plan to destroy the airliner—which would mean one more vote in his favor when the Central Committee was deciding on his fate.

"I can see that there are great advantages with this idea," Eleanor volunteered. "First and foremost, any investigating group—and we've already agreed that the Chinese government will immediately be officially inviting an American accident team into their country—would see for themselves that the airplane had been destroyed by an onboard bomb."

"Yes, we will be most happy to invite the American accident specialists in to look over the wreckage from this unfortunate disaster," the Ambassador said solemnly.

"Thank you," Eleanor answered with mock sincerity. To her, all of this continual facade of *unfortunate disaster* was ludicrous, but she could see that to the Chinese it was a very important factor in their overall method of doing business. The Chinese seemed to be able to live quite peacefully with this dichotomy of conflicting ideas and concerns—as if they hadn't been the people behind the original problem to begin with. "If we go ahead with our first plan, it might be a little bit more difficult explaining away missile holes in the wreckage."

"Possibly." Li nodded gravely, his face still expressionless. "I have already asked my technical people for guidance on that point, and they tell me that there is no way to know for certain, no way to predict what the wreckage will look like. Depending on what specific damage the air-to-air missiles do and how and where the airliner crashes, that will determine whether or not it would be obvious to an investigating committee that external explosives had been used.''

"An embarrassing complication." Eleanor reached for her own cup of tea, raised it to her lips and took a big gulp. It was quite good.

"In addition, there is one other factor," Peng added.

"Which is?" Eleanor already knew what the ultimate decision would be—they'd had no choice from the beginning, really—she just wanted to go down on record as having asked every conceivable question and having covered every possible point. She wondered for an instant who in God's name she was going on record *for*, because if the shit hit the fan then she was sure as hell going to get splattered too—all the assurances from the Chinese Ambassador notwithstanding. Still, it was worth the risk.

"The additional factor is that the shooting down of the airliner requires us to involve more people in the direct execution of the plan."

"More people?"

"Yes. The pilots of the fighter jets at the very least, plus whatever support personnel are necessary for them to complete their assignment."

"Are the Chinese fighter jets already en route?"

"They are. A group of three interceptors is already in the area of the border penetration, and they have been instructed to follow behind the airliner at a safe distance. They are armed with air-to-air missiles, but the fighter pilots have not yet been told of any need to shoot at their target."

"I see."

"There is one other unpleasant possibility also," Peng continued.

"Which is what?" Eleanor asked as her heart sank a little. This list of unpleasant possibilities seemed to be written on a never-ending scroll—in her imagination, Eleanor could see the Chinese unraveling this *scroll of unpleasantries* and reading from it for the rest of the day. Worse than that, she now fully realized that she couldn't stop it no matter what.

"Witnesses on the ground to any intercept operation might easily recognize that it was the missiles from the fighters that shot down the airliner."

"Damn."

"Naturally, that potential for discovery would depend on the conditions of local cloud cover and visibility, plus the unknown factor of how many people on the ground were looking in that direction at the time of the attack." Peng already knew that the area around Yangzhou was covered with a solid overcast, but he didn't mention that fact—he certainly didn't want to say anything that might prejudice the decision against him.

Eleanor blanched at the thought of witnesses to the shooting. "That could be hundreds of people—thousands, even." She was amazed that she hadn't thought of that fact herself—and now she was beginning to get concerned over whatever other important facts she might be overlooking. "We sure as hell couldn't cover up something like that."

Li quickly decided against explaining the truth of that aspect of the situation, which was that no number of Chinese peasants could have the slightest impact on these proceedings. What a thousand peasants in the rice fields saw, or what they thought they saw, was completely irrelevant since no one would listen to what they had to say anyway. Unlike the Americans, Li could and certainly would control what went on inside his own country. But he, too, had no intention of volunteering information that went against the direction of the winds of good fortune. "Potential witnesses to a missile attack are an important factor indeed."

"Damned right."

"Yet if we do what Peng now suggests, then no matter who sees the airliner explode the stories are all in line with what we would want the world to believe." Li wasn't concerned about making things easier on Peng, but he was concerned about keeping China's culpability as easily identifiable as possible by not complicating it with any discussions of "self-defense" or "military error." Li had always lived by the adage that the best food would come from the pot that had only one hand to stir it, and he wanted no others involved in this act of destruction and coverup beyond the group already assembled.

"An excellent point." Eleanor nodded at Vanweele. "This second onboard bomb is really a gift from heaven," she said in a conciliatory tone. "It terminates things in a way that is acceptable to us and acceptable to them, and it also has zero potential for unpleasant discoveries down the road. Doing it this way, the script will read that deranged hijackers detonated their onboard bomb just before the airliner was about to land at the hijackers' destination."

"And when, exactly, will this bomb explode?" Vanweele asked, amazed himself at how quickly he had become a participant in this hideous act. He shivered while he waited for an answer.

Lt. Gen. Peng Ming consulted his computer screen readout, then turned to the group. "The airliner will cross the Chinese coastline within fifteen minutes. From that point on, considering their current speed and heading, they should reach Yangzhou Airfield within twelve minutes after that."

"Twenty-seven more minutes. Very good," Eleanor said calmly. Inside, she was a bundle of nerves—she had never done anything even remotely approaching the magnitude and personal accountability of this act—but she'd be damned if she was going to show the slightest bit of concern. *No pain, no gain.* "Then we don't have much longer to wait." Instead of thinking about the airliner, in the back of her mind Eleanor was already rehearsing her call to the President when she would tell him of the breakthrough with China on the free trade issues. No, she decided, there would be no telephone call to the White House—Eleanor would demand an immediate private meeting with that pompous asshole. Then she would tell him in person. She would get immense pleasure from watching his face drop.

"The sooner the better," Wagner Vanweele added in a low, reluctant voice. In the back of his mind he was also thinking of something else—something not quite as positive as what Eleanor was obviously concerned with at that moment. *If they're going to do this, they should do it right now, before anything else happens. They're taking too many chances.*

16

The Chinese Air Force base at Yangzhou was a bleak and colorless place, with stretches of open concrete broken up by clusters of old and drab buildings. The west side of the field housed the headquarters of the 97th Tactical Air Squadron, a two-story wooden administration building at the compound's center. The building itself dated back to the Second World War, its latest layer of brown paint flaking off in spots as if it were a piece of overripe fruit losing its skin. A large maintenance hangar was directly to the administration building's right, and to the left were several corrugated metal hangars and garages of various sizes and shapes that housed the air squadron's support equipment.

Col. Qi Shui turned up the collar of his green field jacket to protect himself from the chilling northwest wind as he stood on the ramp behind his ground floor office, his eyes scanning the distant horizon to the east. The first hint of morning light had appeared less than twenty minutes earlier and, as he waited outside, the sky in that quadrant had brightened measurably.

"At least the weather is being cooperative," Qi said as he

turned to the young lieutenant who had just walked up beside him. This was, he knew, the only other man at Yangzhou who understood the full truth behind the imminent landing of the American civilian airliner that the airbase had been alerted to through normal, official channels.

"Yes. The weather office reports that the base of the overcast is at least eight hundred meters, with some spots even higher. Flight visibility is more than ten kilometers." Lt. Fei Xiaotong gave his report crisply and efficiently, as was his manner. As the personal aide to the air squadron commander, he knew that it was his job to have answers to whatever questions Colonel Qi might have. More important, he was deeply honored to have been included in this particular mission, an obviously sensitive one. "The surface wind is the only possible complicating factor—northwest at twenty to thirty. But I believe that the American pilot should be able to handle that much easily enough."

"I should say so." Unlike most of the others at Yangzhou, Qi knew well of the Americans and respected their abilities—he had observed them firsthand in Vietnam during several of his covert operations into that country during America's last Asian fiasco. While the pilot of this airliner was a civilian, he imagined that the man must possess the same level of ingenuity and courage as the American fighter pilots he had seen operate in Vietnam. Still, none of that was the point, not once they had received that last message from Washington. "The wind can make no difference now. There will be no landing," Qi said with a shrug.

"Of course." When the lieutenant—whose primary job was to operate the top-secret communications equipment for the colonel—had received the last message, even he had been somewhat startled by what that message had said: *USE BACKUP RADIO CONTROLLER ON PREARRANGED CODES TO ACTIVATE ONBOARD BOMB WHEN AIRLINER GETS WITHIN RANGE OF YOUR EQUIPMENT. AIRLINER MUST BE TOTALLY DESTROYED BEFORE LANDING—THIS IN-FLIGHT DESTRUCTION MUST BE CARRIED OUT AS AN ABSOLUTE FIRST PRIORITY. SIGNED LT. GEN. PENG MING.* Fei showed no emotion as he handed the message over and waited for the colonel's response.

"Do you think that the airliner will be circling the airport or landing straight in?" Qi kicked his boot at a small clod of dirt that had blown across the concrete ramp from one of the collective farms surrounding the airbase. The ball of dirt broke apart instantly and the fragments of it scattered quickly as they were pushed by the wind.

"I would imagine that they will elect to circle, to give the pilot a good view of the entire landing area."

"My thoughts, also." Qi pointed toward a broad empty expanse at the northern boundary of the airfield. "If they circle to the left, which they probably will since that's the side that the pilot will be sitting on, then I'll send the coded signal for detonation when they pass abeam that open area. There's no sense endangering our own equipment from falling debris."

"Very well, sir." Fei looked around the field. In the distance, he could see the fire trucks and ambulances that had already been alerted to the Americans' arrival. Behind them were several army personnel carriers and a few staff cars, with machine gun carrying troops milling around on both sides of the runway. "The army is ready."

"But not for what will actually be happening, I can assure you," Qi said petulantly.

"Certainly not." Fei looked at the ramp in front of where he and the colonel stood. There were a dozen identical F-6 fighters—the Chinese version of the MiG-19—parked in a straight row on the flight line, with three empty slots to indicate the three aircraft that had already been sent aloft. To the rear of the flight line were the squadron's buildings and hangars. A few maintenance men were here and there, but basically, the ramp was empty of personnel—as was most of the administration building at this early an hour.

"If he does attempt to land straight in on the west runway, we will have plenty of opportunity. There should be more than enough time to do the job right from where we are. Do you agree?" Qi always liked to ask his subordinates for their opinion, since he had found that it cost nothing to do so and once in a great while his question would uncover excellent responses that he could then take credit for himself.

"Yessir. You should be able to see the airliner well before

it enters its final approach for the runway,'' Fei answered, eager to agree with the colonel. At best, Colonel Qi was a difficult man to work for—he was headstrong and impetuous, and could be pigheaded beyond belief—but he was also the key to Fei's future, to the lieutenant's next promotion. "The other advantage of staying where we are is that none of the army personnel near the runway will be around to bother us or ask questions."

"A good point. I certainly don't need some old fart of a ground-pounding general peeking over my shoulder or asking me what I'm doing—not that it's any of his damned business anyway."

"Certainly not, sir."

"But there is no reason to subject ourselves to that kind of scrutiny, especially not while we're carrying something that looks more like a computer than a radio."

"Yessir, I agree." Fei paused for a moment, glanced around the airfield, then turned back to the colonel. "I must point out that timing the detonation for the airliner's final approach—if that's what you elect to do—will cause most of the wreckage to fall in the Chungdreichu ravine."

"Unfortunate, but something that can't be helped." Qi wondered if Peng still expected him to attempt to retrieve the remnants of the war games computer from the wreckage, since none of the computer messages from the Washington Embassy had addressed that particular question. "Is there any way to get our people into that ravine within a few minutes after initial impact?"

"I'm afraid not, sir. Men with ropes would take hours, and it's far too windy for helicopters. They tell me that the ravine is notorious for horrible downdrafts."

"I understand," Qi answered reluctantly. Normally, he wouldn't have accepted an answer like that—but this time, it might indeed be for the best. The more the colonel thought about it, the more he realized that Peng had not wanted him to go in after the wreckage after all—which meant that depositing the wreckage at the bottom of the Chungdreichu ravine would be something of a godsend. As both he and Peng had clearly understood from the beginning of this project, the need to detonate the suitcase bomb meant that the problems of getting the war games computer to China had grown too menacing and that the only alternative was total destruction of all the evidence. Anything less would be an invitation for personal disaster—hence, the very understandable phrase in the message from Peng: *AN ABSOLUTE FIRST PRIORITY*.

"I can't imagine that there will be much useful wreckage to retrieve in any event," Fei said. "There will certainly be no survivors."

"Correct." Within a heartbeat of when Qi would send the coded signal, the airliner would be reduced to nothing beyond scattered pieces of twisted wreckage falling from the sky. It was unfortunate for Kao Wei, but his death would be just another unavoidable aspect of the never-ending struggle between East and West. In many of the battles that Qi had seen and been around in his lifetime, civilians had ultimately accounted for most of the casualties anyway—and Kao Wei had been a willing participant in the plan. As far as the others onboard the airliner were concerned, Qi hadn't given them even a brief moment of thought.

"I expect that we should be getting our next message from Jin one-eight at any moment now," Fei said. He was anxious to return to the squadron radio room to get the latest report from the deployed aircraft, and he turned and faced the office door thirty meters behind him. Still, he made no definitive move in that direction until the colonel made it obvious that he wanted him to.

"And what is the status of Jin one-eight?"

"Per your orders, still no change, sir. That flight of three F-6's are maintaining their positions near the border penetration point off the coast. They expect to have visual contact with the airliner within the next few minutes. After that, they will maintain a minimum distance of five kilometers behind the target. Their last report, from approximately four minutes ago," Fei said as he glanced at his wristwatch, "indicated no change in the airliner's heading, altitude or speed. The estimate for the airliner's arrival over the airport is still the same, nineteen minutes from now."

"Then I suppose we should be getting inside." Even though he had logged far more hours at his desk than in an airplane during the last ten years, Qi still put off going into his office for as long as possible whenever he could. He did so especially on days like today, when he was about to do something that he basically didn't want to—the detonation of the suitcase bomb meant total failure of their plan, something that Qi wasn't anxious to admit to.

"Yessir, we should get ourselves totally prepared. With your permission, sir, I'll be leaving the external power hookup attached so that we can get maximum power and therefore maximum transmission range when the time comes to send the signal."

Qi nodded affirmatively.

"I'd also like to check out the portable unit one last time with its self-test function, to be certain that the signal strengths will be sufficient."

"Very well." Reluctantly, Qi turned and strode back toward the administration office and the portable detonation computer that was sitting on his desk. He didn't know where or why the plan that he and Peng Ming had devised to steal the American war games computer had gone wrong, and he didn't know what the ultimate ramifications of this action he was about to undertake would be. All he knew for certain were what his orders from Peng were: to destroy the airliner as soon as it got within range of the backup portable detonator that he had in his possession. That would occur in less than nineteen minutes from now, when the airliner got to within three kilometers of where they were standing. "Three kilometers. Incredible."

"Excuse me, sir?" Lt. Fei Xiatong said, puzzled.

"Never mind." Qi opened the administration building door and stepped inside, preparing himself for the action that would be an admission of defeat when success was so close at hand. For the first time in his career, Qi realized something else, too—how much things had really changed for military men during the last thirty years. He would, he now saw, be conducting a top-level exercise of complex warfare from, quite literally, the swivel chair in his office. There was no chance to see the enemy up close, or to even feel as if combat were taking place—factors in the past that would have helped him accept the failure of his mission. *Three kilometers, then push a button.* The thought of fighting a crucial yet unsuc-

cessful battle by remote control made Col. Qi Shui slightly
ill.

The morning sun had risen above the top of the overcast
cloud condition directly behind the tail of the 787 jet as the
airliner continued westbound. The ambient light conditions in
the cockpit had improved dramatically in the last half hour, to
the point where Ron Jennings could now see everything
around him easily enough. It had gotten light enough in the
last ten minutes that, by looking rearward from where he sat
in the captain's seat, Jennings could also see most of the
damage in the first-class cabin.

"Quite a sight, isn't it?" Barbara Jennings said as she
noticed what her husband was looking at.

"Incredible." Jennings could make out the grotesque details of the mound of twisted debris that blocked access
between the first-class and coach sections of the airliner.
From even that far away, Jennings thought he could make out
areas of blood and gore mingled in with the pieces of aluminum and the sections of fiber glass, and he could hear some
of the shrill air noise from the hole in the fuselage's roof that
made any conversation back at the wreckage nearly impossible. Jennings shuddered, then turned around to face his flight
panel.

"Dad, should I still keep the airplane at this altitude?"
Charlene Jennings asked from the copilot's seat as she gestured toward the altimeter. She had been steering the airplane
for nearly an hour now, keeping it steady at eight thousand
feet, and she had gotten quite good at it. "We're getting
pretty close."

Jennings looked down at the navigation readout in front of
him that showed where they were. It was seventy-nine miles
to Yangzhou—which meant that they were now well inside
China airspace, and nearly to the coastline. The solid overcast
beneath them made everything appear no different than it had
during the last few hours. "No, hold this altitude for a while
longer."

"When do you want to start down?"

"Since we don't know the height of the terrain or the
height of the clouds, we've got to wait until we're just about

over the airport before we descend. Then I'll come down steeply, so we don't get involved in any mountainous areas if there are any around here. I'm going on the assumption that the Chinese didn't build a big airport in the middle of the mountains and that we'll see something when we get low enough." Jennings knew that they were taking a hell of a chance, but if the clouds went all the way to the ground or there were a ring of mountains surrounding Yangzhou, then they were screwed anyway.

"How accurate is this navigation set?" Flight Attendant Kathy Davis asked as she pointed to the readout. It was now reading seventy-two miles to Yangzhou—which meant seventeen more minutes according to the machine.

"Blanchard told me that it was always right on the money. He said that if it wasn't, the set would shut itself down—which it obviously hasn't."

"Blanchard lied about plenty of things."

"Hopefully, this is not one of them." Jennings prayed to God that their single remaining inertial navigation set was correct, because if they broke out beneath the clouds and the airport wasn't around he had no idea what to do next, which way to turn. They still had enough fuel, but they certainly didn't have enough to be wandering around the interior of China for any length of time. If they were really lucky, the clouds below them would break away before they got to Yangzhou. "I'm ready to take it now," Jennings said as he put his hands on the control wheel.

"Okay, you've got it."

Jennings played with the control wheel for a moment before he looked back at his daughter. "Charlene, you've done a really great job. Just remember what we've talked about, how you'll help me with the gear and flaps during the landing."

"I understand." Charlene nodded.

"And I'll be reading off the airspeeds," Kathy volunteered from where she sat in the extra cockpit seat behind the captain's flight chair. "Just tell me when you want me to start."

"I will."

"You'll tell Steven and me when we should go back to sit in the cabin," Barbara said as she fidgeted nervously. She stood directly behind Charlene, with the teenage boy standing next to her. Barbara had placed her right arm with its heavy bandage on the top of the seat back of the copilot's flight chair, and now that daylight had come, she could see for the first time what a mess it was in. The tan bandage was smeared with blood and dirt, and several strands of material were unraveling from it.

"I'll let you know when to go back," Jennings said. "It'll be about ten minutes before the actual landing, just as we start down into the clouds."

"Okay." Barbara wasn't very happy about not being in the cockpit for the landing, but she saw the logic in how things had worked out among the five of them: Ron, of course, would be doing the flying, Charlene would be in the copilot's seat to work gear and flaps, Kathy—who was far more familiar with flight panels than she was—would occupy the extra cockpit chair behind Ron so she could read off airspeeds and whatever other gauges he might want to know about during the landing. Barbara and the teenage boy, who had no available places to sit in the cockpit, would strap themselves into seats in the first row of the cabin. A pure precaution, Ron had said, just in case of a hard landing. It all made too much sense to argue against, although she hated the idea of going back. "We're ready, whenever you tell us."

"Fine."

"Dad, look—another message!" Charlene pointed to the data link screen on the central control pedestal between the pilots' seats. The screen had come alive shortly after they had pushed in the circuit breakers behind the copilot's seat—the circuit breakers that had been out all along, the ones that Blanchard had lied about—and the message had repeated itself any number of times in the past hour:

TO FLIGHT 42. WE ARE RECEIVING YOUR DATA LINK AUTOMATIC CONNECTION MESSAGE THAT INDICATES YOU ARE FLYING WESTBOUND AT EIGHT THOUSAND FEET, AT AN AIRSPEED OF 250 KNOTS. WE ARE AWARE OF YOUR SITUATION/DESTINATION. RESPOND IN ANY WAY THAT YOU CAN TO INDICATE THAT YOU ARE RECEIVING THIS SIGNAL. POE/SAN FRANCISCO DISPATCH.

"Damn, I wish we could answer them." Jennings glanced down at the data link keyboard beneath the screen, where chunks of plastic and pieces of wire had been ripped away by Blanchard's wild shots. As they had realized after the first incoming message had appeared on the screen almost an hour before, the data link unit could receive messages but could not transmit any messages back because its transmitting keyboard had been demolished by the gunfire. Likewise for the normal radio transmitters on the center pedestal—they, too, had been shot up badly and none of them worked even though all their circuit breakers had been pushed back in.

"Should I try sending another message on the data link?" Kathy asked. She knew how to work the unit because the keyboard was identical to the one in the airliner's rear galley—a keyboard they occasionally used en route for passenger connections and ordering supplies.

"No, forget it, it's a waste of time." Jennings could see that there was no hope in repairing the keyboard, that the people on the other end—the airline dispatch office in San Francisco—would have no way of knowing their message was getting through. The bottom line was that it wouldn't make any difference anyway. Whatever information they might have to give them—perhaps the weather at Yangzhou, or the airport conditions—Jennings would need to do without it. "Okay, everyone. Forget the data link messages and forget the bombs and the hijackers. We're just about ready to start down."

"What about the clouds?" Charlene asked.

Jennings peered out ahead, at the solid overcast beneath them. Clearly, they weren't going to get a break there, either— the sky was going to remain overcast. They would need to do a blind penetration over unknown terrain. "Forget the clouds, too. All we're going to concentrate on now is finding the airport and landing. Barbara . . ."

"Yes." She took a half step toward her husband and laid a hand on his shoulder.

"It's time for you and Steven to go back. Strap yourself in tight."

"Sure thing. We'll be okay, don't worry about us."

"As soon as we come to a stop, get that forward passenger

door opened just like I showed you. Get right down the chute and run like hell away from the airplane."

"I'm going to wait for you two."

"There's no need to wait. Charlene and I will be right at your heels. If you slow down, we might run over you."

"You two had better be right behind me, or you'll be in a hell of a lot of trouble with Mom." Barbara squeezed her husband's shoulder.

"I love you, hon."

"I know you do. I love you, too. Both of you." Without saying anything else or looking at any of the others, Barbara turned and walked to the rear.

Ron Jennings waited several seconds to give his wife a chance to get back in the cabin, then put his right hand on the airliner's twin throttles. "Okay, folks. Here we go," he said as he reduced power and pointed the 787's nose down toward the tops of the clouds.

When the red light at the front of the Trans Continental dispatch office in San Francisco had suddenly illuminated again, Wally Poel had been looking directly at it. He had been so totally shocked by the light coming on that it had taken him a full ten seconds to respond, to comprehend that Flight 42's data link equipment had somehow come alive after being off the air for the last few hours.

That had occurred over one hour before. Since then, Poel had notified all the government agencies that they were getting a continuous readout of automatic flight data from the airliner, and had spent much of the time sending out dozens of specific data link messages that requested the flight to respond. As of yet, they had not received a single specific reply to their query messages and Poel had run out of ideas. "Still nothing?" Poel asked his assistant Tom Labitzke as the young man walked toward him from the room in the back where the message printer was.

"Nothing but the automatic status signal. They're still at eight thousand feet, two hundred and fifty knots, heading two-seven-four degrees." Labitzke shook his head in disgust. "At least the data we're getting is correct because it agrees with the information we've received from the Japanese coastal radar and from the military aircraft flying a trail formation with 42. Our aircraft is still flying, still maintaining a steady track—but that's just about all we know.''

"Not true." The other senior duty manager, Byron Stark, was standing near the executive vice president at the far side of the command desk. He looked over at Poel and his assistant.

"What's that?" Poel's words were even angrier than he had intended them to be—he was dead tired, and he knew it.

"We also know what the military and the State Department have relayed to us, that 42 is approaching the coast of China and is headed directly for its original hijack destination of Yangzhou. Since the Chinese are cooperating, it looks like all we've got on our hands now is a simple hijacking.''

"There are no *simple* hijackings, you asshole."

Stark blanched, his face turned white and he took a half step backward. He glanced over at Senior Vice President Reckson but saw that the man had turned away, obviously not wanting to get involved in a public confrontation between two of his top men. Stark decided that this display of immaturity from Poel was something that he could capitalize on. "Calm down, Wally. You know what I meant."

"You're right-on with that one, Byron—I've known what you've meant for years. You've meant shit." Poel stepped off the center command platform and onto the main dispatch floor. He glanced up at the red monitor light at the front of the room—it was still on, which meant that they were still electronically connected to Flight 42. But the bitch of it all was that the airplane was not talking to *anyone*, that all the government agencies continued to indicate that there were no voice transmissions taking place, that the only electronic link to the airliner was the totally automatic readout of the jet's speed, altitude and heading that was continuously coming in to the San Francisco dispatch office. That didn't make any sense, unless . . .

Byron Stark had descended the steps of the command platform right behind Poel. Stark had already sensed that he might lose the vice president's respect if he allowed this buffoon of a man to get away with calling him names, even though any kind of confrontation went horribly against his basic nature. "You know, I've had just about enough of your

goddamn ranting,'' Stark said, trying to make himself sound
more angry than scared. "I don't know who the hell you
think you are . . ."

"I'm supposed to be a *magician,* for chrissake," Poel said
forcefully, his voice suddenly upbeat. He had obviously thought
of something, had just come up with a new idea.

"Huh?"

Poel was looking directly at Stark, although the man in
front of him wasn't who he was actually talking to: Poel was
talking out loud to himself. "God Almighty, what a damned
fool I've been!"

At first, Stark thought that Poel was offering an apology.
After a few seconds, he realized that the man wasn't. "I
don't follow you." Stark took a step backward and glanced
around to see who was watching. Everyone in the room was
watching them, including the vice president.

"Just like we've already figured," Poel continued, "the
crew isn't answering us because they can't—either because
the equipment is broken or the hijackers won't let them."

"We already know that." Stark was getting nervous; if
Poel had stumbled onto something big, that would give him
one hell of an edge in getting appointed to Dunlap's job.
"But there's nothing we can do to change that. If the onboard
equipment is broken or if the hijackers simply won't let it be
used, it's all the same. There's nothing we can do about that
from here."

"Wrong. There sure as hell *is* a way we might be able to
get around it."

"How?" Stark's mouth was open and a bead of perspiration had formed on his forehead. He silently prayed that Poel
was wrong, that he hadn't come up with some way to get 42
to respond to the data link messages.

"The magician's trick, the sleight of hand, the time-tested
way of pulling the Ace of Spades from the middle of the
deck!" Poel was worked up now, his arms were waving and
he was talking fast. Everyone in the dispatch office had their
eyes on him, no one was saying a word to interrupt because
they somehow knew that Poel was on to something big. Poel
himself had his eyes glued to the red monitor light, which
remained steadfastly on to indicate that the data link connec-

tion to 42 was good. "While everyone on 42 is watching the cockpit data link, we'll do what a magician would do—we'll pull the hidden Ace out of our other sleeve! Tom . . ."

"Yes?"

"Address a discreet message to 42's *cabin* data link, just as if we were responding to a request for passenger connection information."

"I gotcha—cabin device only, right?"

"Right. Be sure to code the message so that it goes only to the cabin readout. This way, if the hijackers are watching the cockpit screen, they won't know that a message is coming into the rear unit."

"Exactly. And if the reason we haven't gotten any response is that the cockpit unit is broken, there's still a good chance that the cabin data link might work. We know that the basic unit itself is functional because it's still sending out continuous automatic signals."

"Maybe we'll be able to get a response from someone in the cabin since that's not the obvious way we'd be transmitting to them. Maybe the crew hasn't thought of it either, and that's why they haven't used it. We might be able to learn what the hell is going on by sending a data link message to the rear cabin—and there's a chance we can even be of some help if we can get them to respond and find out what their current situation is." Poel was so exhausted that he had to lean against a nearby desk to steady himself, yet his mind was still working rapidly, still trying to come up with more ways to be of assistance.

"The cabin message will be out in less than sixty seconds." Labitzke rushed toward the back room to send the appropriate message.

Poel stood in the center of the dispatch office with all eyes on him. He had, however, forgotten about being surrounded by Byron Stark and the senior vice president and the dozens of dispatchers and clerks in the room with him. Wally Poel was deep in thought, totally immersed in the logistics of his new plan to communicate with Flight 42. *It'll be just like pulling the Ace of Spades from the middle of the deck,* he said to himself. *Maybe.*

•   •   •

Flight Attendant Fred Lyle was standing less than ten feet from the rear galley when he heard the distant two-tone chime go off from behind him. For several seconds he didn't respond, until the enormity of what that new sound meant hit him.

"What was that?" Max Berger asked as he rushed up. The airliner's rear cabin had been returned to something of a semblance of normality now that there was enough daylight coming through the windows to see. Max had just finished dealing with some of the wounded, moving everyone to the furthest rear end of the cabin which was far quieter, organizing others into an evacuation party for when they landed. He, too, had heard the two-tone chime.

"The data link—God!" Fred rushed into the galley and opened up the fiber glass cover behind which the data link unit was housed.

"What's a data link?" Max rushed up alongside and peered over Fred's shoulder. It was a screen the size of a miniature television, with a numbered and lettered keyboard beneath it.

"An electronic message center. We use it to communicate with headquarters to get supplies at the next stop, to alert them to passenger requests and connections. I don't know why the hell I didn't think about it earlier, except that it's not something we use very often and then only for routine, silly things . . ." While Fred was rambling on, he was also punching buttons on the unit's keyboard, careful to use the proper codes to bring up to the screen whatever the inbound message was that had caused the alerting chimes to sound.

"Look at that, for chrissake." Max watched in awe as the electronic words began to print on the small screen above the keyboard.

TO FLIGHT 42/CABIN UNIT. IF YOU HAVE RECEIVED THIS MESSAGE AND CAN RESPOND, SEND ANY KIND OF ACKNOWLEDGMENT. POEL/SAN FRANCISCO DISPATCH.

"What does that mean?"

Fred's hands were shaking so badly he could hardly work the keyboard buttons. "We can talk to them directly . . . oh, my God . . . why didn't I think of this sooner . . ." As carefully as he could, Fred typed in a short response, then pressed the unit's transmit button.

"Is our message sent?" Max could see that the screen, which had continued the message that Fred had typed, had suddenly gone blank. "Is that what it means when the words disappear?"

"I think so." Fred kept his eyes on the screen, but nothing was happening yet. The airplane rocked beneath his feet and he glanced out the small galley window. "We're in the clouds already. Jesus Christ, we're headed down for a landing, even earlier than we figured."

"Looks that way." Max shouted down the aisle for the few standing passengers to sit, that everyone should strap themselves in for the landing that they had been preparing everyone for. Having done that, Max turned back to the data link screen. It was still a total blank. "Maybe they're not getting our answer."

"Maybe, although it always did take a little while." Fred looked nervously out the galley window again. They were still in the clouds, bouncing around slightly, the aft end of the airliner wiggling just enough to tell him that the landing flaps were probably going down. That meant that the pilots would be extending the landing gear next. "If they respond should we tell them what we've figured out about the bomb?"

"Absolutely."

"And I'll also tell them to send the message about the second bomb up to the cockpit. Maybe we can use this data link as a substitute for the broken cabin-to-cockpit interphone."

"I don't follow you," Max said. He looked out the galley window; the clouds they were flying through seemed to be getting thinner.

"The cockpit has one of these data link screens, too. I've seen it. If the cockpit screen is working and we can talk to San Francisco, I'll transmit a message for San Francisco to send up to the cockpit."

"That's a helluva thing, to send a message thousands of miles to San Francisco and back so we can communicate with the pilots who are only sitting a hundred feet in front of us."

"Yeah, a hundred feet—but through a solid wall of debris and over a noise level that's on a par with a boiler factory.

The cockpit might as well be on the moon, as far as we're concerned.'' At that moment the two-tone chime sounded again. Fred quickly keyed in the proper responses, and within seconds, new words began to fill the cabin data link screen.

TO FLIGHT 42/CABIN UNIT. HAVE RECEIVED YOUR RE-PLY. WHAT IS YOUR SITUATION? POEL/SAN FRANCISCO DISPATCH.

"We're breaking out of the clouds," Max said as the words finished printing on the screen. In the background, he could hear the passengers cheering at the sight beneath them, one that they had been praying for all those terrorized hours that they had spent isolated in the near total darkness: the vivid browns and greens of the gently rolling terrain, a scattering of small buildings, a great deal of lush farmland. "Don't waste time, get them to send our message to the cockpit. Knowing that there's still another bomb onboard might make the pilots want to do something differently."

"Right." Flight Attendant Fred Lyle punched the keyboard as quickly as he could, detailing what they had discovered about a "lower device" onboard and armed. Without bothering to read the message again, he hit the transmit button. Instantly the electronic words disappeared from the screen. "Max, we've done everything we can. We've got to sit down for the landing."

Just then, both men heard the sound of the airliner's landing gear being lowered.

17

"Gear down," Ron Jennings commanded.

"Gear coming down," his daughter Charlene answered as she reached for the big handle on the center instrument panel and pushed it to the down position. After a few seconds she pointed to the indicator lights. "Three green lights, all the wheels are down and locked."

"Okay." Yet even though he had heard his daughter's words and responded to them, Jennings was actually concentrating on the scene ahead. The wide expanse of the multiple concrete runways of Yangzhou lay seven miles in front of them in what was the most welcome sight that Jennings had ever seen. "God, they're beautiful—look at them!"

"What?" Flight Attendant Kathy Davis, who was sitting directly behind Ron in the extra cockpit seat, rose up as far as her cinched-up seat belt and shoulder harness would allow as she peered out the airliner's windshield at the scene ahead. "What's beautiful?"

"The runways. Just like Blanchard said, the airport at Yangzhou is more than big enough." Now that they had found the airport, Jennings wasn't overly concerned with what he had left to do to get the airliner down safely. He would, most certainly, need to pay strict attention to the approach and landing. Even then, he was pretty sure that this wasn't going to be the best landing that he had ever made. On the other hand, Jennings was equally certain that the task was well within his grasp, that nothing disastrous would result. The worst that could happen would be a few blown tires or a scraped wingtip or engine pod. He was now confident that they would get out of this nightmare after all. "It's almost over."

"Thank God." Kathy reached up to lay her hand on Ron's shoulder, but then decided against doing that. She laid her hand back in her lap.

Jennings made a slight adjustment with the engine power as he pitched the nose even lower. They were at three thousand feet, just below the base of the overcast, still descending. "I'm taking us down to two thousand, keep your eyes open for other airplanes."

"Right, Dad." Charlene leaned forward and peered out the cockpit window. There was mostly farmland below them, several scattered clusters of low-roofed buildings, dirt and blacktop roads set at random patterns, a few cars and trucks moving here and there. In one of the fields she spotted a group of people gathered around several tractors, and she watched them until they disappeared beneath the airliner's right wing. Charlene lifted her eyes and scanned the horizon again. "I don't see any airplanes."

"They must know we're coming; they've kept all the air traffic out of our way," Kathy said as she, too, scanned the distant horizon to the left side.

"Maybe." Jennings steered the 787 in a wide descending turn until they had reached an altitude of two thousand feet. "Leveling off," he announced as he pushed up the engine power and steadied the airplane. They were flying through some minor turbulence now, the airframe jolting every few seconds from the continuous minor bumps. "It's windy down here," Jennings said as he recognized the feeling of the wind-induced turbulence. He was, once again, startled by how much he had instinctively remembered from a job he hadn't been near in over five years. "Everyone start looking for smoke or flags or something that'll tell us which way the wind is blowing.''

"There's smoke on our left." Kathy pointed at a group of buildings in the distance, the smoke stack on the largest building giving out a light but discernible plume of grey. "It looks like the wind's blowing at our nose, a little from the right.''

"Yes, I see it." Jennings turned and scanned the runway ahead of them—they were within four miles of it now. "We'll land to the west, on that long runway.''

"We're getting pretty close," Charlene said nervously. She sat further up in the copilot's flight chair.

"We won't land on this pass, we'll circle the airport at least once. That'll give me a good view of the entire airport and the final approach course and also give me a chance to get stabilized for the touchdown.''

"Which way are we going to circle?" Kathy asked.

"To the left." Jennings looked out ahead of them. Between where they were and the touchdown portion of the runway that he had selected to use was a deep ravine that they'd pass over during their final approach. Other than that, the surrounding terrain presented no problems whatsoever—especially the areas straight north and south of the airfield. Those quadrants were nothing but vast expanses of flat fields, most of them barren, a few with a scattering of trees.

"Dad, I think there are vehicles on the runway." Charlene pointed at the tiny figures in the distance that were growing in size with every passing moment.

"No, they're on the sides of the runway . . . looks like army trucks . . . people, too . . . soldiers, maybe . . .'' Jennings concentrated on his flight panel for a moment; airspeed and altitude were good, the engines were working properly, they still had plenty of fuel, the landing gear was down and the flaps were partially extended. Everything was exactly as it should be, including the fact that he, too, felt fine—his headache and nausea were gone, and so was his lightheadedness. "Okay, here we go," Jennings announced to Kathy and his daughter as they approached the eastern edge of the airport. "We'll circle just once, that'll be enough, then I'll turn a three-mile final approach over that deep ravine that we just flew over. Both of you remember to make the call-outs that you're supposed to.''

"Wait, Ron, look!''

Jennings turned in his flight chair toward where Kathy had pointed—the data link screen on the center console. On it was a message, a totally new message, and one that instantly received his complete attention.

TO FLIGHT 42: FLIGHT ATTENDANT AT THE REAR CABIN DATA LINK REPORTS THAT THEY ARE CERTAIN THERE IS STILL AT LEAST ONE RADIO CONTROLLED BOMB ONBOARD, A "LOWER DEVICE," BUT THERE ARE NO HIJACKERS IN THE REAR OF THE AIRPLANE. POEL/SAN FRANCISCO DISPATCH.

Lt. Fei Ziaotong put his binoculars down and turned to the man next to him. "We were right, sir. They obviously intend to circle the airport to the left.''

"Very good.'' Col. Qi Shui took his hands off the controls of the portable detonation unit and let out a measured breath. Now that he was certain that the airliner was circling, there was no need for him to detonate at that time. He could wait the minute or so it would take for that pilot to maneuver his ship over the empty terrain north of Yangzhou. "I'll wait until they get over the northern sector.''

"Not over the ravine?'' Fei asked, surprised.

"No.'' Qi had just changed his mind about detonating the bomb while the airliner was over the Chungdreichu ravine because he decided that he wanted to retrieve the remnants of the war games computer after all—it was the software they were after, not the hardware, and Qi thought that they might be able to salvage that software package if the wreckage wasn't scattered too badly.

"But the orders said that the airliner must be totally destroyed,'' Fei said tentatively. "Perhaps that could be interpreted as meaning that we should scatter the wreckage as much as possible, that the Chungdreichu ravine would be the most appropriate spot.''

Colonel Qi looked at his subordinate with marked disdain.

"Your assignment is to carry out *my* orders, not to interpret the ones I've received," he said angrily.

"Yessir. Sorry."

Qi glanced out at the small black spot on the distant horizon that was the airliner, then down at the portable detonator on his desk. The portable detonator was an exact duplicate of the one that Kao Wei had carried aboard the airliner, and as such, it resembled more a computer than the electronic bomb detonator that it really was. Because of that, the keyboard strokes required to make the machine execute a signal for instantaneous detonation were quite complex and required several sequential moves. Yet Qi knew what those necessary moves were by heart, having studied the handwritten charts extensively.

"They're passing abeam the end of the runway, the landing gear is down and the flaps are partially extended," Fei said, his eyes still fixed to the binoculars. He had no intention of saying anything negative to the colonel, no intention of getting him angry again. "I estimate another sixty seconds."

"I'm ready. Let me know when the target is ten seconds away from being directly over the open fields to the north. That should allow enough time for the falling debris to hit the ground with a proper trajectory. Then as soon as the airliner impacts into that open field, you and I will *personally* go to the wreckage to retrieve that war games software."

"Yessir."

"Ten seconds from that point, no more, no less," Qi repeated. He knew that he had to state his orders carefully and concisely because he knew that he was dealing with basically nothing but fools—even Peng Ming was now acting like an old and frightened woman—. . . *airliner must be totally destroyed . . . absolute first priority . . .*—Peng would wither in embarrassment when he discovered that Qi had not only carried out his orders, but had also managed to save the war games software, too.

"Forty seconds."

"Continue." Even without binoculars, Qi could now easily see all the elements involved in the action through the dusty window of his office. On both sides of the runway were the army vehicles, the fire trucks and ambulances, the columns of armed soldiers. Against the featureless grey background of the overcast cloud conditions above them, the airliner appeared to the naked eye as hardly more than a speck, an annoying insect that was basically no different from any of the countless thousands of insects that had flown through Qi's office window throughout the years. Just like many of those winged annoyances that Qi had been forced to deal with in the past, he intended to smash this particular insect into oblivion with a few quick movements of his hand.

"They're northeast of the field, wings are leveling; they'll be over the open fields to the north in thirty seconds."

Qi nodded, then glanced down at the portable detonator. Suddenly, something nearby caught his eye. "Wait—what's this?" he bellowed.

"Sir?" Fei dropped the binoculars from his eyes, stepped back and looked down at what his commanding officer was pointing at. It was a disconnected cable that was lying catty-corner across the desk, the electronic fitting on its end dangling over the edge like a fishing lure ready to be lowered into a lake. "That cable?"

"Of course this cable!" *Idiots! Fools!* "Didn't you tell me that we needed to be plugged into an external power source for extra range!" While he spoke, Qi had already picked up the plug end of the dangling cable and held it over the portable detonator while he looked for the proper receptacle to plug it into—it had obviously somehow become unplugged. He should have suspected as much, that the lieutenant would somehow screw things up, would leave an important detail undone! He would have Fei's ass for this. "Where the hell does this damn thing go!"

"That cable?"

"Of course this cable, you idiot! Stop repeating yourself!" Qi was shouting now while he searched frantically for the place on the portable set to plug in the external power source. *Incompetent buffoons, every one of them!* There was another cable protruding out of an outlet on the back on the unit's black plastic case, but Qi assumed that this second cable was for other things. The disconnected cable was unquestionably the power source cable since Qi could see the opposite end of that dangling wire plugged into the electric outlet on the adjacent wall.

Lieutenant Fei stammered out a few incoherent sounds, but then finally regained his composure enough to speak. "No, stop! That cable doesn't matter—just leave it alone!"

"Doesn't matter?" Qi stared at his assistant with a combination of belligerence and astonishment. "Why doesn't the external power hookup matter? You said that we needed it for extended range, didn't you?"

"Because it's a *backup* cable, nothing but a spare, an extra that I had ready just in case something happened to the primary cable!" Lieutenant Fei had begun to shout back, his raised voice filling the small office.

"Extra?"

"Yes. This," Fei said as he hurriedly grabbed a second cable and waved it in the colonel's face, a cable that was still plugged into the unit at the one end and into an electric outlet on the opposite wall at the other. "This is the external power cable that we're using! This cable is working perfectly!"

"Damn!" Qi quickly pushed the thoughts of his own error out of his mind and laid his hands on the detonator's keyboard. He concentrated on what he'd have to do next to send the signal. "Where is the airliner right now?" Qi asked, although he guessed that it had already flown somewhat past the open fields, past the ideal spot for the detonation.

"I . . ." Fei picked up his binoculars and scanned the quadrant to the north of the airport. He saw nothing. The lieutenant quickly realized that the delay caused by the colonel's foolish question about the extra cable had probably caused the airliner to fly past the point they had been waiting for. Fei scanned further to the west. Yet he still saw nothing.

"Where are they, dammit!" Qi had begun to bellow in anger once again—he had already managed to put aside the fact that it had been his own mistrust and arrogance that had been the cause of the delay. Qi was now on the verge of punching in the proper detonation code anyway, without accurately knowing exactly where the airliner was. It was only his years of discipline, of his carefully ingrained reaction to follow the prearranged plan of battle whenever possible, that caused Qi to wait as long as he did.

"I . . . don't see . . . maybe . . ." Even though it was against his better judgment, Fei swung his binoculars back to the east. Suddenly, the image of the airliner appeared. "I've found them!" In the distance was a tiny dot etched against the grey clouds.

"Where?"

"Northeast!" The target was now on the opposite side of the airport. It was headed the wrong way! "Send the signal now! Quickly!"

"Here it goes," Qi answered.

But even while he heard the colonel finishing his keystrokes to detonate, Lt. Fei Xiaotong knew that it was already too late, that the signal from the portable unit could not reach out far enough to set off the onboard bomb. For whatever reason, the airliner had turned abruptly away from Yangzhou during those few moments while they were arguing and was now at least five kilometers from them. That was simply too far from them for the limited range of their portable detonation equipment. Unless the airliner turned back, there was no way they could carry out their assigned task to detonate the airliner's onboard bomb from where he and Col. Qi Shui were standing.

"Where are we going!" Barbara Jennings asked as she rushed up to the cockpit. She could see the looks on their faces that told her something was drastically wrong, but she had no idea what. "What's happening?"

"Look." Flight Attendant Kathy Davis pointed down to the message on the center console data link screen, the message that had told them that there was another bomb onboard.

Barbara read the message quickly, then looked up at Kathy. "I don't understand."

"Dad thought we were headed into a trap," Charlene Jennings volunteered from the copilot's seat. She glanced over at her father, who was still intent on his flying, his attention totally focused on the immediate problem of getting them as far away from Yangzhou as quickly as they could.

"Ron, *please*, let's go back and land." Barbara surprised herself by what she was saying, knowing full well that it was purely her emotions talking—she had been within a few hundred feet of seeing herself and her family safe again, and now that sense of safety had been taken away. This time, by her own husband.

"Can't land at Yangzhou . . ." Ron Jennings was breathing heavily, his face was pasty-white and his hands were trembling. Clearly, the decision to abandon the approach and landing at Yangzhou had been the toughest decision of his life. He was now showing the strain of it.

"But why? If there's another bomb onboard, that's even more of a reason for us to get down right now!"

"No!" Jennings took one hand off the airplane's throttles and wiped away the cold sweat from his forehead. The airliner was bouncing around even more than it had been, a combination of the wind-induced turbulence and the increased speed that Jennings was flying the airliner at. The indicated airspeed needle had jumped up fifty knots, and he intended to get it up even higher in his attempt to get away as quickly as they could.

"Why, goddammit! Answer me!" Barbara grabbed her husband's shoulder and shook it to get his attention—something that she obviously shouldn't have been doing with him trying to fly the airliner at the same time. Before she came to her senses and let go of her own accord, she found her hand being forcibly removed from Ron's shoulder by the teenage boy, Steven, who had stepped up beside her.

"Stop that. Don't make it any harder on him. He's the only one who knows how to get us down. Let him decide what to do next." Steven looked around the cockpit at the others. "If he says we've got to get out of here, then that's what we've got to do."

"Charlene, take the wheel," Jennings commanded as he tried to turn slightly in his flight chair to face the others.

"I can't, not now. Not this close to the ground." Charlene could see that they were within two thousand feet of the surface, and at this airspeed, the ground below them was hurtling past at a faster rate than she would ever have dreamt possible. It was nothing like the little Cessnas and Pipers that she flew. "I can't do it."

"Yes, you can. Take the wheel." Jennings looked up from his daughter with pleading eyes, all the color drained from his face. He was having some kind of attack right at that moment, his heart was beating irregularly, he could feel it. "You've got to," he said as he slumped a little lower in his flight chair but somehow managed to hold onto the control wheel and keep the airliner pointed in the proper direction.

"Dad!" Charlene took the copilot's control wheel tentatively in her hands as her father's fingers slipped from the wheel in front of him. Suddenly, she was immersed in the job of flying and she concentrated on that, pushing her concerns about her father out of her mind. Flying this fast, bouncing through the turbulence, the airplane seemed stiffer, more apt to go off on its own, less stable than it had been. But even though she was rougher on the controls then she had been earlier, Charlene saw quickly enough that she'd be able to at least keep the wings level and keep the airplane headed straight in the direction that her father had intended.

"Ron, what's happening?" Barbara pulled her husband's limp body back in his seat and looked at him. He looked like hell, he was trembling all over, and he was totally covered with sweat. "Oh, my God, are you . . ."

"I'll be all right," Jennings answered to cut her off. "Let me rest, get my strength back." He closed his eyes for a few seconds; he could feel both Barbara's and Kathy's hands on him, holding him up, keeping him as comfortable as they could in the flight chair.

After what seemed like no more than a brief instant or two, Jennings opened his eyes again. To his surprise, the scene out the window had changed completely, from the gently rolling hills around Yangzhou to the flatter plains of what must be the coastal region. Beneath them and to the left, a maze of small rivers was running parallel to their flight path. "How long did I have my eyes closed?"

"Five minutes," Kathy answered. "Maybe more."

"God." Jennings sat further upright in the captain's seat.

"How are you feeling?" Barbara asked. Both women still had their hands on him and both were still watching him carefully. His cold sweat had stopped, and there was some color back in his face.

"Better. I'm sure of it." The headache had returned, but the nausea, trembling and cold sweats had stopped. Jennings glanced over at Charlene, who was concentrating on the flying. She was, he could see, doing a good job at keeping them on a steady heading and just beneath the base of the overcast clouds.

"Okay, just don't rush things, take it easy." Barbara took her hands off Ron and took a half step backward as she continued to watch him.

"I'll be okay."

"Kathy explained to us what you realized about the bomb." Barbara gestured toward the data link message that was still printed on the center console screen. "What you said makes good sense. Blanchard must have been working with someone at Yangzhou. The airport at Yangzhou is where the hijack operation must have been run from. If there's another bomb onboard, then the people down there would be the ones to have the ability to set it off. There's certainly a good chance that you're right. We could have been walking into a trap."

"That's what I figured, when I saw the news about another bomb but no hijackers onboard. I know that we were so damned close to a landing, but the chance that . . ."

"You had no choice, we understand that. You'll get us down okay. I know you will."

"I will." But what Jennings failed to add was that he hadn't figured out how yet, that he had no idea where he would take them now that they had turned away from Yangzhou. He had no charts and no ability to navigate. Unless they stumbled onto a suitable airport in the very near future, he imagined that he might even need to put the airliner down in an open field—a hell of a risky maneuver for all of them, but one that he had little option of getting around.

"How's the fuel situation?" Kathy asked.

Jennings glanced at the fuel gauges. "An hour's worth, more or less."

"That gives us time."

"Yes." While he thought about it, Jennings decided that if they hadn't found an airport within thirty minutes from now, he would pick out the biggest farmer's field he could find and make a crash landing while they were still under complete control and still producing engine power. That was the only smart thing to do. "Okay, everyone, keep your eyes open for any kind of airport, even if it's something small where I might have to . . ."

"Dad, look!" Charlene Jennings pointed at what she had just spotted out the left front: a swooping formation of three fighter jets had suddenly appeared, curving in toward them on a gradual intercept heading, the exhausts from their engines tracing straight black lines that were silhouetted graphically against the grey overcast background.

"God Almighty, no." Jennings watched in horror as the three fighter jets came relentlessly toward them. If the pilots in those fighters were part of Blanchard's hijack scheme, then Ron Jennings knew damn well that everyone onboard the airliner would be dead within the next sixty seconds. There was no way he could prevent it.

Wally Poel was so tired that he could hardly see straight. He leaned against the back wall of the Trans Continental dispatch office in San Francisco, the coffee cup still trembling in spite of the fact that he now held it with both hands. The hot, black liquid sloshed over the edges of the cup and dripped down onto the floor. Poel didn't notice; his eyes were locked to the red light at the front of the room, the brightly glowing red light that indicated that Flight 42 was still flying, still connected to the data link.

"Incredible, isn't it?"

Poel turned to the man beside him. Senior Vice President Chuck Reckson had a stack of telephone messages jammed in his shirt pocket, his tie was loosened and his suit jacket had long since been taken off and laid across the command desk. Reckson was pointing toward the data link light at the front of the room, but Poel ignored the man's reference to it. "The incredible part is that you don't look like an ad for men's clothes, you look like an ad for ulcer medicine."

"What?"

Poel knew that he was getting punchy, that he was hardly making sense anymore. "Never mind." He glanced across the dispatch room at Byron Stark, who, at least from a distance, appeared no different than he had nine hours earlier when this nightmare had begun. That, too, was incredible.

"Can you believe that 42 has turned *eastbound,* that they're headed *out* of China now?" Reckson shook his head in disbelief; he never would have accepted it, had he not read the automatic data link readout himself a few minutes before.

"I can't even guess what's going on," Poel answered in a flat, drained voice. The last automatic status messages from the airliner had shocked him, too.

"Nobody can guess because it doesn't make any sense." Reckson paused for a moment, then began to say something that he'd been meaning to. "Incidentally, that was a brilliant idea you had to send the data link message to the cabin unit." Reckson turned to face the red light on the front wall again. Like a bright beacon on a stormy night, the red data link light had become a continual focus of attention to all of them.

"Yeah, brilliant," Poel answered sarcastically. "So fucking brilliant that I let the first eight hours go by without thinking of it."

"Brilliance is relative. Compared to us," Reckson waved his hand around the room, allowing his gesture to pause for a moment in the direction of where Byron Stark was standing, "you were like lightning. None of us could figure out what you were talking about even *after* you began explaining it."

"Is that a vote of no-confidence in my lucid explanations?"

"That's a vote of confidence in your innovation, your clear thinking, your *dedication.*"

"And my magic?"

"Your magic, too." Reckson put on a weary smile to match Poel's—they were both nearly exhausted, both at their wit's end because of the never-ending changes and complications to the fate of Flight 42. Reckson took a half step closer to Poel in order to share a confidence. "Listen," he said in a low voice, "I don't know at this point exactly how relevant that last data link message you sent was, whether what you did had any ultimate effect on the outcome of whatever's going to happen to 42. But what I do know for certain is that you sure as hell *tried,* that you did everything humanly possible to give assistance to the passengers and crew on that airplane."

"For whatever good it might do, we're still trying. I've got the engineering and load control departments trying to work something out on that lower device business."

"Good. I've got to give you credit, you keep plugging away."

"Don't forget to give Byron credit, too." Poel turned from the vice president to look across the room at Stark for a moment—the man was strutting across the dispatch floor, waving a sheaf of papers in his hand as if they were writs from a king.

"Give Byron credit?" Reckson glanced up at Stark, then turned back to Poel with a puzzled expression on his face. "Why? For doing what?"

"For being Byron Stark, for being the final prod that got me working just a little bit harder."

"Oh. I see."

"Yeah. Every time Byron said *no,* that made me want to say *yes* just a little bit more. When Byron said that there was nothing left for us to do, that made me absolutely certain that there must be *something,* some way that we could help those people."

"You were right."

"Maybe, maybe not." Poel nodded toward the command desk where a stack of messages was piled. "I did manage to communicate with 42's cabin data link and did try to send a message to the cockpit. Right after that message to the cockpit went out, 42 turned eastbound again. But that could be just a coincidence."

"It could be. On the other hand, perhaps your message got through to the cockpit and it gave the pilots some information that they needed. Remember, the people in the rear cabin are telling us that they can't get forward because of the electrified debris, that they don't know what's happening or why. All they've told us is that they suspect that there's another bomb onboard, that lower device thing. Regardless, the information you tried to send to the cockpit data link could turn out to be very important."

"I sure as hell hope that they're wrong about another bomb," Poel said as he allowed his eyes to drift back to the red light in the front of the room. It was still brightly lit, still indicating that Flight 42 was in one piece. Wally Poel began to silently pray that the data link light would stay illuminated just a little bit longer, until the flight crew managed to find some place to safely land the crippled airliner. *What in God's name could be happening out there?*

18

From his lead position in the three-plane formation, Capt. Sun Heng knew that he would have a panoramic view of their approach toward the intruder that they had been ordered to intercept. The spy plane that they had been following at a discreet distance since it had penetrated Chinese airspace a quarter hour before was now evidently attempting to escape after photographing secret ground facilities around Yangzhou. Ignoring orders to land and surrender, the intruder—no one knew for certain what country the airplane had come from— was trying to put to shame China's ability to protect its own boundaries. Capt. Sun Heng was amazed that these foreigners would attempt to get away with so brazen a plan. There was no doubt in his mind that he would be able to stop them.

Gaoyouhu Lake was behind them now, with the highway to Yiling just off to their right. They were flying below the heavy overcast, no more than a few hundred meters above the terrain. As Sun had announced on the interplane communications channel a short while before, their flight of three would come in together in a single sweeping attack. The quickly briefed plan he had decided on was for them to fire one missile each when he gave the signal, thus assuring instant and total destruction of the intruder while maintaining a spare missile apiece if anything was to go wrong.

"Safety switches off, automatic missile guidance mode set," Sun ordered the two other aircraft. At the same time, Sun flipped the appropriate switches in the cockpit of his own F-6 fighter jet to get his armament—two K-13A missiles—prepared for the attack. "Jin one-nine and two-zero, are you armed and ready?" Sun transmitted as he followed the engagement rules of the pre-attack checklist.

"Roger, one-nine armed and ready."

"Two-zero, armed and ready."

Satisfied that the missiles were prepared, Sun glanced to his right. The aircraft closest to him, Jin one-nine, was positioned correctly. But the second aircraft, Jin two-zero, was too far back and slightly too low. "Two-zero. Move up and into attack position."

"Roger, two-zero." Sun watched while the furthest F-6 responded obediently. His aircraft, Jin one-eight, continued to maintain its heading, altitude and speed toward the radar target that he was tracking. Sun glanced over his shoulder and saw that the three fighters were leaving a smoky trail as they hurtled over the farmland below. He wondered for an instant if anyone on the ground was watching them, if any of the workers in the fields realized what he was about to do. Probably not. But Sun knew that he would soon be getting all the recognition that he needed: a medal for this at the very least, and possibly even a promotion. Sun looked down at his radar screen again. The escaping target that they were pursuing was still twelve kilometers away.

"Engagement in four minutes," Sun announced to the others on his interplane communications channel. In order to make this mission as failure-proof as possible, Sun had elected to have his group fly slowly and steadily, moving in toward the target at an even tempo, stalking their prey like a wolf would a lamb. "Beginning a slow climb. Keep your eyes open."

"Roger."

"No change in closure rate. Target is ready."

"Understand," his wing man responded.

Satisfied that they were ready, Sun flipped the switch on his radio and changed from the interplane communications channel on his single communications transceiver to the frequency for home base. "Jin one-eight and flight are less than four minutes from engaging the target. Request verification of orders to proceed with combat plans."

"Permission to proceed is verified," the radio from their home base at Yangzhou crackled back, the dull and emotionless voice filling Sun's headset. "The intruder aircraft has refused all attempts to communicate on established international frequencies. You are ordered to use maximum available firepower to eliminate the subject aircraft as quickly as possible. This intruder must not be allowed to escape beyond the border."

"Roger, I copy that the orders for combat engagement are verified." Even through the electronic filtering of the secure military frequency and the background hiss of static in his headset, Sun had recognized the voice as that of Col. Qi Shui, the commanding officer of his squadron. "We will report back when the mission is accomplished."

"Good luck," the radio voice replied.

Sun changed his radio transmitter back to the channel for interplane communications again. "Jin one-eight is back on interplane frequency." He glanced down at his radar again and watched the bright green blip on the screen as the distance between them lessened. "The combat orders have been verified. We are two minutes from the firing point," Sun announced to the other two aircraft in his group. "Anyone see anything yet?"

"Negative."

"Not yet."

"Okay, they should be at one o'clock, slightly above us." Sun fiddled with the controls of his intercept radar—the 97th Tactical Air Squadron had been relegated to older airplanes and older electronics, nothing like what the 123rd at Ningbo had. Still, Sun could make this antiquated radar set work well enough if he was careful with it. "Ninety seconds to the firing point. The target remains at one o'clock, slightly above us."

"There it is!"

"Where?"

"One-thirty, just below the overcast, tracking eastbound."

"Roger." Sun scanned the sky ahead of him for a moment before he spotted the target himself. It was a tiny black dot against the grey clouds, although it was growing rapidly in size as they closed the remaining distance between them. "Get ready to fire, but not before my command." Sun steered his snub-nose F-6 fighter slightly to the right to line up with the target. *This is going to be a duck shoot.*

"Jin two-zero has a positive missile lock-on."

"Jin one-nine also."

Sun saw from his own instruments that his missiles, too, had acquired enough of a signal from the intruder to guarantee a direct hit. "Roger." With every passing moment it was more apparent that the airplane they were targeting was a large one—a bomber perhaps, or maybe one of those converted Russian transports that were used for reconnaissance by Vietnam and Afghanistan. That would be just like one of those countries, to try something this damned stupid. Sun would teach them a lesson that their generals would be talking about for quite some time. "Seventy seconds to the firing point."

Although Sun still wondered why he had been ordered by Colonel Qi to remain at least fifteen kilometers in trail of the target during their initial pursuit after the spy plane had first crossed the border, Sun had followed that order explicitly and done exactly that. Because of the distance they had maintained at that time, this was now the first visual contact they would have with the target. "Prepare to fire in forty seconds."

"Roger, Jin one-nine."

"Understand, Jin two-zero."

Sun watched the silhouette grow. The morning light was dull grey because of the overcast, and the fact that the target was flying directly eastbound helped shadow it even further to wash out whatever visual distinctions Sun might normally see. They were at a distance of five kilometers now, closing slowly, just about to reach optimum minimum distance for a zero-tolerance shot with their K-13A missiles. "Five seconds."

A jet. Very big. Modern. As hard as he tried, Sun couldn't quite make out the markings of the airplane against the background that he was looking at. Nor, for some reason, had he been asked to—which, in itself, went contrary to all their normal methods of interception. But he already had his orders, so he put that aspect of the operation out of his mind. "Ready . . ."

All at once, the target turned. It made a sharp break to the left and, at the same time, began to climb rapidly. The maneuver itself posed no problem to the ultimate combat firing solution because such feeble attempts to throw the pursuers off were easily within the programmed parameters that the K-13A missiles would be able to track. Destroying the target would still be nothing more than a dull exercise, a proverbial duck shoot.

But the new angle between them and the target did cause Captain Sun to clearly see the target's shape for the first time. In addition, he could now make out the markings on the side of the target's fuselage and tail section. *An airliner!* For the first time since the intercept began, Capt. Sun Heng realized what kind of airplane he was about to destroy.

"Disarm—disarm!" Sun shouted into his radio to stop the two other aircraft in his flight from deploying their missiles. In big print along the top of the window line was the name of the airline—Trans Continental—in large English letters. On the transport jet's tail was an American flag! "Don't shoot, I repeat, do not shoot. Return missiles to safe status."

"Roger, Jin one-nine. Missiles are safe."

"Jin two-zero also."

"Jin flight, follow me." Capt. Sun Heng took a deep breath to calm himself, then rolled his F-6 fighter hard-right and watched as the other two jets in his flight followed. What he had to do now was to get away from this American airliner—which had just disappeared into the base of the solid overcast above them—to avoid any chance of an inadvertent collision. "Jin flight, begin descent now, to three hundred meters. We are returning to Yangzhou." He then flipped the switch on his transmitter to call his home base.

Captain Sun knew that he had to immediately report back to Colonel Qi that there had been a colossal, nearly disastrous error by someone at headquarters. What must in fact be an off-course American civilian airliner that had somehow blundered across the Chinese border had nearly been turned into an international incident of the greatest proportions. That could have been an even worse disaster than what the Russians had committed against the Korean airliner a few years earlier—something that everyone at the 97th Tactical Air Squadron had been carefully briefed to avoid at all costs.

The more he thought about it, the more Capt. Sun Heng felt that he might very well be getting that medal and a promotion anyway, after the upper staff found out what he had done. "Home base, do you read Jin one-eight?"

"Roger, Jin one-eight. Has the mission been accomplished?" the voice from home base replied.

"Negative, we have broken off contact."

"What?!"

"Please, Colonel Qi. Let me explain."

"Hold on."

"God Almighty." Max Berger gripped the armrest of his seat tightly as he rode through the increasing forces of the tight turn and rapid climb that the airliner had suddenly begun. "What the hell is happening?"

"I don't know." Flight Attendant Fred Lyle glanced out the window on his right. "We're entering the clouds. What are the pilots doing?"

"Running."

"Huh?"

"We're running away from something, trying to be evasive. That's my guess."

"Yes. Makes sense. Did you hear what they said across the aisle," Fred added as he pointed to the passengers a few rows back who were sitting on the left side. "Did you hear what they saw?"

"Three jets." Max had also heard them and the others on the left who were shouting about the approaching formation of airplanes—the first ones they'd seen since they'd left Los Angeles. But when the airliner turned away and rapidly climbed into the clouds, the cabin voices suddenly fell silent. "Do you think we could be running away from those three jets?"

"There's no way to tell. Maybe."

"Yeah." Max glanced around the cabin. A few of the

passengers were shouting, some were crying again, but most of them weren't saying a damned thing. They were all in shock at the sudden turn away from an airport a few minutes before, and now this. "Maybe we're wrong. Maybe there are still hijackers up front."

"That's possible. I sure as hell hope not."

"Or maybe it has something to do with the message we sent on that data link." Max gestured toward the galley, a few feet in front of where they were sitting in the rear end of the airliner. "Maybe the pilot figured out that we were headed into some kind of trap."

"I don't know." Before Fred could add any more, the two-tone chime of the data link sounded again. He unbuckled his seat belt and moved toward it, being careful to keep at least one hand holding firmly onto something as he steadied himself through the jolts of turbulence caused by the wind and clouds. By the time Fred had opened the access door to the data link, Max was standing beside him in the galley.

"We're breaking through the clouds, we're on top of the overcast again," Max said as he pointed toward the small galley window. A flood of bright sunshine was pouring through the window as the last of the grey clouds fell away beneath them. The ride suddenly got smoother, too.

"He's leveling out." Fred could feel the floorboards pitch down to a level attitude and could hear the engine power decrease from their climb to cruise setting.

"Never mind that. What's the message?"

Fred keyed in the access code. The data link message began to print on the small display screen beneath the keys.

TO FLIGHT 42/CABIN UNIT. UNABLE TO GET ANY RESPONSE FROM COCKPIT. AUTOMATIC READOUT IN-DICATES THAT YOU HAVE TURNED EAST AND HAVE INCREASED SPEED AND ALTITUDE. WHAT IS HAPPEN-ING? POEL/SAN FRANCISCO DISPATCH.

"What should we say?"

Fred did not answer the man standing beside him; instead he punched his reply into the keyboard.

TO SAN FRANCISCO DISPATCH. WE HAVE NO IDEA. WE SAW THREE AIRCRAFT JUST BEFORE WE ENTERED THE CLOUDS TO CLIMB ABOVE THE OVERCAST. WE WILL USE THIS TIME TO ATTEMPT TO LOCATE THE OTHER BOMB AGAIN, THE "LOWER DEVICE." LYLE/ FLIGHT 42 CABIN UNIT.

"Locate the other bomb? Is that what you think we should try to do now?" Max asked as he watched Fred hit the appropriate keys to transmit the data link message to San Francisco. "We couldn't find it before."

"I know, but we should keep trying." Whether or not the pilots up front knew that there was another bomb onboard seemed to be an almost academic point—if they were going to keep flying, Fred knew that he had to find that bomb or at least try to. He glanced over at the hijacker's portable computer screen, which lay on an adjacent seat.

The small hard-plastic case of that portable computer was lying face-up. Although it was still switched off and its grey face was still totally blank, in Fred's mind's eye he could clearly see on it that last computer message—a message that had come as such a damned shock to him. *SIGNAL CLEAR; AUTO-SEQUENCER DISARMED* was what the screen had read for the first few seconds after he had turned the portable unit back on. Then, suddenly, the words on the screen had gone to something far more ominous before Fred hurriedly shut the portable unit off again: *SIGNAL CLEAR; UPPER DEVICE DISARMED, LOWER DEVICE ARMED.*

It was then that he and Max knew for certain that there was still another bomb onboard, and that this bomb had the potential for being armed and, most probably, being detonated. All it would take would be another one of these portable units somewhere to execute the commands. Even though they had checked the rear cabin and the passengers thoroughly to verify that there were no more portable units around, Fred had no idea if there might still be one up front in the first-class area or the cockpit.

"Do you still think that this lower device can be exploded?" Max asked. The two of them had talked that idea over at great length—and with great secrecy, too, in order to keep a full-scale panic from developing in the rear cabin. If the survivors back there even suspected the possibility of yet another bomb, there would be no predicting how frightened, how wild, how violent they might become.

"Who knows?" Fred paused. "Yeah, I think so." He looked around the cabin anxiously, wondering where in God's name this second bomb could be. Maybe it didn't even exist, he prayed, although he realized that thinking like that was probably too good to be true. It was the kind of thing they could put out of their minds with an airport beneath and a landing imminent, but not anymore.

"Since we're obviously not going to be on the ground very soon," Max said as he pointed at the galley window and the view of the solid overcast cloud deck a few thousand feet below, "we should keep trying to find this other bomb. Makes sense. But we've got to be careful as hell not to give any indications to the passengers that we're looking for another bomb."

"Right."

"And what the hell we're going to do with it if we ever do find another bomb, I'm not so sure."

"We'll worry about that when we get to it." Fred was going to look under all the passenger seats again—the thought of the under-the-seat bomb on that TWA flight out of Rome a few years back came to mind—even though they had searched nearly every square inch of the cabin pretty thoroughly during the last few hours. Fred had taken just a few steps from the galley when the two-tone data link chime sounded. He wheeled around, punched in the acknowledgment code and waited for the message to appear.

TO FLIGHT 42/CABIN UNIT. ENGINEERS SUGGEST THAT LOWER DEVICE MIGHT BE IN CARGO BAY WITH CHECKED BAGGAGE. CARGO MANIFEST SHOWS MOST BAGGAGE IN AFT BAY. ACCESS TO AFT BAY CAN BE ATTAINED BY REMOVING FLOORBOARDS IN AISLE, ADJACENT TO SEAT ROW 35. THEN FORCE SEAM IN CARGO BAY PLASTIC LINER FOR ENTRY. POEL/SAN FRANCISCO DISPATCH.

"Let's go," Fred said. He picked up a crash axe from its

holder on the side of the galley, then turned into the aisle and headed aft toward row thirty-five.

"What do we tell the passengers when they see us ripping up the damned floorboards?" Max whispered. He could see already that any number of heads were turning in their direction; it would be no more than a handful of seconds before the entire coach cabin knew that he and the flight attendant were attempting to get access to the cargo bay below.

"Tell them that we're looking for wires to splice the cabin-to-cockpit interphone with," Fred said as he picked up the carpeting around row thirty-five and began to inspect the seams in the floorboards.

"That doesn't make any sense."

"So what?"

"But what if they don't buy it?"

"Then I'll tell them that I'm looking for my bags."

"Huh?"

"I'll tell them that I'm desperately in need of clean underwear."

"Once again, you are absolutely correct." Max Berger pushed the carpeting aside and began to work at the task of separating the floor seams above the aft cargo bay.

Col. Qi Shui stomped on the wheel brakes of his F-6 fighter, bringing the aircraft to a sudden halt on the ramp at Yangzhou. Ahead of him, waving his arms wildly, was Lt. Fei Xiaotong.

Qi pushed the button to raise the canopy of his fighter jet as Fei ran directly toward him. As soon as the canopy began to rise, the inside of the F-6 filled with the shrill, irritating noises of the jet's twin engines. "Has the airliner crashed?!" Qi shouted above the din as Fei scampered up the internal steps built into the side of the jet fighter. Qi was hoping that somehow his problem had been miraculously solved for him.

"No." Fei leaned awkwardly into the small cockpit as he hung onto the tiny handrungs just below the raised canopy.

"Then what do you want!" Qi bellowed before Fei could add any more. "We have no time to waste!"

"Take this!" Fei shouted. He thrust a small plastic sack toward the colonel.

"What is it?"

"Batteries."

"What?"

"Replacement batteries for the portable computer," Fei said above the noise of the jets. "I just realized that the batteries inside the unit might be weak. I didn't replace them before because we were using external power," Fei explained as best he could from where he hung precariously on the side of the fighter.

"Will the batteries inside the unit work?" Qi demanded to know.

"Probably."

"Then get off, you idiot! You've wasted enough of my time already!" As soon as Fei had dropped to the tarmac, Qi lowered the canopy of the F-6 and then pushed forward on the throttle. With the wing swinging rapidly around and missing the lieutenant's head by no more than a meter, Qi taxied hurriedly to the end of the runway at Yangzhou.

Qi glared at the plastic package of spare batteries in his hand, then shoved them into the top pocket of his flight suit. *Idiot.* Qi then glanced over his shoulder, at the backup portable computer sitting beside him—crammed into the corner behind the switches for the aircraft's generators and electrical circuitries.

As he continued to taxi toward the runway, Qi allowed himself to fume even more. *That fucking Sun Heng, I'll hang his ass.* Yet even though he wanted to, Qi knew that there was nothing he could do to Captain Sun, since the man had simply used common sense in not firing his missiles at what was obviously an airliner. *Damn.*

Once the airliner had gotten out of range of the portable detonation transmitter at Yangzhou, Qi's first thought was to simply have the three airborne fighters in his squadron shoot the airplane down. *Just a horrible mistake, a foul-up.* If Qi pretended that he had no idea that this was an American airliner—that he had somehow never gotten the official word about the hijacking—then he could order the shooting.

Qi realized that he might then be subjecting himself to a court-martial for not following the proper intercept procedures that called for positive target identification, but he imagined that Peng Ming could use his influence to lessen that charge. Shooting down the airliner "in error" was exactly what Qi had attempted to do—and his plan would have worked perfectly if Captain Sun had not recognized the target just moments before he launched his missiles.

Right after Captain Sun radioed the news that he had broken off the attack, Qi still considered ordering the flight to reverse course, intercept and shoot the airliner down anyway. If he was forceful enough and gave them a direct order, they would most probably comply. But giving that order would make his own eventual escape from prosecution absolutely impossible. There was no excuse whatsoever for him giving an order to shoot down an airplane that Qi had been pointedly told was an unarmed American transport. For a few desperate moments, Qi thought that he had run out of options.

If only I hadn't seen that damned extra cable! Qi cursed himself for being so close to the ultimate solution a short while back, and, of course, cursed Lieutenant Fei for allowing a deceptive cable to be so near to the real one. For nearly two minutes the airliner had been in view directly outside his office window and Qi's fingers had been poised over the portable computer's keyboard. By now the smoldering wreckage would have been spread across at least ten-square kilometers of desolate land, and most probably, Qi would have been able to find the war games software too. Instead, that moron Fei had allowed that American pilot to turn away undetected. Once the airliner had gotten a measurable distance past the edge of the airport boundary, it was simply too far out of range for the portable computer to send the detonation codes.

Too far! But now Qi realized something else, too—that his problem was not one of *how* to destroy the airliner, but simply one of *where* to destroy it from! Although he could no longer bring the airliner back to him, Qi had realized that he could get the same results by carrying the portable detonation transmitter out to the airliner!

"Roger, Jin zero-one is cleared for takeoff," Qi transmitted as he began his roll down the long west runway at Yangzhou. Within half a minute he was airborne, in a hard

right turn to an easterly heading, the F-6 fighter climbing into
the base of the overcast with its engines locked at full power.

Qi turned on his aircraft's intercept radar and aimed it
straight ahead. While he adjusted the set, his F-6 broke
through the tops of the overcast and into the clear sky above,
the blinding morning sun directly on his nose. Qi ignored the
sun and concentrated instead on the sweeping green lines of
his radar set as he picked up the first impulses from what he
assumed must be the airliner that he was after. *Thirty-six
kilometers, straight ahead.*

Qi then punched several buttons on his tactical display and
watched as the F-6's onboard weapons system did its job of
determining the intercept solution. After a few moments, the
answer flashed on his screen: if this airspeed and closure rate
were maintained, the weapons system predicted that interception would occur at a point eight kilometers inside the Chinese coastline, which was well inside Chinese territorial airspace
limits.

Reaching behind him for the portable computer, Qi laid it
in his lap. While he continued to steer his F-6 directly toward
the target, he got himself ready for the final phase of the
operation. When he got within the necessary three-kilometer
range of the target, Col. Qi Shui would punch in the proper
codes and detonate the airliner's onboard bomb. Then, as far
as everyone would assume, it would appear as if the hijackers
of this American airliner had simply gone crazy and committed mass suicide. *Perfect.* The final event to end this unfortunate incident would occur in six more minutes, at the very
most.

19

It was too horrible to accept, yet impossible not to. With her hand laid against his neck, Barbara Jennings could feel the clamminess of her husband's skin, the cold sweating, the weakening beats of his pulse through the artery that was just beneath her fingertips. ''Keep your head back,'' Barbara kept repeating as calmly yet as positively as she could, knowing full well that she was giving useless advice. ''Stay quiet. You'll be all right.''

But Ron Jennings hadn't heard a word of what his wife had said. He lay slumped back in the captain's flight chair, his body limp, the fragmented thoughts that flashed through his mind nothing more than a series of disjointed memories, hopes and fears.

At that moment, the vision that was going through Jennings's mind was of the polished brass ship's bell that Barbara had bought him for Christmas last year. In one instant he was looking at it on his boat, in the next it had suddenly turned into the head of a sea monster that was moving directly toward him, its scaled and discolored body slithering back and forth across the only avenue of escape. That surreal vision, in turn, transformed itself into a bottomless pit that Jennings was being pushed toward by a fierce wind from behind, his legs stumbling out from under him as he pitched forward toward his certain fall.

As he continued to hallucinate, Jennings felt his body sail over the edge of the imaginary abyss, then tumble through the black nothingness of what he knew must be the entrance to hell itself. Faced with that, Ron Jennings suddenly began to sob out loud, the incoherent noises coming up through his throat in spasms as he struggled to catch his breath with what little strength he had left.

"Stop it!" Flight Attendant Kathy Davis held on to Ron from the other side of the flight chair, her hands wrapped tightly around his left arm and shoulder as she tried to steady him, to keep him from pitching forward into the flight controls. "Stop it!" Kathy shouted again, her own words rising above Ron's hysterical, delirious sounds. He had begun to flail around awkwardly in his seat, and Kathy was struggling to contain him—and contain herself, too, because she was on the verge of crying and screaming herself.

"Hold him, don't let go." Barbara leaned forward to increase her leverage, and as she did, Ron's right arm swung out and knocked her backward. But she had put herself in a good position to keep her balance and her husband had hardly any strength left in him, so the initiative stayed totally with her: in just a few seconds she had grabbed his arm again and held it down, forcibly keeping it away from any of the crucial aircraft controls that surrounded him.

"Mom, help him. Please." Charlene Jennings glanced sideways from the copilot's seat toward where her father sat and her mother stood next to him. She was making a nonsensical, irrational plea for her father's safety and well-being because there was no possible way that she could help him.

"I'm trying!" Barbara was attempting to stay calm, but she could tell from the sound of her own voice—it seemed hollow and far away, as if it belonged to someone in the cabin, not to her—that she was losing it. *He's dying. Please, God, no.*

Charlene hardly heard her mother's answer; instead, because she couldn't stand to watch her parents a moment longer, she turned quickly back to the flight panel in front of her. Even before her eyes took in the meanings and trends of the gauges, she sensed that something was going wrong with the airplane again. Airspeed was now a little lower and dropping, while altitude was a few hundred feet too high.

Charlene pushed forward on the 787's control wheel in order to get the airliner back to the position that her father had told her to keep just before he passed out. But in her haste and fear, Charlene made the inputs with the control wheel far more violently than was necessary.

"Be careful!" Barbara shouted as the airliner pitched rapidly down in its pursuit of Charlene's instructions through the flight controls. Barbara's stomach seemed to rise up into her throat and her feet nearly left the floor. She continued to hold onto her delirious husband with both hands, now as much to steady herself in the pitching airliner as to protect him and keep him from falling into the flight controls.

"Be steady. You can do it." Steven Stidham was standing directly behind Charlene's seat, with both his hands firmly anchored to the top edge of the copilot's flight chair, his fingers brushing against Charlene's back as she moved around in her seat in an increasing display of near-panic.

"No—I can't!"

"Yes, you can."

"Not anymore! Someone else has to do it. Please . . ." Charlene was crying, her eyes were filling with tears. She could hardly see the gauges on the flight panel, and the view out the cockpit window—the brilliant white overcast beneath them, the sun directly in their faces, the cloudless blue sky above—was becoming nothing but a hazy blur. "Help me . . ."

"Just keep doing what you've been doing. You're doing a good job. You've got to do it, there's no one else. You've got to give your dad a chance to recover." Even Steven could see that her father was in bad shape, but that was something that none of them would allow themselves to think about for even an instant. Her father *had to* recover, because he was the only one onboard who could land the airplane—that was what Charlene had told them over and over when she first took the controls, and that was what they all now believed because even flying straight and level had become nearly too much of a job for her.

"I can't do it, it's too hard!" Charlene was fighting with the control wheel now, making inputs far too late, far too excessively, or not at all. That was causing the airliner to jolt from side to side unmercifully, and its nose to repeatedly wallow up and down.

"I'll help you." Steven leaned closer, his head bare inches from Charlene's. "I'll read the gauges to you, just tell me which ones you want to know about. You can watch out the window." Steven had seen enough of her flying to tell that the airplane was basically kept straight and level by positioning it in relation to the tops of the cloud deck and keeping the wings and nose on an even keel. That was the obvious first priority, although the stuff on the instrument gauges also seemed to matter too.

"Airspeed and altitude! These two gauges!" Charlene stabbed a finger at the only two instruments on the complex panel that meant a damned thing to her. "We need to keep the airspeed at two hundred and fifty, the altitude at eight thousand." That was what her father had told her. What she didn't know was how far those figures could vary before they were in absolute danger—and now with her father unconscious there was no way for her to find that out. She had to keep the airliner as close to those numbers as she possibly could. "Tell me if we begin to get away from the right airspeed and altitude!"

"How far away?"

"I don't know!" Charlene was nearly crying again as she continued to wrestle with the flight controls.

"Calm down, I'll figure it out." Steven began to read the flight gauges out loud while Charlene concentrated on working the controls to keep the view out the window reasonable. At first they still wallowed around the sky just as much as they had been, but then the airliner began to settle down, to fly correctly again—the measured patterns of Steven's voice as he read off airspeeds and altitudes seemed to settle Charlene down a bit. "Altitude and speed are very close to the numbers you asked for," Steven said.

"Are they staying close?" Charlene resisted the urge to

peek at the gauges herself and concentrated instead on the view out the cockpit window.

"Close enough," Steven answered in a firm, reassuring tone.

"Let me know if I begin to drift off again. If all I have to make are small corrections, I'll be able to keep us steady."

"I know you can." Steven kept his own eyes glued to the flight panel, concentrating on his job of watching the flight gauges, although his thoughts were now on something else. It had become more than obvious to all of them that Charlene's father—the man in the captain's seat who seemed to be on the verge of dying—was their last chance, their only chance to survive. "You keep holding the airplane level until your father can take over."

Charlene took a few breaths to steady herself a little more, then took one hand off the control wheel for a brief moment to wipe away the residue of tears that was smeared across her eyes and down her face. "Okay. I'm okay now . . . I'm sure I can hold it." Charlene could feel Steven's hand lying against her back. His touch was reassuring. The boy was a few years younger than she, but he was strong and smart—strong enough to give her courage, smart enough to make her believe in herself again. "Mom, keep working on Dad," Charlene announced in a voice more positive, more assured. "I'll be able to hold the airplace straight and level until he revives."

"Good," Barbara answered. "We'll be all right," she said without much conviction. She was trying not to sound negative, but as she glanced to her left toward Kathy, she saw a look in the stewardess's eyes that must have been a direct reflection of her own. As their eyes locked, the two women subtly acknowledged between themselves that they now shared the certainty of one single and horrible concept: no matter what they said or what they did from that point on, it was an apparently indisputable fact that Ron Jennings was on the verge of death.

In addition to that, both women also understood and conveyed between themselves something else: that when Ron died, then everyone else onboard the airliner would die soon thereafter. Charlene didn't stand a prayer's chance of landing the airliner—that was obvious enough—and the rest of them were even less qualified to get it down than Charlene was. If and when Ron died, all of them would die when the airliner's fuel supply ran out or when something else happened to upset their status quo.

"His breathing is getting worse," Kathy said in a voice too low for anyone beyond Barbara to hear. "More labored. Erratic." Kathy closed her eyes and dropped her head a few inches forward, laying it lightly against Ron's shoulder, the dampness from his shirt brushing against her face and mixing with her own sweat and tears.

For just an instant, Kathy had the flash of a memory of having done exactly that—her head lying gently against his shoulder while he sat in the airliner's captain's seat—any number of times in the past when she and Ron had flown together. It was a memory that seemed a literal lifetime ago.

A lifetime ago. It almost seemed to Kathy as if it were someone else's life that she was remembering now or, more accurately, that the memory was from her own life but from a time when she was a totally different person. That person was the someone that she had never wanted to stop herself from being.

No matter what else happened to her, Kathy knew now that the time she had spent with Ron years before was the basis of most everything that still meant a damn to her—and anything that would ever mean a damn, for that matter. Kathy's hands were wrapped tightly around Ron's arm, and she could feel the life in him ebbing out like a slowly receding tide.

"He loved you a great deal, didn't he?" Barbara said, also in a very low voice, as she took one hand off her husband and laid it gently on the back of the young stewardess's bowed head. Barbara's fingers stroked through the long strands of the woman's blonde hair. "I know he did," she continued without waiting for an answer, her voice soft, sincere and without the slightest hint of acrimony. "And I can see that you loved him, too. Very much."

Kathy slowly tilted her head up. She raised her eyes, then looked at Barbara. "Yes." A fresh flow of tears had formed, and they had begun to trickle slowly down Kathy's cheeks. "Yes, we were in love," she answered in a choked voice.

"You're right, I loved him very much. I know that he loved me, too. But he didn't love me as much as he loved you."

The two women remained in deep silence, their eyes locked on each other, their hands laid gently on the man whom they both loved so overwhelmingly. The airliner continued flying eastbound above the solid overcast of brilliant white clouds, directly into the bright morning sun. They were all headed toward an unthinkable destiny that was, at the very most, only a short period of time away.

Col. Qi Shui dealt with the flight controls of his F-6 fighter in a cursory, automatic manner, most of his attention being focused on the portable detonation computer that now lay in his lap. The F-6 continued due eastbound, directly toward the target on the aircraft's intercept radar. *Eight kilometers straight ahead. Two more minutes.*

Qi watched the green sweep line of his tactical display radar as it pulsed twice more across the target, confirming the distance and altitude between him and the American airliner. At this rate of closure, Qi would be within the three-kilometer range of his portable detonation device while they were still well inside Chinese airspace—the omens of good fortune were finally unmistakable, the final solution to this nightmare of theirs was only moments away.

Qi glanced outside the bubble canopy of his fighter jet. The cloud cover beneath him was impenetrable and it stretched in all directions unrelentingly—which meant that there could be no witnesses from below to what was about to happen. That was also an excellent bit of good luck since it meant one less potentially complicating possibility—witnesses on the ground—done away with.

Qi peered straight ahead through the jet's windscreen, to see if he could spot the airliner itself. But it was still slightly too early for that, especially considering that he needed to look directly into the sun. *Very soon, get ready.*

The portable detonation computer on his lap was still shut down, its display screen a blank grey. Qi intended to keep it shut down until he was within useable signal range, on the outside chance that Lieutenant Fei—his fool of an assistant—

had been correct about the weakening battery power of the set.

Qi took his left hand off the F-6's throttles and pressed it against his left breast pocket. Inside that pocket, the plastic pack with its four spare cylindrical batteries could be felt. Even though Qi was certain that he wouldn't need any spare batteries to execute this single detonation signal, touching them was a reassuring gesture.

The green sweep line of his tactical radar screen passed across the target once more, showing it at a distance of five kilometers, slightly to the right and a few hundred meters above the F-6. Qi looked out at the spot where the radar was telling him.

There they were! A black dot against the brilliant glare of the morning sun; even as he watched, the marked contrast and resolution of the target had increased dramatically. The American airliner was flying straight and level, emitting only the thinnest trail of smoke from its engines, the long wings beginning to sprout visually from opposite sides of the visual dot as the F-6 continued to close in on its target.

Qi sat mesmerized for a few seconds before he finally sprung into action. One more time he checked his tactical radar, this time to be certain that they were still a considerable distance from the boundary of Chinese airspace. According to the screen, the city of Rudong had just passed beneath his aircraft and the coastline lay a few kilometers ahead. *Detonate just offshore, so there will be no wreckage to find, no evidence to be concerned with.*

Since there was no longer any opportunity to salvage the war games software out of the wreckage—Fei's idiocies with the extra external power cable had ruined that chance—Qi knew that he might as well bury all the evidence beneath a few hundred meters of sea water. Detonating over the ocean, he would still have a buffer of fifteen kilometers of Chinese airspace before the American airliner reached international waters.

"Jin zero-one, do you read Yangzhou?"

"Roger," Qi replied to the hollow, metallic voice in his headset. He recognized the voice as that of Lieutenant Fei, transmitting on a secure and scrambled voice channel; even if he hadn't recognized the voice, Qi knew that Fei was the only person at Yangzhou who knew where he was going and knew what frequency he would be monitoring. "Go ahead with the update."

"I have verified that the secondary orders from Lieutenant General Peng Ming are being complied with by all squadrons, that no other units are being allowed up to intercept the target. You are alone."

"Excellent." While he spoke, Qi kept his eyes on the airliner. The big tail and horizontal stabilizer had grown from an indistinct blur to clearly visible appendages, and it was now possible to see a faint stripe of color along the side of the fuselage. "What about the American fighters?"

"Fifteen kilometers offshore, just outside the airspace boundaries. A flight of eight, orbiting. They are directly in line with the target's flight path, they obviously know that the target is headed toward them."

"The target will never get that far." Qi clicked off his transmitter and glanced up at the airliner. The sun glinted off the wings and the metal trimwork around the engines, and he could almost make out the row of passenger windows along the fuselage. *Less than three kilometers.* Qi turned his attention to the portable detonation computer in his lap.

Turn the unit on, key in the code. Qi fumbled with the small slide switch on the side of the unit as he watched the grey viewing screen. Letters that indicated a quick self-test filled the screen, showing that the unit itself was completely operational. A single discrepancy did appear at the end of the test cycle, a discrepancy labeled *internal batteries weak— strength 2.* Qi ignored that message, since he was confident that he had more than enough power remaining in the unit to use it once from this close a range.

Qi then hurriedly hit the keys to acquire the signal. He needed to get the portable unit into the detonation loop with the airliner's suitcase transmitter and its bomb. Qi watched as the unit's grey screen filled with letters again:

SIGNAL CLEAR; UPPER DEVICE DISARMED
LOWER DEVICE ARMED

Seeing that he had reacquired radio contact with the airliner's onboard bomb and that he had now established a useable link with it, Qi quickly typed in the proper detonation code. *Now.* Without even glancing up at the target again, Col. Qi Shui pressed the final button in the prescribed sequence; in one swift move he had sent the electronic signal to the American airliner that would detonate its onboard bomb.

20

When Flight Attendant Kathy Davis finally realized that there was something she could do to help the situation, she lunged for the access door on the cockpit's side console to get at what she needed. "Here!" Kathy pulled the emergency oxygen mask from the molded plastic pocket in the side console at the left of the captain's flight chair, then hurriedly pressed the inflation button that expanded the mask's straps and turned on its oxygen flow. "Get this on him."

"Let me have it." Barbara Jennings took the mask from Kathy and pulled it down across her husband's head. Barbara had, just the moment before, finished wiping away the residue from around Ron's mouth from when he had begun to gag and vomit, a small quantity of bile retching out of him and puddling on the floor around the captain's flight chair. Ron was moaning now, rocking his head slowly from side to side, his eyes still closed.

"Watch him. We've got to get that oxygen mask off if he begins to vomit again."

"I know." Barbara wiped away the sweat from her own forehead, then glanced behind her. Charlene was still in the copilot's seat, with Steven standing directly behind her giving advice and encouragement.

The airliner was flying more or less straight and level at that moment, although they had experienced several loss-of-control excursions in the last several minutes. Even though Charlene had announced that she would be able to keep them flying normally until her father could take over, every few minutes she seemed to suddenly run out of confidence and give up completely. On each of those occasions, it had taken overwhelming shouts and continuous pleading from all of them—and some actual physical prodding from Steven—to get Charlene to take hold of the wheel again. In each case, she had managed to barely get them out of the deteriorating situation just as things appeared to be going beyond salvation. Charlene was clearly at the very edge of her limits.

"We can't hold out much longer." Kathy glanced beyond Barbara, directly toward Charlene. "We can't expect her to keep this up. She's losing it, letting it go too far," Kathy said in a low, frightened voice.

"Do you think you should try to do the flying?" Barbara asked.

"No. Charlene's the only one who's got half a chance to keep us straight. I wouldn't know where to begin."

"We've got to just hang on until Ron comes around. That's our only chance."

"Right." Kathy looked at Ron Jennings, his features drawn and white, the oxygen mask strapped snugly around his nose and mouth. Over the last several minutes Ron had periodically opened his eyes, although none of those times did he seem to know where he was or why. At that moment his eyes were tightly shut and he looked like hell, but his breathing did seem to be improving, growing deeper and more regular, the movements of his chest now a regular rhythm of expansion and contraction.

"His breathing's much better with the oxygen on, there's no question about it," Barbara said as she correctly guessed what was on Kathy's mind. "Definite improvement," she continued, trying to sound clinical and uninvolved—as if everyone's life wasn't on the line. "The oxygen was a damned good idea."

"It's our last chance."

Reluctantly, Barbara nodded her agreement. "I know." Barbara had one hand lying on her husband, the other on the young stewardess's arm. She squeezed hold of both of them, in a gesture meant to take encouragement and give it, too. "We'll make it, if we can get Ron to help with the landing. As soon as he comes around, we'll dive below the clouds and land in whatever open field we can find." Barbara had phrased her comment as a statement, although it was really more of a question since she had very little idea of what they could do or how they should do it.

"We might be over the ocean by now."

"Don't say that, I don't want to think about it." Barbara turned and looked behind her. "Have you found the fuel gauges?" she asked Steven, getting back to the question she had asked him a few minutes before, after she remembered that Ron had been concerned about the fuel, too.

"Yes." The teenage boy pointed at several dials on the bottom of the center instrument console. "The fuel gauges are here, I've been watching them. They're low, but not at the very bottom. At the rate they're dropping, my guess is that we should have at least thirty more minutes of fuel." Steven paused, then pointed to his left. "Is he almost awake?" he asked, hardly wanting to look at the man whose life they were unquestionably depending on. Charlene's father was still slumped down in the captain's flight chair, an oxygen mask on him, his eyes closed.

"Yes, I think he's coming around," Barbara lied. She squeezed her hand against her husband's shoulder, her bandaged arm against the top of the flight chair. *God, please, let him wake up. Don't let us die like this.* "Anytime now, I'm sure of it."

"The engines are holding up, too. That's good news." Kathy pointed to the vibration gauge for the left engine, as she tried to add something else that was positive. Listing the things that were going right for them was the only way that they could stop themselves from panicking completely, the only way they could find the strength to stop themselves from giving up and letting the airplane crash.

"What do you mean?"

"The vibration problem, don't you remember?" When Kathy had remembered about the engine vibration problem a few minutes earlier, it had taken her quite a while to even find the gauges on the flight panel. When she had found the vibration gauges, it took her another minute to figure out what they were saying as she tried to remember what Ron had told her. Finally, Kathy put it all together and realized that at least the vibration problem had gone away, that the needles showed that both of the engines seemed to be working normally. "Ron thought that we might have to shut down one engine."

"Right. I remember." Barbara looked at where Kathy was pointing; she saw the needles, but none of the readings made the slightest bit of sense to her.

"Obviously, now we don't have to."

"Good." Barbara pushed that thought out of her mind, it was way beyond her ability to handle. Instead, she turned back to watch her husband. "He's moving again," she said in a flat voice, not wanting to invest too much emotion in what might be another false alarm.

"Yes." Flight Attendant Kathy Davis leaned over, held her breath and watched Ron Jennings closely. She, too, was afraid to get too excited, afraid to make too much out of Ron's random movements. Still, he now had more of his color back, his breathing was more regular, he was definitely looking better. *God, I beg of you. Please bring him back to us.*

Col. Qi Shui played gently with the flight controls of his F-6 fighter, keeping its relative position to the airliner the same, as he watched for the first signs of the airborne detonation. *A few seconds. The bomb's relays need to close.*

Yet as he stared straight ahead, nothing changed. The American airliner continued to fly eastbound, its wings level, both its jet engines producing a thin black line of exhaust thrust. *Nothing!* Qi forced himself to look away from the target; his eyes dropped down to the portable detonation computer in his lap.

Qi could hardly believe what he saw. In the center of the

grey screen, in addition to the original lines of text that had shown a workable connection to the airliner's onboard bomb, was something new. It was an added phrase—one that Qi had stubbornly refused to acknowledge as any more than remotely possible, even though Lieutenant Fei had told him otherwise.

SIGNAL CLEAR; UPPER DEVICE DISARMED
              LOWER DEVICE ARMED
              TRANSMITTER POWER
              INSUFFICIENT

Batteries! That damned Fei had been correct after all; the portable computer's internal batteries were barely strong enough to receive the signal being sent from the airliner's suitcase bomb—but they were too weak to transmit the detonation codes across the three kilometers between them and the airliner's cargo bay! Qi realized now that he had been dead wrong, that *strength 2* had not been enough power to transmit a message to the airliner—it had been barely enough power to even receive the incoming signal from the airliner's onboard radio bomb!

Qi knew that he had to change the batteries *now*, and he was suddenly very thankful that Fei had handed him the spare batteries just before he had closed the jet fighter's canopy at Yangzhou and taxied away. Qi touched the left breast pocket of his flight suit to assure himself that the spare batteries were still there. They were. Yet before he began changing to the spares, he couldn't stop himself from frantically punching the buttons on his tactical radar. The Chinese coastline had already passed beneath them, and Qi now had less than fifteen kilometers of airspace remaining before he would run headlong into the American fighter jets that were orbiting over international waters. *Hurry!*

Qi grabbed the flight stick of the F-6 with his left hand, then reached across with his right hand and yanked open the zipper on the breast pocket that contained the batteries. His fingers fumbled with the long, thin cylinders until he finally managed to grab them and pull them out. *Fei should have changed these before, damn him!*

There were four of the cylindrical batteries, a complete set, and now all Qi had to do was transfer the spare batteries to his left hand, flip over the portable detonation computer, open its rear case, then slip the old batteries out and replace them with the new ones. *Fei should have done this before I left Yangzhou!*

Yet the job of transferring batteries was hardly an easy one in the cramped confines of a jet fighter. Worse yet was the fact that Qi needed to keep his own aircraft under control, that he couldn't use both his hands freely to get the old batteries out and the new batteries in.

Two in, two more to go. Qi glanced up at the airliner—it was still flying level, approximately three kilometers ahead. *A few more seconds.* Qi hurriedly looked back down at the portable computer, and it was at that moment that it happened.

The two additional fresh batteries, plus the four old ones, were crammed into the palm of his left hand—the hand which was also wrapped lightly around the flight stick. A slight motion from the fighter caused Qi to respond with the control stick, and when he did there was a sudden pressure against the palm of his hand. That slight pressure caused all six of the long and thin batteries to pop out. The batteries then fell to the floor of the jet fighter.

Aiyyh! Qi had yelled out loud to himself in astonishment and horror as he watched all six of the batteries—the new and the old alike—roll across the floor and slide somewhere beneath his flight chair! He looked around frantically, moving in his seat as much as his cinched-up straps would allow, but could find none of them. Qi looked up at the airliner again, it was still in formation, still headed east; he then glanced at his tactical radar. He had begun to pick up the targets of the orbiting American fighter jets, now displayed as clear targets no more than twelve kilometers from where he was now flying.

Think! Stay calm! Qi knew that he absolutely needed at least two more batteries inside the portable detonator in order to make it work at all—without four in the case, there would be no continuity, no electrical flow, nothing. *Find the batteries!* Yet the more he looked, the more he realized that he had nearly no chance of getting them out from under the complex array of braces, struts and plates that constituted the bottom of his flight seat.

Then Qi realized what the solution would be, although he did so more with his hands than with any level of recognizable thought. His left hand yanked hard against the control stick, and the F-6 fighter responded instantly. In less than a heartbeat, Qi was hanging upside-down in his flight chair, the F-6 rolled on its back. He then continued to jiggle the flight stick back and forth in order to induce more motion to the airframe.

Suddenly, one of the batteries came out from where it had been and fell straight down, hitting the Plexiglas canopy a few centimeters to the side of Qi's helmet. With his left forearm pressed against the portable computer to keep it firmly in his lap, Qi quickly scooped up the battery with his right hand. *Need one more.*

Qi jiggled the airplane's flight stick again. Nothing. Twice more, still nothing. Finally, on his fourth attempt, Qi managed to dislodge two more of the batteries from wherever they had been trapped beneath his flight chair. He quickly grabbed those two off the canopy, then rolled the F-6 right-side up again.

Which ones? Qi looked at the three batteries in the palm of his hand. There were no markings on any of them, so there was no way to tell which were the new ones and which were the old. For no reason that he could think of, Qi decided on the two batteries on the left. He quickly pressed them into the back of the portable computer, then closed the case and flipped the unit over. Qi shoved the extra battery into his breast pocket, then switched on the unit and watched anxiously as the self-test began. After a few moments the error message appeared:

INTERNAL BATTERIES WEAK—
STRENGTH 4

Enough! Qi suspected that one of the two batteries that he had just put into the set was from the old batch, which would account for the slight decrease in power from optimum.

He had no way of knowing whether the additional battery in his breast pocket was new or old. Yet suddenly Qi realized that none of that mattered anyway, that the portable detonation device *was* more powerful now—strength 4, rather than strength 2—so it certainly should be able to easily work within the three-kilometer range, except . . .

Out of the sky ahead, from above him, swooped down the squadron of American F-15 fighters that Qi had been watching on his tactical radar. All eight of the powerful, maneuverable jets came hurtling down out of the sun directly toward him and the airliner ahead. Qi sat immobile for a few moments, not knowing what to do next.

Within seconds, the American F-15's had split into two groups, three of the aircraft maneuvering near the airliner, the other five aircraft joining up alongside Qi. As he watched, Qi saw that the aircraft up front were obviously giving lead, providing the airliner with a path to fly that would undoubtedly take them to Japan and the American airbase on its northwest coast.

The five other American fighter aircraft swept in on both sides and above Qi's F-6. Qi could clearly see the pilot of the aircraft to his immediate right, and as he watched, that American pilot gestured his instructions by pointing down and aft. The five jets of the American squadron were flying a tight box formation around him, with only the area behind and below now open for Qi to maneuver into. *Too many, I have no chance. I cannot fight them.* The American jets were forcing Qi to descend, forcing him to trail much further aft, forcing him to increase his separation from the airliner with every passing kilometer that they traveled. Qi cursed himself as he watched the silhouette of the airliner recede in the distance—a distance he now judged to be at least seven kilometers and increasing.

"Yangzhou, do you read Jin zero-one," Qi transmitted on his secure-channel radio, his mouth dry, his voice cracking. While he waited for an answer, Qi hit the proper keystrokes of the portable detonation computer in his lap. What he saw was the signal that he already suspected would be on the unit's readout screen—a signal caused by the increasing distance between him and the airliner.

```
SIGNAL CLEAR; UPPER DEVICE DISARMED
         LOWER DEVICE ARMED
         TRANSMITTER POWER
         INSUFFICIENT
```

"Go ahead, Jin zero-one. This is Yangzhou."

"Contact the Washington Embassy immediately. Tell them that I am being blocked too far aft from the airliner by a squadron of American fighter jets." Col. Qi Shui omitted any mention of how he had gotten into that situation or why. Instead, he continued to transmit the message that he needed Lieutenant Fei to relay to Peng Ming. "The portable detonation device *is* working, but I am being held out of range. Unless the American jets break off for some reason and allow me to fly closer, I will not—repeat—I will *not* be able to detonate!"

"No, we must!"

"Don't be a fool—this is insane!"

"Wagner, stop it!" American Secretary of State Eleanor Cameron grabbed hold of her young assistant and shook him. "It's too late to turn back, we've got to go ahead with this. Remember the trade issues, that's all that matters."

"No!" Wagner Vanweele looked at the two Orientals in the room, then back at Eleanor. "We're going to get *caught,* for chrissake! We're going to go to prison!"

"That is not true." Ambassador Li Ying-teh raised his hand, a gesture meant to restore some calm to their discussion. Ever since the message from across the Pacific had appeared on the embassy computer screen a few moments before, all four of them had been in near pandemonium over the involvement of the American fighter jets and the apparent flight of the airliner toward Japan. "Nothing has changed, we still have all our cards to play. We have just not had an opportunity to play them yet."

Lt. Gen. Peng Ming stepped forward. "The message tells us that the onboard bomb will function as soon as we do something to allow Colonel Qi to execute the detonation commands." Peng's words had been carefully chosen; he pointed at the computer screen on the rosewood desk, as if he were verifying what he had just said.

"What are you talking about?" Vanweele said, his voice a mixture of anger, fear and dread.

Peng looked directly at the young American assistant. "Even though our people onboard the airliner are obviously no longer in control, they must have done something earlier to cause all of the airliner's radios to fail. That's why the airliner is still totally out of communications. That fact is a very significant development for our plan." Peng wondered how Kao Wei had managed to do something so complex as to cause the airliner's radios to fail, although he doubted that he would ever know for sure.

"Forget that kind of crap—just tell me how we can get your fighter to detonate the bomb!" Eleanor said hurriedly.

"By giving the order once again that you gave earlier." Ambassador Li glanced at the computer screen himself, then back at the American Secretary of State. "Get the American fighter jets to back away, get them to allow Colonel Qi up closer to the airliner."

"On what goddamn pretense!" Vanweele shouted, his booming voice filling the conference room. "This woman is the *Secretary of State*, for chrissake, not the Secretary of the Air Force! She has no *legal authority* to order the Air Force to do a damned thing!" Vanweele ranted on, frightened out of his mind by the single haunting vision of them being caught and sent to prison. Yet he also knew now that he would never find the courage to defy Eleanor directly, that he needed her to lead them both out of this.

"He's right," Eleanor answered nervously. "I'd have to go to the President, and he'd need to give the order to the Air Force. That's how we'd have to do it."

"And what should we tell them," Vanweele added, his voice still loud, angry and frightened. "That we're ordering the U.S. Air Force to back off so the Chinese Air Force can detonate the airliner's onboard bomb and open up free trade! Christ Almighty, you've got to be *reasonable!* They'll lock us up and throw away the fucking *key!*"

"Your assistant has made one good point," Li answered calmly as he ignored Vanweele and concentrated instead on the American Secretary of State. "You do indeed need a justifiable reason to ask your Air Force to back away."

"Damned right." Eleanor stared at the Ambassador, praying that he had come up with something.

"Then we must correct ourselves, must change our thinking." Li was speaking slowly and softly, using all his powers of persuasion to get his point across. *I am too close to allow this to slip past me now. All of China, all of the world will benefit from our actions. I must see it through.*

"Change our thinking?"

"Yes. You have no authority to *order* your Air Force, so you must make a *suggestion*—one that would be quite appropriate to be given by a person of your position."

"I'm all ears. It better be good."

"It is the ultimate concern of an American Secretary of State. It will put you beyond criticism." Li paused for a moment, checked the computer screen one last time, then went ahead with his idea. "A public display of international cooperation, a continued firming up of ties between our nation and the United States . . ."

"What the hell are you talking about?" Vanweele slapped his hand down on the rosewood table, attempting to resist any turn in the conversation. "Don't be a . . ."

"Stop." Li pointed an accusing finger at Vanweele. "Your fears are speaking, not your rational mind. You are so badly shaken that you are not even hearing the words. You are too young and inexperienced to be involved in the destiny of two great nations." The Ambassador glared at Vanweele for a moment, then turned toward the American Secretary of State. "Nothing has changed, except that some Air Force general in Japan has decided that no other aircraft other than his own shall escort the hijacked airliner. That general is acting on his own also, since there could obviously be no ironbound procedures established for this sort of thing."

"Correct." Eleanor nodded; she was already beginning to understand the Ambassador's point. "Our military people in Japan are undoubtedly doing what they consider prudent, nothing specific has come from above."

"Exactly. So when you *suggest* that your Air Force jets back away enough to allow that single Chinese airplane nearer to the airliner—for the sake of the concept of international cooperation, for the sake of a continued display of cooperation between China and the United States in this hijacking situation . . .''

"Public relations?''

"In effect, yes. All you are stressing with your military people is that this unfortunate event has opened up a wonderful opportunity to continue displaying solidarity with China by simply allowing them equal access to the final rescue of this troubled airliner. You will be reminding your military men how cooperative the Chinese have been throughout this ongoing situation.''

"And I'll also be stressing the point of potential loss of face,'' Eleanor added enthusiastically. "A distinct possibility if we allow ourselves to do anything that could be later construed as a sign of reluctance to work with the People's Republic of China. I'll point out to this Air Force general that his operational decision to keep the Chinese airplane isolated from the airliner had the effect of barring a Chinese representative from the final moments of the rescue, even though the Chinese had been completely cooperative up to that point.''

"Well phrased.''

"I will, of course, be *suggesting* that the general change his plan while there's still time—although I'll be *hinting* that any reluctance on his part could later be interpreted by the President and the Pentagon as a rather narrow vision for a person in his position.''

"All of this more than justifiable, from your point of view. International relations are certainly a proper concern for a Secretary of State.''

"Naturally.'' Eleanor nodded.

"When the airliner does explode, we will all feel deep regret that the insane hijackers had inexplicably detonated their onboard bombs.''

"Right.''

"And by doing this we even *further* our basis for complete and open trade. A formation flight of both American and Chinese aircraft alongside the doomed airliner would be the first gesture, the beginnings of the complete and open relationship between our nations.'' Li stopped, knowing that he had said all he could, that he had exaggerated here and there but had basically spoken only the truth. Li's biggest worry was that she might well fall back on the Western notion of being totally concerned over each and every human life regardless of the bigger consequences—the Western concern over that sort of thing had never ceased to amaze him. Li shrugged; he doubted that she would, and besides, he had either convinced her or he had not.

Eleanor paused a few moments, deep in thought. "What do you think?" she finally asked in a low, calm voice as she turned to Vanweele. "Nothing has changed. Not really. The excuse for letting the Chinese airplane up close is reasonable— no one will think anything about my making that suggestion to the Air Force. In fact, now that I think of it, people might wonder why I *didn't* suggest something like that."

Vanweele stood where he was. His eyes were locked to the words on the computer screen, his thoughts were a mass of jangled, conflicting ideas. *Open trade. Throw away the fucking key.*

"Well?" Eleanor said, pressing him. She suddenly knew that she intended to go along with the plan anyway, no matter what he did or said. But Eleanor did want Vanweele to be involved too, if it was at all possible. For an instant she wondered why—was it the sex and some variation on the age-old theme of love, or was it pure power and total control over the destiny of a handsome young man—but then she dismissed that thought as too trivial to be concerned with at the moment.

Vanweele still did not answer. Instead, after several seconds, he turned to face her. Their eyes locked together for quite some time. The beginnings of tears were welling up in the corners of his eyes. *Walk out of here. Right now.*

"Well?"

Vanweele still did not answer her; instead he turned and began to walk away abruptly. But instead of heading toward the conference room door and the embassy exit, he walked in the opposite direction, even further into the interior of the room. Wagner Vanweele now had his mind completely focused on a single idea—the only idea that he would allow to run through his thoughts for the remainder of the duration of this nightmare. *Open trade with China.*

21

Damn! Flight Attendant Fred Lyle had cut his hands several times on the ragged pieces of fiber glass as he worked on breaking through the nonstructural covering that separated the rear cargo area from the airliner's passenger compartment. Fred pulled his hand away from the debris and looked at the gash and the fresh blood that was oozing out of it.

"Don't worry about the cut," Max Berger whispered tersely as he reached down and pulled on more of the fiber glass sections, exposing a bigger area for him and Fred to work their way through. Max then picked the crash axe up and began to hack away at the corners of the expanding hole. "If the second bomb goes off, we won't need to worry about what our hands look like."

"Right." Fred glanced over at Max. His hands, too, were cut and bleeding—even worse than Fred's were. "Workman's compensation . . . sure as hell going to file . . . for both of us . . ." Fred said, slightly out of breath from the exertion. He turned back to the floor area between them and continued ripping away the last of the protective panels that were blocking them from getting into the aft bay. "Are the

U.S. fighter jets still in close formation with us?'' Fred
asked, although he knew damn well that the passengers in the
airliner's cabin would be screaming hysterically if the three
jets in formation around them suddenly left the area.

"What do you think?" Max nodded toward the rows of
passengers with their faces pressed to the cabin windows.
"Those people sure ain't looking at the clouds, I can assure
you."

"Guess not." Fred pulled up another sheet of fiber glass,
and it, too, was smeared with his own blood. He watched the
fiber glass panel crumble in his hands. "Maybe we're nuts
for doing this."

"Maybe. Can't hurt."

"I suppose." Fred took a moment to glance along the
aisle. Everyone but him and Max were firmly strapped into
seats. Dozens of people were talking loudly, excitedly—the
mood in the cabin was still one of fear, but the undertone was
positive now, upbeat, hopeful. Those who were too injured to
sit up and look out the windows were being spoken to by
those who could. "Put a few sophisticated fighters on the
wingtips and everyone feels great. It's really not too logical.
We're still trapped inside this aluminum tube, and the fly-
boys outside can't do very much to help."

"I know." Max Berger glanced to his right, toward the
window where one of the fighters had been visible moments
before. It was still there, its bright aluminum body glinting
magnificently in the bright morning sun. Even from this
distance—the United States Air Force jet was a few hundred
feet away—the American flag on its tail looked more beautiful than anything else Max could have imagined. He could
make out the helmeted head of the pilot beneath the bubble
canopy. "A hell of a sight, though. I've got to say that I'm
feeling pretty good about it myself."

"Me, too." Fred concentrated on what he was doing—he
was nearly through the fiber glass liner now, he expected to
be totally into the aft cargo bay in just a few more moments.
"At least now we know that we're headed somewhere reasonable," he said without looking up at Max. Beneath his fingers
he could make out the first hints of empty space as he clawed
through the last layers of fiber glass.

"This is a waste of time. I don't usually like to waste time." Max, too, had just broken through the last layer of fiber glass, and he thrust one hand into the empty area of the cargo area below. "I'm in."

"So am I."

"Now what?"

"Do you really think this is stupid?" Fred asked.

"I'm beginning to."

"I've go to admit that I am, too." Fred shook his head; a strange sensation of surreal calm had descended on him—and it was a very comfortable sensation, like being beneath a warm blanket on a cold winter's night. "We were probably wrong about another bomb being onboard; we got ourselves excited and jumped to a dumb conclusion. We should put a stop to these pseudo-heroics and sit with our noses against the windows like everyone else, admiring our boys flying through the wild blue."

"Maybe." Max looked around the cabin at the other passengers. Only he and Fred had any notion that there might be another bomb onboard—and that idea was fading pretty fast for both of them, too. The positive mood in the cabin was infectious, which was a reasonable response considering how damn bad things had been before. Even during the periods of wild flying, the recovery and subsequent return to straight and level immediately brought the mood back to one of hope. By this time, everyone in the cabin was expecting to survive, none of them were expecting that they wouldn't get out of this horrible experience alive. "It's pretty tempting to do just like you said, shit-can this exercise and just sit on our asses for the rest of the ride back to civilization."

"Yes." Fred thought about what they were talking over, forced himself to go beyond the obvious. "But if we're being honest, the only thing that's changed for us is this false sense of hope that we're subjected to now. We're high on survival, and we're probably not thinking straight. We should keep doing what we figured out before, when we weren't kidding ourselves quite as much."

"Good thought. I like your style." Max nodded in agreement. "That's pretty much what June used to tell me when I was ready to make some piss-poor business decision—that I should stop kidding myself. Besides, what's the worst that can happen? By keeping this up all we'd be doing is wasting our time, people will call us jerks, and this company of yours will want us to pay for the floor damage.''

"Right." Even though neither his nor Max's heart was in it any longer, Fred suspected that he already knew what they should be doing. "Keep ripping. Use the crash axe on that side over there—we'll need more room if we're going to crawl down to check things out."

"Okay."

"Another upbeat thing," Fred said as he continued working on his side of the fiber glass, enlarging the hole to make it big enough for them to fit through, the sense of urgency in their situation all but gone for both of them. "At least now we know for sure that the world knows about us, they know where we are and what's happening." Fred gestured toward the sight of the jet fighter outside the cabin window.

"Yeah. They know where we are, that's for sure."

"Right." Fred had already thought about that subject—that they could have gone down somewhere over the Pacific last night, without anyone knowing exactly where, without anyone ever finding a trace of where they had crashed. That idea was disquieting enough, but then Fred had also realized that there was *nobody* in the entire world that he particularly cared enough about to want them to know for sure what had happened to him. The man helping him at that moment—Max, a plumbing contractor from San Diego who he had met a few hours before—seemed more a friend to him than any of the other guys from his past. Was something basic in Fred beginning to change, or was it that he was just frightened? He didn't know. "Do you think the hole is big enough?"

"A little more." Max paused; he felt the preliminary telltale motion begin as he quickly looked around the cabin again. "Oh, no! Here we go!" Max felt the airliner begin to wobble slightly, then pitch down.

"Hang on!" Fred grabbed hold of the opening in the floor to brace himself—they had been tossed around wildly several times since they had begun the job of breaking into the aft cargo area—but this time he could somehow tell that this particular bit of irregular flying was going to be relatively mild. The nose seemed to pitch up and down a few times, and the tail wagged from side to side, but the 787 seemed to be back under positive control within just a few seconds of when the wild flying had started. A few people in the cabin had screamed, but it had all ended so quickly that a few others in the cabin had actually begun to laugh soon after—as if this wild flying were nothing but a carnival ride. "People are amazing."

"What?"

"Never mind."

"That wasn't too bad." Max quickly went back to his job of ripping away more of the fiber glass. "Maybe whatever's wrong up in the cockpit is finally straightening out."

"Maybe." Fred hadn't said anything to Max about what it felt like to him—that someone who wasn't much of a pilot was handling the controls, tossing them around, letting the airplane wallow and shake and get away from them every now and then. It was not an idea that he even wanted to entertain. "The hole's big enough. Let's get down there, go through enough lady's lingerie to satisfy ourselves that we've become irrational doomsayers, then get back up here and strap ourselves in for the landing."

"Here we go." Max Berger lowered himself through the hole and into the airliner's aft cargo bay.

"Jin zero-one, do you read Yangzhou?"

"Roger, Yangzhou. Jin zero-one reads you," Col. Qi Shui replied as he pressed the transmit button on his F-6 fighter's control stick. "Go ahead."

The metallic words coming in on the secure communications channel filled Qi's earphones. "An updated message from the Washington Embassy has been received. It is signed by Lieutenant General Peng Ming. He advised that the American fighters have been ordered to allow you access to the airliner. He also advises that you are to execute the detonation code as soon as you are within range of the target. You are then to land at the American base at Sasebo, refuel, then return immediately to Yangzhou. Permission for this landing and refueling has been granted by the American commander of the airbase, all of it approved by the Japanese." There was a slight pause in the transmission from Yangzhou before the final portion of the message came through. "Is there any indication as yet that the American fighter jets are following the orders that have been issued to them?"

Qi glanced outside the cockpit of his own jet. The five United States Air Force F-15's around him were rigidly maintaining their positions: one on either side, one in the front, two above. The closest of the fighters was the aircraft on his right—that pilot was holding to a formation of no more than twenty meters—and he was keeping his head turned toward Qi's aircraft most of the time. "Negative, Yangzhou. No change in the position of the American jets—I am still boxed in."

"Understand," the hollow, synthetic voice from Yangzhou replied. "What is the distance of the airliner? This is a request from the embassy that I must respond to."

Qi glanced ahead. The black dot that represented the airliner was nearly invisible to the naked eye; the dots that represented the additional American fighter jets around the airliner were already too small to be seen. "Stand by." Qi leaned forward and adjusted the settings on his tactical radar. He waited until the green sweep line passed over the targets twice before he transmitted again. "Fifteen kilometers," he transmitted in a flat, emotionless voice that did not indicate how tied up in knots his insides were. *We are doomed, unless something happens very soon.*

"Jin zero-one, can you also verify your position? How far are you from the Japanese coast?"

"Talking will not solve our problems, you idiot!" Qi shouted into his microphone. Inside his flight helmet, sweat was rolling down his face—yet his hands were cold and clammy. "Get them to do something *right now!* There is no more time for talk!"

There was a pause of a few moments before Yangzhou replied. "Jin zero-one, this request is directly from the Washington Embassy. State your distance from the Japanese coastline. I must reply to them."

Qi slammed his hand hard against his tactical radar screen before he grabbed hold of its control knobs and forced its antenna to tilt downward toward the ground below. *No won-*

der we are failing! "Seventy-two kilometers to Japan—are you now satisfied! Will the fools in the Washington Embassy wait until we are overhead the American airbase at Sasebo before they get off their asses to do something!"

There was no reply from Yangzhou.

Qi watched his radar set a moment longer, then looked outside. To his amazement, there was now activity out there. "Yangzhou, the American jets are breaking off!" Qi shouted into his helmet microphone. The F-15's ahead and above him had already peeled away; the pilot of the fighter jet on his right side was motioning toward Qi, gesturing ahead, pointing toward the distant airliner! "I repeat—the American fighters have broken off; they are motioning me ahead to the airliner!"

Without wasting another breath, Qi released his transmit button and slammed forward on the twin throttles of his F-6. He kept his eyes focused outside for the first few moments, watching the American fighters to be certain that they would stay away from him, and also verifying that the tiny black dot in the distance that he was headed for was indeed the airliner.

It was. Within a minute, Qi had gotten his own jet close enough to the target to make out its wide wings and the thin line of exhaust from its engines. *No mistakes this time.*

Qi glanced down at the portable detonation computer on his lap. The unit had already been switched on, the self-test done, the battery condition verified as more than adequate for a close-in detonation, since Qi had used the lengthy delay to replace all the original batteries with new ones. Qi pressed a few keys and watched the words on the unit's grey screen.

SIGNAL CLEAR; UPPER DEVICE DISARMED
LOWER DEVICE ARMED

Everything was ready. By now he was closing in quickly on the American airliner. Qi's F-6 was slightly below the target, and from that vantage point he had a good view of the three additional United States fighter escorts—a silver F-15 on each wingtip, and one in the lead. That lead escort was presumably showing the airliner's pilot which way to head to get to the American airbase at Sasebo. *They will never make it. I will stop them right now.*

The distance between the Chinese F-6 fighter and the target was hardly more than one kilometer. Col. Qi Shui reached down and began pressing the keys on the portable computer that would send the detonation signal to the suitcase bomb inside the airliner's cargo bay.

22

It was dark in the aft cargo bay of the airliner, although not pitch-black. Through the hole in the fiber glass lining above them, Flight Attendant Fred Lyle could see enough to make his way around.

"Nothing over here worth looking at," Max Berger announced in a loud voice from where he stood at the other end of the cargo compartment, the fiber glass ceiling panel a few inches above his head. The area he worked in was cooler and noisier than the passenger compartment, but not uncomfortable. Max picked another suitcase up; it was too light. He put it down and picked up another. That one was heftier. He shook it and felt something heavy inside being moved around. "This one meets the profile."

"Bring it over. I've found two others that do." Fred picked up the two suitcases that he felt were within the limits that they had agreed on—a large, solid suitcase that was heavy and, possibly, unbalanced. More than likely it would be securely locked, too.

"Here." Max stepped into the empty center area beneath the hole in the fiber glass lining, a spot they had cleared of bags a few minutes before. The daylight from above them shone down, although by the time the light reached them it had defused enough to cast everything in deep shadows. "While I was shaking that last bag, I had the sudden feeling that maybe I shouldn't be." In spite of the coolness of the cargo bay, Max was sweating profusely.

"Yes, I had the same thought." Fred knelt down and looked closely at the locks on the bags at his feet. "But we should stick to our first plan. If there's a bomb down here— which we both doubt, I might remind you—it couldn't be too sensitive to the touch or it never would've survived the loading."

"Right. I remember watching those clowns on the ramp at Los Angeles while they were packing us up."

"We don't call them baggage smashers for nothing." While he spoke, Fred was fiddling with one of the suitcases. The lock on it popped open. Gently, he released the clip on the other side, then raised the lid. Clothes. A travel kit, a travel iron. Fred let out a low sigh. "I wish to hell it was a little brighter in here."

"Makes no difference," Max said. He glanced around the dark cargo bay. "We ain't going to find nothing."

"Thank God."

"Right you are."

"Nice of you to say so." With every passing moment, with every additional bag that they searched, Fred was feeling better. Now, he also felt confident that they were going to get out of this thing alive.

"Do you want me to look at any more bags?"

Fred glanced around. He was just about to say no, that it wouldn't be necessary, when he spotted one more group that he thought neither one of them had gone through. "How about that batch over there? You haven't looked at them, have you?"

"No."

"Give them a try. I'll pry open these two locked bags with the crash axe, although neither one of them feel very suspicious."

"Sure thing." Max stepped over the luggage that was in the way, carefully working his way toward the small pile of

suitcases that Fred had pointed at. With every step it grew
darker, since he was leaving the small circle of daylight
behind him. *A waste of time, right, June?* Max said to himself. *I know, dear. I should stick to the plan—it's the only
way to do business. Whatever you say, doll.* Max moved a
few soft-sided suitcases first, then reached for a big, solid bag
in front of him.

His heart stopped. As soon as he picked it up, he knew
damned well that he had found something. *Bomb.* He instantly knew that he had found what they had been looking
for, what they had almost talked themselves out of believing could possibly exist! *God Almighty.* "Fred."

"What?"

"I found it."

"What?!"

"Stand still, I'm coming back with it." Max maneuvered
himself backward, stepping over and around the piles of bags.
He held the heavy, unbalanced suitcase gingerly in his hands.
"God Almighty, this is it. I'm sure of it,. I'd stake my life on
it."

"You are. Be careful." Fred had already pushed aside the
bags he had been working on to make an empty spot for what
Max had found, for what Max had decided was the real thing.
"You're absolutely sure?"

"Yes." Max was breathing hard now, his eyes riveted on
the suitcase. "It's got a big lock on it, too. Just like we
figured it would, and look at this, the name on the tag is
Oriental."

"Stay calm, we've got to stay calm." Fred's hands were
suddenly shaking so badly that he could hardly keep a steady
grip on the crash axe.

"I *am* calm, for chrissake! Open it—hurry!"

"We've got to be real careful." Fred took a deep breath,
then knelt down beside the suitcase. With trembling hands he
forced the point of the crash axe into the lip between the lock
and the suitcase. Once it was wedged there, he attempted to
pry it up. He tried it twice, but neither time could he get the
hardware around the lock to budge. "Shit!"

"Let me have it!" Max knelt down beside Fred. He grabbed

the axe handle and pushed hard. A few seconds later the lock sprung apart.

"Okay. Let me open the lid." Fred unclasped the side latches, then gently lifted the suitcase's cover.

"Jesus Christ, save us." Even in the dull light, Max could see the suitcase contained a very large array of electronics, an antenna, a battery and, at the very center, a large mass of grey putty wrapped in black tape. "The grey putty must be the explosives. What do we do?"

"We've got to disarm it." Fred's voice was surprisingly calm, considering how he felt. What he wanted to do was to put his hands over his head and run screaming out of there as quickly as he could. Instead, he stayed where he was, gawking at the bomb.

"Do you know how to disarm a bomb?"

"I haven't got the slightest fucking idea."

"We've got to try."

"I know." Fred peered into the case, laying his hand first on one part, then on another. ". . . if I could only see a little better . . ."

"Here." Max took out his last pack of matches. As he struck the match, it became more than obvious that his hands were shaking quite badly also. The area around them lit up, the contents of the suitcase now plainly visible. "I'm glad I didn't give up smoking yesterday . . ."

"It's radio controlled, that's for sure. This must be the battery."

"I've heard that sometimes if you try to pull these things apart, that they're rigged to explode right then."

"I've heard that, too." The sweat was pouring so heavily off Fred's forehead and into his eyes that he could hardly see. "We should pull the battery wires off."

"Are you sure?"

"No." Fred wrapped his fingers around the wires that lead from what he suspected was the battery to what he suspected was the radio portion of the suitcase bomb. Yet he made no move to disconnect them.

The match in Max's hand burnt down. He quickly relit another, both men remaining motionless until he had. The bright light from the new match illuminated the contents of the suitcase bomb again. "I'm not sure that we should pull off any wires."

"Well, I . . ."

"Look!" Max pointed directly at a small red monitor light that he had spotted in the center of the radio portion of the bomb. What made the tiny red light so suddenly visible was that it had just flashed on, its ominous color flooding over both their faces as they stared directly at it. "God!"

Flight Attendant Fred Lyle responded to the sudden glow of the bomb's red light by shutting his eyes, then impulsively yanking back on the wires that his fingers were still wrapped so tightly around.

"Jin zero-one, they have received the signal!" the voice on the secure communications channel transmitted. "Signal terminated! They have verified the reception of that message at the Washington Embassy!"

Col. Qi Shui sat motionless in his F-6 jet while the voice of his assistant at Yangzhou squawked excitedly into his earphones, the man's tones artificially flattened by the scrambling and decoding devices that were protecting this transmission from any eavesdroppers. Qi fidgeted slightly in his flight chair, then glanced down at the portable detonation computer in his lap.

The unit's grey readout screen contained a message that was crystal clear, the words that he had for so long wanted to see now etched across it in big, bold print:

SIGNAL TERMINATED

The airliner's suitcase bomb was no longer connected to the orbiting Chinese satellite and, hence, was no longer connected to either his portable terminal or the computer terminal in the Washington Embassy. Qi kept his eyes locked on the sought-after electronic message on his portable computer screen while his hands played lightly with the flight controls of the F-6 to keep the jet fighter flying straight and level.

"Jin zero-one, do you read Yangzhou?" came another transmission from Lieutenant Fei, this one slightly bewildered because of the previous lack of response. "If you read me, answer."

"Yangzhou, I read you," Qi finally replied. With great effort he raised his eyes and looked above him, slightly ahead. There, at a distance of less than one kilometer, rode the American airliner. It maneuvered through the sky majestically, the bright sun gleaming off its aluminum frame. The airliner continued eastbound on its direct path toward Japan— and it was totally undamaged, totally without any signs of an explosion from the suitcase bomb!

"Roger, Jin zero-one, understand that you are reading me. Your mission is accomplished. Refuel at the American base at Sasebo, then return to Yangzhou as soon as possible. Say nothing to anyone while you are on the ground at Sasebo about the explosion of the airliner. Those orders come directly from Lieutenant General Peng Ming."

"Yangzhou, I have a message for Lieutenant General Peng Ming."

"Go ahead with your message."

Qi ran his tongue across his parched lips. *The bomb must have been internally disabled just before the detonation cycle was completed. There is no other explanation.* Qi pressed the transmit button on his control stick. "Inform the Washington Embassy . . ." he said. Qi then paused and, after a few moments, allowed his finger to slip off the control stick's transmit button.

"Jin zero-one, you are breaking up. Say again?"

For several long seconds he sat motionless, watching the coastline of Japan begin to appear on the distant horizon. The layer of clouds beneath them was also beginning to break up rapidly, exposing large areas of the deep blue sea. *There is no hope.* Finally, Col. Qi Shui pressed the button on his control stick and transmitted a brief message to Yangzhou. "We have failed completely."

The good news was that the weather was breaking. Also, there was a coastline clearly visible straight ahead, and Barbara Jennings suspected, shortly thereafter they would be seeing an airport—the one that the United States fighter jet in front of them was obviously intent on leading them to. "How's the fuel?"

"We better get down pretty soon," Steven Stidham answered from where he stood behind the copilot's seat. He glanced at the center panel fuel gauges, forcing himself to look at a pair of needles that were nearly at the bottom of their scale. "There's still a little left, but not much," Steven said nervously.

"Right." Barbara glanced over at Charlene, who was concentrating totally on flying the airliner, keeping the wings level and the nose pointed at where the fighter jet was taking them. "Everyone keep your eyes open," Barbara announced to all of them. "As soon as we see an airport, we should try to land right away."

"How is Dad?" Charlene asked without looking over. A rugged coastline was sliding beneath the nose of the airliner at that very moment; the rolling green hills beyond it were an immensely beautiful sight. "Is he ready to take over yet?" Charlene had managed to keep her courage up because she hadn't allowed herself to believe anything else—her father *would* be ready for the landing, because there was no way in God's name that she'd be able to do it.

"He's just about ready." Barbara leaned toward her husband, who was now sitting upright in the captain's seat. His eyes still had that vacant stare, but he seemed to have more color back, his breathing was more regular, his responses more predictable. "Ron, can you hear me?"

Flight Attendant Kathy Davis was standing on the other side of the captain's flight chair, her arm around Ron to hold him up, the oxygen mask that she had removed from his face a short while ago in her other hand. "I think he can hear us," Kathy said, knowing full well that she wouldn't have allowed herself to believe anything else in any event. "I'm sure he's coming around."

A constant stream of thoughts were going through Ron Jennings's mind, and a good deal of them were directly connected to the preceptions that he was receiving from his eyes and ears. *Barbara. Landing. Fuel.* Jennings blinked a few times, then sat further upright in the captain's seat. He gazed out the cockpit window at the ground below. *Headache.*

Nauseous. Got to land. Low on fuel. ". . . airport . . ." Jennings said, the single word coming out in a low but firm voice. ". . . where . . ."

Barbara knelt down close to her husband on his right side and glanced over at Kathy on his left. The two women's eyes met, and both of them shared the same expression—a mixture of fear and hope. "Ron, we need help," Barbara finally said. "You've got to land the airplane. Charlene doesn't know how." Barbara had said the words without emotion, although she understood too well that she was on the verge of totally losing her self-control. If she did, she knew that Charlene would lose her self-control, too—and then they would all die before Ron would have a chance to take over.

"Yes," Kathy added. "You must land the airplane. Very soon now." Kathy watched Ron's head turn toward her. All at once, she could suddenly see the change in him—his eyes were alive and alert! He was sitting further upright now, under his own power, moving his arms, picking up his head! He *was* coming around, there was no question about it! "Thank God!" Without even realizing it, Kathy had begun to cry; the tears of joy ran down her face.

"I . . . can do it . . ." Jennings blinked a few more times, then looked around the airliner's cockpit. Memories flooded back to him, and for the first time in nearly an hour he understood where he was and why. He glanced over at his daughter in the copilot's seat, and Charlene looked back at him. She, too, was crying now—and Jennings could feel the involuntary pulses she was putting into the control column, could feel the airliner's nose jerking mildly up and down. Jennings licked his dry lips. "Charlene."

"Yes," she answered in a choked voice.

"I need help. Both of us. Together." Jennings closed his eyes for a brief moment; the effort of talking, of thinking, was quickly draining him of what little energy he had left. He opened his eyes again. ". . . need help. From everyone. We can do it."

"How?" Barbara asked. She wiped away her own tears of joy. "Tell us what to do."

Jennings put his left hand on the control wheel, his right

hand on the airliner's twin throttles. "Charlene, keep flying. Feel my inputs. Go with them."

"Yes, Dad." Charlene nodded; she understood what her father wanted—exactly what one of her flight instructors back home would often do. He would ride the controls while she was flying, making little nudges here and there to give her a hint as to what she should be doing next.

"Throttles. Barbara."

"Yes?" Barbara leaned closer to her husband to be able to hear him clearly.

"Put your hand on mine. Follow me."

"Like this?" Barbara laid her hand on top of where her husband's were lying on the twin throttles.

"Yes. More power, forward. Less power, back." Jennings closed his eyes again and took another deep breath. There was a ringing sound in his ears, and he was lightheaded. *Stay alert. Got to.* He opened his eyes again. "Power is airspeed. More power, more speed."

"Should I read the speeds off like I did for Charlene?" Steven asked. He fidgeted where he stood behind the copilot's flight chair.

Jennings nodded.

"What speed should we be at for the landing?"

Jennings looked at the captain's flight panel. He began to study the markings on the airspeed indicator as he tried to remember what Blanchard had briefly mentioned to him so many hours before. "Full flaps for landing. Between one hundred fifty and one hundred seventy." At least that's what he thought he remembered that Blanchard had told him would be a good compromise between being too slow and stalling or being too fast and not having enough runway to stop.

"Got it."

"Kathy?" Jennings turned slightly to his left, until he managed to catch a glimpse of her blonde hair. His arms were tingling now, and he was having trouble moving.

"Yes?"

"Need your hand here."

"On the control wheel?"

"Yes. Follow me, also." Jennings paused to catch his

breath again. "Might need help . . . to pull back . . . on touchdown . . ."

"Right, I understand." Kathy nodded. She could see that Ron's eyes were still alert, but his color seemed to be draining from him. "Do you want any oxygen?" she asked.

"Yes."

Kathy laid the oxygen mask against his face and turned on the valve. She watched him breath deeply a few times as she listened to the hiss of the oxygen flowing through the tube. Finally, Ron shook his head slightly to indicate that he wanted the oxygen mask taken off.

"Look!"

Everyone in the airliner's cockpit glanced up at where Steven was pointing. Ahead, in the distance, the lead fighter had begun an abrupt dive. Beneath that fighter was a large airport, with several crisscrossed long and wide concrete runways.

"Should we . . ."

"Yes!" Jennings sat up as best he could. "Landing gear down!" he commanded to Charlene. "Put down the flap handle. All the way." Jennings shivered violently; he could feel a strange, hollow sensation begin to edge through him from somewhere deep inside. *No. Fight it.*

"Ron!"

"Throttles. Descend." Jennings ignored Barbara and Kathy and Charlene and the boy; instead, he focused totally on the runway ahead, totally on the need to get the airliner established in a stable descent, established at its proper speed and angle for touchdown.

"Too high! We should circle the airport!" Kathy shouted, her hand firmly locked to Ron's. She could feel his dwindling inputs to the control wheel, she tried to help, but she was confused. The airliner began to wallow, its nose pitching lazily up and down.

"Daddy!"

Jennings didn't answer any of them. He pulled farther back on the twin throttles, and he could feel Barbara's hand assisting his.

"Speed, two hundred and ten!" Steven announced in a loud, frightened voice. "Too fast!"

Jennings also felt the airliner begin to pulsate, its nose
hunting laterally across the horizon in periodic swings. He
began to pull backward on the flight controls, and as he did,
he could feel Kathy's response going along with him. She
was helping him, pulling back on the wheel, giving him
leverage where he no longer had strength enough to provide it
on his own. The runway that Jennings was desperately attempting to get them to was five miles ahead, still approximately three thousand feet below them. *Too high, too fast.*
Jennings shivered again, another spasm passing through him.
No. Instinctively, he knew that this would be their only
chance.

"Speed, two hundred!"

Four miles to go. The hollowness inside Jennings was
spreading fast; he felt as if his body might begin to float
away, that he was being eaten alive by something. He tried to
put that out of his mind and concentrate totally on the picture
out the cockpit window, the view of the approach and landing
that everything was now so completely dependent on. Jennings's vision had begun to blur, and there were white spots
beginning to encroach at the sides of most everything that he
attempted to bring into focus.

"Speed one-eighty!"

The wings began to rock slightly, but Jennings could feel
Charlene correcting even before he did. Out of the corner of
his eye he caught sight of the airspeed indicator on the
captain's panel a brief moment before the boy behind him
announced the sudden loss of airspeed that Jennings had felt.
He pushed the twin throttles partially forward, with Barbara
pushing along with him, to stop the negative trend.

"Speed one-forty! Too low—but increasing!" Steven paused
for a moment. "Speed one-sixty!" he announced in a wild,
joy-filled tone when he realized that the disastrous trend had
been caught. "Speed is now stable!"

Three miles. The large painted numbers on the runways
were clearly visible, and so were the crash and rescue trucks
that raced all over the airport, their red lights flashing. Jennings felt his right hand begin to sag off the throttles, but he
also felt Barbara's fingers wrap even tighter around his,
keeping him securely where he needed to be. On his other

side, he could feel Kathy leaning closer to him, her arm nearly an extension of his own, as she helped him push and pull on the control column to keep the airliner's nose exactly where it belonged.

Barbara. Kathy. Charlene. Tears were beginning to well up at the corners of Ron Jennings's eyes, diminishing even further what little clear view he had left of the runway. Two miles until touchdown. *Barbara. Kathy.*

"Speed one-fifty and stable!"

One mile. The giant airliner slid down its descent path toward the broad concrete runway as if it were on hidden rails that would allow no other flight path, its wings rock-solid, its nose steady, its engines producing continuous thrust with the final remnants of its fuel supply. As they finally crossed the edge of the runway apron, Jennings was on the very edge of losing consciousness.

Barbara. Kathy. Yet, through sheer determination, Jennings did manage to forcibly hold on to the final impulses of his conscious mind; he kept his eyes open and he kept his hands responding accurately to the complex array of patterned instincts that would enable him to make a hint of a final input to the control wheel and the throttles. Those small movements allowed the others whose hands were on those controls to understand exactly which way they should be moved, and exactly how much.

Touchdown. Ron Jennings slumped forward in his flight chair just as his daughter began to apply the wheel brakes. At 7:52 A.M., local time, Trans Continental Flight 42 finally came to a complete stop on the United States military airfield in Sasebo, Japan.

Epilogue

Kathy Davis paused at the top of the long set of aluminum steps as she exited the airliner in Daytona Beach, Florida. She took a moment to deeply inhale the late afternoon's warm and scent-filled air, then glanced around at the tall palm trees at the corners of the low white terminal building.

"Can I give you a hand with that, Miss?"

"No, I can manage." Kathy smiled at the airline agent on the steps beside her who had offered to carry down her suitcase. "Thank you anyway." Kathy scooped up her bag and quickly moved down the steps and into the terminal building. Even though she hadn't told them what time she'd be arriving today, Kathy glanced around to be certain that none of the Jenningses had come out to meet her. Naturally, they hadn't.

"Taxi, lady?"

"Please." The ride from the airport was a pleasant one. The taxi driver pointed out a few of the sights, but mostly he remained silent and drove sanely—a change that she could immediately appreciate from her experience with wild rides through Los Angeles in beat-up cabs driven by men who hardly spoke English. *Ron was right, it's a big world with lots of nice places if you go looking for them.* Here, at least, she could make herself understood to the cab driver. "How far is the ocean?"

"Four miles, straight ahead." The cab driver glanced at her in his rearview mirror. "But that address you gave me ain't the ocean—you know that, don't you?"

"Yes. They told me that it's on a river." Kathy remembered back to what Ron had said about his home and dock, and she wondered for a moment if it would look anything like what she had pictured in her mind. She would know soon enough.

"Right. A river, sort of. It's the Intercoastal—you've heard of that, haven't you?"

"Yes."

"This address that you're going to is on the Peninsula, on the Intercoastal side. The ocean will be about a quarter mile east. I take it that you've never been here before?"

"Never." Kathy could have added that she never would have guessed that she would be, either. She had known that Ron had moved to Daytona Beach after he left the airline, but she had pointedly resisted giving that fact any thought.

"Been good weather lately. A high of eighty-four degrees today—pretty good for mid-December, huh?"

"Yes."

"Should stay pretty good for the next couple weeks, right on through Christmas. You staying till then?"

"I think so." Kathy turned away and looked out the side window. Car dealers, fast food chains, commercial buildings of all kinds lined the wide street. Kathy sat in silence and watched the scenery go by. They crossed over a drawbridge and she spotted the Army Corps of Engineers sign that marked it as the Intercoastal Waterway. There were boats on both sides, although none of them looked like the one in the picture that Ron had shown her. The taxi then began to weave around several side streets. The big orange sun was a good portion of the way down in the western sky already, and Kathy watched it reflect brightly off the Intercoastal whenever she caught a glimpse of the waterway between the rows of houses that they were now passing.

"Here we are."

Kathy paid the driver, then waited while he sped away before she made a move toward the house. It was a nondescript brick ranch, neat and clean, with several trim plantings of flowers on either side of the walkway. Kathy stepped up to the door and rang the bell.

Barbara Jennings broke into a radiant smile when she opened the door and saw who was standing there. Without saying a word, the two women hugged each other for quite some time. Finally, they stood apart and both began to speak at once. They laughed, then they started talking in quick, clipped sentences as they each tried to get in more words than the brief few moments together could possibly allow.

They had hardly stepped into the house when Kathy spotted it immediately, through the double-width sliding glass doors at the rear. "It's beautiful."

"Yes, it is."

"It's just like I remember from the picture." Kathy stepped through the sliding glass doors, then up to the dock at the back of the house. She glanced down at the name on the stern of the boat, painted in gold letters against a black backdrop: *Flying Low*.

"Had I told you the name?" Barbara asked.

"No."

"It was my idea. At first, Ron didn't like it. Then he did, very much." The sun was edging closer to the distant horizon. Barbara looked back at Kathy. "How are you feeling? The scar's mostly gone."

Kathy touched her forehead, her fingers touching the bare remnants of what had been a gash and, it turned out, the concussion that had kept her in the hospital. "I feel good."

"You sure?"

"Yes."

Barbara paused, turned around to watch a pelican swoop down into the waterway as it dove in after a fish, then glanced at her wristwatch. "Have you gone by to see Ron yet?"

"No. I thought I'd come here first."

"Do you want to go together?"

"Now?"

"Yes."

"What about Charlene?"

Barbara thought about that for a moment. "She's with friends, she won't be back for a few hours. We can be back before she gets here."

"Fine." Kathy glanced at the boat again, then nodded. "I'm ready."

Barbara drove, and the two of them talked almost continuously during the short ride—mostly about the interviews with government investigators, the press, the attorneys, the incredible discoveries about what had happened and why. They talked at length about Captain Blanchard's involvement in the scheme: the payment to him of a quarter of a million dollars in cash for doing two things: bringing the cabin bomb onboard the airliner so it would get past the security checks, then going along with what the hijackers publicly demanded, that the flight divert to Yangzhou, China.

"Just like the government people said, it should have been just about no risk for Blanchard. Once the hijacking began, all he had to do was take the airplane to the hijackers' destination—exactly what everyone expected him to do."

"It was supposed to be no risk, until the copilot screwed things up for him," Barbara replied.

"Yes."

With every passing mile they spoke less and less, until finally they sat silently and stared at the passing road. Barbara left the main highway, steering down several side streets, then finally drove through a set of double iron gates. She pulled over to the tree-lined curb. "You go ahead. I'll park the car."

Kathy opened the door and stepped out. "Which way?"

"Down there." Barbara pointed. "C-36, on the left."

There were large pines and oaks on both sides of the path. Birds were singing noisily, and from behind her, Kathy could make out the slight murmur of the street noise from the road. But with every passing step, things got quieter around her. Finally, all she could hear was the rustling of the wind through the trees, and the beating of her own heart. Kathy followed the well-marked route, periodically checking out the signs that showed her which way to go.

The headstone was suddenly in front of her, the words jumping out more powerfully than she could have imagined. For the entire four weeks that she had spent in the hospitals—the first two in Japan, the next two in California—she wondered endlessly how the words would look, how it would feel when she first read the message that she still had hardly been able to accept.

The name Ron Jennings was engraved in the granite gravestone, with the date of his birth and the date of his death—the date of Flight 42's landing in Sasebo, Japan—beneath it. Kathy began to weep softly, and did so for some time.

From behind her, Barbara walked up the path quietly. She stood to one side for a moment, then gradually stepped toward Kathy. Kathy turned, her face red, her eyes swollen with tears.

Barbara Jennings and Kathy Davis embraced, neither one of them making any move to step away from the front of the gravestone. Several minutes later the sun finally set below the horizon, leaving scattered rays of light spread across the clear western sky.

"It's time that we go."

"Yes. I guess it is." The two women walked slowly, hand-in-hand, toward the cemetery's exit.

TWELVE MONTHS LATER

Ambassador Li Ying-teh was recalled by the government of China and forced into retirement. He died of natural causes nine months after the Trans Continental Airlines incident, in the city of Beijing.

Lt. Gen. Peng Ming, Col. Qi Shui and Lt. Fei Xiaotong were arrested and tried by a Chinese military court. Lt. Fei Xiaotong was sentenced to a dishonorable discharge and ten years at hard labor. Lt. Gen. Peng Ming and Col. Qi Shui were executed.

Thomas Nicholetti was never apprehended because of a lack of direct testimony from the Chinese and insufficient evidence. He is currently living in Las Vegas with an aging showgirl, where he sells sports cars as a sideline.

Wally Poel was promoted to department director at Trans Continental Airlines, in addition to receiving a cash bonus and an all-expense-paid trip for him and his wife to the International Magicians' Conference in London, England. Byron Stark opted to take early retirement from Trans Continental Airlines, and he is now engaged in the sale of real estate in the San Francisco area.

Charlene Jennings was awarded a scholarship by Trans Continental Airlines to continue her flight training. A confidential memo from the company's president, which is on file in the employment office, has directed that she be immediately hired as a first officer for Trans Continental as soon as she is suitably qualified.

Secretary of State Eleanor Cameron and her assistant Wagner Vanweele were tried and convicted in federal court for violation of civil rights and obstruction of justice, and are serving sentences of eight and six years, respectively, in federal prisons.

Steven Stidham was provided with a full scholarship to a private boarding high school and then the college of his choice, paid for by Trans Continental Airlines.

Fred Lyle resigned from Trans Continental Airlines and began working for Max Berger in San Diego, where they are in the process of creating one of the largest design and installation centers for plumbing apparatus in Southern California. Three months after the Trans Continental incident, Max Berger met a woman whom he fell in love with and the two of them were married five months later. Fred Lyle participated in his partner's wedding as best man, and soon after that he allowed his social life to settle into a routine that included a nearly equal number of male and female lovers.

Barbara Jennings used her insurance proceeds and a special bonus from Trans Continental Airlines to open a golf and tennis shop in Daytona Beach, not far from her home on the Intercoastal Waterway. The golf and tennis shop has expanded to one additional location in Daytona Beach, and further expansion in the future is expected.

Kathy Davis resigned from Trans Continental Airlines,

moved to Daytona Beach, and used her severance pay and special cash bonus to become partners with Barbara Jennings in the expanding string of golf and tennis shops that they jointly own. Kathy purchased her own home on the Intercoastal Waterway and, shortly after moving in, also purchased a half share in a power boat. The vessel, a twenty-eight foot Bertram flybridge cruiser, still has the name *Flying Low* painted in gold letters against a black backdrop on its stern.